THE HIVE QUEEN

BOOK TWO OF THE BOND TRILOGY

D1248799

THE HIVE QUEEN

A Novel

ROBIN KIRK

Blue Crow Books

Publisher's Cataloging-in-Publication Data
Kirk, Robin 1960-.
The Hive Queen.
p.____ cm.____
ISBN 978-1-947834-48-4 (Pbk.), ISBN 978-1-947834-99-6 (Ebook)
1. Science Fiction. 2. Young Adult Fiction. 3. Fantasy Fiction. I. Title
813.6 ׀ LOC PCN 2020933018

Blue Crow
Books

Published by Blue Crow Books
an imprint of Blue Crow Publishing, LLC
Chapel Hill, NC
www.bluecrowpublishing.com
Cover Design by Lauren Faulkenberry
Map Art by Travis Hasenour
Cover Photo Credits: rdrgraphe/Shutterstock; Tithi Luadthong/Shutterstock

Also by Robin Kirk

The Bond Trilogy

The Bond
The Hive Queen

Nonfiction

More Terrible Than Death: Massacres, Drugs and America's War in Colombia

The Monkey's Paw: New Chronicles from Peru

The Shining Path: History of Peru's Millennial War, by Gustavo Gorriti, with a forward and translated by Robin Kirk

Poetry

Peculiar Motion, a poetry collection

Praise for The Bond Trilogy

The Bond is imaginative and fresh, and Dinitra is my new hero. What a beautifully tense, wistful, creative, and genius story!

-Karla F.C. Holloway, Ph.D., author of A DEATH IN HARLEM

Fans of *The Handmaid's Tale* and *Never Let Me Go* will devour *The Bond.*

-Lisa Williams Kline, award-winning author of ONE WEEK OF YOU

An adventure and a masterful exploration of what it means to be a human being.

-Constantine Singer, author of STRANGE DAYS

Kirk brings the reader into an intricate, well-imagined world— a landscape so credible it instantly feels like a classic.

-Beth Kander, author of the Original Syn Trilogy

Kirk's dynamic world-building will transport you to a place you've never been before.

-A.M. Rose, author of ROAD TO EUGENICA and BREAKOUT

A rollicking adventure story whose underlying questions make for a read that is as thought-provoking as it is highly entertaining.

-Carolyn O'Doherty, author of REWIND

A riveting, dark, post-apocalyptic romp that hooked me from its very first line.

In this dynamic sequel to *The Bond*, Kirk takes readers on an intricately-plotted journey as warrior Fir leads his brothers to escape servitude and finds himself faced with a decision with potentially devastating consequences for those he loves the most. Readers will revel in the lush world-building and carefully woven plot. *The Hive Queen* delivers on every level!

Contents

To Frances and Ray
& my own ferocious 12
RoZee

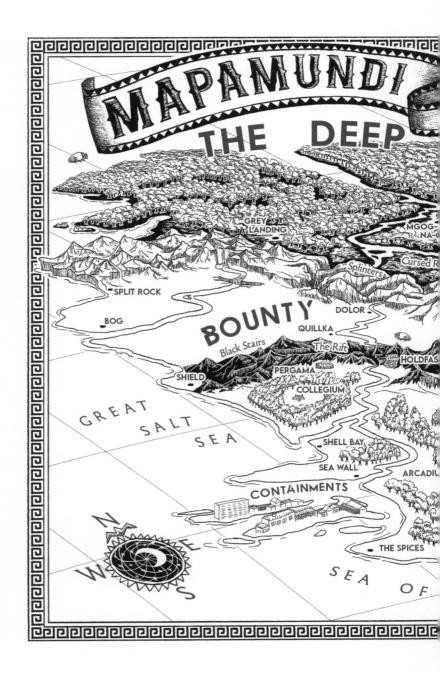

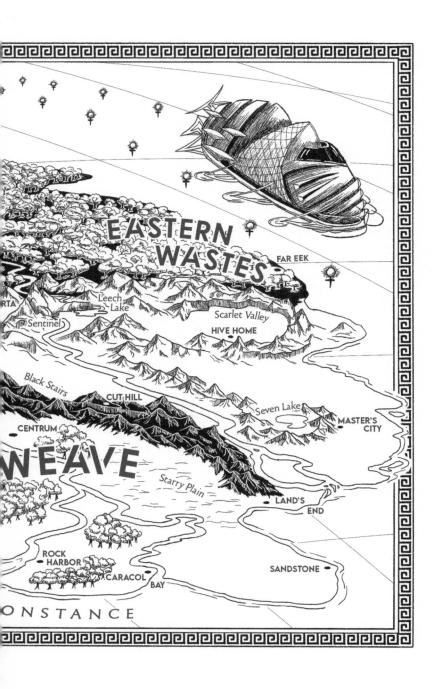

...War's grim gates will close,
Tight-shut with bars of iron, and inside them
The wickedness of war sit bound and silent,
The red mouth straining and the hands held tight
In fastenings of bronze, a hundred hundred.

- Book I, THE AENEID by Virgil, Translation by Rolfe
Humphries

Cursed River

I never meant to kill my brothers.

But that's what I may have done. Seven days ago, I ordered all nineteen of them to flee east with me from the city of Dolor. The only way we'd ever be free, I'd told them, was to escape before the Weave's fleet arrived like a thousand small and murderous suns. We'd seen what those helios and their pulsar guns could do at Quillka: turn everything to ash. Not one of us, not even our mother, would survive another attack.

Our mother is a Captain of Bounty. By escaping, we escaped her, too, and escaped Bounty, our home.

Seven days ago, I asked my brothers, "What good is freedom to the dead?" *Freedom:* the shape word is a fist opening.

Tanoak is strongest and most like our mother: red-brown hair and green eyes, slow to anger and terrible once the fury takes him. *The Living Wood follows where you command, Fir. To freedom or death. Give us the order.*

I have a tongue since our mother bred me to be commander and left me undocked. I gave the order in word and shape language: *We go now.*

Only seven days in, a hyba pack has us pinned against a river. A scout swings into the branches above our heads. They're big as tigers and have massive hyena snouts. Their long, muscular monkey tails make them excellent climbers. And killers. The scout chuckles greedily. A cub, still snowy white, appears next to it. Then the pack. One hyba is so black I glimpse only a grin of white fangs against the dark canopy of branches.

My brother Thorn jabs his finger at the river, overflowing with rain and white with froth. His hair went white at Quillka, where we lost three brothers. *Hybas won't touch water. We have to get to the other side. Now!*

Tanoak's finger circles his ear. *Can't you hear the waterfall? I count two breaths before anyone who stumbles is swept away.*

On his shoulders, Tanoak carries Cedar, our youngest. My brothers have been switching off since Quillka, where Cedar took shrapnel to the hip. The injury never healed. Every morning, Thorn, our fysic, doses him with tincture of forgetting. One drop of the clear liquid makes a warrior smile as if he's never felt pain or grief. Two erase the world, at least long enough to amputate a limb or stitch a gash.

Cedar swallows just enough forgetting to bear the pounding he gets riding a brother's shoulders. Cedar's bright red hair is lank as plucked weeds. *Have we found the Master?* he asks groggily.

I touch his burning cheek. "Just a little further," I lie.

When we were still warriors of Bounty, wildmen would creep close to our grub fires at night and in exchange for food and clothing tell us what they'd seen in the east. In the east, there's no mother-bond, they promised, the duty for life a warrior-son owes his Captain and mother. Men eat what they want, sleep when they want. There was a Master of men, a whole city of men.

And this: the Master can cure the virus our mothers breed into our bodies.

We could find this city if we survive. If this Master exists. If he lets us be free.

But are we truly free if someone lets us be free? What do you have to do to get this virus cure?

Loyalty, a wildman told us. The shape word for *loyalty* looks a lot like the shape word *blind:* a palm cut across the eyes instead of blocking them.

The wildmen also spoke of drafts, the Weave's failed laboratory experiments discarded like trash on the slopes of the Black Stairs. Some, like hybas and derak, flourish. There's a draft Queen: part human, part animal, maybe even part plant. She lures wildmen to her secret fortress, never to be seen again.

Other drafts—without lungs to breathe or skin to protect their insides—perish.

I wish we had a wildman with us right now. My brothers' lives are like weights that get heavier with each step. We're twenty-strong, but I feel alone. We don't have a single map for the east. We've found no trails, no villages, no markers. I can't even describe what we're running to. What does freedom feel like? Will freedom bring us peace? A place? A fire and good grub?

The hybas scrabble down the tree trunks. Right now, freedom feels like a sour burn at the back of my throat. We've passed their kills, bloody snow and dirt and the broken teeth they shed. Hybas don't leave behind even a sliver of bone. Their smell, burnt butter, makes my blood run cold.

I order Tanoak to set a rope across the river so we can cross. "I'll take him," I say, reaching for Cedar.

Tamarack can, he answers.

"I need Tamarack's arm." Tamarack is best with the huaraca. He swings the slingshot over his head so fast it screams, then releases the stone with deadly precision.

Gently, Tanoak drapes Cedar across my shoulders. The weight is suddenly real. Fever-sweat makes Cedar slippery as a just-caught fish.

Tanoak loops the end of the rope around the tree trunk nearest the water, then strides into the current, coils of rope spooling off his back. The rest of us form a human wall. One hyba tries to flank us and force us back underneath the trees, but Tamarack strikes it with a stone straight through the eye and it yelps away.

What I wouldn't give now to have 12 at my side. Dinitra's draft is part hyba, part battle dog, part whatever else her Sower brewed into her formula. I don't think even the largest or the craftiest of the hybas could kill 12. Each of her paws is the size of a griddle. 12 weighs twice what I do and is quiet as breath.

But Dinitra and 12 are far away. They were going to escape Dolor, too. But Dinitra decided to head north to The Deep, not east. One of the Captains, Rek, had vowed to slaughter the hyba cross.

I tried to convince Dinitra to come with us.

"What life could this Master of men offer me?" she countered. The fear in her eyes was like a knife stab. Yet she was determined to head to The Deep to save 12's life.

I couldn't disagree. Still, I wanted freedom to be a path we could walk together. There it is: a boy, a warrior, wanted her along with his freedom.

Maybe my brothers and I should have gone to The Deep. Maybe we all should have gone west, to the great Salt Sea. Anywhere but here, trapped between a hungry hyba pack and a river high in flood. Dinitra made our escape possible by drawing the secret plant our mothers call Remedy. We need Remedy to quiet the virus. She stole a sack of the Remedy powder, too, enough to last until we could find more.

Without it, we'd break into fever and bone-breaking shakes. We'd die.

"Search near the ridges," Dinitra told me. She'd seen the Remedy bush there on her walks with 12. The bushes were heavy with hard, red berries.

In return, I gave Dinitra a miserable thing: a scrap of my tunic. She knew what it meant. Someday, somewhere, somehow, 12 could use the scrap to follow my scent and find me.

Unless I've passed to the Far Lands. Not even 12 could find me on that smoky path to the after-life.

Tanoak fights against the river's hammering. When my brothers and I run out of rocks to hurl at the hybas, we scoop up frozen mud lumps. They fall apart with gritty sighs. Then we load the leather cradles with fistfuls of pebbles, flinging them rat-a-tat.

The pack pays the pebbles no more mind than fleas. Tanoak's not even halfway across. We have to ford or be a meaty meal.

"Into the river!" I scream at my brothers.

Cedar's fevered skin burns against me. I see sunlight through the flesh of his hand as he motions, *The water looks fine.*

"You always did like a swim."

I'm the best swimmer of all.

My brothers can't grab the rope since that would jerk Tanoak off his feet. They slip and slide, go under, then scramble to stand again. We trained for this. If there's nothing to hang on to, they have to resist trying to help each other, not even if a brother cries out. That only risks having two brothers die instead of one. They struggle, falling and staggering with froth pouring from their hair.

But we never trained for what lies on the river's far bank. At our grub fires, wildmen would describe how hyba packs encircle their prey. Grabeen flocks blacken the skies and howl like wolves. Big as barn cats, grabeens have bright yellow, green, and red feathers. Striking until you realize that if you've seen them, they're already hunting you.

Then there are lithers: tall as horses, with constrictor bodies and leathery bat-wings. Speluks, cave-dwellers in human form but with bright blue skin and huge, lidless eyes. They suck their prey into husks. Worse than any of these creatures are hunger and exhaustion, they told us. Fear. Fear rises in the small hours, sticky as Cedar's fever sweat. This river is to be feared. There's not a single drop of mercy in it.

I'm the last one on the bank, with Cedar on my shoulders. Two bees slowly circle my head, attracted, I think, by the sweetness of forgetting on his breath. I hear Tanoak chuff as he finally claws his way up the far bank. Quickly, he loops his rope around a tree and pulls tight, the rope lifting as water springs from it like sudden tears.

Freedom is a rope across a river.

My brother Willow, our cook and grub master, seizes it, the lone satchel of Remedy powder hoisted above his head. A week's worth of life in rough burlap.

I wade in backwards, my stave up and facing the hybas as they close in. I have one arm hooked across the rope, to steady myself. The water is so cold, my crook contracts. Froth splashes Cedar and he squeezes my neck.

"Careful," I manage, "not to kill me."

Why kill my favorite brother?

The hyba cub, the white one, creeps close. He's less cautious than the adults. I've seen this a hundred times: the bravery of inexperience. Separating from the pack. Too eager.

With a snarl, the cub leaps.

I shove my stave up and catch the cub through the upper palate. The stave point blossoms between its ears like a red and gray flower. The cub crumples. The pack falls on the cub's still-quivering body.

The first good news in a week is a steaming meal for a hyba pack.

Tanoak's rope feels taut as a bow string. Over the roaring river, I promise Cedar: "There'll be fire and hot paddle loaf waiting on the far bank. Hold tight, my brother."

His hand flicks: *tight as a hyba's tail.*

I slip. Cedar's nails pierce my shoulders. I stagger up only to slip again, this time taking both of us under. I shove my boots hard against the river bed, hook my wrists over the rope, and haul up.

You didn't tell me we'd swim together, Cedar sputters.

"You didn't tell me you grew claws."

I promise Cedar honey, pounds of it, and fresh cheese we don't have and last summer's apricot jam, also a bold lie but I know it's his favorite. I've seen him lick every last morsel from his fingertips. For him, freedom means having as much food as he can eat. I intend to give it to him. I lie that when we reach our brothers, there will be dry blankets and greasy, hot, roasted derak and a jar of frothy pogee, just cracked opened and milky with corn sap.

"We'll be drunk as Captains by moonrise," I bellow over the river's din. "No training, no patrols, no cook-and-clean duty. No digging, no sewing, no sharpening, just bellies full to bursting and sweet, sweet sleep."

Every warrior's dream.

Lazy you are. Cedar's trying to give me strength. *I want to be free and meet this Master. Tell me what he looks like.*

I want to tell him something funny or wise or confident, but I'm at the deepest point. The water's so wrenchingly cold I hold my breath. Every shred of energy goes to staying upright in this cursed river.

Cursed River. A good name. Through clenched teeth, I say, "He looks like you, sweet Cedar. A male with a crook."

I'm thinking of something more to lie about when I lose my grip on the rope. I fall, my knees impaling on the rocks. I gulp water, foam, and tiny tree twigs. My thighs scream as I push up, hands grasping wildly.

Cedar slithers off my back with a sickening groan.

I lunge for him but brush only his right heel. The current tumbles him: leg, back, shoulder, ass, face in froth. Once, his leg flails upwards. The knee joint bends like a dog's hind leg. Then Cedar vanishes.

Two breaths, just like Tanoak said.

Several brothers race downstream. Gasping, I fight my way to Willow, who hauls me out. My knees burble blood where the rocks slit me open to winking, white bone.

Willow says, *They'll find him.*

I know Cedar's dead.

I carried him. I killed him. I have no words, shape or otherwise, for what I feel. How many more brothers will die for this freedom I promised? We'll face more cursed rivers, more hybas, dwindling Remedy, and us without even a coil of usable rope. My main job as commander is to keep my brothers alive.

I failed our youngest brother, the one who most needed me.

My gut clenches with shame. More than shame: disgust at myself for falling. Longing, too, to spin the forest and the river and the hybas back to the moment Cedar settled on my back. The rope shed tears when Tanoak pulled it tight, but I can't cry, not in front of my brothers. If only I'd let Tanoak carry him so I could set the rope across the river myself. If only we'd gone north instead of east, escaped a week ago, a month, a year.

I belch out river foam. Until I make my final journey to the Far Lands, I'll remember the slide of Cedar's skin against mine.

If I could take it all back, return to those lava beds at Dolor, erase this week of running and hiding, would I? Would I trade freedom— flimsy as breath, a far mountain on a moonless night—for the slim possibility that my brothers would survive the Weave's next attack?

If they survived, they'd still be trapped by the mother-bond. Its own death.

I vow: not one brother more will die because of me.

2

Brother-Bond

After finishing their gruesome meal, the hyba pack leaps back into the trees. Their raucous hooting quickly fades.

We should make a fire. Without it, there's no paddle loaf. We need paddle loaf because Willow mixes into the dough the Remedy powder we must eat to keep the virus asleep. Without a fire, there's no warm water to clean my wounds, no heat to stop our shivering.

I don't give any order. The Cursed River runs orange and red with the setting sun.

My brothers return carrying Cedar's broken body. He's drained of blood. His skull caved in over the right ear.

Willow kicks rocks into the river. The willow tree he's named for has a slender trunk and bendable branches, but my brother is thick as a barrel and spitting mad. *We should go back to our mother. There's nothing here for us: no Master, no Remedy. This freedom is only suffering.* His palm swipes across his chest. *We can cross back on Tanoak's rope. We'll beg our mother's forgiveness. We made Cedar choose between us and our duty and now...*

His jaw clenches. *If we'd stayed, Cedar wouldn't be dead.* A sharp clap: *dead.*

But a return to Dolor is also death. The Weave means to exterminate all males. I don't need to remind him that Captain Rek destroyed what Remedy stores she had in Dolor. She doesn't need it since she brews her sons without virus. By putting us at risk, she meant to weaken our mother and the other Captains and take Bounty for her own.

Two kinds of death no matter where we go: back to the mother-bond or to this Master.

"I'm not going back," I tell him.

Can you make that decision for the sprigs? Willow demands. The sprigs: our youngest brothers. I often go to Willow for advice, but right now he has no patience for me.

"I'm their commander." I struggle to speak calmly even though it feels like the Cursed River is still battering me. "And yours. Our brothers are free."

If they survive freedom, Willow says.

"They won't survive the mother-bond, brother Willow." No warrior I've known lives past thirty. At seventeen, I have only stubble on my chin, yet I command.

I wish my brother wouldn't argue any more. With Cedar's broken body at our feet, I have only failure to show for my decision. I can't point to the place freedom stands. I can't hand freedom out like a sharp stave or rope. It's not something I can grasp or swallow.

Willow doesn't give up. He's always been stubborn. He has to be. He's in charge of safeguarding our food, drink, clothing, and Remedy. He keeps us fed in the worst of winter. No begging ever parted him with so much as a dry crust unless it was to keep one of us alive.

He says, *You ordered us to follow. Is that really the freedom you mean, where you still tell us what to do and when to do it?*

He's right. When my brother Ash commanded, more than once I felt his stick on my back or a boot on my ass for not obeying quickly enough. Ash's job was to make us into fighters, not free men.

Now, I command. Are my brothers really free if the only reason they're here is because they obey me as we once obeyed Ash? Can I command them to be free against their will?

My wounded knees make squishy sounds as I stand. I manage several paces, then pick up a fallen branch and lay it at my feet. I look at each brother in turn. "Return to Dolor if you wish. You aren't slaves here. You can all go back. Or come with me to find this Master. You choose. May the Mother protect you either way."

Slaves, Willow spits. *That's your word. I choose the word sons. I choose the word warriors. Our mother brewed us to defend her. To defend Bounty. We wouldn't draw breath without her. Did that Captain tell you that you're a slave?*

That Captain: Dinitra. "She didn't teach me that word. I taught her." *Slave:* wrists crossed as if bound.

Shadows darken my brothers' faces. "Since I was a boy, a thousand things told me the mother-bond made me a slave," I tell them. "I couldn't go where I wanted, sleep when I wanted, eat and shit when I wanted. We despise wildmen for their rags. They were rejected by their mothers and so we rejected them. But they have something we don't have: freedom."

I ask my brothers, "What separates wild animals from wildmen and wildmen from warriors? Why is our mother free and we, who share her blood, are not?"

Because that's the way of things, Willow fires back. *That's always been the way.*

"Have hybas always been the way?"

You know they're drafts. Willow folds his arms angrily. *They're brewed. They're mistakes the Weave dropped onto the Black Stairs long ago. Without a care for their suffering or the harm they cause. They're free—and miserable. Are you comparing us to drafts?*

I speak with my voice and my hands. "Hybas were brewed. We were brewed. But they're free. Why are we any less than them?"

My youngest brothers, the ones who were closest to my mother, silently weep. I understand how they feel. Before I became a warrior, our mother Timbe was gentle and loving with me. She'd bring me the sweets I craved, hold and caress and kiss me, call me her own precious boy. Ash, our leader, was all discipline and duty compared to her.

But once I became a warrior, Timbe rarely spoke to me. As second-in-command of her Living Wood, I obeyed her orders without comment or complaint. That was the way of things.

It's the way no more.

Dinitra didn't teach me *slave,* but she helped me see the truth. Like so many daughters, she'd been kidnapped from the Weave on her mother's orders, so that she could come to Bounty and learn the truth. Dinitra believed what the Weave taught her. Males were violent and a danger to everyone. Once the Weave could make daughters without males, there was no need for males anymore.

But in Bounty, she learned that was only part of what the Weave planned. The Sowers weren't just making daughters. They were brewing all manner of drafts in their laboratories.

The Bounty rebels, all former Sowers in the Weave, brewed warrior sons to fight back. As my brothers stand before me, I see them as the Weave sees them: muscled and broad-shouldered, fast and deadly quiet, trained killers who don't think twice about obeying an order to slit a Weave soldier's throat.

I quickly realized that Dinitra was different from the other daughters we'd brought to Bounty. For one thing, she came with her own draft. Kesh, her mother, had made them both: daughter and hyba draft. Dinitra and 12. The other Captains argued about having 12 in Bounty. Why bring a dangerous draft, just the kind of creature that convinced them to rebel against the Weave?

Kesh argued that warriors needed to train with 12 because this was exactly the kind of weapon the Weave would use against us in battle. When I first saw 12, my heart leaped in my chest. She was twice the size of any battle dog and had a heavy, hyba snout. Her powerful tail swished back and forth, tipped with a surprisingly delicate tuft of white hair. She loves Dinitra with a single-minded intensity I've seen in no other creature.

We saw her power that first day in the Quillka training pen. 12 thought Dinitra had ordered her to attack Ash. My commander and brother. I watched in horror as 12 tumbled him, then ripped out his throat.

Once she starts a kill, nothing and no one can stop her. Our mother stepped in to end Ash's suffering with her knife. A mercy, she called it.

That day, I became commander of the Living Wood. Commander of the brothers who stand before me.

As yet, they don't see themselves as I came to see myself. Dinitra drew pictures: 12, the warriors, the mountains we call the Black Stairs. And she drew me. When I saw my face in charcoal, I was stunned. Using only nubs from a fire, Dinitra captured me, Fir, and the longing in my eyes I couldn't hide.

A longing for freedom.

Gradually, I found myself craving her voice, her nearness. Dinitra was the only person in the world who saw me, the real me, the Fir who could be free. Sometimes, my craving for her infuriated me. I wished I could pull her from my thoughts as one pulls out a splinter. Warriors couple together as do Captains with other females. But male with female is for beasts alone.

Then my thoughts would drift to her again and I'd find myself wondering what it would be like to touch her hand. Kiss her as warriors kiss. I longed to wind her brown curls around my fingers. My breath would quicken as I thought these things and I'd feel the heat in my crook.

Shameful. Unnatural. Like a beast of the field or forest.

Dinitra feared me at first. She'd been taught that men were violent and dangerous. She believed in the Weave's Great Quest, that exterminating men was for the good of all.

Despite all of this, we talked. We grew to trust one another. I'd find her training alone with 12 and find ways to help. One day, I blurted that I wanted to be free. I wanted my brothers to be free. To escape, we needed to know the source of Remedy. We meant to go east and find this Master of men.

Dinitra discovered that Remedy is made from rose hips. The bush was common, she said. She'd come across it on frequent walks with 12. The hips are like sour berries. Once dried and ground, the berries become Remedy powder.

I still have the drawing she made of the plant so that we could find it. In Dolor, Dinitra stole a satchel of Remedy, enough to last, we hoped, until we found the bushes.

As we stood in the shadow of Dolor's lava rocks, she cradled my hands in hers. She cupped my cheeks and kissed me. I tasted her: dust and flowers. "Maybe there's a place we could both be free that's not the end of the world," she told me.

It was then that I ripped a strip of cloth from my sleeve. I vowed we'd meet again.

But even powerful 12 and her magnificent nose can't scent over jungles and mountains and the rocky crags between here and The Deep. Dinitra's north, I'm east, and that's the end of it. *Enough.* I can't kill a hyba pack with freedom. We can't eat it. I can't light freedom on fire to cook our grub. Freedom doesn't tell me anything about which path to follow or this mysterious Master.

I have to think of my brothers, not Dinitra. I want them to see freedom as I do, know that freedom is the only way we can truly live. I need them to believe.

Most of all, I need to believe in freedom myself.

I snap my fingers, the signal that I'm about to speak. "I loved Cedar," I tell my brothers. "I mourn him. But I won't go back."

I don't give a greasy fart for freedom, brother. Willow's eyes blaze as he sets himself like a boulder in front of my puny branch. *We followed you. There, I said it. We followed our commander. We obeyed your order. We don't follow freedom.*

When wildmen crouched at our fires at Quillka, Willow grumbled louder than anyone about their stink and rags, their matted hair stuck with leaves and who knows what tree sap. Some were rejected as warriors and a handful were beast-borns, product of the shameful union of male with female. But in the morning, the wildmen would find fresh carry-cake in their pouches and a mended shirt or cloak. Willow pitied them, but never envied their freedom.

Tanoak gives a shrug, then strides over the branch and turns to answer Willow. *Why not? Better than going back, I say. I want to get a glimpse of this Master.*

Willow glares. Thorn and Hawthorn, my deputy commander, join Tanoak. Soon, Willow is the only brother who hasn't stepped across.

After a long pause, he swears, *Very well. But there's one more thing.*

He hoists the Remedy pouch he carried across the river. It's as if I'm seeing the worn fabric for the first time: dripping pale pink water. *I tried to keep it dry. The current was too strong.*

Having no Remedy is as much of a death sentence as a hyba pack or a helio blast. I reach for my pouch, where I kept Dinitra's drawing of the Remedy bush. The paper is sopping, the charcoal washed away. "How much Remedy is left?" I ask.

Three days. Maybe four. Willow's caught the pink drips in a bowl. He begins to scrape out the Remedy sludge and heap it on a rock to dry. *Do I have to leap over your blasted branch? I have Remedy to dry and a meal to prepare. And a brother to send to the Far Lands.*

I tell two brothers to gather wood and water for Willow's grub fire. Two more prepare a place for us to sleep. "The rest of you," I say. "Bathe our brother and prepare his pyre."

Wait. Tanoak goes to his haunches at the water's edge. He's found a fresh print in the mud. Something—someone—crossed before us. *This morning, I reckon.*

Tanoak lays two fingers on a palm. *Human.*

Wildmen? I ask.

Tanoak points to the boot tread: zigzags like lightning bolts. *Blazes carve that symbol.*

The Blazes are Captain Rek's warriors. It's possible Rek sent Blazes to capture or kill us before we could reach this Master. She claims to have an alliance with him. She may fear we'll complicate her plans.

But this make no sense. We've been running for a week. "How can Blazes be ahead of us?"

This one's no more than a boy, I'd say. See how the print is shallow? I see just the one. Blazes travel in pairs.

Tanoak shapes the next words carefully. *The boots don't fit him.* He traces out the place where the boot sole slipped under the foot. *I'm thinking these boots aren't his.*

A lone boy can't hurt us. But what if the boy has brothers? Or maybe this is a turn in our luck. Maybe the boy can lead us to the Remedy plant. Maybe he knows this Master. Hope and worry twist in my gut. This boy could be very lucky for us or a taste of very bad news.

I push my questions aside. Right now, our attention has to be on Cedar and his pyre.

My brothers have settled Cedar's broken body on branches thatched around him like a cradle. We form a circle around it. The pyre will be visible for a long distance, possibly alerting those who would do us harm. But we have to risk it. Cedar is the first among us to die free. He deserves a proper ceremony to start his journey to the Far Lands.

If I don't send Cedar off properly, my brothers will worry that freedom not only takes them away from all they've known in life. Freedom will separate them from what awaits them after death: rolling hills, peace, and plenty.

As is our custom, Cedar's shoes and tunic go to our tailor and cobbler, Whitebark, for repairs and reuse. I parcel out his other belongings from youngest to oldest: his sharpening stone, strips of dried derak meat, flints, and a spare shirt and socks. I'm left with two stick figures. One is a warrior, the head a striped pecan carved with eyes and a mouth. For hair, black dilidot fur is stuck on with pine sap and woven into a top knot braided with shreds of old red and black ribbon.

Our mother's colors, red and black. The stick figure is Ash, our former commander, unmistakable.

The other toy is 12 herself. With a pine cone, Cedar captured her tiger stripes. Her tail is old rope stiffened with beeswax. It even has a dandelion tuft.

I keep the toy figures for myself.

My brothers were careful to point Cedar's feet east. We pass a burning stick around the circle. One by one, my brothers touch the flame to the wood. Soon, he will be with Ash. I think of Ash as he was on his last day: his dark red hair like our mother's, like Tanoak's, in glossy braids that fell from his top knot to his waist. He roared as he ran the training pen, just as he'll roar in delight when he sees sweet Cedar, all of the boy's fear and pain burned away.

My mother chose Fig to be our singer, so she left him his tongue. Now that Cedar's dead, he's youngest. Of all my brothers, Fig looks least like our mother. His eyes are rimmed in bright blonde lashes and seem to float on the milky lake of his face. They sparkle with welling tears.

He leans close to me and whispers. "There's no more mother-bond," he says. "What else binds us, Fir?"

A simple question. I speak so that all of my brothers can hear. "We're brothers."

I shape a word: the pointer fingers parallel and joined. "We have the brother-bond."

If I say it enough, maybe they'll believe it.

Fig has composed a new verse for our praise song, adding Cedar's name to the long list of brothers we've lost.

Timbe's son, the warrior Cedar.
Content was he, to love his brothers.
His spirit escaped from suffering, he was

first of the Living Wood to die free.

Tamarack and Tanoak, our largest brothers, gulp in air as they weep. My brothers will follow me tomorrow. Maybe they'll follow for a week or more.

But they won't follow forever. Freedom has to mean something. Something more than death.

Some of my brothers may come to regret their choice. As I look at their faces in the light of Cedar's pyre, I wonder: who will be first to say it?

3

Sprig Tales

Once Cedar's pyre collapses into coals, we return to Willow's grub fire. My brothers drag stones close to the hasty pit they dug and warm themselves. Willow first checks the pile of Remedy he hopes will dry, turning it to make sure it doesn't burn.

The hands of my brothers are still, silent. This is a night for sadness. For thinking about Cedar as he walks the smoky path to the Far Lands. We'll have no time for any of that in the morning.

Silently, Thorn goes from brother to brother to treat cuts and scrapes from our river crossing. To stop infection, he first douses the gashes on my knees with tincture of starry white. I refuse the forgetting he offers. I won't dull my wits. With a grunt, he pulls out his curved needle and gut to stitch. I grit my teeth, his needle swift and sure. Where Cedar's fingernails dug into my shoulders, Thorn layers a compress of bitter comfort leaves. He binds the leaves tight with cloth cut from Cedar's tunic.

Willow uses a leather pouch to mix flour from his pack with a pinch of precious salt, another of rosemary. Though he's done it a thousand times, we stare as he adds a scant handful of Remedy, still dark with river water.

Remedy turns the dough a pale pink. Willow drops the dough onto a flat stone and kneads. He sprinkles the iron griddle with water.

When the droplets sizzle, he pats the dough into paddles the width and length of his palm and slaps them onto the griddle to cook.

Sometimes, he'll make a crescent moon or a triangle. Tonight, it's only paddles. He stabs each paddle with a fork, to keep bubbles from forming.

It's a poor meal—paddle loaf and a cold strip of dried derak meat—that barely blunts our hunger. I examine my brothers in the flickering light. We look older than we did yesterday. We look older than we did two hours ago, on the edge of Bounty, with the hyba pack hooting above our heads.

As my brothers eat, I pull our tracker map from my boot. Unlike Dinitra's drawing, the map is resistant to water and still intact. My mother gave me the map because I was her commander. I had to know where my brothers were at all times. I had to know where she was since our first and most important duty was keeping her alive. The thick, spongy paper is infused with our cells, ours and our mother's. My brothers and I appear as twenty dots at the river's edge. Cedar's dot is going ashy and will narrow into an X.

Our mother's symbol, a tiny maple leaf, winks at Dolor.

With her own tracker map, she could be staring at us even now. But by tomorrow, we'll have run beyond the tracker map's reach. It's of no use to us any more, just a link on the chain that once bound us to her.

I place the map on the fire and watch it flare and burn. When she looks at the map now, it will be as if we never existed at all.

Bitternut is first to form his hands into a question. From where I sit, I see only the side of his face that was burned by a helio blast. The skin is scaly and permanently red. *Tell us again of the Master, dear brother. Will he welcome us?*

The truth is that none of us know. I'm beginning to shape a response—*patience* or *let's talk about this in the morning*—but Bitternut doesn't wait for my answer. He babbles, hands moving in jerks. *Wildmen say the Master sees into the hearts of men. Secrets are nothing to him. Sometimes, he walks far from his city to find men and bring them to his halls. He's neither young nor old. His city stands beside a lake. Or in it. I didn't understand that part. He walks without being seen. He sees with his eyes closed. And there's a draft Queen no one escapes.*

Spruce cuts him off. Like Tanoak, Spruce is a skilled tracker. He's shorter than Bitternut, but has his features and chestnut skin. Like all of us, his neck is ringed with a tattoo of our mother's name: *TIMBETIMBETIMBE*.

The Master heals with a touch, the wildmen told us, Spruce says. He speaks with confidence, though I know he's learned all of this from wildmen tales told around a grub fire. *He can take the shape of any animal or draft and roams with them, taking on their speed and strength. His eyes are the color of fire. He flies without any craft. He has a potion that makes men strong, so they say.*

Willow jabs the coals, sending up a swirl of sparks. *Tales from when you couldn't wipe your own ass. I don't believe a word.*

Spruce shrugs. *Who thought the Weave could harness the sun for their helios? Who knew that Captain Rek would deny Remedy to the sons of her fellow Captains or that the Weave's helios would cross the Black Stairs? Fir,* he says, kicking a log to get my attention. *I know we're free. But...* He grips his hands. *What does that mean? We still have guard duty, right? I'm still a scout? Or...*

Tanoak interrupts. *Free means doing what you're told but without all the complaining.*

Spruce flushes red as our brothers snicker.

But not Willow. Spruce's innocent questions rekindle his anger. *Heed your own words, brother Spruce,* Willow says, impatient. *Are his eyes fire or are they those of a draft—say that frog draft, Sil? The one we found and brought to Bounty?*

Willow mocks him by bugging out his eyes, like Sil's. This is a sign of Willow's fatigue and fear more than anything. I know he loves the frog draft we left behind at Dolor. Sil had a keen intelligence Willow appreciated. We'd often see Sil teaching the other drafts shape language. He brought fine fish to Willow to cook and the tender leaves of water plants for his stews. Because of his delicate skin, Sil would often rest in a stream or water barrel, chatting with Willow as he went about his chores.

Willow's angry at me, not Sil. He's angry at the dark trees, the murderous river. At the pyre still crumbling nearby. *So this Master of yours has wings. A hawk's or a bee's, Spruce? How about dragonfly?*

Spruce stares obstinately at the fire. Willow is being cruel, but he can't help himself. I know he's afraid, for himself and for our brothers.

It's all nonsense! Willow slaps his floury palms together. *Sprig tales, nothing more.*

Tanoak interrupts with a sharp snap. *It's not all nonsense. Here's what a wildman told me about this Master. This man fought under the Master's command.*

Willow challenges him. *How do you know he fought? You've never told us this before.*

I never had cause to. Tanoak's eyes narrow. *The wildman had the scars to prove it.*

The shape word for "Master" is one pointer finger over the other. *The Master leads the Hundred-Hundred,* Tanoak says. *They fight in spectates, one hundred men each. Ten spectates form what they call a Millennium, a thousand men. Of these, he has at least ten, or so it was told to me directly.*

My mouth hangs open. By Tanoak's numbers, the Master has 10,000 men. A Hundred-Hundred. The Master's army is at least as large as Bounty's was before the first Weave attack at Quillka.

I challenge him. "You never spoke of this before, brother."

We never cared about this Master before. The wildman told Tanoak that the Hundred-Hundred uses speluk drafts as a kind of battle dog. *Except the speluks eat what they kill. They have enough spider in them to spit out a liquid that turns prey into mush. They suck the juices through their snouts, so all that's left is skin.*

I cry, "Enough!" In the darkness, it's as if every haint out of a sprig's tale has crept to Willow's fire. "It's time to rest. We'll leave at first light. Spruce and Whitebark, you have first watch. Bitternut and Pine are next. I'll take last watch."

Before they can say anything more, I warn them: "No more tales. Double duty to whoever tells one tonight."

For warmth, we lie side-by-side on a heap of pine needles, layering our cloaks like feathers. On one side of me is Willow, asleep almost instantly though his hands twist as if he's kneading dough. On my other side is Tanoak, a stinky boulder. A kind of rest comes to me, sleep on the skin of sleep. Tiny creatures rustle the underbrush. The grub fire softly crumbles. The brothers on watch pass on their rounds. A shift in the wind wreathes us in smoke.

Bitternut wakes me for my watch. My knee wounds scream when I stand. But once I'm up, I relish the time to think. Our lives used to be simple. The Captains brewed us and placed us as seeds inside their Vessels. The Vessels carried us and birthed us and gave us to our Keepers. Keepers brought us to our mother's chamber to kiss and hold, to spoil with treats and teach us shape language and the glory of the mother-bond. This is the life we all knew as sprigs.

When I came of age, my mother led me to the warrior pen to learn to fight for her, to obey my brother, Ash, and through him always her. My brothers were docked, their tongues taken to mark them as warriors.

But my mother whispered in my ear, "To you, I give the gift of a tongue, to always hear and obey and protect me."

And now? We have wildmen's tales and a word none of us truly understands: *freedom*. We could just as well be saying *bozzle* or *wendigar*: nonsense. We speak of a Master who walks unseen, who sees into men's hearts, who has eyes of fire.

And a Queen—a draft of who knows what mixture—no man escapes.

Nonsense. Tales to scare sprigs. If there's a master, then surely he and his men are men like us. And no draft Queen can keep us from freedom.

But with the scars to prove it, Tanoak said.

I push the doubts away. I have real things to fear. Things I can touch and see. As I look over the Cursed River, I go through my deadly list. Will we find the berries to replenish our dwindling Remedy? I think of Dinitra and 12 heading north for The Deep. Not a land of males or females, but drafts and who knows what wild creatures. Are they safe? Should we go there instead?

Who left that boot print in the mud? Could it have been the Master wandering far from his city? The river's roar is my questions and doubts threatening to drown me.

Out of the corner of my eye, I glimpse something. I creep closer to the river. Where we found the footprint, I see the shape of a lone figure. It's a warrior: tall and broad. His top knot falls in a thick braid down his back. The braid is studded with beads: red and black.

The figure is Ash. My brother. I smell him, too: sweat and the pungent rosemary salve we use to ease our aches. I feel in my pocket for Cedar's toy, the stick figure of Ash. My pocket is empty. It's like the stick figure came to life, Ash as I remember him and feared him and loved him.

"Where are we?" my dead brother asks.

I know I'm dreaming. Ash's tongue was docked by our mother. I never heard his voice in life. Even though he could have kept it as commander, he insisted my mother take it, to prove his loyalty.

It's me who has no tongue. *East of the eastern border,* I tell him.

I want to touch him, feel his pulse. I want to ask: did he hear of this Master? Did he speak with wildmen and learn their secrets? Which are true and which are tales?

But what if my touch makes him disappear? I saw him last on the ground of the training pen. 12 planted her paws on his chest as his life drained out. Our mother's name is inked on his neck: *TIMBETIMBETIMBE.* I feel a surge of love and relief. He's come back to us in our moment of need. He can help me.

Ash says, "You seek the Master."

Yes. A nod.

My brother's eyes are still pools. I try and fail to keep from seeming panicked. *Our brothers are afraid. The trees are filled with hybas. We're running out of Remedy. I'm leading our brothers to their deaths.* The truth is I don't know where I'm leading them, death or otherwise. *Remedy, Remedy, without it, we'll die.* A sprig's rhyme we're taught from our first steps.

"You'll find the cure," my brother tells me.

What? A cure for virus? We won't need Remedy at all?

"You'll find the cure," Ash repeats. "It won't save everyone."

I feel like screaming. Why won't a cure save us? Who's next to die? My brother won't take his eyes off the far bank. There, another figure stands: Cedar.

I must have eaten something rotten. There must be some conjury in the mist. Could this be the beginning of Remedy sickness? Is some conjurer at work, the Master himself on one of his long journeys?

Tell me what comes next! I plead. *Will this Master welcome us? Will he take us prisoner? What of the drafts loosed in the forest, the speluks that eat men like soup?*

"The Master isn't the cure." Ash's body is a map of his loyalty: helio burns, the puckered scars of battle dog bites, our mother's tattoos.

Tell me what to do, brother! My pointer fingers are parallel and joined. *Tell me where the Remedy bushes grow. Who left the boot print on the bank? I'm afraid,* I say. I feel like a boy again, desperate for answers. *I'm not ready.*

To say the words aloud would be to die of shame. Ash doesn't even look at me, his eyes fixed on Cedar.

What about this Queen? I reach out to him but feel only cold river mist. The Queen makes the nektar the Sowers use to brew their drafts. In exchange, they send cloth and pergama, the precious metal they use for their helios. But any male who comes within her grasp vanishes, the wildmen say. How many dangers must we face to be free?

Ash raises his hands to his chest. I think he's making the word for *courage,* fists joined and moving outward, when a sudden gust tosses the branches above our heads. I look up, afraid the hybas have somehow managed to leap across the Cursed River.

When I look back, Ash and my brother Cedar are gone. I walk the bank again and again looking for boot prints, snapped twigs. I speak aloud: "Brother!"

I find nothing.

Before I can change my mind, I go to the tree where Tanoak lashed the rope. I cut it free. The rope is pulled straight by the river's current, still fixed to the far side. To Bounty.

For us, there's no going back.

4

Burn & Hunger

The morning fog that blankets our camp is sweet compared to the stench over my sleeping brothers: sour breath, foot reek, farts. Bitternut was supposed to fetch water for breakfast. I find him snoring open-mouthed under the feathered cloaks.

Ash would have whipped him. I can't bring myself to, especially after what happened to Cedar. I must have been hallucinating about Ash and Cedar walking the banks and speaking with tongues. Addled by grief and the pain that sears my knees every time I take a step. Maybe there's something in the air, the river water, that cold mist.

I can't help thinking: I wish I could speak to my brothers in riddles and be gone by first light. My brothers' lives would no longer be my responsibility. Maybe, they'd be better off.

I kick Bitternut's boot to wake him. I'm still commander, at least today. At least this morning. "Get up, you lazy sack of bones."

Bitternut gives a terrific sneeze, then scrambles to his feet. *I was just resting my eyes, brother.*

Resting your ass more like it. I jerk my hand toward the river. *You should have brought Willow his water by now. Our brother's not so forgiving in the mornings. Be quick.*

At home, the Living Wood would have been up before dawn for stretches and a fast run. That's how I came to know Quillka's farmers and bakers, the laundry workers and the cheese-seller carting fresh milk from her goat pen to her kitchen. They weren't bound by the mother-bond. They served the Captains by choice. It was good business.

Occasionally, I'd notice a shuttered house, an empty barn. Some of Quillka's traders and farmers quietly slipped away. People whispered that there was no war in The Deep, the jungle north of Dolor. To get to The Deep, you had to descend the Splinter Range. There, Bounty's high plain fractures into valleys so narrow and deep they look like black splinters driven sideways into the ground. Once, Ash took us to the Splinters to climb ice. We roped together, then chiseled our way up and down the ice falls.

He pointed to The Watcher, the last peak before the plunge into The Deep. He told us creatures sacrificed a human child and left it there to watch over the pass.

"What creatures?" I asked. Ash's story made me afraid.

The ones who eat boys like you, he told me with a grin.

If I stood where we lashed our ropes that day, would I glimpse Dinitra and 12 winding their way into The Deep? Dinitra planned to bring Rek's Vessel with her, the Weave girl she called Susalee. Dinitra said she wouldn't leave Dolor without her. Otherwise, Rek would force her to bear more sons.

What creatures live in The Deep? The dangers we face might be nothing compared to theirs.

At the grub fire, Willow grunts unhappily. He's managed to coax up a single lick of flame. The wood's soaked with heavy mist. Then Bitternut runs up, breathless. *Blazes,* he says. *On the far bank.*

The Captains can't allow an escape to succeed or go unpunished. In thick brush, I crouch with my brothers. Two Blazes stand at the spot where the hyba pack fed on the cub. They're tugging at the rope we used to ford the Cursed River.

I know them: Burn and Hunger, both warriors.

Burn has a thick braid of orange hair to his waist. Despite the cold, his broad chest is bare. A snake tattoo coils around his chest and back, then up his neck, jaws opening over his jaws.

Hunger is thin, his face and neck decorated with his mother's blue swirl tattoos. A dozen metal studs glint in his ears. His black hair is loose.

Both Blazes carry distinctive blades with wicked hooks at the tip.

It's no secret my mother despises their mother, Rek. The feeling is mutual. Rek defied Timbe and the other Captains by sowing sons without virus, bragging that love alone bonded them to her. Rek refuses to dock their tongues, too. I have no love for Blazes—crude braggarts, for the most part, who relish a fight. Yet they're fellow warriors. This far east of Dolor, they'd be free if they wanted to be.

Tanoak quietly scoffs. Rek's sons are fierce fighters, but poor trackers. Burn and Hunger trample the spot where we backed into the water, churning up our trail.

I ask, *Have you heard any hybas?*

Likely sleeping off yesterday's meal, Tanoak says.

Too bad.

Hunger cries, "Left this behind, so they did!" He hacks at the tree trunk where the rope is tied. The rope slithers into the current and is gone.

Tanoak sighs. He loved his rope. *If those idiots make any more noise, every hyba pack within a day's journey will come.*

Hunger jabs his sword at Burn. "Have you a look on the other side, brother."

Burn's laugh is harsh. "You ain't the master of me. I'll hold this bank for you case that scuttle's creeping about after the walloping he got from my blade. Them Trees can't be far."

Scuttle is slang for wildmen. Tanoak taps my arm. *Look at Burn's feet.*

Burn is barefoot. Whoever he smacked with his blade also stole his boots. It has to be the scuttle who crossed the Cursed River ahead of us. A barefoot Blaze is the first hopeful thing I've seen since we left Dolor. Maybe that scuttle knows about the east. Maybe he knows how to find Remedy plants.

Hunger jabs his blade at his brother. "I said git and I mean git! You let that sly boy steal your boots, so you get in there and get them boots back!"

Without warning, Burn launches himself at his brother. Hunger's blade spins up, then smacks the water and sinks. Their fight is brief and vicious. Burn wins by trapping Hunger in a chokehold, then squeezing until his brother's face goes tomato-red.

Burn aims a kick at his brother. "You git!"

Even mighty Tanoak struggled against the powerful current.

Hunger thrusts his arms up, as if keeping them dry will help him against the water's pounding. Immediately, he stumbles and falls to his knees, struggling to stand again.

"Aw, dancey, dancey," Burn guffaws. "Now who's crying? Them fishes nibbling at your toes? Hungerin' for Hunger, hoo!"

Hunger takes small steps, then falls again, this time going completely under. This is exactly what happened to me when I cracked Cedar's head open. I feel sick. If only I'd managed to keep my feet, my brother would be alive. I don't want the Blaze to cross but I also don't want to watch another warrior die. A *person*. I feel my own thighs ache in sympathy as Hunger braces himself, every shred of energy spent on just standing.

Burn hoots again. "Don't come back without word of them miserable Trees. Or I'll tell our mother you was weak, so I will, and she'll skin you, tan you, and trim you into a little drum for our baby brothers! Scream will tap, tap, tap it, tappity tap your hide all the way 'round Dolor. Gorgeous, so it will be with your lovely tattoos for decoration."

Burn is so taken with his taunts that he doesn't hear a faint howl from above. When Hunger looks up, so do I. I glimpse flashes of red, green, and yellow.

Grabeens. This time, Hunger's dive is purposeful.

Burn's mouth looks like an open sack. If he'd had time to put his finger in front of his lips, the gesture would mean *surprise*. The flock howls as it falls on him. There must be thirty birds, each the size of a barn cat, with talons and razor-sharp beaks. Burn vanishes in a frenzy of what looks like bright yellow breeches.

I grip my stave, a reflex.

Tanoak rests his huge hand on my throwing arm. *This is our lucky morning.*

The three of us could kill a dozen grabeens from where we crouch. But we couldn't kill them all. The ones we didn't kill would come for us. Within a minute, all that's left of Burn is bone, some bloody orange hair, a shred of breeches, his water flask, and his peculiar blade.

They even eat his leather belt.

Hunger surfaces twice to breathe, then quickly sinks again

beneath the froth, letting the grabeens finish their grisly meal. As quickly as they came, the grabeen flock takes to the air and is gone.

Cautiously, Hunger pops his head above the water, then clambers up the bank. His blade's long gone. His soaked breeches drag low over his ass. He's shivering so hard he can barely walk. Hunger goes to the bloody mess left by the grabeens and fishes out his brother's blade and water flask. Then he unlaces his breeches, pulls out his crook, and douses his brother's remains in steaming piss.

"Haw!" he grunts.

Once he's finished, he kicks apart Burn's bones. Hunger looks quickly across the water. "Too bad them Trees killed my dear brother. Savages, they are, since he'd already surrendered. That'll get mother's blood to boiling, so it will. I'm guessing she'll want their skins for her little drums."

He lopes back the way he came.

They'll come back, more of them and with the taste of revenge on their tongues, Tanoak says. *We have to leave now.*

We do, without a bite of breakfast.

For the next two days, we only stop to eat, nap, and piss. We run as far into the night as we can without pitching ourselves over a cliff. Once, we slow down near a tree heavy with grabeen nests. The lower branches and trunk are coated in white excrement. Sun-bleached bones pile at the tree's base. I hear soft peeping as we creep past.

On the third day, we climb a rocky ridge. In the distance, the Cursed River winds like molten pergama through the pines. Tanoak finds another boot print with a distinctive zig zag pattern. The print is fresh, only a couple of hours old.

We're on our last day of Remedy with no sign of the Remedy plant. We need to find this scuttle. That afternoon, a derak fawn peeks out from behind a bush. Tamarack is quick with his huaraca, the fawn making a single cry before it falls dead.

We make camp immediately. That evening, we eat well, starting with the heart, kidneys, and liver and ending with a fatty slice of haunch apiece. If we can find meat, surely we'll find the scuttle wearing Burn's boots. Surely, we'll find Remedy.

We have to.

Willow buries the fawn's hide even though Whitebark begs for it, to repair our clothing and shoes. We don't have time to tan it or supplies enough to do more than watch the hide rot. With the Blazes pursuing us, we hide our tracks as best we can.

Whitebark does harvest some intestine. Cross-legged by the fire, he strips and slices the coils to make lacings and wound stitchings.

While my brothers settle down to nap, Tanoak scouts ahead.

Willow sits next to me. *The fawn ate well,* he says. *Plenty of fat.*

Young, I answer. An adult would have tusks as long as Willow's knife, not ivory nubs.

The young are weakest. So it's been and so it always will be.

It's a grim peace offering after our fight. *I should have bound him to me,* I tell my brother. *The pack came too quickly. There were too many.*

Maybe we'll come to envy him. He didn't suffer.

I don't tell him I spoke to Ash at the river bank. I saw Cedar healed. I'm tempted to ask Willow what to think about how Ash spoke of a cure for the virus. But I hold my tongue. He already thinks I've put him and my brothers in danger. I don't want him to think I'm going crazy.

Tanoak tells me Hunger pissed his brother's bones, Willow says. *He rejoiced in his brother's death.*

"They're Blazes after all." Then I regret it. For many months, Willow had Bonded with their cook. He and the Blaze would steal away to be together. Before escaping Dolor, I didn't even ask myself if some of my brothers were leaving behind more than the mother-bond.

I wish I could say or do something to show that I understand he's also grieving this lover. But what is there to say? The silence is long and uncomfortable.

My hand brushes my pocket. I feel the stick figures. At seventeen, I'm no sprig, but I still remember my own warrior toys. I had one of Ash, too, and my mother. The legionaries they fought were no more than rocks and pine cones.

I take the warrior-shaped toy out and run my finger along the pecan-shell head. If Cedar had used corn silk in the top knot, the figure would be one of the warrior Dreams. More metal and a tuft of orange thread and Hunger himself would stare back at me.

Cedar would want you to have this, I tell Willow, placing the toy on the stone between us.

Willow examines the toy. *I remember when Cedar begged me for a pecan to make the head. For the hair, he wanted yellow moss, what I use to flavor stew. The moss was too fragile, I told him. It wouldn't last. A cook I know from the Blazes gave him the dilidot hair.*

It's the gentlest of rebukes. The cook helped Willow make a toy to please our young brother. Willow loved him. Willow moves the toy's arms to make it look as if Ash means to speak. Then he hands the toy back to me. *This could be useful.*

What use do we have for toys? "What do you mean?"

We saw the mother-bond in Timbe's face. We knew she made us from her body. What do we have now, with no mother-bond? We're like apples and oranges and pears and fine peaches. Different hair and skin and bodies. Some like our mother and some... He scans his own broad belly. *I always thought they took extract from a Harvest warrior to brew me.*

I rarely think about the warrior my mother used to make me. I look enough like her to know that I'm her son: her slender body, her pecan-colored skin, her gray-green eyes.

You won't take us back to her. I accept that, Willow says. *But we can't replace the mother-bond with only words. Words are easily twisted. We need something more, something we can all believe in.*

"Are you saying we should believe in a toy?"

It's a toy that means something. This isn't just one warrior, but many. Made by many. It's not just Ash, but all of us. Any of us. We see ourselves in it. We see our Bond. We need something to believe in, dear brother.

"We have the brother-bond."

But we don't see it. This, he says, pointing to the toy, *is real.*

"So it's Ash?" Would my brothers still think of me as commander?

He thinks for a moment. *We should call him Fire Brother. It doesn't really matter what the name is. Just something we can all see.*

I still don't understand. "It's a play thing."

Look. This is Ash, then, he says, covering the hair, *it's also sweet Cedar. Bitternut and even poor Burn. You, too. He could be any of us: lost, slave, or free. He's every brother who's been born and suffered. He's every brother who's died or been killed. He's you and me together, Fir. All of us.*

"But the toy will fall apart. What do we do then?"

Willow thinks for a moment. *We have to tell a story. Fire Brother's story. And the story of us, the Living Wood. Like the praise song Fig sings when one of us dies. The song binds us. We are our stories and Fire Brother reminds us. Like your freedom, dear brother. It's an idea we need to make real.*

Willow pulls a small cloth from his sack and hands it to me. *A cloak for Fire Brother. To keep him safe.*

My brother's only two years older than me, but so much wiser. Yet still I don't tell him about the other toy I found: 12. That's a private thing, a secret thing, to keep close. 12 and then the Captain who was always by her side: Dinitra.

Whitebark has been following our conversation. Curious, he comes to stare at Fire Brother. *Let me show my brothers,* he says, reaching for the toy.

Whitebark is careful to wrap the toy in the cloak. He shows the toy to our brothers. A light snow starts to fall. Willow and I watch as our brothers as they examine Fire Brother.

Then Willow rests his hand on my shoulder. *Tomorrow, we'll eat the last of the Remedy. Four more days and we're dead, brother Fir, Fire Brother or no.*

5

Scuttle

Tanoak returns to our camp. He's breathless. *The scuttle's close.*

He shows me a stone spattered with blood. I touch a drop with my finger: still moist. *Wounded,* Tanoak says. *Even a nick of a Blaze's blade leaves a fearsome wound. He's slowing down.*

"Let's go get him then." My voice is tight with excitement. Maybe Fire Brother really is bringing us luck, I think to myself.

With Tanoak and two other brothers, we race up the scuttle's trail. The trail follows the curve of a rocky slope. Though the sun is setting, I don't need Tanoak to point to the marks. On the ice-crusted snow, blood drops freeze like tiny red candies.

The scuttle is canny. He's trying to lose us in the crags above a lake. But he's no match for Tanoak. Once, Tanoak hunted a wild boar through a marsh, the trail no more than a crushed lily pad or two and bubbles in the soft mud. Yet that night we feasted, harvesting enough fat for Thorn to render a season's worth of healing salve.

We reach a high lake rimmed in snow. Tanoak goes straight to a boulder fall. There, the scuttle is wedged into a crack. Tanoak grabs and pulls. A bit of sacking becomes a leg and an arm red with blood.

The scuttle's got enough life in him to spit and bite. The left side of the scuttle's face is swollen and bruised a greeny-black. By the look of him, the Blazes sliced through his left cheek and down his upper arm to the bone. The edges of the wound fester pus-green. The boy's hair is like a nest of tiny snakes, black as his furious eyes.

He wears Burn's stolen boots. He's no older than Cedar. Across his nose and cheeks scatter copper-colored freckles.

I say, *Calm yourself.*

The scuttle stops biting, though whether that's because of my command or exhaustion I can't tell. Wildmen have their own shape language. Maybe he doesn't understand. If a boy's abilities don't develop properly, he's expelled after the docking but before any time is wasted on warrior training. The ones who survive find their way to other wildmen. They must learn the new words that keep them alive.

Tanoak trusses the scuttle like a derak kill, hands and feet bound. Then he throws him over his shoulder. The boy tries to bite, so Tanoak tells him, *You can bite my ass, little one.* He swings him head down over his lower back, gripping him by the ankles.

We return to our camp. Eyes big as fists, my brothers crowd in to stare. With a thump, Tanoak drops the scuttle in the dirt beside Willow's grub fire.

He's woozy from the ride and blood loss. "Are you hungry?" I press my fingertips to my lips. *Eat?*

The scuttle's expression is savage. I start to step closer, but Tanoak holds me back. *They've been known to take out a warrior's eyes.*

Willow hands me a strip of yesterday's cold paddle loaf. The loaf is pink with Remedy. "Good loaf," I say to the boy. To prove it, I take a bite. *Good loaf.*

There's no mistaking the boy's revulsion when I hold the loaf out to him. His thumb and short finger join. It's our word, too: *poison.* Willow looks from the boy to the loaf and back. *The scuttle means Remedy. It's Remedy he calls poison.*

Thorn peers at the boy. *If Remedy's poison, he needs none. He has no virus. This one's beast-born.*

Other than Rek's Blazes, the only males without virus are beast-born. No one selects their qualities, brews them with care in the laboratory, then evaluates if the mixture runs true. They're like pots where anything can be tossed in to cook: twigs and stone, a bit of gristle, hard berries, spit to loosen the mix. Disgusting and unnatural.

Warriors shun them. Petal, son of one of the Bounty Captains, was beast-born. The only reason he was tolerated was because he was

Anku's: a Captain few were reckless enough to challenge. Anku had no other sons. She'd take Petal with her on secret journeys into the Weave.

She and Petal were the only ones Dinitra's mother trusted to bring her daughter and the hyba cross to Bounty.

We suspected Anku lay with a Sea Hunt warrior, since Petal was born with webbed fingers. Petal even looked wild. Skinny and knob-kneed, he had a bright red thatch of hair and a sideways grin. Petal always hung over Dinitra's shoulder when she was drawing. He pestered her so much she taught him to draw just to give herself a break.

I grew to like the boy. Dinitra wouldn't mistreat this beast-born scuttle even if he did try to bite her. "Give him meat," I tell Willow.

The boy can't shove the derak strips into his mouth fast enough. Even as he chews, tears spring from his eyes from the pain of his wounded cheek.

Only when there's no more derak does the scuttle speak again. *He won't spare the likes of you.*

My brothers shift uneasily. "Who won't spare us?" I ask.

The scuttle repeats himself as if these are the only words he possesses: *he, spare, likes of you.* Then his eyes roll up and he passes out.

Don't let him die, I tell Thorn. I don't have to add: the scuttle's our last hope for Remedy before we start to see signs of Remedy sickness.

As a fysic, Thorn treats everyone, even a scuttle. Even a beast-born. One brother grinds a fresh poultice of powdered starry white for swelling, bitter comfort and telling tree bark for infection, and laurel to ease the pain. Willow stokes his grub fire, to melt ice.

Will the scuttle live? I ask Thorn.

Even if I break the fever, blood loss may take him. Look at his hand.

The scuttle's hand reminds me of Cedar's. The fire glows right through it. *He won't lose the arm, I don't think. Sleep and food are as important as any poultice I can prepare.*

My brother doesn't need to say that a starved, sick scuttle may not be worth what little food and medicine we have. Healing him doesn't make him our friend. It may not even loosen his tongue. But it's clear from the path he took to try and escape that he knows these lands. He's the best hope we have to find Remedy and this Master of men.

"What do you think he meant about the Master? When will he wake up? I need to speak to him."

Speak all you like, Thorn says. *He'll wake when he wakes.*

Over his grub fire, Willow stirs a healing broth of derak bone and wild garlic. Once it cools, he siphons the liquid into the boy's mouth with a hollow reed. The scuttle is what we call *pure*—no tattoos or scars save the ones he'll bear from these wounds.

As he withdraws the reed, Willow looks up, incredulous. One pointer finger slips over the other. *The scuttle is tongued.*

"By the mother's breath," I whisper. Petal is the only beast-born I know still with a tongue. Could this be the child of a Captain like Anku who refused the docking knife? How did the boy come to know this Master? I want to shake him awake, but all night the boy sleeps. Willow and Thorn sleep on either side, their cloaks feathered over him.

In the morning, Willow holds the empty Remedy satchel over a bowl he's using to catch the water he's using to rinse the fabric. Our last taste of Remedy. *We're out of time, brother*, he says.

I ask Thorn, "Can we move him? The Blazes won't be far behind us."

His gray eyes are steady. *If you want him to die.*

I can't sit any more just staring. I take two brothers to retrace our steps down the slope and check for any sign of Blazes. The skies are low with snow clouds, making it impossible to sight smoke from a distant grub fire.

We find a shallow lake. The surface is iced over except for a steamy spot along the bank where a hot spring burbles. I dip in my feet and watch my brothers hack a hole through the center. They sink in their arms and wriggle their fingers, waiting for a hungry fish to bite.

Bees eagerly harvest the bit of sweet spire left from summer. I distract myself by thinking of names for this place: Marsh Lake, Fish Lake, Hot Spring Lake. My brothers and I found Sil at a lake like this. On the southern slope of the Black Stairs, the lake formed over the pergama mine where Sil had worked as a miner. He'd been brewed for his ability to dive into the underwater caves. After the last bit of pergama had been carted away, the Weave abandoned him. The Weave wanted only pergama, not the creatures brewed to mine it.

Pergama is precious to the Weave. They use it to build their helios and the Concave that feeds them fuel. The fleet, in other words, built to end all men. We felt pity for these creatures. When we rescued Sil, he was no more than a bit of dull green skin over bone. His gills were singed black by the sun.

If Sil almost died, how could a mere scuttle manage alone, with no brothers to heal him or hunt with him? No friend to protect him? No mother to guide him? Is that the kind of freedom we seek?

The scuttle seems to be a boy without a Bond. At least, no Bond I recognize. What kind of life is that?

Something tickles me. Dozens of fat brown strings dangle from my shins. I swish my legs, releasing a cloud of muck. The strings are latched on.

Leeches. They hibernate in mud. My fresh blood drew them out.

Thorn will be happy. He can draw more saliva for his forgetting.

I slide backwards onto the frozen grass. One by one, I place my thumb besides their lips and force them to release. They pucker and squirm. I drop the leeches into my pouch, then layer them with stems of dry grass.

Leech Lake. Perfect.

Back at the camp, the scuttle is still asleep. My brothers hand Willow a fine string of fish to roast.

Thorn nods when I show him the leeches. One by one, he touches their sucker mouths to the scuttle's wounds. They'll help keep blood flowing and hasten healing. Once the leeches have their fill, one by one, he milks them, filling his bottles with their cloudy saliva.

When the scuttle stirs, a full moon is high. His cheeks are pink, not blazing red with fever. His eyes are clear. Though still red, his wounds are no longer inflamed. When the boy motions for meat, Willow gives him a whole roasted fish.

"My name is Fir," I tell the boy. "We are the Living Wood. I know you speak. Tell me your name."

The contempt in his voice startles me. "You'll die like all the rest. Even if you survive, he'll never let you go."

I swallow my shock. "Who do you mean?"

"You'll see."

"The Blazes attacked you. We saved your life. We're not here to hurt you."

"You're all the same, in the end."

I don't have time to waste on riddles. I could beat the answer out of him, but I suspect he's faced far worse than fists. "At least repay us for saving your life. Where can we find Remedy...the poison, as you call it?"

"Not a fair trade." The scuttle speaks like he's in charge. "I'll show you poison if you've got something to trade. I'm looking for a man who went to your lands. But I found only ruins there. What happened?"

"You mean Quillka?" Our home, destroyed by the Weave's fleet weeks ago.

He shakes his head. "The place called Dolor. Home of them cursed Blazes."

"There are no ruins there."

"There are ruins now."

I step back. If Dolor is a ruin, that means the Weave's fleet has attacked. I knew our mother would likely die there, but the news still shocks me. Despite everything, I still love her. She made me: she made all of us. But something doesn't fit. If the Weave destroyed Dolor, why are Blazes hunting us? *Don't come back without word of them miserable Trees,* Burn told his brother before the grabeens killed him.

"Did you see the helio fleet?" I press him.

"You haven't answered my question. About the man on the painted horse."

"Describe him." We've seen no such man, no one at all. But any information he has could be useful.

"The man I seek rides a painted horse: black, white, and red," the scuttle says. "One black eye and one white, he has. He was near here not two weeks ago for a talk with that Captain Rek."

"Captain Rek," I repeat. A man had a secret meeting with Rek? Rek told the Captains she wanted an alliance with the Master. Is that the painted man? "A talk about what?"

The boy reminds me of an angry hornet. "You got nothing to trade."

I healed you, Thorn says. *And I can unheal you. Answer my brother's question.*

The scuttle squirms. "I'll show you your poison berry, but that's all. That's the trade. Then I'll be on my way."

There's no way I'm letting the scuttle go. My heart races. He'll find us the berries then tell us more about the Master. He might even lead us straight to him if we beat him enough. Or stuff him with derak. For the first time since escaping Dolor, I feel a glimmer of hope. If Dolor is in ruins, there's nothing to return to. Maybe, we escaped just in time. Now we know there's a real Master and he's on a painted horse.

Whether he'll spare us or not is a question for another day.

"Agreed," I lie to the scuttle.

The scuttle rides Tanoak's shoulders back to the boulders where we caught him. He points at the ridge behind the lake. The slope is almost vertical and covered in grit and small pebbles. For every step we take, we slide a half one back. The snow near the top is hip-high. There, the scuttle tells us to dig.

About a foot down, we uncover a network of black branches. On them are rose hips frozen hard as pebbles.

Willow cracks one between his teeth. I taste a hip, too: bitter and sour. It's the Remedy plant just as Dinitra drew it. We dig out about twenty bushes, and harvest several sacksful of rose hips.

There's enough Remedy for months of paddle loaf. Months of freedom.

The scuttle turns surprisingly chatty. "Poison likes wind. Places that stay buried in snow until summer. You'll always find bushes at the heights."

At our camp, Willow grinds enough berries for a week's worth of paddle loaf. The rest he packs so that each of us has Remedy in our pouches. I can tell Willow's hopeful by the way he cooks, slitting the fish down their bellies, scooping out the guts, and stuffing them with a paste of chopped broad weed, wild garlic, and ground Remedy berries. He stitches the bellies closed with grass stems so that he can roast them speared along their spines.

As a treat, Willow buries moon root under the coals. The roots cook until the outer husks char black. When he chops through, the inner flesh spills out bright orange and sweet as custard. The scuttle eats his fill of everything except the Remedy stuffing. Then he curls like a puppy at Thorn's feet and sleeps.

Thorn covers the boy with his cloak.

Before taking my rest, I make a final circuit of our camp. I hear small animals scratching and scrambling in the bushes. For them, this is home. The thought comforts me. We're looking for a home. Perhaps it's as simple as that: settling somewhere. *Home*: the fingertips of one hand pressed to the back of the other. We could even make a place for Fire Brother in the boulders where we found the scuttle. He would be safe there, I think.

We have full bellies, Remedy aplenty, fresh forgetting, and the scuttle, whatever his name is, to guide us. He'll spit and even bite, but that's a small price to pay. Willow will give him moon root enough to quiet his complaints. He'll tell us everything we need to know about this Master, the draft Queen, even this mysterious man on the painted horse.

Like a scent, Dinitra drifts into my thoughts. Maybe it's not so crazy to think I'll see her again. When we find our home, I'll make sure my brothers are settled, then look for her in The Deep. The minute 12 scents me, she won't rest until she finds me. Dinitra won't be far behind.

With those thoughts, I find my place among my sleeping brothers.

It's almost dawn when Thorn wakes me. The leeches he set on the scuttle's wounds before going to sleep lie dead and frozen on the ground. Next to them are Burn's old boots.

The scuttle is gone. He's traded Burn's boots for Fig's, a better fit.

Tanoak growls, pointing to the scuttle's trail. *We'll never catch him now.*

6

Fire Brother

Tanoak tracks the scuttle past the Remedy bushes. On the far side of the crags is a steep drop and a narrow valley shrouded in thick mist.

We pause. Should we follow him? He's going somewhere.

Avoiding danger or leading us to it?

Might as well follow, Willow says. *If he's not eating my paddle loaf, he's eating what someone else cooks. We should find out who that someone is.*

As Tanoak suspected, Fig's better-fitting boots mean the scuttle moves fast. A herd of derak has kicked away some of his footprints, but it's clear that the boy is running.

He has three hours on us at least. Tanoak has been trained to read a trail without emotion, since any commander has to make decisions that aren't swayed by the tracker's panic or anger. *He's weak, but he knows this land. He knows where he's going.*

I swear loudly. I kick at stones. I should have put a guard on him. I should have laid beside him, I should have lashed him to my own body as I should have lashed Cedar. Battle-tested and highly-trained, the Living Wood was outwitted by a starving, wounded scuttle.

Willow doesn't share Tanoak's calm. He slams a fist against his palm. *We don't even know his name.*

The wind carries a bite of fresh snow. Every time we gain, we lose. We gained freedom and lost a brother. We gained Remedy and lost a guide. We're on a terrible scale where every advance costs us.

Tanoak places one pointer finger horizontal to the other. *Surely, the scuttle goes to this Master.*

I have my doubts. If this Master is so powerful, why is the boy alone and starving? Why would he sneak to Bounty alone? Who is the man on the painted horse he seeks? No wildman ever spoke of such a man to us.

Tanoak is startled by the groan that slips slick and miserable out of my mouth. If someone promised we'd end this uncertainty by standing on our heads or building an elaborate dwelling for Fire Brother, I'd do it. Anything to get answers.

With that sound from you, brother Fir, the Hundred-Hundred will think an army of lunatics approaches, Thorn says. *What can we do but follow the boy? He's headed somewhere.*

Here we are, warriors, and a scuttle, beast-born at that, slipped through our fingers. As if to layer misery upon shame, snow starts to layer around our feet.

My brother Tamarack—a deep feeler, with an explosion of coal-black braids—starts to laugh. No: he throws back his great head and lets out a blare so loud jackadaws roosting in the crags nearby burst into the sky. Tanoak echoes him. What else can we do? Willow laughs too, his great belly jiggling. Then another brother, a nasally peep. And another: a snuffle. Fig, our singer, makes a *he-he-he* high as bells.

Tears sparkle in Willow's eyes or perhaps those are melting flakes of snow. *Look at us. Laughing our asses off the edge of the world.*

The land ahead is pathless but for the scuttle's trail. Since the scuttle traded Burn's boots for Fig's, the tread printed in the dirt is the Living Wood's, a tree trunk that spreads into branches to the east: right, left, right, left, like a marching song.

Someone hurls a stone high into the air. I can't say why but the clatter when the stone hits the ground lifts my spirits. In our pouches, we carry fresh derak meat. There's plenty of Remedy thanks to the scuttle's knowledge. We're well-watered. We've eaten, we've pissed. There's fresh gut in Thorn's fysic pouch and freshly-milked forgetting from the leeches.

We're going to find this Master, find a home, no matter what stands in our way.

Tonight, we'll run. Tomorrow, we'll run again and eat and piss and sleep. And the tomorrow after that and after that until the Master stands before us.

At least, that scuttle will tell this Master a fysic sewed him well, Thorn says. *He slept on a lake of forgetting as the leeches did their work. He has fine boots. And the fat one,* he gestures at Willow, *made sure he ate his fill. The Master should welcome us on that alone.*

By afternoon, we're climbing again, to a saddle deeply banked in snow. Wading through it exhausts everyone, but there's nowhere to rest. On the far side, the wind is brutal, but there's less snow. The scuttle's trail leads us down a narrow, dark canyon. Just as we're beginning to get nervous about what's on the other side, I smell something sweet and soft, like early spring.

The smell comes from the valley that opens to the east. Crags to the north and south shelter it from the winds. A stream curving through is banked by tree groves, meadows, and carpets of red flowers.

When I touch my cheeks, they're damp. It's so warm, the snow melts just before reaching the ground.

Willow plucks a red flower and sniffs. The flower has long petals that end in delicate curls. Each flower has three pink stalks inside the cup, coated with bright yellow pollen. When Willow rubs the flower between his fingers, there's an explosion of scent: like roses but muskier, sweet, and with a metallic edge.

Willow knows the name of every flower and tree, but he's never seen this one. The flowers are everywhere. As we follow the stream, our legs and boots take on a yellow sheen that starts attracting bees.

Low brambles still bear juicy blackberries. My brothers pluck them and eat as we walk. Willow pauses to turn over some fallen logs, then snorts with delight. He's found a yellow fungus he calls butter bell: delicious. Willow sends one of our brothers into the thickets to search for duck eggs.

We camp at a bend where the stream runs broad and shallow. Willow beats the duck eggs into a froth, mixes them with wild herbs, and fills the cored husks of green apples. The apples bake upright in the coals. The custard is savory, slightly charred, and delicious. With fresh fish caught in the stream stuffed with butter bells and paddle loaf pink with Remedy, the meal feels like a feast.

Afterwards, no one wants to sleep. My brothers sit shoulder to shoulder around the fire. I've posted two brothers as guards. Even then, they don't stray far from the fire's flickering circle.

Willow points his fork at me. *Tell a story about Fire Brother.*

I'm in the middle of a burp. *What?*

Fire Brother. His pointer fingers are together while the rest wriggle. I realize it's the new shape word he's thought up for Cedar's toy: *Fire Brother.*

My brothers are eager to hear a tale. "Once upon a time, there was a warrior who discovered fire," I start. The story comes gradually, like a path that only reveals itself a step at a time. "He led his brothers into the Splinters." The Splinters are where the mountains fall into The Deep. "They were so tired. The warrior found them a place to camp. He gave them his own cold food and his own cold water, but it wasn't enough."

"This could be a song, brother," Fig says. He starts to sing, but Spruce claps sharply. *You limp crook, you're ruining the story.*

Spruce looks at me eagerly. *What did Fire Brother do next?*

"Patience." Do my brothers understand that I'm making this up as I go? Willow winks at me, urging me to continue. I close my eyes, as if the story's whispering to me. "What they needed was warmth. A fire like this one." My fingers curl into *fire*: palms up and fingers wriggling.

What would warriors who don't know fire actually do? They'd eat everything raw. "Until then, they'd lived like beasts, eating uncooked flesh and moon root still tough from the ground."

My brothers are transfixed.

"The warrior remembered how in some places fire flows from the Mother's crevasses. Fire strikes in lightning bolts, igniting trees. Sometimes, fire from below makes pools steam and mud pots bubble."

Sometimes, it comes out of Balsam's ass, someone smirks.

Shut up. This from Tamarack. Tamarack has a temper quick as his throwing arm. *Or I'll twist your ear off and toast it here and now. I'm still hungry. Leave our brother to tell his tale.*

"Fire is in the Mother, the warrior realized. Beneath the dirt and even in a twig or leaf. The warrior took a stick. He cracked it against a stone. No fire. He struck a stick with another stick: no fire. He hammered the stone with his own fist: only blood and pain. In his anger, he flung the stone. When it hit a boulder, he saw a blue spark."

Fire, Tamarack says eagerly.

I nod. "He hammered stone on stone. Each time, the spark flamed and died."

What is fire without fuel? asks Tamarack. *I could teach that dolt Fire Brother a lesson.*

My brothers laugh. Tamarack can coax fire from a single dry leaf with his flints. "Just so. Like warriors, fire needs sustenance. Fire needs care, as the warrior cared for his brothers, as his brothers cared for him."

Twigs are what he needs, dry things, crackly things, Willow says.

Pine straw, Tamarack adds.

"With a bit of dried grass and patience, the warrior captured the fire. He made it grow. His brothers brought him sticks and chaff, whatever they found that could burn. The light kept the beasts at bay. The light kept them warm. They ate their fill. The light gave them hope."

Fire brother gave them hope, Willow nods, a bit too firmly. Stories are best when the teaching inside them is hidden.

"All night, the hybas howled and lashed their tails and sharpened their terrible claws, but they were afraid of the fire. Over the flames, the warriors cooked their food and found it delicious. That night, they slept in the fire's light and were comforted."

And lived, says Juniper. He came from the group of sons after me and still has the gangly appearance of a young boy.

"And lived," I repeat.

"We honor him every time we kindle a fire." As I'm telling the story, I understand better Willow's point about Fire Brother. Having Fire Brother gives us something to thank, something to hope for. Someone besides me to bind and protect them. "Fire Brother leads and sustains us," I say.

"Like our mother?" Fig asks.

My brother's face is without cunning. He misses our mother and wants something to believe in. He's grasped the core of what Willow and I are trying to do. We're using a story to replace our love for our mother and our obedience to her with Fire Brother and the Bond we share as brothers.

But this won't happen quickly. I can't expect my brothers to change the way they think as easily as we might change a pair of boots, a worn pair for a fresh one. "Fire Brother," I say, "is the spark trapped in the stone. He's always with us. Always has been. More than our mother, for he's never far. He's one of us, equal to us. Just as we suffer, so does he. And when we triumph, he shares our joy."

I point to Whitebark. He's been carrying Fire Brother all day. As he unwraps it, my brothers' eyes shine with new wonder. For a long moment, I let them stare at the toy, the fire's light turning Fire Brother's hair from black to orange to black again.

"Fig will carry Fire Brother tomorrow," I say. "Each of us will have our turn to keep him safe."

Fig looks pleased and a little frightened. As my brothers bed down, I see Whitebark's quick instructions to him. *Don't put him so close. You'll roll on him. You must pack him properly in the morning. Careful or the arm will snap. Fig, you're a dolt if you leave him in the pine straw. Some mouse will make off with his head!*

Willow and I sit alone as the fire crumbles. *You did well, brother*, he tells me. *That story will buy us at least a week's worth of hard walking, I think.*

Still, I don't reveal that there's a second toy, a 12, in my pocket. That's for me alone.

The next day, we continue down the spring-like valley. Tanoak sees only the scuttle's footprints, no others. Yet I begin to feel like someone—something—is watching. I think about this draft Queen. The bees humming at the red flowers seem the same as any others. Tanoak assures me he's seen no signs of dwellings or drafts, no trails, just the scuttle's foot prints. All I see is plenty: laden fruit trees, a stream teeming with fish, and the perfume of the red flowers.

That night, I tell another story about how Fire Brother learned the healing arts. The next night, I make up an adventure story about how Fire Brother caught and tamed a fearsome speluk, a cave dweller in the shape of a man but who eats like a spider, sucking the juices of his prey. Fire Brother lit the speluk's cave on fire, forcing it into the sunlight. There, he speared the speluk and tanned its skin for a fine new coat.

It's a good story.

On the third day, we stop on a small rise to eat a cold lunch. My brother Birch, Fire Brother's bearer for the day, cuts fresh, green grass to cushion the toy. Apprenticed to our blacksmith, my brother has powerful arms and fine, neatly tapered fingers, capable of great delicacy. He sits with his back to a tree and weaves a protective twig cradle.

All we need to do is catch the fruit when it falls and welcome the fish as they leap from the water, Willow says, patting his belly contentedly. *I could grow fond of being free in a place like this.*

I have to agree. I've even considered staying. But the scuttle's steady trail east means one thing: he's heading for something more than what's here. And he's going fast. He must have meant that the Master wouldn't welcome us. Why? Could the scuttle warn the Master's forces and urge them to attack us? We're just a handful of warriors. If Tanoak's right about the Hundred-Hundred, we're no threat.

A deeper worry scratches at me. Are we safe in this valley? The scuttle seems to have a plan, but is it to avoid something or lead us to it? It's strange that this valley stays so mild in the middle of winter. Can those red flowers be dulling our senses with their powerful scent?

Willow stretches out for a nap, but I'm too restless to sleep. I want to look around. On the far side of the stream is a dense stand of pine, then a sharp rise to a set of high crags. Perhaps there's an outcropping where we can get a better look at what's ahead.

Oak's eyes dance when I point to the trees. *Pine honey,* he says. On patrol, we'd often gather pine honey from bees that harvest the sugary secretions of insects that live on pine sap. Willow claims honey is a way of distilling time. When we eat it, we taste a season's warmth and every rain condensed into golden drops.

Honey wouldn't be a bad treat for the next several days.

I'd like to see Willow dance when we bring him honey, Oak grins.

I feel a prickle of unease. Yet we've seen no signs of habitation, not even footprints other than the scuttle's. Not humans and certainly no drafts. And Thorn needs more pine sap, which he uses to close small cuts.

What harm can there be in getting a look around? Oak and I grab our staves and some sticks to light to make smoke to gentle any hive we find.

Once we're under the shadows of the pines, Oak kindles a quick fire. We coat the ends of the branches in pine pitch, then light them. Although the valley is bright with midday sun, under the trees there is a permanent gray shadow.

Listen, Oak says. Under the rustling of the branches, we hear a hive hum.

I remind myself: we've seen no evidence of houses or farms. No soldiers, no fortress. No Queen. I can almost taste the honey we'll harvest, honey I promised to poor Cedar.

Oak scrambles up a steep slope. He's spotted the distinctive white scaling of the insects the honey bees feed on. He unties the leather strap around his waist, which he'll use to climb. I leave my smoldering stick propped against the trunk he chooses.

I move further on to get a better view. As I climb a rise, I see the sparkle of water. Beyond are crags I can climb to see the valley and whatever lies further east. The sparkle comes from a lake. I'm thinking it's another Leech Lake, but the water looks much deeper and colder. The crags beyond are an unusual color, more yellow than gray. A breeze coaxes wavelets from the water's surface. Strangely, the humming of Oak's hive seems louder. The sound isn't behind me, where Oak is beginning to climb, but ahead.

Then I see that the crags aren't made of rock. The surface is too ordered. They look more like fungus, like butter bells, but enormous, hanging in great yellow lobes. Each lobe is striped yellow and orange and is pocked with thousands of six-sided holes. The holes seem to shiver as bees—human-sized, with spindly arms and legs—crawl in and out. I smell honey and mold and something sharper, like perfumed metal.

The red flowers.

Then I know. We've stumbled on the draft Queen. This is her fortress. With a sick lurch, I realize that her fortress isn't made of stone, but of yellow and orange honeycomb.

This is where males like me vanish. Males like us. Just then, a fish fin breaks the lake's surface. By the look of it, the fish is the size of a full-grown cow. The beast propels itself partly up a sandy bank, to a pile of what looks like corn cobs. The fish sucks them up. I see arms and legs and heads flopping.

The cobs are bodies.

I run back to Oak's tree. I hiss loudly. *We have to get out of here. Drop me your stick.*

He shakes his head. He thinks the hive he seeks is just a little higher up.

Drop me your stick. Now. Then I add: *danger*: two fists, one in front of the other.

He drops his stick. I shove the ends of both sticks into the soft pine dirt, to extinguish the smoke. Oak drops down beside me, his eyes wide and terrified.

A bee lands on his forehead. Then another.

A bee lands on my wrist. Bees push through my fingers and force me to drop my stave. They push under my tunic, into my breeches, into my boots.

Oak's eyes are bright with terror. They're the only part of him not completely skinned in bees. He shapes a word, thumbs crossed. The word seems made of humming, twitching, black and yellow-striped bees.

The word is *afraid*.

7

Hive Home

A dozen figures separate from the tree trunks. They're taller than my tallest brother. Yellow fur rings their necks and ankles in dense ruffs. Their arms—four apiece—are shiny black and quadruple-jointed, each ending in a set of three claws. They wear armor and carry clubs the dark yellow of the lobes of honeycomb on the heights.

The largest of the creatures levels a spear at us. The tip is cruelly barbed. The thing's body is encased in black armor plates that shift as it moves. Instead of a mouth, it has mandibles, curved and set like a sideways beak. I see myself in the creature's eyes, big as Tanoak's fists and sectioned into dozens of black hexagons. "We've been expecting you," it says.

The voice: pebbles swirled in a metal cup.

When I raise my hand to shape a word, a bee stings me. Venom courses through me and I shudder. I open my mouth only wide enough to speak. "We're travelers. We mean no harm."

"You follow the boy."

It must mean the beast-born scuttle. "The boy," I repeat. I should have tied up the scuttle. I should have put him in a sack and knotted it well. I would gladly deliver him to this thing in exchange for freedom.

Again, I open my mouth, just a bit, to keep the bees from crawling past my lips. "We're looking for..."

"We know what you seek."

Dozens of times I'm reflected in the creature's eyes. My skin seethes with yellow and black bees. With the spear, the creature jabs west to Bounty. "A day from here, others like you steal fish and derak. They harvest our fruits, defile our grasses. Men with markings and metal in their skins. So says the Swarm. One," the creature says, leaning close, "rejoiced as the other was eaten."

Hunger watched as grabeens tore his brother apart. I feel like I've gulped a bellyful of icy water from the Cursed River.

"One you burned," the creature says. *Cedar*.

"My brother fell when we were crossing the river." I will my voice to stay calm. "That's our way with the dead. That's how we show respect. The fire starts the path into…"

"Fire," the creature hisses, "destroys."

I remember how bees circled my head as the hyba pack closed in. There were bees at Leech Lake, bees when we first saw the valley's red flowers, pleased at our good luck. *The Swarm*. They've been following us and reporting back since we left Dolor. "We mean you no harm," I blurt.

"Yet harm you bring. Thieving. Polluting. Destroying. The ones who hunt you leave a bone trail. They kill for joy. Filthy creatures with your shit and leavings. *Humans*."

In the creature's mouth, *humans* is an insult. "The bone trail poisons. Nothing grows until the ground is cleansed. Many sun-hours of work. The bone trail stinks worse than *fire*."

The creature's eyes take in our charred sticks, evidence of our purpose: to steal honey. Against these creatures, against the Swarm, we'd need a forest fire.

"Hive Home gathers and stores. Hive Home cultivates. Hive Home protects," the creature says. "The Queen lets the boy Lark come and go," the creature finishes with a clack of his mandibles. "Lark leads the wildmen to her. That is his work for the Hive."

My eyes drop to the ground. *Lark*: the scuttle. *Curse Lark*. He led us straight to Hive Home. Where men vanish. I should have brought Willow with me. He knows about bees and hives. Frantic, I go through what I know. There's a single Queen to a hive. The bees are her children. Some are workers, some are scouts. Bees are gentled by smoke and terrified by fire. A hundred stings would be the death of me.

What about draft bees the size of humans? What about this creature, who looks like it would rather spear us through than hear another word? I see nothing that makes it male or female. Nothing that tells me how many generations lie between it and an ancestor concocted by the Weave in their labs and discarded on the Black Stairs. Some drafts are peaceful, like the derak we hunt for meat. Others became predators, like the hybas. Dumping their mistakes on the border with Bounty was also the Weave's way of weakening the Captains.

I've only seen a few drafts with the power of speech, like that frog draft, Sil. But Sil could never be as fearsome.

There are at least a thousand bees on me and another thousand on Oak. "My greetings to your Queen." I bow my head slowly, my bee skin shifting. "We come in peace."

The creature grips the spear, seeming to listen to a far-off sound. "My lady wishes to see you. Follow me."

I'm about to say, "But my brothers..." I bite my tongue. If we're gone for too long, they'll come looking for us. These bee creatures may not be so willing to talk before attacking them. Or maybe my brothers will be more cautious and realize they have to escape the Hive Queen. The creature said they'd been watching us for days.

"My brothers," I say. "They must be safe."

The creature hisses again. "My Queen decides. They are watched."

In the next breath, the bees lift from our skin. The two swarms, Oak's and mine, combine into a single cloud, then spiral into the pine branches. The soldiers spread the translucent wings they kept folded on their backs and hover just above the ground. Their commander also lifts, the spear pointing toward the Hive.

No wonder we saw no trails on the ground. There are no trails in the air. These creatures fly.

Beyond the lake, Hive Home rises under snowy crags. Enormous lobes of yellow comb hang vertically from the rock. There are dozens of them: striped yellow, amber, and a deeper color I've only seen in Thorn's potions, like honey darkened by a long simmer over a fire. Everywhere, there is motion: bees crawling, landing, hovering. Some bees are like the ones that covered my skin. Others are the size of human children, with filmy, amber-colored wings.

The buzzing grows louder as we approach.

At the Hive's base, the creature orders us into a large, conical basket of woven sweetgrass. The basket has a sturdy wooden floor that's scuffed with use. As one, the soldiers grasp the handles in the sides with their claws. Their wings beat the air as the basket lifts. We stop halfway up the enormous hive, just above the peak of one waxy lobe. There, the comb is elaborately carved into an entrance around a cleft in the rock.

I swallow the dread in my throat. The Queen sends nektar to the Weave. The Weave uses nektar to make drafts, though how or why it works I don't know. Does the Queen agree with the Weave that men should be exterminated? The wildmen say one thing about her: males who enter her hive never leave.

Were those cobs I saw the fish feasting on actually men? What danger have I brought upon my brothers?

Once again, my desire for freedom may have sentenced all of us to death.

Inside, I smell the sweet metal tang of the valley's red flowers. This is the largest city I've ever seen. What light there is pulses blue and cold from the walls. A sweet stickiness coast my lips. My heart races and not just from panic: the sweetness quickens the pumping of my heart.

The creature leads us into an enormous cavern. To either side, steps spiral up and link the Hive's many terraces. The same blue light pulses from the ceiling, a great unmarked dome. As we climb one of the staircases, I see that each hexagon scored into the walls and ceiling marks a chamber. Some are empty and some are capped with yellow wax. Everywhere, human-sized bee drafts work: smoothing the caps, cleaning empty chambers.

They ignore us. It's as if we don't exist

As we approach one chamber, workers are pulling off the waxy outer lid. They reach inside to drag out a body. The body's curled in on itself like a new leaf. With it comes a gush of golden liquid. The liquid drains through holes in the floor.

The red flower's metallic scent is so thick it makes the air itself feel heavy. Just as we pass, the new creature uncurls its legs and arms.

The workers clack their mandibles. With flat paddles, they scrape off the remaining liquid, then rub the creature's arms and legs vigorously.

We make a sharp left turn into a narrow hallway. Oak's fear is so intense he stumbles.

I steady him. "Keep your wits," I murmur. "Don't say anything. I'll talk for both of us."

There's a sting at my neck: the barb of the creature's spear. "No talking."

The next arch is also elaborately carved. I recognize wildmen and Captains, hybas, grabeens and lithers, waterfalls, trees and mountains and fish twisting exuberantly over a lake. I see the figure of a great ape, too, thick through the belly and dense with hair. Flowers twine everywhere, some set with red gems and others with polished hyba teeth.

As we enter a large room, a dozen pairs of eyes blink at us. These creatures aren't bee-like at all. They're like ground mammals scurrying on two short, chubby legs. Each one is completely covered in dense brown hair that curls tightly over their bellies. Colored half-moons of skin sit under their eyes and match the color of their beaks: blue to blue, pink to pink, purple to purple.

Around a low platform, a dense curtain of bees undulates. The bees move in rhythm, like a heartbeat. I can't make out the figure seated behind the curtain.

"Kneel," the creature behind me hisses.

Oak and I kneel. The creature rests the butt of the spear beside me. "My Queen."

The red flower smell slicks my skin, coats my tongue. The Queen's voice is a low thrum. "Tell me, warrior. Have you eaten well from my lands?"

My cheeks go hot with shame. We ate her fruit, her fish, her derak. Her butter bells, her sweet herbs. She cleared the forest of hybas and the skies of grabeens, and we passed unscathed and ungrateful. We stole from her and never once asked permission or gave thanks. Instead, we praised that ridiculous Fire Brother toy. I thought that our skill, my skill, kept us safe.

It was the Hive Queen all along.

If only I had some gift for her, a new cloak or knife. The bitterness in my throat is heightened by the sweetness coating my lips. Ridiculous! Shall I present a Queen with dried derak? How about a slice of day-old paddle loaf dusted in grit from Willow's grub fire?

The walls and ceiling pulse their sickening blue. I yearn for a bank of snow to clear my head. What can I possibly say to save my brothers? "We didn't know these were your lands. We'd heard of you, of course. Your fame, your nektar..."

My heart races so fast I have to catch my breath. "I beg humble pardon. We are fleeing..."

The words *our mother* stick in my throat. What is a Hive Queen if not a mother? Again, I curse the beast-born scuttle, Lark: liar. If he'd only warned us, I never would have hunted honey. I would have skirted this terrible red valley. I wouldn't have led my brothers into a trap.

All who come in peace are welcome here. Have you eaten well?

I can't see through the curtain of bees. Did she speak aloud? Did I hear her in my mind or did she speak?

Fear prickles down my arms. Even Willow's knowledge of bees wouldn't help me. What good is a practical brother who knows of honey bees when I'm faced with drafts? Part human, part bee, part bancat by the look of the soldiers' yellow fur. I can't stop thinking about what the wildmen said. Men who enter the Queen's fortress never leave. Will I ever see my brothers again?

The bee curtain seems to move to my pounding heart. Or hers. Still, I glimpse only an outline of her head and shoulders. The tip of the commander's spear stings me again. "Answer my Queen, intruder."

I thought we were lucky. I never once imagined that the land already belonged to someone. Helplessness and misery tangle in my gut. "I thank you," I say. "We've eaten well."

I hear her reply and feel it too, a buzzing inside my head. "Tell me your name," the Queen says. "It's something small to start, warrior. A name. What is your name?"

Her words are soothing. Yet I'm surrounded by her soldiers, her children, her Hive. I can only see an outline that's human-shaped, with a head and shoulders. Through the Swarm, she watched me from the moment we crossed the Cursed River. Does she know I saw my dead brothers on its banks? Did she see me dreaming of Dinitra and 12 and the Vessel descending into The Deep? What deadly game is this?

I clench my fists, willing myself to resist the scent of the red flower, the pulsing of the Hive walls. Her voice. "Fir," I say. "My name is Fir."

I feel her pleasure. As if parted by an invisible hand, the bee curtain opens. There she sits: no more than a girl. I see myself fractured into dozens of Firs by her faceted eyes. Her skin is glossy and black as polished jasper. She wears a red gown cut low under her collarbone, revealing the swell of her breasts. Around the Hive Queen's neck is a pergama chain. In everything but her strange eyes, she seems human.

I try to stand, but with a snarl, the commander shoves me down. Angrily, the commander uses a boot to grind my face into the floor. I taste the comb: must and sweetness. Beside me, Oak whimpers on his knees.

"My Queen, these *things*, these *things* cannot be trusted. All they know is killing. *Fire*. They mean to take Hive Home, the Scarlet Valley. They'll trample your precious lilyfire. They'll devour our food, poison our water, kill our children. Criss-cross with the bone trail. They bring only suffering."

The Queen's voice is mild, but I can tell she expects to be obeyed. "Jarvon, my most loyal protector. We have much to gain through friendship."

My breath comes wet with blood from where I bit my tongue. Jarvon's boot sole is molded into the hexagons of her Hive. My cheek is patterned in hexagons.

"These are guests," the Queen says. "Please help them stand."

The boot lifts. Claws slip under my arms and haul me up.

"I wish to see your name, Fir." Her lips are full and red as ripe raspberries. "Shape it for me."

I obey and feel immediate relief. I've done what she asked and quickly. This pleases her. *Fir*, pointing and middle fingers angled across one another, thumbs overlapped. The empty space shapes a fir cone.

"Is this correct?" I lift my eyes high enough to see her hands: narrow, with long fingers and a ring set with a large red stone. She has four fingers, not five. *Fir* is inked in black by her skin.

"Yes," I say.

"My dear Fir, that's no shadow crouched next to you. If my eyes don't betray me, that's a brother. What's your brother's name?" There's a lightness in her voice, almost playful. This isn't what I expected from a Queen I thought would murder us.

I place my right palm up, then meet it with the left palm flat, a mighty plank: *Oak.*

"To Oak, then." She shapes his name. "To Fir." Echoed by her voice, our names are a graceful hand dance. "To all who come in peace, my Hive bids welcome. You've heard tales that men come and never leave. I feel this in you. Do not be afraid. These are lies. You're safe here."

The Queen laughs with a child's lightness. I can't help but smile. I see none of Jarvon's violence in her. "What's my name in your language?" she asks.

I think back to what Jarvon called her: *my lady.* We call our mothers Captain. In the Weave, they were Sowers, the most powerful. We fight the Weave's legionaries: soldiers. For farmers or cooks, female is enough. But there's no shape word for lady, whatever that means. "I don't think we have a shape to match you," I say haltingly.

Then I regret not being more flattering. I should have praised her wisdom or her kindness, the size of her Hive. My eyes follow the curves of the red dress and my breath catches.

I have to say something. "I don't know your name, lady."

"Odide." This time, I hear her whisper in my mind. *Odide.*

Odide steps from the platform, the bees moving like a second shadow. She's taller than me by a head and slender as a sapling. As I look up, I imagine circling her small waist with my hands. Like a girl, but not a girl. A Queen.

She reaches for my hand. There are tiny hairs on her palm that move against my skin. Her face is heart-shaped. Yellow pollen bands her eyes. In them, I see two dozen Firs, all with a mouth agape and eyes full of wonder.

I see and feel her amusement. My fear melts away.

"Come warrior Fir. Let's talk just us two."

8

Odide

I follow Odide deeper into the Hive. In a small room, Odide settles on a low couch. The fabric looks like hair, but is a deep purple, like no creature I've ever seen. Chittering, the furred creatures adjust her dress and smooth her hair, which falls like a black curtain down her back.

The Queen releases my hand. Suddenly I miss her touch and crave it. In the corner, a bird sits on a perch of silver pergama. A pergama collar rings its neck, attached to the perch with a delicate pergama chain.

Jarvon stands silently in the doorway.

"Don't leave a Queen sitting alone, warrior Fir," Odide says mildly.

Jarvon growls from the doorway. "My lady, your safety."

"I have nothing to fear. Do I, warrior Fir? Leave us, Jarvon."

I feel her command, too: *leave*. Jarvon withdraws and we're alone but for the furry creatures. To me, Odide gestures at the space beside her on the couch, so that I will sit. I move before I can even think of what it might mean to be so close. What am I afraid of? I want to feel those tiny hairs again on my hand. Really, there's nothing more in the world I want than to sit beside her.

But I can't. There's something else I need to think about, but it escapes me, like a name I can't remember. I feel taut as Tanoak's rope across the Cursed River. Except this river is soft and warm and scented with the red flowers. "My lady," I stammer.

I remember now: Oak. Oak didn't follow us.

Odide's irritation is sharp as a bee sting. "I told you your brother is safe."

She reaches for my hand again, the tiny hairs on her palms moving with some internal current. A sense of well-being washes over me. "Let us talk about my shape name."

In Bounty, we learn shape speech by watching others and having our mother and brothers fold and move our hands and fingers into words. The shape we used for *Queen* is the same as the shape for *nektar*, the substance she trades to the Weave and that they use to brew drafts in their laboratories. *Nektar* is the fingers curled, palm up, mimicking the sacs used to grow the drafts in a nektar bath. To us, the Queen was nektar and the nektar was the Queen, something far away that we'd never have to worry about.

But that shape word doesn't fit Odide at all. Her name can't be *bee*, the thumb and index finger tapping. She's no human female, either, or Captain. I could call her *draft*: a V of fingers cut horizontally across the eyes. Not human. A concoction, an experiment. Sometimes, a mistake to be discarded.

Odide flinches. Thinking those word, *concoction* and *mistake*, hurt her. The captive bird trills high, then low, agitated.

"Forgive me," I splutter. "I'm no good with words."

This time, I see that her lips don't move. She speaks in my mind. *I'm no mistake. No concoction.* The sweetness on my lips has a slight burn. Odide is losing patience. *All I ask is a name to call my own.*

"Forgive me. I've known no Queen before." I make the word *Captain*, my free hand outstretched and angled up. *We have Captains, the mothers who brew us and train us for war.*

Mother, I hear her in my mind. The shape for mother is the flat of the hand horizontal and circling the ground. *I am Captain to no one, warrior Fir. Jarvon leads my soldiers. I am mother to my Hive. But you are no child of mine. You must make me a different name.* She smiles as if she's shared a lovely secret. *My name is neither draft nor mother nor Captain nor concoction nor precious nektar. Fir must make a name for me alone. A name like no other.*

I'm woozy with her scent: the red flower and behind it, around it, underneath it the musk of the comb. I dig into my memories, something I lost and they come to me: my brothers. I remember the bodies I saw the giant fish pull into the lake. There is more, much more, but Odide's voice is like a moving curtain between now and whatever was before.

"Even drafts die, dear Fir," she says aloud. "We drafts are born and we die, just like you. My children are dear to me. They stay in the lake, in the earth, in the fish, in the air. To be near me, my dear ones."

The bodies are her children. Of course, what else could they be at such a large Hive? I gaze at her breasts, her slim waist, her burnished arms. Where are her laboratories, her Sowers?

"Come, dear Fir!" Odide says brightly. "I've brought you into Hive Home. I've welcomed you. I didn't bring you here to bore you with lessons on this and that. The Hive prospers, that's what you need to know. I sit beside you asking only for a name."

The desire to give her a name pulls me like a slow current. At the same time, I see the current and understand that I am being borne by it. I can adapt to this power, let it bear me. Or I can resist and fail. I try to empty my mind like I'd empty a pail of water, thoughts and ideas gone as I ride the current of her desires. She wouldn't have me here, in her private rooms with me close enough to touch, if she didn't want more than a name.

She's intrigued by me. A seam of tension links us. "I understand that a commander concerns himself first and foremost with his warriors. His brothers. Jarvon," she says softly.

In an instant, the huge draft returns, filling the doorway. "Escort Fir's brothers to the lake so they may take their rest. I wish these brothers to be provided with food and plenty of hilt."

"Hilt?" Is this conjury?

This time, her smile reveals perfect white teeth. "Hilt, my dear Fir, is distilled from honey. Aged in a barrel. A refreshing drink, nothing more. This vintage is especially fine since the lilyfire nektar we gathered last year to make the honey was quite potent. Hilt is a drink one feasts with," she says. "You must have something like it."

"Pogee." Made of corn milk, a thick, sour brew. Pogee-belly is when a warrior who drinks too much sees their belly burst from their breeches.

I repeat: "Lilyfire."

"Yes," she smiles. "You've seen it. The red flower from my valley. Lilyfire is what gives the nectar its special powers."

Odide turns to the furred creature with a blue beak and blue crescents under its eyes. "Delphinia Arc, bring your special salve to me directly. The warrior Fir's legs," she says, pointing to the still-bloody seams Thorn sewed into my knees. "I wish to treat him myself."

Delphinia Arc scampers away.

There's a sly twist to Odide's lips as she turns back to me. "Hilt may loosen even your tongue. Helleboria Arc, Achillea Arc," she says, beckoning the pink and purple-beaked creatures, "bring us food and hilt."

On the low table, the Arcs place a fat fish glistening in honey glaze, roasted carrots, a cake drizzled in honey, a still-warm loaf of bread, and a round of white cheese wrapped in laurel leaves. In crystal goblets, the drink she calls hilt is golden with bubbles that rise like backwards rain.

With a fork, the Queen teases white meat from the fish. She chews, then sets the fork down. Her gaze is merry. She means to show me the food isn't poisoned. The scent of lilyfire hasn't faded. It's just layered on the luscious aroma of the food. My brain feels packed with wool. I need fresh air, fresh air and cold water.

I don't remember where I laid my stave.

Odide lifts a goblet of hilt and drinks deeply. She pierces more fish with the fork. This time, she holds the fork between us. "Will you not eat?"

I reach for the fork, but she pulls it away. "Eat?"

She's asking for the shape word. Two fingers press to my lips. *Eat.*

"Eat," she repeats, then *eat*, her fingers to her lips. "Warrior Fir, do you not understand the words of your most avid student?" *Eat.*

I open my mouth. She gently feeds me.

"Now teach me *friend*." She spears a carrot. Again, the captive bird trills.

Friend: the pointing fingers curled around each other.

Before I know it, I'm savoring everything: the moist fish, the bread, so different from paddle loaf, with a lightly browned crust and supple, soft interior with no ash or grit. The hilt bubbles up my nose.

The drink is delicious, a bit sour and sweet at the same time. Soon, only the fish's watery bones lie uneaten on the platter.

Delphinia Arc brings the Queen a large clam shell filled with an amber-colored salve. The Queen dips in her fingers, then gently dabs the salve on my knees. The salve is cold and slick. Almost immediately, the ache that lingered there vanishes.

A hunger grows in my belly and it's not for food or drink. It's for her, Odide, this girl Queen who's so welcoming, so caring. I can still feel the warmth of her skin, the thrum of her voice in my head. When Dinitra touched me, I didn't feel this powerful longing, to be one with her, be next to her, be inside her voice, her scent, to never leave her. I can't help staring at the pulse at Odide's throat.

She tips her head. "That's not a word I understand. Dini...?"

Something in me steps back. I shouldn't think that name, indulge that memory. I feel the danger like a prickle on my neck. This Queen wants my full attention. Even the memory of Dinitra provokes her. The toy figure of 12 is in my pocket, still protecting her.

Odide puts aside the shell and takes both of my hands in hers. My body is drawn to her, as if she's always been the thing I wanted. As she speaks, the salve on my knees warms. *You need not fear, warrior Fir. We have no secrets, you and I. Tell me your story.*

It's a relief to say something that takes me away from craving the Queen's embrace. I think of my brothers being escorted to the lake. I think of our purpose, to find this Master. To be free. But something tells me I can't let Odide know about the young Captain heading for The Deep. About how I felt the same pull toward her, but without any lilyfire.

I close my eyes, and still the Hive Queen is in my mind: her red dress, the stone flickering in its pergama frame like purple fire. She's watching. She wants to see what I see. This is what the Swarm does, I understand, let her use their bodies and eyes to see and travel far from Hive Home.

I see the river we forded to escape the hyba pack. That's where I want to start my story. Abruptly, Odide stops me. "The river isn't where your story begins. Tell me of your mother."

The hairs on her palms shift against my skin. I bring up my first memory: my mother caressing my cheek. I was a sprig when she folded my fingers into the shape of my name. My mother taught me about plants and stars and how to read a trail. I showed special talent for leading my brothers. None of us could match Ash, though. His hair was dark red, like my mother's. He was tall and strong.

"Ash," Odide says aloud.

I nod. Then I show her. *Ash:* four fingers straight with the thumb crossed over the palm.

"I'd like to meet this Ash." I feel Odide's sudden pity as she senses my grief. "You saw him die and mourn for him. How awful."

"He was killed by a battle dog. A draft, really. The only one of her kind."

"A draft," the Queen says, now intensely curious. "May I see her?"

I call up 12 as she once lay at my feet. Her blue-black tongue hangs from her heavy snout as she pants. In the afternoon light, the orange of tiger stripes glows. She's content, the white tuft at the end of her tail gently ticking.

"She is…magnificent," the Queen murmurs.

"She's like nothing you've ever seen." I've never told this story to anyone. I move my hands as I describe how 12 rammed into my brother and ripped out his throat. Her great tail lashed with delight. It was a mistake that no one could take back.

I close my eyes and remember my mother taking out her knife. When she put an end to my brother's suffering, I was glad. But the more I thought about it, I wondered why he had to die. Why do any of us have to die for her? It wasn't 12's fault. My mother killed Ash. "Now I'm commander," I say.

Only in nightmares have I revisited Quillka and our lost brothers and fellow warriors. My story spills out: the attack on Quillka, when the helios crested the Black Stairs for the very first time, like a hundred separate suns. Their pulsar guns blasted our world to bits. I can still see the flames and taste the smoke that billowed gray and bitter from the Council Hall. The townspeople of Quillka, their bodies strewn everywhere. The grit and ash choking me. The fires that consumed our home.

The Queen releases me abruptly, hands at her mouth. *Fire, fire.* Suddenly, she's vanished from my thoughts. I feel abandoned, then desperate for her to touch me again, be in my mind.

"What's wrong?" I reach for her. "Have I offended you?"

The Arcs chitter with concern, wedging between us. They stroke her bare arms. Achillea Arc's purple beak gently nibbles her hair, as if the perfectly straight strands must be returned to their proper places.

Odide blinks rapidly. "Fire is… Fire destroys."

She stumbles when she stands. The Arcs steady her. "Come, let me take you to your brothers, dear Fir. I don't wish to cause further worry. We'll speak again later."

This time, I follow the Queen out of the Hive. When she steps into the woven basket, everyone in Hive Home, from the smallest bee to the tallest soldier, stops to stare. As before, Jarvon and his soldiers lift the basket, then lower it to the ground.

My brothers gather at the lake, just as she promised. I see the look in their eyes that must have been in mine when I first glimpsed her: amazement and terror combined. Jarvon is at her side as she greets each one, asking to see their shape name. The welcome is so gracious that even my brother Willow grins like a moon-struck boy.

All the while, Jarvon's insect face is unreadable.

Her soldiers have erected tents for us. Odide explains that the tents are made of a fabric that's light as leaves but impervious to rain and dense enough to deflect all but the sharpest spear. The tents trap heat, too, so that my brothers will sleep warm even in the cold of winter.

To one side, the Arcs have set up a small pavilion. There, my brothers feast as I did, on roast fish arrayed fin to fin on platters of tempered comb. There are baskets of sweet apples, a great wheel of white cheese, and five barrels of hilt, heady and delicious.

"It eases weariness." Odide lifts a goblet. "And comforts, when you are grieved. You have lost dear ones. So have I. Welcome, warriors of the Living Wood. May we always be friends and allies."

She sips hilt. Then the Arcs take her by both hands to lead her back to the Hive. I feel a stab of jealousy. I want to be with her. Before she turns away, I hear her: faint this time, like a whisper from the trees. *We'll continue our conversation once I'm refreshed, warrior Fir. And you'll show me my name.*

9

Conjury

The Queen's conjury fades quickly. I feel peeled, like the part of me that was with her and wanted her is a soft, warm cloak she's taken with her back to the Hive.

Willow, too, is free from her temporary spell. *We must leave,* he tells me. *Now.*

Her soldiers stand guard between us and Hive Home. I don't know if they're watching us or guarding her. Or both. No soldier stands between us and the Scarlet Valley. But I know we can't just run. Jarvon and the Swarm would be on us in an instant.

Besides, my brothers are goggle-eyed from the Queen's hilt. We're stuck here, at least until my brothers sleep off their stupor.

Willow shapes more words, but I place my hands on his, to silence him. My shape words are hidden by his cupped palms. *Beware the bees. They're spies and messengers. Everything we do, everything we say, they see and she sees.*

I purposefully speak aloud so that any guard listening can transmit what I say to the Queen. "If the Queen wanted to kill us, we'd be gutted and packed in preserve in her storehouse by now. She welcomes, us, brother. Those tales we've heard from wildmen are lies. She feeds us generously. She gives us hilt. Look at our happy brother, Tanoak!"

I couldn't have arranged him better. Mighty Tanoak slumps half-asleep against a tree, his arms cradling his full belly like a furry bancat nestled atop his thighs. An empty goblet of hilt tips in the pine straw beside him.

"If we leave now," I say, "we'd have to carry his belly in its own separate sack."

Willow tries hard to arrange his face into agreement. He looks a bit like he's about to belch. In my cupped hands, he replies: *I won't trade a Captain's command for a Hive Queen's no matter how rich her offerings. We can escape tonight when it's dark and they're sober again. Bees don't fly without sunlight. That's all the time we need.*

Willow wasn't with me in Odide's chamber. He doesn't understand that she's no normal bee. I can still hear the soft wool of her voice. I can feel her slick hairs on my palms. Aloud, I say, "She's offered peace." But in his palms, I motion, *We must be careful, brother. At least for now. We have to talk our way out of Hive Home. She sees all.*

I press the back of my fingers to an eye: *patience.*

My brother's opinion is clear on his face. Willow wouldn't trust Odide if she laid crumbs of paddle loaf to mark the path all the way to the Master's gate. *I'll give you a day. No more.*

In Bounty, such disobedience would earn him a beating. But things have changed. The Living Wood has changed. I've changed. Our Bond is no longer to our mother alone, but to each other, to brothers. My brothers are not like the Queen's children, who bend to her will like branches bending to the wind. I'm my brothers' leader, but I also have to prove myself to them. I have to lead them well.

Willow refused both food and hilt. He gets busy on a small grub fire and begins to mix paddle loaf dough. My brothers may have eaten and drunk their fill, but we all still need Remedy.

That night, Jarvon returns with his soldiers. The lake is quiet. Hive Home softly hums. Willow's grub fire has crumbled to embers. My brothers stare at it, their faces slack from the after-effects of hilt.

The Queen's commander keeps his distance from the fire. "She summons you."

Sober after his long nap, my brother Tanoak stands. *I'm going with you.*

Jarvon's faceted eyes flicker dangerously. "You are not summoned."

I touch my brother's arm. "Just tell our brothers no more hilt."

Again, I'm lifted in the basket. As I suspected, the Hive is still active at night. This time, the scent of the lilyfire flower soothes me. I feel my heart beat just a little faster in anticipation of seeing Odide. I think I'm prepared now to resist her conjury. I'll let the current of lilyfire lift me, but I'll keep my wits. Perhaps the Queen will reveal the right path we need to take to reach the Master. Perhaps she'll tell us more about him.

In her small chamber, I find Odide resting on her low couch. The Arcs lie around her like beloved pets. When she left our camp, she looked drained. Now, she's lively again, a fresh spray of yellow pollen around her eyes and lips as red as the stone on her finger. Her new gown is silver and clings to every curve of her body. The same pergama chain adorns her neck, with its purple stone. Lilyfire still makes me woozy, but a part of me stays apart. I say to myself over and over, *That's lilyfire. Lilyfire. Keep your wits, Fir.*

In her eyes, I see dozens of Firs, watchful and entranced.

"Your story didn't come easily, I know," the Queen says. "The best ones never do. I felt your pain and grief, warrior Fir. Your longing."

Delphinia Arc nestles her head on the Queen's hip. For an instant, I'm horribly jealous. The Queen senses this and wakes the little Arc. "Bring hilt for our guest, dear Delphinia. Sit beside me, Fir."

I take the spot warmed by the Arc's body. Odide's arms are like a lovely vine as she reaches for me, the sun to my eager plant. Again, the soft hairs of her hand slip against my palm. I hear and feel her words. I feel the current of her longing even as I stand apart from it, watching.

She notices. Surprisingly, this pleases her. "My lilyfire has a powerful effect. But you know that. This I promise you. You make your own choices with me, Fir. I won't force you."

Delphinia Arc returns with a tray bearing two goblets of golden hilt. "Forgive me for what I did earlier. I didn't fully understand who you were. What you want. I didn't know you. You're not like the others I've known."

"Others?" I ask.

"I think you guessed, dear Fir. Other males have come before. This is a necessity for Hive Home. As Queen, I must search out the qualities I need to make strong children. It's not so different in Bounty, no?"

She's right. The Captains brew the warriors they need: the Living

Wood for speed and ferocity, the Sea Hunt for their mastery of the ocean, the white-haired Dreams, spies and carriers of secrets. No warrior ever chose to be born to his mother. I know nothing about how my mother chose a male to make me. Captains use the sons of other Captains to brew fresh warriors. But no warrior ever knows or even questions what other boy could share their blood. My brothers Tanoak and Tamarack—tall, broad, fast, and strong—were frequently requested by other Captains. After each session with the Sowers, they returned to us boasting of the strong boys the Captains would make from their seed.

We don't even have a name for that male. *Mother*, yes. But what of the male?

She lifts her goblet to mine, then I sip. My lips burn with fiery pepper and I splutter.

Odide laughs. "The sweet is nothing without the spice. This is the Queen's special vintage."

I will myself to calm even though what I'm about to say is a horror. "You told me you didn't take men by force. You said those were lies." I can't help imagining how that would be done: Jarvon with his clacking mandibles, the soldiers, the spears.

Odide thinks for a moment. "By the time I'm finished speaking to them, men choose to remain. I give them good lives, Fir. Every comfort. I'm no monster. No *concoction*."

In her mouth, the word has an edge, like *scuttle* or *beast-born*. Something bad or unnatural. "I'm telling you the truth when I say I've met no man like you. No one who's moved me like you have."

Moved her? By my story of loss and failure?

She smiles gently. "Everyone loses someone. Everyone fails. Yet you still lead your brothers. You want them to be free. You worry about them. You encourage them. That's what I'm talking about, Fir. You have a good heart."

No one has ever said such a thing to me. This is both more complicated and more dangerous than I thought. It's not just lilyfire. Odide has a keen intelligence. "You conjured those men," I say carefully. "Like you conjured me."

"Show me that word," she says, curious.

I circle my flat palm at my left ear.

She considers her answer. "My lilyfire is strong. That's true. But I have no powers beyond what lilyfire gives me. Truthfully, I can't live without it. Lilyfire feeds my Hive. The nektar we distill from it nourishes my children and makes them strong. How can I *conjure* with something that to me is as important as water is to you? Or... what is the word? Remedy?"

"Remedy only keeps me alive," I tell her. "It gives me no strength."

"I have much to learn from you, Fir. Is there something that makes you strong?"

"My brothers," I answer quickly. "Their love." I keep the memory of Dinitra far away, even though that also gives me strength.

"You see?" Her eyes flicker with amusement. "You have a good heart. You could be a partner, a true partner to me. My mother had one, and her hive was strong. If you choose to stay, perhaps you could help me make Hive Home what it can be. What it should be."

I don't know how to respond. To say no right away would be an insult. I pretend her offer is something I'm willing to consider.

"This I promise, friend Fir," Odide says. "I won't enter your mind without permission. There will be no ... *conjury*." Her hand circles her left ear.

"Were these males happy?" Too late, I realize I'm implying that she's lying.

"I never gave them reason to complain," she says, a sting in her tone.

I'm quick with my apology. But the sting aches. There are layers and histories here I can't even imagine.

Delphinia Arc pours more hilt. This time, I'm ready for the burn. Bubbles fizz deliciously on my tongue.

I take her hand again. In my mind, she enters and waits for permission to go any further. I say, *You could have warned me about the spicy hilt.*

I'd halve the pleasure. So much joy rests in surprise.

The thrill exhilarates and frightens me. I crave her attention, her touch, but I also want to be separate. I see myself entranced by her and also watching myself, wondering: can I manage this? Is being part of Hive Home something that would be good? Is this the place my brothers and I should settle as free men? Willow and I discussed this before we learned that the valley belonged to Odide.

Odide assured me she'll only enter my mind with permission. But at any moment, she could take that promise back. She could inhabit me and nothing I could do would blunt the power of the lilyfire.

What I feel for her is nothing like what I felt for Dinitra. With Dinitra, there was no lilyfire, no hilt, no faceted eyes examining me from within my own mind. I felt no need to defend myself from Dinitra. Yet somehow, we walked each other's thoughts. At Dolor, with her hands on my cheeks, I could no longer say where I stopped and she began. She would never enter my mind without permission and I would never enter hers. There was no need. She saw me as I saw her. I saw her as she saw me. That was everything.

I sip more hilt, this time prepared for the burn. I must keep my wits. I can't accept the Queen's offer. My loyalty is to my brothers. My good heart belongs to Dinitra. I have to find some way to convince the Queen that it's better to let us go than to keep me at her side whatever her purpose.

Odide speaks softly. "I owe you an explanation. For my... weakness earlier. When you spoke of fire."

Fire: spoken and thought. A shiver of fear goes from her hand into mine. "Come, let us get some air," she says. "I would have us both clear our heads."

Delphinia Arc scurries to pull back a curtain. I follow Odide to a balcony just off her chambers. It's the middle of the night. Below, the lake is a pane of dark glass. The white half-moon gleams like an arched doorway into the depths. The air has a bite, but is still warmer than it should be in the middle of winter. A sweet, musky steam rises from the great lobes of comb to either side.

"May I?" She holds out her hand and I take it.

For generations, we've been free. We know where we started, with the Sowers and their laboratories of glass. We were the first. They wanted to use our nektar to make more and different drafts. But those first drafts couldn't make enough nektar in captivity. The first nektar was like water compared to what we make now.

You trade with the Weave, I say. *They use the nektar you make from lilyfire.*

She nods. *Yes. They discarded us like they discard so many. Then we found this valley. We found lilyfire. Lilyfire only grows here. Now, our nektar has special powers of healing. And youth. The Weave would not have discovered lilyfire's power without us.*

Through the trees, Willow's grub fire flickers in the distance. Her great eyes darken. *The Sowers are no more, Fir. The Weave, all of it. The Swarm brings me news of Dolor, too.*

I pull my hand from hers. I don't want to see my mother die in a pulsar blast.

"Dear Fir," she says. "She lives. Your mother lives. The Captains live. They were victorious. They defeated the Weave."

I take a step back and the balcony's bannister digs into my back. "That can't be true. The Legion. The helios. They're too powerful. The Weave meant to end us: end males. And our mothers with us."

"The Weave's fleet was indeed powerful," she says softly. "What they wanted to do was a terrible thing. But they failed, Fir. Perhaps it would be easier to show you. Jarvon saw it all."

Odide extends her hand. I hesitate, then lay my hand in hers. Through the eyes of the Jarvon and his guard, I see the Weave's fleet appear south of Dolor, like a huge pergama blade radiating with sunlight. As it did when the fleet crested the Black Stairs for the first time, the sight fills me with panic. The Concave hangs high above the helios, collecting a thick and pulsing cord of light. The cord reaches all the way over the mountains to the capital of the Weave, the Centrum itself.

The Concave splits the cord of light downward into a hundred separate streams, to fuel the helios and their pulsar guns. The vibros, too, already emitting their piercing blasts. The air shivers, then seems to turn to metal as the pulsars begin their barrage.

Behind the helios comes the Legionships, black cylinders with a thousand Legionaries apiece and as many battle dogs.

Death in sunlight and dog-fangs and bloody sound.

The helios blast Dolor's lava bed walls. They crumble. The Captains and their sons stand exposed and defenseless beyond the gates. Through Jarvon's eyes, broken into a dozen panes, I glimpse Petal, Anku's beast-born son, his face slick with tears. I see my mother alone, her fists raised and her mouth fixed in a scream. With a gasp, I see Dinitra and 12 racing through smoke and fire.

All this time I imagined them fleeing north into The Deep. My hand goes to my mouth, as if to keep my heart from leaping out in shock and despair.

Suddenly, the thick cord of light winks out: there, then gone. It's as if someone dropped a curtain. There's only sky and smoke and rubble. The Concave wobbles, a sickle gash against the winter sky. Without the light, there's no fuel to keep the ship aloft. There's no fuel for any of the Weave's helios or vibros or Legionships. The Concave starts to drop, then the helios with it, no longer glowing with light but dull streaks of pergama.

The Weave's entire fleet smashed to bits outside Dolor. The Legionaries and all of the battle dogs went with them, wiped out.

"Your mother lives, Fir." Odide pauses for me to compose myself. "There's more, if you wish to see it."

I gulp more hilt, the burn nothing now compared to my shock. Did Dinitra and 12 survive? Where are they now?

"Warriors hunt you," Odide tells me. "The ones Jarvon spoke of, who leave the bone trail. They mean to force you back. They mean to make you what you once were: slaves."

Though Jarvon's eyes, I see the Blazes, over a dozen of them, following our trail. They camped at the lake where we captured the scuttle.

Now? I ask.

She nods. *Three or four days away.*

The Blazes pursuit makes sense now. Bounty is victorious, the Weave defeated. Of course, the Captains won't allow a single warrior to escape. And they need them, now more than ever, to occupy the Weave.

Odide examines me closely. "Yesterday, you spoke of the creature that killed your brother Ash. The hyba cross with the long tail. The only one of its kind."

I let my breath come out slowly. I see 12 in her mind: her heavy snout, the orange and black brindle of her ribs and flanks, that long, powerful tail with the white tuft at the tip.

"This creature, too, was seen by Jarvon," Odide says.

As if from a great distance, I see 12 and two humans walking through a heavy mist. One of them has red-gold hair. It's the Vessel, Susalee. She birthed Rek's twins at Quillka. Behind them, her hand on 12's massive shoulder, walks Dinitra.

I can't hide my relief.

"They are friends of yours." Odide is curious. "How can that be? Are warriors friends with Captains who aren't their mothers? Didn't this draft kill your beloved brother, Ash?"

Inside this curiosity is something hard and demanding: the Queen I first met, who delivers orders with sharp efficiency. A Captain who befriends a warrior and a draft no one has seen before, one that's killed a warrior, are unpredictable and therefore dangerous. A surprise and not a welcome one. If Odide learned that Dinitra and I have a Bond, she could order Jarvon or the Swarm to kill her to eliminate a rival.

I have to protect them. Odide assumes I want 12 dead because she killed Ash. I let her think that.

"That Captain helped us escape," I tell Odide, keeping my voice cool. "I'm grateful."

Odide isn't satisfied by my answer. But she keeps her word and doesn't probe my thoughts further.

For now. I hesitate to beg for their safety. That would acknowledge that the Queen may consider harming them. Better that she think I'm hers, so I close my eyes and breathe in pure lilyfire. Every thought goes to her and away from what she showed me. Away from Dinitra.

Gently, the Queen lays her palm on my forearm. The touch feels wonderful, like the first warm day after a long winter. *Can I go no further in your thoughts? May I not see this friend as you do? When she gave you your freedom?*

All that matters is that I'm here now.

For a long moment, a silence grows between us. She's used to obedience. But she knows that I bring her something more. I bring her strength.

Tanoak is a master tracker, but his skill is nothing compared to Odide's ability to track my thoughts. I take her hand in mine, turning her palms with the tiny hairs away from my skin. "We said goodbye in Dolor. I'll never see her again."

Then I press my lips to her palm. In that moment, Odide is everything: the room, Hive Home, the black conjury of her faceted eyes. I have to keep Dinitra tucked safely away, beyond Odide's reach.

But I can't lose her. If I lose her, I may lose myself.

10

Zong

Odide shivers with the night's chill, so we return to her rooms. The Arcs fuss over her as she sits on the low couch.

Again, she wants me to join her. "There are things about the Hive you should know, Fir, before you make your decision. Jarvon didn't want to build Hive Home here. He said only my children with wings could escape such a place. The rest—my Arcs, as you see, who can only walk—would be trapped. But I knew no other place would be as safe."

I wonder what force could possibly threaten Hive Home. Then I remember: fire. If there were still helios to threaten them, fire from the Weave's helios would cut through the comb like hot knives.

But the Weave and their fleet are gone. Through the eyes of the Swarm, I saw the Weave's entire fleet fall. "Who would attack you?"

"Many desire lilyfire nektar, dear Fir. The Master you seek, principally. Though he hates and fears drafts, he craves nektar." In the cold blue light of the Hive, her face is impossible to read. "Cranox, his general, cruelest of them all."

"Cruelest," I repeat. "Tell me about him."

Odide searches my face. "So that you will leave me and join him?"

"So that I know who threatens you. Who makes you afraid. I would do what I could to protect you."

What I mean is me and my brothers. Perhaps we can make an

alliance with Odide. Maybe we can agree to come when she calls, when the Swarm calls us. Is that so much to pay for freedom?

Protect me, I hear her say in my mind. *That pleases me, Fir.*

Could you tell me more about this Master?

She takes a sip of hilt before continuing. "The Master's city is near Seven Lake. Only males may live there. Cranox, his general, comes as far as the Scarlet Valley looking for males."

The Scarlet Valley, scarlet because of lilyfire. Lark told us we wouldn't be spared. By Cranox or this Master? Yet the Queen says the Master's general searches for males. Who should I believe? Could they both be correct? "Do the males come willingly? As free?" I ask.

Odide shakes her head. "Cranox stays to the edge of the Scarlet Valley. He searches for bone trails. The males he finds? They never reach the Hive to tell me what he wants."

I sense she knows more than she's saying. The Master craves the nektar she sends him. Yet she fears him and this Cranox. Why? "If the wildmen make the Master stronger, why let them pass?"

I think again of the pile of bodies where the lake fish fed. She needs males to make her children and maintain Hive Home. The males may choose to stay here, but under what conditions? With what conjury?

Her hand squeezes mine. "I don't kill them, Fir. They live as members of the Hive. They're cared for, protected. I like to think they even come to like it here, where there is food and hilt and warmth. Bounty—your Bounty—asked you to give your lives. I would never ask that of my males."

"Could they not..." I don't know how to put this. "Could they not serve you, then go on their way. Free?"

She shrugs her shoulder. "None asked for that."

I can feel that the Queen is speaking honestly, but I also sense that there are things she is staying away from, harder things, just as I'm staying away from Dinitra and 12. I haven't seen any human males in the Hive who aren't my brothers.

I return to questions about this Master. "Does he have a name? Did he also pass through your valley?"

Odide shakes her head. "That was before I was born. To me, he's Master. I've only seen him through the Swarm."

"And Cranox?"

Her loathing of Cranox comes across as nausea that I also feel. "I understand that any male who wishes to join his Hundred-Hundred must fight for the honor. They say he feeds the losers to his speluks. And the other drafts he keeps for sport." Her revulsion turns to icy anger. "They say the only drafts he loves are the ones who kill for him. The Master is to be feared, Fir. Not me."

"They? Who is they?"

She smiles. "The Swarm, dear Fir. And my spies. I have excellent spies."

I can't help feeling admiration for her. What would any commander give for spies like the Swarm? They are everywhere yet rarely would anyone notice.

"Do you fear Bounty?" I never heard any Captain speak of attacking the Queen. But now that the Captains have defeated the Weave, are they a threat?

"Bounty had no interest in the Hive until recently. One of the Captains seeks an alliance with the Master. To seize command from the other Captains. To seal a new alliance, she would take Hive Home and our nektar with it. She hates drafts like us."

"Captain Rek," I blurt. "The Swarm saw her meet with the Master?"

"With Cranox. Many times."

I take a moment to absorb this. Captain Rek's betrayal goes deeper than defying the other Captains. She's seeking alliances to defeat the other Captains. Bounty may think it's ended the war by defeating the Weave. But another war brews with Rek and this Master.

Odide is caught between them.

"Hive Home seeks only peace, but even perched on these cliffs we seem destined to be drawn into fighting." A smile plays over her red lips. "I know you feared me. With all that I've told you, are you still afraid?"

My face flushes. "My lady. You are…the delight of a surprise."

I'm learning her way of speaking. "We seek the company of males, yes. At least to know the Master's land. To see it for ourselves. There, men are free. Or so we've been told."

"And what do you think of drafts?" Odide asks. "The Master abuses them and makes them fight in his arena. Rek hates them and would exterminate them all. Not just me and Hive Home. All drafts."

I know Rek's hatred all too well. She wanted to kill 12, Dinitra's hyba cross. She wanted to rid Bounty of all of the drafts we'd saved on the Black Stairs. "We don't hate drafts. We rescued them in Bounty. We befriended them. Rek is not our mother."

"Your mother." Odide draws close to trace my tattoo collar with her fingertips: TIMBETIMBETIMBE. I shiver with delight as the effect of the lilyfire courses through me. "Did you love your mother?"

As a boy, I adored her. I craved every moment I could sit near her, feel her hand on my cheek, hear her say my name. Then I grew to resent her. She was the reason I was bound. She didn't care for me, not really. I was a tool, something she brewed up to fight her wars. I never saw her weep over my dead brothers. She treated us like cattle or sheep: beasts.

"I loved her," I tell Odide. "I'm ashamed of that now."

She drops her hand to mine. A second, silent conversation runs like a stream beneath our spoken words. She's in my mind and I'm in hers. I look for treachery and find none. I look for a lie, even a small one. She's telling me the truth.

"You spoke of your mother," I say. "Of a male who joined her by choice. Who partnered with her to make her hive?"

Still the word for this male escapes me.

"My mother was Tyr," Odide says. "Her hive was to the west, at the entrance to the Scarlet Valley. She tended it, protected it. The fruits you ate were from trees she planted. Fields she planted. It was a strong, good hive. My mother and her partner gave each other strength. I've always wanted that. Not just a way to make children, but to have a partner. Together, we'd strengthen the hive, protect it. Make us strong."

Her palm rests on my cheek. The warmth of the tiny hairs suffuses my body. "You are beautiful, friend Fir. We would make beautiful children."

I have no words in my mouth or my hands. No one has ever called me beautiful. Not even Dinitra talked to me like this.

"Beautiful," she repeats. "Your hair is the brown of pine bark. There is red there, just a little. You face is well-shaped, like someone knew they were making a thing to be admired. And your eyes." Her lips part. "I have no emeralds as beautiful as the green I see in your eyes."

I can see myself at her side. I can see myself cradling a babe with burnished jasper skin and a heart-shaped face: a little female. She has green eyes like mine with sparkling facets and red lips like her mother.

A new Queen. My daughter. My child. I never even dreamed about having a child. No male knows his children in Bounty.

But what about the brothers who also look like me? What about finding the land of men? What about freedom? I pull away from Odide and the vision vanishes. When I saw myself holding a new Queen, I didn't see a single one of my brothers.

"But don't you see, Fir? This could be your home. You could be free here with me," she says, hurt darkening her eyes.

My words are wet with emotion. "What of my brothers? You spoke of my good heart, yet you want me to abandon my brothers."

"Don't you want a home? Don't you want children? Children who will have children of their own? You wouldn't simply vanish, Fir. You would build something. Isn't that part of being free from your mother's bond? Don't you get to choose?"

Is it a choice if someone says they've given you a choice? My home was always with my brothers. For a time, before we escaped Dolor, I imagined that it could be with Dinitra in some other land. But we haven't found that land. Maybe, that land doesn't even exist. I know through the eyes of the Swarm that Dinitra barely escaped Dolor. By now, she and 12 are far into The Deep. Lost to me.

If I can't have Dinitra, maybe I should choose Odide.

Odide takes my hand again. An ominous figure enters her thoughts. He is broad-chested and wears black armor, like Jarvon. He has Odide's human mouth, but his scowl exposes sharp, white fangs.

"That is Zong." From her thoughts, I understand that he is Odide's brother. "He seeks to destroy Hive Home. I need your protection, Fir."

Brother is the pointer fingers parallel and joined. The urgency she feels makes my heart race. "Zong and I are linked by my mother, as you are linked to your brothers."

Odide sips her hilt, then rests her goblet on the low table. "Zong was full-grown when I was barely walking. Zong commanded my mother's soldiers. That last day, the day my mother died, she'd given him a gift: a dagger with a blade forged from pure pergama. The most precious, beautiful metal of all, from the Weave's own mines. But that wasn't what he wanted. He wanted her hive for his own."

Even with a belly full of hilt and entranced by the thrum of her voice, I know Queens rule hives, not kings. But these are drafts, I remind myself. They have different rules. "Zong demanded she give him her hive a thousand times. A thousand times, she said no. She knew he would use it for war. She wanted only peace. As do I."

I feel time passing, though I couldn't say how many hours. Have I been with Odide more than a night? With a sick lurch, I wonder if my brothers think I left them. Willow gave me a day. Do they think I've chosen her?

But there's no way I can leave her now. She needs my protection. "My mother taught me that each one of us has a duty. Some are born to farm or care for animals. Others nurture our young or guard us from harm. We have our cooks and fysics, as do you. Our brothers are equal to us in every way except one. They cannot rule. I was to be Queen with Zong as my guard and protector."

But Zong made a new ally: the Master and his Hundred-Hundred, commanded by Cranox. "They surrounded my mother's hive. While my mother's soldiers battled the Hundred-Hundred, Zong betrayed and attacked her. Before my eyes, he killed her. He killed our mother. He killed her with the very dagger she'd given him as a gift."

The grief in her is bottomless. I feel suffocated by it, a blinding storm of grief. "To this day, the Master sends spies to search out my weakness. To test the border of the Scarlet Valley. To destroy me. Only in that way will he fulfill his promise to Zong: to help kill me and deliver Hive Home."

I think of Lark. Is he spying on her? I would gladly strangle him.

Odide sees Lark in my mind and shakes her head. "No. The boy is dear to me. He came to me after losing his mother. For a time, I became a kind of mother to him. My Swarm can see but they can't hear. Lark does me this service. Lark listens. He reports. He brings me wildmen and for that service I shelter him. Sometimes, he asks for nektar to trade and I give it to him. He is loyal to me."

"Yet you send nektar to the Master who would destroy you?"

Her smile turns bitter. "We have been trading partners, not friends. Not even allies. He wants—he needs—large quantities of lilyfire nektar. I supply what I can. But with the fall of the Weave, he sees an opportunity. He couldn't attack before because he knew the Weave protected me, they'd send their fleet against him. But the Weave is gone. Zong has promised him all the lilyfire nektar he wants in exchange for killing me, burning my Hive."

I feel her tiring again. Odide rests her head on the arm of the couch. "Zong won't wait much longer to take what he's always thought is his. My Hive. I must prepare."

I've never heard tales about this Master brewing his own drafts, only the Weave. "Why is nektar so important to the Master?"

"Nektar has many qualities, Fir, first among them healing. It was nektar I spread on your wounds. Look at your knees now."

My knees aren't just healed. Nektar has wiped away any trace of the wounds. And more—my knees and legs feel stronger. I could run all the way back to Leech Lake without tiring.

"Nektar preserves youth, too," Odide says. "At least some. That's what the Master desires most of all, dear Fir. Youth."

Odide takes another sip of hilt. Her lidless eyes gleam. "I would protect my children and avoid my mother's fate. To do that, I need your help, Fir. I've made mistakes, it's true. I've brought wildmen here who weren't strong like you. I didn't do what my mother did, partner with a worthy man. I'm asking you to choose me. To choose a place where you could be happy. Where we could thrive together."

She reaches for me. I take her hand in mine, the tiny hairs stroking my palm. I see Zong: huge and enraged. His wings carve the air. Zong stabs his mother's guards one by one. Odide is quite young in this memory, no more than a sprig. She's helpless before her brother's fury. There's a terrible hissing as Zong tries to grab his sister's head to rip it from the slender reed of her neck.

Odide glimpses her mother: sectioned eyes dull with death. Odide wants to die with her and starts to crawl toward her.

Then suddenly Odide is swept up. Her protector leaps into the air. Odide screams for her mother though she knows her mother is dead. The arms holding her are armored, a living shield. Odide slips her fingers between the protector's chest plates to reach the skin beneath. Soon, the two breathe as one, hearts beating as one.

I know him, circling high above Tyr's burning hive. *Jarvon.*

I smell the acrid crease of honey burning. In their six-sided chambers, white larvae, Odide's sisters and brothers, writhe. Wax courses down the hive like water.

Fire.

My breath twins with Odide's. We are three now: me, Jarvon, and the girl Queen, gasping wildly. I feel the great lift of Jarvon's wings as gains altitude, to escape Zong. He'll do anything to save the young Queen. I smell smoke, I feel panic, and I'm back at Quillka, the helios and pulsars blasting us to bits. The Weave's vibros zound and blood courses from my ears. I want to kill the Weave's Legion, I want to kill Zong. I want to feel the armor on Zong's chest crack under my fists. I'd pound his face until it was pulp. If I were 12, I'd rip out his throat. I'd plant my paws on his chest and pant, triumphant. I'd hurl the helios and the vibros and the Concave against the lava rocks of Dolor.

It's bloodlust, I know it. We're trained as warriors to fight with cold precision, never for anger or revenge. We fought for the mother-bond. We fought for each other. Not for emotion. Never for anger.

Yet in my mind, I fight for Odide. I fight for loyalty, for desire. I fight for the Bond. *They are your brothers, but that doesn't mean they can't betray you,* Odide says. *Like Zong.*

Odide pulls me close. Her breasts press against my chest. Like tender vines, my fingers encircle her waist: so delicate, so inviting. I've never felt such desire, such wanting, such thirst. Blood rushes to my crook. Being with her would be like being in a lovely dream. Never parting: lilyfire. I would be hers.

It is you I want, warrior Fir, Odide whispers. *To make my Hive great as my mother's once was. To protect against Zong and my enemies. I need more children, more and better children. Children that you can give me. A daughter. A new Bond, Fir. A beautiful daughter with your hair and green eyes. With your strength. Help me, Fir. Choose me.*

11

Jarvon

She's exhausted by the memories of her mother's burning hive. I scoop her up. She weighs nothing. The Arcs chitter and fuss as they lead me to her bed. It's low and wide. I lay her there, and the Arcs immediately press close to her body as if to warm her.

Already, she's fading from my mind. She's asleep.

The captive bird trills. I once thought Odide was a girl. She can't be. She has hundreds of children. Thousands? Her face is unlined, unscarred. But building this massive hive must have taken years, decades. Ever since I was a sprig, I heard whispers of a draft Queen. Tyr or Odide?

She never told me the name of the male who partnered with her mother to make her. To her, I must seem so young. What does the name of the male even matter? I never knew who my mother used to make me. I never cared. Which Captain sowed him? What were the qualities that my mother wanted for her son?

It's pointless to wonder. What matters is what comes next, the choice I'll make for me and my brothers. With the Queen asleep, my mind is clearing. I have to go and tell my brothers I'm alive.

I'll never talk my way out of Hive Home. Willow was right. We have to run.

I make my way quickly back to the straw basket. There are no soldiers to lift it, so instead I climb down the face of Hive Home, using the edges of the six-sided chambers as a ladder. I understand why Odide brought us here—brought me here. She wants me to mate with her, to help strengthen and defend Hive Home. To fight Zong. this Master, this General Cranox.

And Rek and maybe even my mother and the other Captains. Three wars? I didn't escape Bounty to keep fighting the wars of others.

I vowed to keep my brothers alive. I vowed to find a new way to live. The further I get from Odide, the clearer my thoughts become. Odide didn't lie to me. But what does that matter if she has the power to conjure me with her touch and scent, her body pressed to mine, the low thrum of her voice? Can I really tell what's a lie and what isn't?

Or what truths she left out?

What of the mound of husks I saw at the lake's edge? How many were her children and how many the males she used to make them?

Only Oak, bleary-eyed, is awake to greet me. Far from the Queen, hilt still sloshing in my stomach, all I want is sleep. But there's no time. We have to run. As I climbed down the face of Hive Home, I saw no Swarm or guards. Jarvon didn't track me through the trees. No Swarm flits among the trees surrounding our camp.

Perhaps the human-sized drafts work inside the Hive through the night. But the Swarm rests. We have the night to flee.

What news? Oak asks. *We thought there'd be more food. When can we have more of the bubbly drink?*

We're leaving. Wake your brothers.

What about breakfast?

You'll breakfast on my boot if you don't move. Wake your brothers.

Can we take the tents? The blankets? They are fine.

By the Mother's breath, if you don't move now, I'll feed you to that giant fish myself. Take only what you can carry. I know my face is thunder as I step toward him. *Now.*

Willow rushes up, sleep crusting his eyes. *Have you come to your senses? Let me make breakfast.*

No. We have to leave now.

But before Willow can collect his cooking gear, I hear the beating of wings. My heart sinks. Jarvon and his soldiers land at the edge of the trees where we're camped.

Jarvon points his terrible spear at me. With Odide asleep, I think he may kill me and slaughter my brothers out of spite. I remember him as he was in Odide's memory: her savior and protector, their hearts beating as one as he flew her away from her murderous brother. He would do anything for her.

Still, I don't feel Odide is watching. There's no Swarm. Jarvon seems to have come on his own.

"We thank the Queen for her generosity," I tell him. I keep my voice low and calm. "Now, we must go."

Jarvon inclines his head. The black carapace over his chest and arms looks freshly polished. "My lady told you of Zong."

Tanoak appears beside me. Even he seems small compared to Jarvon. "Take our brothers down the path," I tell him. To Jarvon, I say, "Yes. Zong. Her brother."

"She told you everything?" Jarvon's mandibles open and close with a clack.

"She told me enough." Tanoak doesn't move and I feel my brothers gathering to me, preparing to fight.

"A few details may have escaped her." Jarvon's voice scrapes metal on metal. "She was young."

His tone doesn't change. But I sense a tenderness in him for Odide. He'll do anything to protect her, protect Hive Home. "Go on," I say.

"He wants my lady dead." Jarvon has no eyelids to blink. His stare makes my skin crawl. He can't walk my mind like Odide, but I feel him drilling into it. "Zong waits for his moment to strike. You have given it to him."

"I've given him nothing. I've never even seen him." That's not true, though. I've seen him through the Swarm. I've felt the Queen's terror. But I won't be shamed into sacrificing myself or my brothers.

"If you leave, you'll give him everything. You'll weaken her in her time of need. Her Swarm spies and so does his. They've seen you enter and they will see you leave. She needs a mate. You rob her of a new Queen."

"I would help her if I could. But we can't stay." *I can't stay*, I think. I can't betray my brothers. I can't break the brother bond. I can't be that partner she craves. If I said yes, I'd betray my brothers. I'd betray Dinitra.

I feel a hand on my shoulder: Tanoak's, heavy and with a grip that goes through to the bone. He's warning me to stay calm.

"She said I could choose," I tell Jarvon. "She promised not to conjure me as she did the others."

"Conjure," he rasps.

She promised. Jarvon didn't. "We are free to go," I repeat.

"Run." Jarvon fingers his spear. "You are free to *run*."

This is between me and Jarvon. My pulse quickens. "We've never run from a fight," I snap back. "But these were *our* fights."

His laughter rankles me more than any word could. He's right. I've only fought for our mother.

"Coward, I call you." Jarvon steps toward me. "You would leave my lady to die. Show me you're no coward. Fight me for the privilege of leaving."

Come any closer to my brother and I will end this chatter. Jarvon doesn't have to understand shape language to see the menace in Tanoak's face.

"You aren't worthy of being her mate," he rasps. "Better you skitter away like some fearful night creature. You will never know the richness of the Hive. Of children. You will die alone, great warrior Fir. Alone and forgotten. Even your brothers will leave you."

He's trying to provoke me. Why? Odide didn't choose him. He's jealous of how the Queen wants me and not him.

"You can't be her mate," I spit. "She looks at you and sees a servant." Cruel, but I revel in it. I try to remember what Willow taught me about bees. There are Queens and workers and... drones, that's it. "You are nothing but a *drone* to her."

Jarvon opens and closes his mandibles. His chest shakes, but it's not because of fear. A laugh rooted in his belly spreads up his hard thorax. "You understand nothing, Tree."

I must seem drunk with hilt, stumbling in my words, woozy, soft with nauseating bubbles. How can I leave without a fight? I can't resist another encounter with Odide: the thrum of her voice, the press of her body against mine. Her skin is like the softest, sleekest petal.

I force myself to step back. "My life is my own as a free man." Even to me, this sounds ridiculous, like a sprig mouthing off to his Keeper.

"Your life has never been your own." Again, the Queen's commander laughs. "My life is the Queen's to do with as she pleases. I am no drone. I am a vagabond. Hive-born, but without a Hive to call my own. I wandered until the Queen's mother took me in. I stayed because I love and obey my Queen."

Jarvon's rasp throbs with misery. "I see the males that come to her one after the other. Not one has won her heart. Not one could break her. Until you."

Jarvon take a step towards me. He can't kill me without angering the Queen. But he can hurt me enough to keep me from leaving. She'll be angry, but he'll save her from breaking her promise. He wants me to fight him. With horror, I realize that Odide doesn't need me to be whole to be her partner. Jarvon never promised what she did, to let me choose.

I push away Tanoak's heavy hand. "This has nothing to do with me."

Jarvon's strange laugh makes his armor shake. "Why do so many who love you die, warrior Fir? Your brother. That girl and her concoction heading to The Deep. Yes, I've seen them, too. So, I assure you, has Zong. They leave a bone trail, warrior Fir. Easy to follow."

He's threatening Dinitra and 12. "The Queen has no reason to hurt her."

"I'm not speaking of the Queen." His mandibles clack. "Even your brothers wonder. They doubt you, warrior Fir. They speak of their doubts and I see. The Swarm tells me everything. They fear you'll lead them to their deaths."

He lies, Tanoak says. *We were only worried about you. Filthy draft.*

I hear the lie in my brother's voice. Jarvon's words sink deeper than any spear. While the Queen conjured me, my brothers planned to leave me. As I think this, Jarvon hands his spear to a soldier. "You were never worthy of the honor my Queen gave you. You were always unworthy."

I'm unworthy: my secret fear. I've failed. I'm torn between wanting to rip his head off and wanting to run away in shame. Jarvon has exposed me for what I really am.

He presses in. "Your brothers see what a weakling you are. They never should have followed you."

He reaches out with a claw and shoves my chest. I stumble backwards. If I leave now, will my brothers even follow?

Again, Jarvon shoves me. The Queen's protector is twice my size. Half of the fight is imagining it and there I am, savoring how I'd crack his armor, rip out each one of his vicious, curved claws. Fury spreads like fire along my arms and legs. My mind is saying no, this is crazy. Leave now with your brothers.

They won't follow me.

Left on the rocks of the grub fire is Willow's cooking knife. I turn to reach for it, but Willow shoves in front of me. *Brother, what's the meaning of this? Walk away!*

"Out of my way."

He slams words into my chest. *This is conjury!*

He's wrong. The Swarm saw my brothers talking. Jarvon can hear what they say. "I can beat him," I say to Willow, my words thick with rage. I already see myself pounding Jarvon's face into the ground. I'll prove my loyalty to my brothers. I'll prove I'm no weakling.

Willow shoves me backwards. *We have Remedy, fool. We can leave! Do not do this, brother.*

"Listen to the fat brother," Jarvon hisses. "They are leaving you."

In Willow's face, I see dread. Or guilt? Willow has always doubted me. Willow has always suspected that weak part inside of me.

I shove my brother so hard he falls on his ass.

Tanoak stares goggle-eyed. *I want this,* I say savagely to him.

"To my two arms, you have four," I snarl at Jarvon. "On your back, you have wings. You wear armor and all I have is the skin I was born in. Still, I will crush you."

"Bold talk for a warrior who can't even save his own brother from *water.*"

I'm on Jarvon before he can grin with triumph. He reels backwards, wings flapping wildly. Then he pivots, using my forward motion to twist and slam me to the ground.

My breath explodes from my lungs. Red veils my eyes from a gash. Jarvon jams his claws under my arms, lifts, and whirls, until I don't know up from down or right from left. Again, he slams me down.

I've fought my own brothers in the training pen. I've fought 12. Instead of pushing him away, I embrace him. *So much joy rests in surprise,* I think in Odide's thrummy voice. Jarvon's claws try to rake me, but all he gets is dirt. Against my arms, I feel the roots of his wings, scaled and sharp as blades.

I won't let go.

His chest deflates just a little. I don't react quickly enough. Jarvon has just enough time to pull back and slam his forehead against mine. My blood slicks his black armor. I lose my grip.

I twist to my left. Jarvon is already there. Claws slice through my shoulder. Again, across my face. My front two teeth dangle and I spit them out in a gob of flesh. I raise my forearms to shield my face. Jarvon flays off the skin in ragged strips.

He yanks at my left arm. The joint leaves its socket with a nauseating gulp.

Jarvon seizes my right hand with his mandibles and bites down. The pain makes me yelp, then I grind my teeth together. I won't give him a single sound of weakness. Something drips from his mouth into the open wound: venom, a bee sting times a thousand. I start to shake. Jarvon steps back to watch me die, joy unmistakable in his faceted eyes.

Only then do I feel the Queen. With Jarvon's venom coursing through my body, I feel my mind and body separate. I see myself even as I feel myself slipping away. Odide is horrified and thrilled, angry at Jarvon and so deeply grateful to him for stopping me from leaving that her heart feels a physical pain. He's almost killed me; he's stopped me from leaving. He has served her, without her asking. He's allowed her to keep her promise not to force me.

His bloody gift to Odide is my broken body.

I feel the moment Jarvon thinks he's won. He shifts his attention to how he'll celebrate the Queen's favor. He'll kneel before her. He'll receive her deep thanks. One day, she might even allow him to feed my spent body, my husk, to the great fish in the lake.

No. Not all in combat is strength, Ash would remind us. Cunning can be our greatest weapon.

I force my knees up and flip to my feet. Ash taught me this move, to force my body up. I can only see a black smear where Jarvon stands. I slam my broken shoulder into Jarvon's belly, bellowing in agony. Then I throw a leg behind him and force him down. Suddenly, Jarvon is beneath me, his four arms and wings pinned.

My shaking is worse now. Everything I see is red with my own blood. The joy of killing him is all that's keeping me moving, at least until the venom stops my heart.

I scrabble for Willow's knife and find it just where I remember. My hand goes to the gap between two plates of Jarvon's armor, just where Odide, as a girl, touched his skin when he saved her from Zong. I wedge the knife there. I want to cut through his skin and drag out the heart that once beat with hers.

But killing him solves nothing. If he dies, only I will be left to protect the Queen. Only I would stand between her and Zong. "Yield," I grunt.

That single word causes me splitting pain. Jarvon's head leaches a thin, yellowish liquid. His blood and mine mix into a livid orange soup that dribbles into the pine must.

I press harder. "Yield."

A hiss come strangled through my fingers. "You were always mine for the taking. When you ate, when you slept. I could have slit your throat. I could have scattered your bones."

"Yield."

Jarvon's great eyes dim. For a moment, I think he'd rather die than yield. He's given the Queen what she wants: me.

But we're not alone. The Queen is awake. Above our heads, the Swarm swirls.

She loves him. He's done everything she's ever asked. Now this: sacrificing himself to keep me from leaving. She cannot watch him die.

"As my Queen wishes," Jarvon growls. "I yield."

I collapse to the blood-spattered ground. My arms shake, my legs shake. Thorn kneels beside me, pulling open his fysic kit. I see the words he shapes through a haze. He can't contain the amazement, dismay, and grief that twists his face. *I have never seen such a fight. Fir, stay with me!*

The places where Jarvon's claws split me gush blood. I try to move the fingers on my dislocated arm. Three of them are gone. Even Thorn's gentle touch causes excruciating pain.

"I'm dying," I try to say. What is hear is a gasp. I want to tell him I'm sorry. I've failed my brothers. I fell into Jarvon's trap. They were right to doubt me. Dinitra was right to go to The Deep instead of coming with me. They were all right about me.

A hand goes to my chest. Rough, callused: Willow. *Brother, not even Ash could have bested that creature. I wish you could have seen yourself. We honor you.*

Something grasps my arms. I'm lifted with a sickening lurch. I vomit a thin stream still tasting of the Queen's sweet hilt but mixed with venom, bile, and blood.

I hear her voice, only her voice: soft and soothing. She didn't break her promise that I could choose to leave. But Jarvon couldn't bear her grief. Now that my body is broken, she has no choice. She won't let Jarvon or me die. It feels as if she herself holds me in her lovely arms.

The last I hear is this: *Take him to the Arc.*

12

The Arcs

Warm and slick. Liquid but not water: sticky, yielding. My arm travels the substance I'm submerged in as I open my eyes. The substance is amber colored, swirling, and has a weight to it, like syrup. I hear muffled voices.

No: *chittering*.

The liquid fills my mouth, ears, nose. Deep into my lungs. My chest is still: no breath. Yet I'm not drowning. My heart beats steadily. I feel strong. Around me, a blue light pulses.

I move my hand: amber, too, glistening. I feel no pain. My fingers aren't severed by Jarvon. More: I have all of my fingers, including the three he bit off. I put my hand to my face. Every slash is healed. My tongue searches for the gap where I know I lost two teeth.

There's no gap. I probe the hard surface of two new teeth, resprouted and perfectly smooth. The chamber I'm in is narrow. I feel its texture with my feet: pebbled and slick. I'm naked.

Faces appear above me. Furry, beaked, in bright blue, yellow, and purple. The Arcs. The last thing I remember is being lifted from my brothers' camp. I was soaked in blood, Jarvon's and mine. My body shook with venom. The Queen murmured to me of an arc. The Arcs? As I lift my other arm, I see that the skin that Jarvon flayed is also healed. More: there are no tattoos. No scars. My skin is pure.

The chittering intensifies. Hands grasp my shoulders and haul me up. The amber liquid coils off my skin in perfect loops. I taste no sweetness, only the familiar scent of lilyfire and its metallic edge.

Honey can't breathe for me. Honey can't heal me.

I was submerged in pure nektar.

I recognize the Queen's Arcs, the size of children and completely covered in curly hair. One—purple-beaked, Helleboria Arc the Queen called it—pounds my back smartly. The little drafts are surprisingly strong. I cough up more nektar. Arcs scrape my skin, careful to keep every drop in the chamber.

I feel strong. No—I feel wonderful. No hunger, no thirst. No pain. No dizziness. What I lost I have again: fingers, teeth. What was broken is healed, better than before.

The Arcs help me climb out of the chamber and seat me on a stool. They squeeze nektar from my hair, then douse me with warm water and scrub everywhere, ignoring my efforts to protect my crook. The water mixed with the last bit of nektar drips through a screen beneath me and into a channel that runs like a stream out of the room. Once there is not a speck of nektar left on me, the Arcs use their beaks and chubby paws to plait my hair with new ribbon: cream-colored.

No Captain I know wears this color.

Delphinia Arc hands me a fresh tunic, the same pale hue as the ribbon. The other Arcs push my feet into new leggings and cream-colored leather boots. Around my neck, they drape a hyba-tooth chain with a purple jewel set in a pergama frame, identical to the Queen's.

My old clothes lie in a shredded, bloody, stinking heap.

More Arcs tend other nektar chambers. The sides of each chamber are translucent through the dark orange comb. In each chamber lies a body. From the faces and jointed limbs, I recognize the Queen's soldiers. They move languidly, as if to the pulse of the Hive's blue lights.

"Where are my brothers?"

"Asleep you've been, warrior Fir," says Delphinia Arc. The blue of her eye circles seems especially vivid. Everything seems vivid, as if my eyes have been peeled to fresh tissue. "Here, all things are made new."

They cock their head. "What dreams did you have? Nektar dreams are the loveliest."

I remember no dreams, only the fight with Jarvon, then his words: I was a coward. My brothers doubted me. I let Cedar die.

I cough. A bit of the nektar slaps against my palm. Immediately, Delphinia Arc seizes my hand to scrape the liquid into a pail. Their chittering travels like ripples on a lake. "Eh-eh-eh, precious nektar. Mustn't waste a drop. Sick and wounded, we make them whole. Better than before. Better, eh eh eh."

Delphinia Arc places a furry paw on my knee. Like the Queen's, the paw pads are covered in silky hairs. "Shall we bring Fir food? Hilt?"

I'm not hungry. I'm not thirsty. What I want is… nothing. I need nothing.

Delphinia Arc's blue beak opens and closes in delight. She's pleased. The Arcs smooth a lotion onto my face and hands that smells of the comb itself, deep and rich. I feel how my arms feel to their hands. I see myself from behind and above and staring at Delphinia Arc. Through their eyes, I am young and beautiful. Young: the same height and weight, but my skin newly plump and smooth, the color a rich brown. The name of my mother, once tattooed in blue ink around my neck, is gone with the rest of my tattoos. Where Jarvon slashed me, I have no wound. Not even a scar. "What have you done to me?"

"Stronger you are," chitters Delphinia Arc. "Nektar heals not only skin and bone."

I examine my hands and legs. "I don't understand."

Delphinia Arc's beak opens and closes. "Poison men come burdened with sickness that can't be cut out, eh eh eh. No sickness is too deep for nektar. You are healed."

Delphinia Arc's eyes are alight with amusement. Then I understand: they mean the virus. The nektar leached out the virus my mother brewed into me.

The eh-eh-eh is joyful. "Just so, warrior Fir. You have the cure."

Stunned, I inspect again my arms and legs, as if by doing so I could see through the skin to the tissues beneath and through them again to the deepest parts of me where the virus lived. I work the muscles Jarvon shredded down to the bone. I slip my tongue over my resprouted teeth.

"How can this be?" The ghost of Ash talked of a cure. He told me not to look for the cure from the Master.

The Queen gave me the cure. The cure is nektar.

The Arcs chitter, "Eh, eh eh."

I must get my brothers to the Arcs. The Arcs must cure them in the nektar chambers. We won't need the Remedy we gathered on the heights. We won't need Remedy at all. We will finally, truly be free of our mother.

"Are there enough chambers?" I ask Delphinia Arc. "We'll need nineteen." Then I correct myself. Eighteen. Cedar is dead.

Delphinia Arc's furred ears swivel. "The chambers await the Queen's orders, warrior Fir."

"Then I must go to her." There are no windows in the Arc to tell the time of day. Is this even the same day I fought Jarvon? "How long have I been here?"

Delphinia Arc blinks. "Seven sun-days."

Seven sun-days—are those twelve hours or twenty-four? Shorter in winter? Every one of the chambers already has a body in it. Only Jarvon and I fought. But the Queen's soldiers I see have terrible wounds. Some lost limbs. The nubs of new ones are only starting to grow. "What happened to them?" I ask.

"Zong raided the Scarlet Valley while you healed," Delphinia Arc chitters softly. "These are the ones we could save. He grows bold."

I feel like a child repeating its Keeper's lesson. "Zong raided Hive Home."

Delphinia Arc nods. "Zong and his Furies."

"Furies?"

"Furious they come, to kill and burn us. Zong's Furies. His children. That is why the Queen can no longer wait, warrior Fir. Oh, but you will fill the Hive with strong children! Zong knows the Queen searches for a mate. Zong knows she's found one. Without a daughter, my Queen is weak. A new Queen must come. Your daughter, warrior, or Zong will burn us all."

Delphinia Arc pauses. "The Lady Odide knows you have risen from your nektar chamber. She bids you join her."

In the chamber nearest the door, I recognize Jarvon. His faceted eyes fix on me. I remember what he said to me: I will always be weak. My brothers plotted to leave me. The nektar healed me, but didn't erase my memories.

If I could spear Jarvon where he lies, I would. I vow to prove him wrong.

I must tell the Queen my decision is final. We're leaving. I will hold her to her promise. I get to choose.

The nektar sings in my blood. I'm connected to Hive Home even more firmly than through Odide's touch alone. Somehow, I sense the path to her chamber. As before, Hive Home teems with activity. Yet I notice a subtle change. There are more empty chambers. There are fewer workers. I smell an edge of decay.

Odide is seated on the platform in the large room. The Swarm flows like a curtain behind her. At her feet are piled bolts of brightly colored cloth.

Her smile is radiant and welcoming. I understand that she's been following my recovery closely. Suddenly, I crave her touch and there it is, her hand curling in mine. The tiny hairs tremble with delight. There's a fresh spray of yellow pollen around her eyes. Her hair is wound with a glossy ribbon the same cream color as my own.

I am so glad. She draws me to her.

The Arcs chitter and clap their furred paws. I want nothing but this: her hand in mine. Her body presses to me. Her eyes drink me in and I see myself: entranced.

We have so much to do.

From Odide, I know the others in the room are seamstresses, cooks, gardeners, bakers. Aloud, she says, "My people wish to celebrate the alliance of the Hive and the Living Wood. Our partnership. The Jule is being prepared. There will be feasting, music, dances. These are gifts for both of us, from my people, who rejoice."

"Jule?" I don't know this word.

Her throaty laugh soothes me. "Why, a Jule is our union, our coming together. It starts with a day of great happiness for Hive Home. And then…more happiness for the two of us, dear Fir."

I feel the preparations through her. Special perfumes are being mixed, meats roasted and carved, fruits stewed and made into jams. New songs are being written. Her children practice their singing. A hammering in her private chambers marks an expansion, so that I may have my own rooms in Hive Home. Once our first Jule day is complete, we will live in Hive Home in perfect harmony.

The Hive and the Living Wood will be one. "A Jule," she says, leaning toward me, "is the most wonderful celebration, my love. It celebrates new beginnings. And it lasts as long as our union. For many, many years, dear one."

My crook and the sac it nests in tingle with anticipation. I'm to be joined in Jule with my beloved Odide. I'll have children, more children than I can count. A green-eyed daughter. A new Queen. Odide squeezes my hand. We'll fight our enemies together.

Seven sun-days the Arcs healed you, she murmurs to me. *Every morning and evening, I came to see you. The Arcs promised and so they've delivered. My love, healed and whole. Stronger than ever. Were you not pleased about the cure?*

I struggle to put into words how I feel. How my body feels, vibrating with strength and desire. Desire for her. Our Jule can't begin soon enough.

Patience, my darling, she smiles. *By tomorrow evening, we will be one. Dear Fir, are you happy?*

I wish my brothers were here to see our joy.

In her eyes, I look younger than my years, almost a boy. She takes my cheeks in her hands and we kiss: deep, delicious. When we part, her eyes dance with joy. *What I have waited for,* her voice thrums.

Then Odide points to a bolt of blue cloth, then one of orange. *Which do you prefer? I want my dress to please you.*

I care nothing for any color but the color of her skin, her lips, that I may caress them and taste her. Her lilyfire nektar is a marvel! I wonder when I might have more nektar. Then I think of my brothers: the cure. Once the nektar chambers are free, they must lie in them and be healed of virus. How happy they'll be! I will have truly accomplished something. I'm no longer weak. They won't doubt me. I've led them to freedom. I'll see them cured.

"The nektar healed every wound, too." I blush as I say this aloud. She knows the power of her own nektar. I show off my pure arms, my pure neck. "I even grew back two teeth!" I laugh.

I feel the teeth with my tongue, making sure this was no dream. So much of this feels like a dream!

Odide strokes my arm, her eyes admiring. "Don't you feel it, a new sensation? Something delicious, like hunger, but..."

I pull her to me, and she gasps with longing. I can't keep my hands from stroking her back, her bare shoulders. My hands stray to her breasts, firm and round. Her great eyes flicker with pleasure as I feel their weight. I want to be inside her, to revel in her smell. I want to wind her hair in my fist and gently pull her head back, baring the lovely stem of her neck to my eager mouth. I want to stop thinking and let only her thoughts guide me. I want to live inside her, to share her skin. I would rather lose every limb, my sight, my hearing, than lose her.

The taste of her is sweet and dense, deep. A whole valley of lilyfire in her precious body.

That too the nektar gives you. What your mothers said you couldn't have. What they made you fear and despise. Desire. There's a delicious tremble to her thoughts.

I lean in determined to taste her again. I did this before: a kiss. Did I not just kiss Odide? There was the taste of flowers, of dust. For a moment, I'm lost. There was someone who wasn't Odide. Where are my brothers?

Odide lays her hand on my chest, under the tunic so that the little hairs touch me. "After our Jule, we may lie together for days, weeks and months, if you wish. You never need leave my side again. There's nothing I want more than that."

I feel disappointment but also anticipation. Lying with her will be all the sweeter for waiting. That's the only thing I crave.

Odide asks me to admire the jewels in the chest. She points to an emerald big as a walnut. "Green like your eyes. I asked for it specially. I shall make for you a jeweled knife and this shall be on the hilt. Twinned with red."

Helleboria Arc rummages in the chest and brings up a chain made of hyba teeth. There's something about hybas I remember, so I reach for it.

Odide is pleased. The chain shall be my gift. She places it around my neck, then pulls me close to kiss again.

How wonderful is my Queen. How generous, how insightful and wise! I bring her hand to my lips. I can't help placing the tip of my tongue on her palm, to feel the black hairs that curl there. I am her little bee tasting her, savoring her.

She lets out a soft groan of pleasure. *You choose me,* she whispers.

Again, I notice that she has four fingers, not five. How delightful, how perfect. Eight times she can touch me. With each touch, I want her more. *Odide, Odide, shall we stay in this embrace forever?*

I want to give her something of mine. Something beautiful. But I have nothing. Compared to everything she has, everything she is, I am nothing.

The Swarm buzzes with contentment. Odide's skin tasted of honey and the musky tang of comb, nektar, the hilt's fiery spice. All of these are now as much a part of me as my own skin and blood.

Odide. Odide. The shape word for her name comes to me. I press the base of my palms together. My fingers splay above them like a fresh bloom. Like petals of lilyfire.

Her eyes gleam with pleasure.

"Odide," I say aloud. *Odide.*

My name.

13

Jule

Odide leads me to her private chamber. There, the Arcs have laid platters of fruit, jellies, honeyed nuts, and honey-crusted cheeses. "In the morning, you will taste a banquet unlike any other," she says happily. "Food, hilt. My love, this will be a Jule no one will forget!"

Her pet bird trills on its perch. Through her thoughts, I understand that she's trained the bird to imitate different sounds. To my delight, Odide uses her right hand to speak to it. The bird runs through songs in quick succession: bobolink, hawk, jay, crow. When Odide switches to her left hand, the bird sounds like a bell, a bee, and the unmistakable chuckle of a hyba.

Then she uncouples the little chain and has the bird dance on her fingers. I feel a twinge of jealousy. I want no other creature to touch her, to delight her. Her lips are red as ripe summer strawberries. Is she not mine alone?

She takes my hand, smiling. *I'm yours alone.*

Odide lifts a delicate bone spoon to feed me pink jelly frosted in sweet corn cream. The taste is like a thousand raspberries and summer's heat in one bite.

"This and all of your favorite foods we'll serve at our Jule," she says. "And hilt of the Queen's vintage. Three years ago, we had an especially hot summer. The lilyfire was so laden with nektar that we had to store the juice in plum wood barrels. You can still taste the plums. Of course, also the pepper I ordered mixed in. For the spice."

"Lilyfire," I marvel. So much is new! In her mind, I see an endless carpet of blooming lilyfire, so filled with nektar that her children have to return again and again to collect it. Our life together will be like that, endless and beautiful and rich. It seems like I've always known about lilyfire, but that can't be the case. I first saw it... when? I wasn't alone.

The Queen strokes my healed arm and laughs, low and sweet. "Once we've sealed our Jule, we'll invite your brothers to the Arc to be cured. Perhaps, Willow himself will thank me." Odide is playful. "Yes, I learned their names. Tanoak and Oak and Fig. They'll be my brothers, too. I'll tell my cooks to teach Willow the secret of our dishes. Especially the pink jelly my love favors."

"And he'll teach them the secret of paddle loaf." I wish I could see them now and have them see me with Odide, so happy. Why paddle loaf? The memory of the taste disgusts me: grit and ash and sour Remedy. I want to tell Willow this, that he should prepare moonroot or roast fish, not paddle loaf. I remember that I could see the camp from her balcony.

Odide pulls my arm around her waist. "And Thorn the arts of the Arc. Tell me, my love. What more can my cooks to prepare to tempt you?"

Once, I considered Thorn so skilled, so knowledgeable. Compared to nektar, our forgetting and salves and poultices are like spit and dirt. With nektar, Thorn can heal anyone of anything. Perhaps even death itself will be no more.

Odide laughs. *Spit and dirt—surely, his healing skill amounts to more than that.*

I wish I could bring Thorn here to hear her amusement, to feel her praise. Odide strokes her cool fingers along my bare arm. "For Thorn, whatever my love desires. Your brother has no small skill, I know. With nektar, he'll be a healer for the ages."

Her hand moves down my chest as she leans closer, as if to share a lovely secret. But there are no secrets between us. She walks inside my mind as easily as if I had opened doors and windows. As if there were no walls at all. If anything, she is more beautiful inside my mind than in the flesh. The Queen: graceful and warm, her laugh a balm.

Odide, my world. No longer do I even need shape language. What we have is finer: heart language, a language of skin-on-skin, thought-to-thought. Shape language is crude compared to it, rough spun beside one of her silks.

"Blue," I say suddenly.

"Blue?"

"Have your dress for the Jule ceremony made of the blue cloth."

Odide squeezes my hand. She's delighted I remembered. "My love, Jarvon will be at our Jule. I want no more anger between you."

I pull away. "I should have killed him."

I don't want Jarvon near her ever. Odide is mine. He said terrible things to me, terrible, hurtful things.

It pleases Odide to feel my devotion. Through her thoughts, I know that Jarvon has stepped from the nektar chamber and is being dressed by the Arcs. He begs permission to come to her, to be at her side.

She withholds it. "I'll speak to him in time. Right now, I'm with my dear one."

Odide strokes my cheek. "I've long wished for this, to find someone whose strength and wisdom complements my own. I despaired of wildmen. Violent minds, like the Master they seek. And weak, their most persistent flaw."

Someone once called me weak.

"Look," Odide says, her voice a salve of pure nektar. "The Arcs have brought more of what you crave!"

She means a new plate of pink jelly. The taste is sweeter, denser, as if each time I eat it I'm compelled to eat more. Raspberries harvested just as they plump and weigh down their branches, a faint twist of something unforeseen, perhaps a bit of leaf or thorn that got caught in the mix. I've lost track of my questions. Her eyes seem to shimmer in their pollen mask. There's no reason to fear or doubt. I feel like I'm walking through a delicious haze. Why would I ever want to leave? Odide loves me as she has never loved another. What do I feel? Like I'm perfect. Like I'm her world. She's cured me, wiped away my scars. My tattoos. I must repay her with devotion. Love. The nektar rooted this in me: desire, for her touch, her smell, her pliant lips.

I watch as Odide lifts again her delicate bone spoon with its quivering jelly. I will love her or die.

"Shall we tour our new chamber?" I've eaten all of the jelly, all of the nuts, all of the cheeses. No longer will she use the chamber where she once slept alone. Together, we will live at the very peak of the Hive.

We climb a spiral stair to a large room where workers are busy carving comb with their pincer jaws. "This is where we will talk and rest. And here," she says brightly, "we will take our daily meals. And here," she says, her voice lowering, "we will make our children."

At the foot of a wide bed sits an elaborately carved cradle. *For our daughter*, Odide tells me. *The new Queen*.

I marvel at how the cradle is carved with the same creatures and twining vines as the entrance to Hive Home. Once, I saw a child born. I try to remember when, where. The stench of smoke. Thorn was there and Captain Rek's Vessel. What was the Vessel's name?

Odide is beside me, soothing. "See, dear Fir? All this is ours."

She leads me to a balcony. Far below, the lake is a brilliant blue. Odide tells me that this will be the exact blue of the gown she'll wear tomorrow, for our Jule. Herdsmen drive cattle into the lowest level of Hive Home to be fed and milked, so that tomorrow's feast will be at its freshest. Some workers dive from a high rock into the water, their cries joyous.

Often, I saw my brothers do the same at Quillka. There was a swimming hole where we'd bathe and talk. I search for the name of it and then the names of my brothers and it's all just out of reach, like the figure of Ash beside the river that I dared not touch. At my brothers' camp, I see no movement, not even smoke from a fire. It was Oak who did not want to leave and miss breakfast. How long ago? Where are my brothers?

Odide presses my hand to her lips. *They need no fires, my love. I send all the food they could ever wish for*.

Then Odide circles my wrists with her hands, feeling the quickening of my pulse. "Tomorrow is our Jule. We will be one."

Delphinia Arc scampers up to her. All of this talk with me has drained the Queen. I take her by the waist, guiding her inside. "Will you sit by my side as I rest, dear Fir? Promise you won't let go of me." Her eyes are pleading.

"Of course."

By the hand, Delphinia Arc leads Odide to her sleeping chamber.

Odide keeps talking to me as the Arcs remove her silver gown. For an instant, I glimpse the naked curve of her spine, her narrow waist flaring like a flower into her hips.

Then the Arcs lay her in her bed and snuggle against her, drawing up the blanket. She looks like a flower with her head where the petal opens. Not once does she release my hand. As her lovely eyes grow dim, the Arcs' chittering grows softer. Soon, the room is quiet.

As Odide sleeps, I admire her. Everything about her is perfect. Even her eyes, so strange at first, are lovely: sectioned into hexagons just like the comb. After our Jule ceremony, what will sleeping with her be like? I know nothing of lying with females much less a draft like Odide. Males come together for love and pleasure, but there's no child produced. There must be something strange that happens to fashion a whole other being.

Like my brothers, I felt disgust when I saw beast-borns. No science selected them, no Vessel bore them. All I know of birth is what I witnessed when the Vessel delivered Rek's twins in the smoke and fury of the Weave's attack on Quillka. Odide spoke of many children: hundreds. And then the cradle. A new Queen.

I feel the pulse of Hive Home. I feel every worker, every drone, even the animals penned below and rustling through their ricks of hay and sweet grasses. Nothing can be shameful about this. This is what she wants—what we want. To join in Jule and make a new Queen.

Then Odide's hand slips from mine.

The little Arcs seem to be sipping the moisture from her skin. The little bird opens and closes its mouth, but makes no sound. What will happen when this new Queen takes Odide's place? Who was the male who partnered with Tyr, Odide's mother? What happened to him? I saw nothing of him through her memories.

Is it day or night outside? I kept my promise. I didn't release her. She released me.

Where are my brothers? The Arcs told me seven sun-days have passed. Do my brothers know I was healing in a nektar chamber? Do they know about the cure for virus? Odide promised they could choose to take the cure.

Quietly, I make my way back to the balcony. Before, I remember seeing Willow's grub fire through the trees. With each step away from

Odide and her lilyfire, my memories grow clearer. Dinitra is the name I was searching for. I was remembering the taste of Dinitra when I kissed her. Dust and flowers. When the Swarm saw Dinitra with 12 and Susalee heading into The Deep, I remember the wild hope that I might find her again.

Then the dismay when Jarvon told me Zong saw her, too. She was in danger.

I see no fire or any movement at my brothers' camp.

Odide tried to erase Dinitra from my memory. Not erase: hide. Drown. Borne away on the steady current of lilyfire. Did she tell my brothers I died?

A hole opens inside me. Odide tried to erase everything. Once she finishes with me, will I be erased? In the sky, there's a single star winking through broken clouds.

And no moon.

There's one way to know for sure. I swing my leg over the balcony wall and climb down the face of Hive Home.

14

Old Bone

W ith each step, fury and shame close in on me. Delphinia Arc told me I was suspended in nektar seven sun-days. Seven sun-days dozing while my brothers worried and wondered.

Or left. Or died. Long enough for the moon to vanish.

My boot—my ridiculous cream-colored boot, chosen by Odide for our Jule—slips on the edge of a hexagon. But my nektar-healed fingers, the ones that grew back after Jarvon bit them off, catch an edge. I scrabble for a foothold.

It's as if my nektar-healed eyes have replaced my old ones. I see more than what's in front of me. I see inside myself, around me, above: I hate it all. I betrayed my brothers. I let the Queen conjure me. I even liked it. More than liked: I reveled in her. I dreamed of lying with her, of being inside her, coating myself in her smell and taste.

I gave everything to Odide, including my brothers. I shed them like I once shed worn-out boots. Jarvon said it. I'm weak. I served my fresh freedom up like pink jelly.

Worse that behaving like a beast. I behaved like a traitor to my brothers.

To Dinitra. 12. To the Living Wood. Now the worst has happened. I've lost them all.

Never before have I wished to be docked but at this moment, I'd rip out my own tongue if I could, since I still taste her. I'd peel my skin like a fruit and toss the rind into the lake, because I still feel her. I'd trade my eyes for fish eyes, frog eyes, snake eyes, eyes ignorant of Odide's beauty, her conjury. Even now, with the Hive behind me and my brothers' camp in my sights, Odide makes my heart race.

On the bank of the lake, I strip off my clothes and boots. Only then do I remember: the toy 12 was in the clothes Jarvon shredded. Gone.

If I've learned one thing about Hive Home, it's this: smell is everything. If I mask my scent, I might be able to slip by any guard. I dig up handfuls of muck to scrape my skin. To make sure my back and ass are covered, I wriggle in it. I even swallow a bit, to make my breath smell of mud. I rub it to my scalp and make sure my top knot, grown thick with nektar, is coated in mud.

Then I shove my fingers down my throat to puke up pink jelly, hilt, even a last bit of nektar, gone slightly green. I wade into the lake and dive, the water so icy I stop breathing.

The Queen said Willow and Thorn would welcome our Jule. They would be a part of Hive Home.

A lie. Willow would never agree. He refused to even sample her hilt. And Thorn? He would use every potion and salve in his fysic's kit to save me from her.

I'd be like some beast the Queen harvested to make her children. Like males in the Weave, used for their extract until they were no use at all. The bodies I saw the fish feed on may have been Odide's children. But can I really be sure that some did not belong to the wildmen who helped her bear them? Or my own brothers?

Every time Odide touched me, every time she fed me, every time she kissed me, my doubts drifted away. The closer I got to her, the more I desired her, the more the lilyfire addled me. When she said we would always be together, it was like the warmest of blankets.

Swaddling me. Binding me. Imprisoning me. Suffocating me. Caging me.

Never again. I empty myself again, down to a sticky string of spit. I can't risk being stopped again. I'd be back in the Arc by the time the Queen woke. She'd never let me wander. Maybe she'd even fit me with a collar and chain, like her pet bird.

Love, obedience, desire, nektar: pergama links to bind me.

Silently, I approach my brothers' camp. I hear no sentries

patrolling, smell no fire. The awful truth is clear. They've abandoned me.

How Dinitra would despise me if she knew I let the Queen conjure me. This is a part of me her sharp eyes never saw. Fir gave up his dream of freedom to be a pet bird tethered on a chain. No more than a beast a draft Queen could conjure. A thing to be sucked dry and, when there was no more use for him, fed to a fish.

I feel like groaning with anguish but I make no sound. Did my brothers think I was dead? Or did they understand that I betrayed them?

Near the hastily dug latrines, I find a pile of discarded things: derak skin scraps, splintered staves, a knife with a shattered hilt. Before any journey, we check our supplies to make sure we're prepared, discarding what we must.

The pile contains a message: a full fysic's kit with a small fir cone on top.

My brothers are alive. They think I'm alive. To them, I just vanished. There's a small sack with cold paddle loaf, an old tunic and breeches, a ragged cloak. Tanoak's huaraca is frayed in the cradle but still usable.

They left me Burn's old boots.

I kiss them, shaft and sole. I pull on the clothing and the boots. At least I know this: my brothers held out hope that I'd escape.

And find them.

Willow left a Remedy pouch with a week's worth of brown powder. More than the clothing, this gift shakes me. They couldn't know that the Queen's lilyfire nektar is the cure.

I make a silent vow: to my brothers, to Fire Brother, to anyone who'll listen. Somehow, I'll find a way to get them the nektar cure. I'll take whatever punishment they want. I deserve nothing more.

But first, I have to find them. I take what I need, then slip down the rise that Oak and I climbed as we looked for pine honey.

My brothers' tracks are faint, but my nektar-strong eyes find the prints easily: boot soles marked with our distinctive tree. Like they did, I run the southern side of the valley, above the lilyfire flowers.

Hours later, still running, I feel a stab when the Queen wakes. Like a rising fever, I feel her confusion, then despair. She lashes out at the Arcs. She calls for Jarvon and he kneels before her, pressing his face to the floor and begging her to kill him for allowing me to escape.

Maybe our mothers were right. Maybe males aren't fit for freedom, since we're so easily conjured. In that bath of nektar, my body betrayed me. My mind cleaved to her.

As I run, Odide's anger grows fainter. As yet, I've seen no Swarm in pursuit. By morning, I'm climbing out of the Queen's valley to a steep rise marked by frequent avalanches. It's no longer false spring but bitter winter. I see in great detail. A tree at least an hour's run distant is laden with thatch nests and a trunk streaked with white feces: grabeens. Beyond is a thicket of Remedy bushes. Everything looks etched by nektar.

I feel no hunger or thirst. All day and then all night I run. At this pace, I might catch up to my brothers in two or three days. In the back of my mind, I'm starting to crave nektar: just a taste. I wonder if that scuttle, Lark, would give me some of the nektar he gets from the Queen. I have a feeling I'll see him again, though I can't pretend to know when or where. Perhaps he's the one who will cure my brothers.

I feel my brothers' path like the vibration of a silent drum. When the air is still, I can even smell them: musty, sweaty, afraid. I've never been so alone. Yet I've never felt so accompanied. I have the breeze. A single bug skitters in a vein of a tree's bark. I feel inside the tree, where sap draws up water and food. I hear the high peep of bats, the quiver of a snake's tongue tasting the air.

The Queen changed me. Can I even pretend to be what I was before? A Fir who's loyal to his brothers yet still loves a young Captain he'll never see again?

The rocky slopes flatten into a plain with only a few trees. I'm exposed, but there's no alternative. My brothers go east straight as a stave.

On the second morning, I'm tempted to keep running. Since leaving Hive Home, I've seen no bees. Once, a grabeen flock appears like a murderous rainbow on the horizon, then vanishs. I argue myself into caution. Jarvon promised the Swarm would pursue me. I have to assume they're searching.

But the Swarm won't search at night. Better to lie low for a sun-day.

I find a ravine where I can lie partially hidden in a thicket. At first, I think the lumps in the earth are oddly shaped rocks, but when I lift one, I see that these are bones. One leg bone—derak, human?—is hollow. I console myself with this: the bone is too old and dry to belong to one of my brothers.

The bone gives me an idea. What if I empty my mind just as the bone was emptied of its marrow? What if I hollow myself of every feeling but what's around me, what I can see and feel? Will that rid me of Odide?

I press the old bone to my chest. At first, my mind is as busy as the Queen's chamber, with the Queen, of course, her love and fury, the nektar, my shame, Jarvon's disgrace, and my worries about my brothers, what they must think of me. The Arcs chitter. My brother Willow glares as Fire Brother watches. Cedar flails and Ash turns his broad back.

Dinitra is there, too, her face framed by brown curls.

I grip the old bone so tightly it snaps. I have to get used to my new nektar-fueled strength. I dig up another bone, and it snaps, too. Then another, more slender: a foreleg. I try to fill my mind with sky, cloud, wind, snow. Sky, cloud, wind, snow for hours. By the time the sun sets, I'm surprised to see that snow piles around me like a cradle. I'm not at all cold. Though I haven't slept, I feel refreshed.

Thoughts of the Queen still follow from a distance, like a dust trail. Maybe someday, I can outrun them, too.

On the third night, the plain fractures into hills. I try to vein myself between them, but quickly realize that I'm running in circles. I climb each hill so that I can pick up their trail more easily. At the summits, Remedy bushes grow thick and heavy with frozen berries. At least there's this: my brothers have all the Remedy they need.

I crack a berry between my teeth. The taste is bitter and oily, and I spit it out. Lark called the berries poison and that's what they taste like now, to a tongue healed with nektar.

But the taste of the berry does awaken my hunger. I have no flints to make a fire, no pot for stew, no meat for the pot. I stake out a place beside a burrow and wait. I can hold my breath for several minutes. When a head darts out, I snatch it: a lizard. The lizard's snout is long and narrow. On its body are four filmy wings the color of new peas. I wring its neck, then the neck of the next one and the next.

I slit their throats with the knife my brothers left me and suck out the blood. The blood is salty and tastes like sweat. Then I swallow the lizards from beak to tail tip. There's a pleasing crunch to the wings.

At sunrise, I enter a forest of tall oaks. I haven't had water since vomiting next to the Queen's lake, so I search out a spring. I find one burbling from under a rotted log. A depression between some tree roots has created a small pond surrounded by reeds gone brown and dry with the cold. Ice skins the pond's surface.

With Tanoak's huaraca, I bring down a dozen small birds. I don't want to risk a fire that would draw the Swarm. I brace myself to eat the birds raw. It's disgusting, but the quicker I swallow the better. I suck blood through their necks. Then I pluck the feathers and gulp the bodies whole.

Once I'm sated, I climb one of the oaks and find a broad limb. I watch the sun rise over the hills I just crossed. From the tree, I piss a hot stream onto the ground. I position myself securely against the oak's central trunk, the hollow bone clutched to my chest like a charm, and immediately fall asleep.

When I wake hours later, the sun is just setting. For a moment, I'm disoriented. To the north, over the steaming jungle of The Deep, I see a land of lakes and fiery hills laid out like an enormous tracker map. It's as if the land has suddenly appeared from behind a curtain. The scene is a mirage, the effect of a setting sun on clouds. But it's wondrous. I let myself imagine that this is the new land I'm searching for. This is where I'll be free. This is where I'll give my brothers the cure.

My brothers would be with me, Dinitra, too, delighted by the orange lakes and cloud islands. I'd build my city on the peninsula made of a darker cloud against a spread of brilliant purple. The dwellings of my brothers I'd build at the tip, so they could take a daily swim. Dinitra would live at the very top of a hill, with all of the light and space she needs to draw. 12 would live with her, able to survey the surroundings and protect her master.

A darker spot to the west looks like a marsh. There I would fish. We would learn to cultivate, we would store our harvests. As the sun dips lower, my land shifts, revealing a deep blue of what could be bell flowers and ridges that flame orange and yellow.

The marsh grows darker, as if veiled in smoke. The dark cloud narrows and bulges, rising like a column of black flame.

It's the only thing that's not fading. It's moving. With sick feeling, I realize it's the Swarm.

The Swarm flattens, then skims low to the ground. Faster than any man can run, faster than a hyba pack. Heading for me.

I scrabble to the ground. There are no thickets, no caves to hide in. I can't outrun the Swarm. I can't out-climb it. If I don't find somewhere to hide, the Swarm will have me in a matter of minutes. I'll never see my brothers or Dinitra again.

I'll never be free of the Queen.

I remember the little spring. Water may hide my smell. I think of how I pissed on the ground. The Swarm will find it. *Stupid.*

The spring is two bodies wide and half as long. I have to curl up. Even then, some of my skin is above water. I draw up fistfuls of muck and smear myself. How will I breathe?

The old bone.

Tanoak would shake his head at my poor planning. I should have looked for a hiding spot before resting.

But the old bone, I'd say. Pretty resourceful for someone who's escaping a draft Queen.

The thought of my brother's laugh fills me with resolve. I'll survive this. I'll see him again. I'll see all of my brothers again.

I sink into the green algae with my pouch clutched to my belly. Any warrior would notice. But maybe not the Swarm. Bees smell but don't see well. At least normal bees. For good measure, I scatter dry leaves over the pond surface.

Before nektar, I wouldn't have been able to stand the cold. Now, the cold is nothing to me. I place the old bone between my lips and slow my breathing. There's a squirm at my hip. A creature leaps to my left cheek. A frog-like face stares down at me. Above its pink eyes quaver thin pink antennae. The creature makes a *shesh shesh* sound.

Then the Swarm arrives like sudden night. The buzz is so loud I can hear it through the water. If I weren't the prey, I might think the Swarm lovely as it dips and hovers over my piss and the bird feathers scattered from my meal.

Found, found, found, they tell the Queen. *We are one, we are yours! His smell is here. Fresh.*

Where? the Queen demands. Her voice is thick with fury. *I'll send Jarvon to get him.*

Through the algae, I see the black cloud of bees swoop over the tree branch where I slept. They dip, and I lose sight. They must be at the spot where I knelt and drank from the pond.

Breathe. I try not to blink, to keep from attracting their attention. So far, Willow is right. They are relying on smell, not sight, to search. Several bees hover over my submerged face, then leave.

The pond creature snaps its pink tongue and captures a bee.

WANT, Odide is saying through the Swarm. *WANT. Bring him back, bring him back, bring him back!*

I can sense the Arcs stroking the Queen's long black hair, chittering softly. The nektar still binds me to her, still connects us. But she can't see me.

Want, want, WANT. Then Odide catches herself. *My love. You can have what you want. The cure, your brothers. Just come back to me.*

I feel her need, her desperation. I have to fight myself to remain still. The pond creature swallows bee after bee. I wonder if it understands that it's helping me. Sated, the creature continues to pick off the bees, dropping their bodies on the pond's surface. In a matter of seconds, a blanket of yellow-and-black bees adds to the algae screening me from the Swarm.

Then the Swarm lifts. The voice of the Queen grows faint. *Come back…*

Then nothing. The Swarm is gone.

The creature leaps away before I can thank it.

15

Horse

That evening, I come across a hastily-doused grub fire. On a flat rock, I find a telltale smear of pink paddle loaf.

Just beyond is something more ominous. My brothers' trail is trampled by horses. Maybe ten or twelve, though only Tanoak would know for sure. Lark said he was searching for a man with a painted horse. Since fleeing Bounty, I've expected this, wanted it: evidence of men, maybe the Master himself and his Hundred-Hundred.

Now that I have it, there's a sickening surge in my gut. The horses crossed my brothers' path, then chased them. Here and there, a human print survives. Tanoak taught me: they were running too fast to leave a clear print on the dry ground.

Lark warned us, *He won't spare the likes of you.*

The trail leads to a little dell and the first human village I've seen since escaping Dolor. A low blanket of smoke clings to tumbled-down walls. Timbers have burned to ashy heaps. I pass a collapsed chimney next to a charred beam with a single, embedded arrow. Orange-crested conloors squabble next to it. They are large with a wing-span the length of a human and an eerie, high-pitched cry. Unlike grabeens, conloors are scavengers and not normally dangerous to living things.

As I approach, the conloors fly off, revealing a body. I know him: my brother, Tanoak. His chest and arms bristle with arrows. I feel numb. I never promised Tanoak honey, as I did poor Cedar. I never carried him. He wasn't the smartest or the fastest of my brothers. But none among us could equal his strength. None among us could better follow a trail. Tanoak could swing a huaraca with deadly precision with either arm. He was tender. He loved Cedar, he loved his brothers. He was loyal. He loved me.

If he found me dead, I know he'd weep in deep, wet gulps. I'm dry as my old bone. The brother who betrayed the Living Wood with a draft Queen isn't entitled to tears.

I touch his forehead, just below the stripe of raw flesh where someone sliced off his top-knot. What I feel is cold fury, at myself for betraying him and at whoever did this.

The arrows are not from Blazes. The fletching is made of grabeen feathers sharp enough to cut flesh. I see what look like bite marks on Tanoak's thighs and upper arms. More than bites: places where something fed. Something that's bigger than a conloor.

Tanoak's pouch is flung to the side and split open. I recognize a bit of black fluff: Fire Brother's hair. My brother's a carcass, but Fire Brother's unharmed. There's no justice in that. There's only truth. Another brother dead because of freedom.

Because of me.

Guilt settles like a stone in my gut. I'll always carry it no matter how fast or far I run.

I have nothing to light a pyre. But I manage to shift Tanoak's body so that his feet point east. I slip Fire Brother into my pouch.

Before leaving, I press words into his chest. *My turn to carry,* I tell him. *I'm sorry.*

When Tanoak reaches the Far Lands, will he tell Ash and Cedar that I went to the Queen eager for a collar and leash? That I turned my back on my brothers for segmented eyes and lips ripe as summer strawberries?

I'm no singer. I whisper to him: "The warrior Tanoak, strongest of all. His arms protected and embraced his brothers. He followed…"

The rest is a fist in my throat. "He followed Fir until the Queen conjured him."

I make my way through the deserted streets of the village. The air is sharp with cold. Snow glistens on the collapsed roofs. I see what must have been a bell tower like the one at Quillka. The tower is a mound of rubble, the bell tipped on its side. With red and white paint, someone's made a grinning face with two red horns.

I hear human voices. They're followed by the thump of horse hooves. The horses aren't galloping, just walking. I slip inside what once must have been a bakery, burnt loaves scattered in the wreckage. Through a hole, I watch the road.

The riders are like no males I've ever seen. They are huge and broad-shouldered, with thickly muscled arms. Their heads are shaved and scrolled in tattoos. All of the hair they seem to have is on their faces and chests, like fur pelts. They're heavily armed, with spears, staves, knives, and cross bows. One has huaracas draped over his shoulders, with the Living Wood's red and black cradles.

They must have my brothers.

The horses are massive, thick-legged, with pan-sized hooves fringed in long hair. Steam erupts in dense clouds from their nostrils. The horses are painted like the bell, grinning white faces with horns.

Painted horses. Lark was searching for them when we caught him. Which one does he want to kill?

Behind the horses slink four speluks. Though I've never seen one, I recognize them from the wildmen's tales. They are human-sized and completely naked, their skin a bright blue. Their arms and legs are stretched like spider legs. The speluks use both arms and legs to walk, their spines ridged and serrated like a row of teeth. They keep their dog-like snouts close to the ground to sniff.

Poor Tanoak's flesh was torn from him in chunks. If wildmen are to be believed, the speluks eat human flesh. The rage in me burns quick and hot. But I remain where I'm hidden. Behind each speluk walks a handler holding a thick chain connected to the metal collar clamped around the creatures' spindly necks. With whips, the handlers keep the speluks moving.

Behind the speluks shuffle my brothers. Willow's limping. One arm presses tight against his bloodied tunic. After him comes Yew, Bitternut, and Thorn. Like the speluks, they're collared. A single rope connects all seventeen of them by the necks.

Two horsemen bring up the rear. One is larger than any of them. His bare scalp is covered in tattoos. Gray flecks his bushy beard.

The final rider is smallest. He's the oldest human I've ever seen. He has no hair on his face or any visible tattoos. His black fur cape mounds around his body. Like the others, his head is shaved. Dark circles ring his eyes. His jowls tremble with the horse's steps. A flap of skin droops beneath his chin, like the wattle of a turkey.

Just as the speluks are passing me, one freezes and whines. Its milky eyes turn to me.

"Halt!" the handler shouts.

I can smell the creature: putrid meat, curdled milk, rotten eggs. The creature's fingers are long and knobby. The speluk strokes my prints with them, then extends its thin black tongue to taste the rubble I stepped on.

The small rider rests his pale hands on the saddle. "Poison man, come out."

The speluk creeps closer to me.

"Speluks smell human flesh from a surprising distance," the small rider comments. "I won't stop it if it finds you. Fair warning."

His horse stamps a hoof impatiently.

"We have no more brothers." I recognize the voice of Fig, our singer. His words are thick, as if he's been badly beaten.

The small rider cocks his head. "I'm tempted to call human flesh a delicacy, but of course a delicacy is something eaten only on special occasions. The speluks feast daily."

He motions to his rider with the gray-flecked beard. "Decan, bring me the prisoner who spoke. Feed him to a speluk. They need fattening."

The rider, Decan, dismounts and strides up to Fig. "You won't be harmed, whoever you are," the smaller man says. "But this one will pay with his life. Come out, if you don't want to watch my speluk eat him. I'm very tired. I need my rest."

I have no choice. "Call off your creature!"

Without revealing myself, I keep my tone bold. I have to prepare my brothers for what they'll see: Fir alive and without tattoos or scars. I can't let myself be chained with them. My best hope of freeing them is to seem different, to not be one of them.

It will be another betrayal, but I see no other way.

"What cause have you to threaten me?" I shout. "I'm no poison man. I've made no attack against you, horse rider. I am a traveler in these lands. Do you threaten every traveler who crosses your path? No wonder you are tired."

My insult draws a smile. "Then show yourself." He waves his hand to the man he calls Decan. Decan approaches the bakery where I'm hidden. His grin is terrible, teeth black and filed to points.

As I stand, I keep my voice loud so that all eyes are on me. These men can't see my brothers' faces when they recognize me. My palms press together at my waist: *trust me,* I'm telling my brothers. My brothers need time to understand what I'm doing.

"I heard this is a land of free men. A land where a strong arm is welcomed."

The rider doesn't hide his curiosity. His left eye is completely black, the white inked away, his only tattoo. His right eye is white with narrow black lines, like a cracked egg.

"Decan, have you seen the like?" he says. "Tongued and pure. And without a shred of respect. We take strong men. Not sharp tongues."

"I saw the man you killed." I fold my arms across my chest. I have to keep my emotions hidden. "He looked strong to me."

"Strong and stupid. He ran."

That doesn't sound like Tanoak, but I let it pass. The lives of the seventeen brothers I have left rest on my behavior. "And these creatures ate him."

Under the speluk's snout, saliva pools. I challenge the rider. "What reason do I have to trust anything you say?"

The rider shrugs. "What would you have me do, thank him for resisting? The speluks didn't eat everything. But tell me—you're no poison man, you say. Where do you come from? What are you doing here? Do you," he says, nodding at my brothers, "know these wretches?"

"My story is my own."

"Well! That's a new one." He coughs deeply, for a moment struggling to breathe. "My camp is near. I need food and a comfortable bed. A long drink of cranny. Come and be my guest."

"Your guest." I keep my face blank as I look over my brothers. Spruce cradles what looks like a broken arm. Bitternut's face is so swollen he can hardly open his eyes. Thorn keeps his eyes downcast. He understands they can't reveal that I'm their brother. "I would know who you are and ask guarantees for my safety before accepting your... hospitality." I force myself to shrug, as if my brothers' injuries are nothing to me. "Your other *guests* don't look so well-treated. Not a good sign."

The rider's horse paws the ground. "Come, stranger! I grow weary. These poison men ran. Unfortunate, but this is the Master's land, after all. We live by the Master's rules. They must be obeyed. What's your name?"

All the times I played with names for places and I haven't spent a single second concocting a new name for myself. The horse shakes its head, its bridle jingling.

"Horse," I blurt.

The rider blinks. "Horse?"

"A worthy animal, wouldn't you agree?"

"These ones here," the rider says, meaning my brothers, "are trees. Oak and Elm and that one…Willow, though I've never seen a willow so thick. Are you sure you're not a tree?"

"Do all men who journey become your prisoner?" I counter.

He smiles, but not with amusement. He doesn't believe anything I've said. Yet he's intrigued. At least the nektar gave me this: pure skin. Nothing connects me to my brothers.

"Let me see those boots," he says.

"What? What need do you have for my boots?"

"Decan," he orders. "Take them."

Decan strides toward me. Before he can touch me, I have the boots off. Decan rips them from my hands. I silently thank my brothers for leaving me Burn's boots. The tread is a lightning bolt, not our tree.

The soles make the old man curious. "Are you one of Rek's Blazes?"

I scoff. "I'm no Blaze. They come and go between here and Dolor carrying everything I need. All it takes is a little night-time visit to their grub fire to steal it. You may want smarter allies, friend. That Blaze walks barefoot while I wear his boots."

The rider barks a laugh. "Just so, Horse." He throws the boots back to Decan, who returns them to me with a sneer. "Tell me, what brings you to the Master's lands?"

"I've heard of his city." Odide named it: Seven Lake. She also said Cranox was the general of the Master's Hundred-Hundred and patrols as far as the Scarlet Valley. Odide called him *cruelest of them all.*

I wonder if this rider is Cranox. If so, he's the rider of the painted horse Lark was looking for. Lark vowed to slit Cranox's throat. Quite a desire given the number of fierce-looking soldiers who protect the rider. "You're Cranox," I say.

"Ha! Lucky you have that tongue, Horse. Else I would have fed you to my speluks." The rider jangles his reins, impatient. "Yes. I'm Cranox. Come. I give you every assurance. Eat with me tonight, then be on your way. Horse."

"What happened to this place?" I ask. "Did poison men live here? Were they your guests?"

"They helped our enemies." His horse steps forward and he winces.

I save this detail. Cranox is ailing. "The punishment is death," Cranox says. "Come now or I will make a meal of you, not for you."

I walk at his side. Because of the ropes binding them by the necks, my brothers shuffle. But Cranox is in no hurry. His horse takes slow, deliberate steps, careful not to jostle him.

"It's no easy task to survive in these lands," Cranox says to me. "You must be quite skilled. Or lucky. Both things, the Master values. Tell me about your journey, Horse. What wonders have you seen?"

Truth is less complicated than lies. Besides, Cranox is no fool. I've seen good commanders and bad. Cranox may be cruel and ruthless, but his men seem loyal to him.

I sprinkle lies like salt over roast meat. "I've seen hybas and grabeens. A water creature unlike any other. The feet were human. There are...many in the wild that come from no natural design."

"Of great concern to the Master," he nods. "We're surrounded by dangerous drafts. Some we've trained and put to use. These speluks, here, for instance. But only with the aid of a whip. Most drafts are worthless. We do what we can to get rid of them." Cranox examines me closely. "No thinking creature did you encounter, Horse? None capable of speech?"

I shake my head.

"You come from somewhere, Horse. Have you a mother?"

"Long dead," I lie.

"I saw my mother killed. I was, I think, five or so. The wildmen saved me just as they saved the Master. You are...beast-born? Else you would have the markings."

He means the tattoos, the docked tongue. "I know nothing of my birth," I lie again.

"That is indeed remarkable, Horse. The Master will have many questions. By his breath, I have questions. Every man in the Horned Mask will have questions."

"The what?"

"Look around you, Horse. The Horned Mask is my Spectate. The best in all of the Hundred-Hundred and the lead of all of the Master's forces."

"The Master." I try to quiet my breaths. "He's far from here?"

"Not far." Cranox coughs, wincing. "Too bad you didn't meet this Queen so many speak of. Some say she's the most beautiful creature to have ever lived. Others say the most terrible. Few who see her live to tell."

"I wouldn't know."

Cranox mulls my answer. "For one so brave, you have no scars, Horse. Curious."

I tell him the boldest lie yet. "I've always been a free man."

16

Cranox

At his camp, Cranox orders his men to remove the rope that binds my brothers. Guards shove my brothers into cages fashioned from thorn branches. The handlers stake the speluks near each cage, with enough chain to reach the bars, sniff, and drool at the smell of human flesh.

At least a dozen wildmen already huddle there, filthy and in rags. I use the back of my hand to wipe my brow as Cranox's men lock the doors: *patience*, I'm saying.

My brothers are careful not to stare, all except Willow. The Queen conjured me and dishonored me in his eyes. Every inch of me wants to go to him, explain, show them all that I'm still Fir, loyal, and their brother. I will do whatever I must to make this right.

Patience, I repeat. It's too much to ask, but I'm their only hope. Willow spits and turns away.

Cranox's horse ambles to a stop at a large tent. A horse boy holds it by the reins as Cranox dismounts, his face contorting with pain. He uses Decan's thick forearm to steady himself.

"Show Horse to the baths, Decan. Fresh clothing and the rest. Horse will eat with me once he's bathed."

Decan moves to support Cranox but the old man waves him away. "This much I can still manage, Master be blessed. Tell that boy extra oats for my horse. Or I'll whip him myself."

The baths are in a temporary structure of split saplings hung with fat skins of water. Each skin has a chain that opens a nozzle at the base. Water warmed by the sun gushes out. In Quillka, we had a similar system, goat skins smeared on the inside with pine pitch to make them waterproof. These skins look like hyba juveniles, the white fur still sleek.

Decan hands me a rough cloth and a square of black soap. Even the flares of his nose and the inner cups of his ears are tattooed in reds, yellows, blues, and greens.

It's risky, but I ask, "Were you all poison men once?"

As his answer, Decan opens his mouth to show me a charred stump of tongue the same color as his blackened teeth.

You speak...I mean to see if he understands our shape language, but he barks a laugh and turns away.

Alone, I take a moment to quiet the thumping of my heart. I have to be careful with my gestures. These men are not so different from us. At the same time, Decan's markings and his bushy beard, the horses and the sharpened teeth, are as strange to me as the Queen's children. There's so much I don't know.

I must seem as strange to my brothers, cleansed of tattoos and scars. Nektar: I can still feel it, still taste it, and with it the taste and scent of the Queen.

I peel off the ragged clothing my brothers left me. When I pull the chain, I'm doused in sun-warmed water. The water smells of dried meat. I move to the next skin and the next, scrubbing myself at each one. I want every bit of Odide washed away.

Cranox will question me. I plan out my story. I should keep it mostly truth, with only the lies necessary to get what I want.

What combination of truth and lies will free my brothers?

Decan returns with clothes in the style of the Horned Mask: long tunics, baggy pants, and heavy-soled boots that lace just under the knee.

The new boots I leave. I've come to think of Burn's boots as a good luck charm. Who would have thought that Lark would save my life with stolen boots?

Cranox's tent is wide and well-lit by flame lamps. A guard motions for me to remove my boots before stepping inside. The floor and walls are layered in thick rugs. Cranox himself rests on pillows piled beside a flaming brazier where meat skewers sizzle. Around him, the men of the Hundred-Hundred relax beside their braziers. The air smells of roasting meat, wood fire, feet, and wet wool.

"Come, Horse. Sit beside me." Cranox pats the pillow next to him. "By now, you'd eat a bancat raw, I'd wager. Lucky this is fresh-caught derak."

The raw birds I ate turned my stomach. But my mouth waters as Cranox hands me a skewer of roast meat. A man brings a platter of roast vegetables and soft bread dotted with black seeds. There are horns of cool water to drink. Cranox rips off a piece of bread, then leans over the platter to scoop up the juices. The tent fills with the sound of men chewing.

Once the platter is empty, a man brings a bowl of minted water to rinse our hands.

Cranox settles back, his strange eyes on me. "You speak the language of a Bounty warrior. Decan there," he says, "says you use your hands to speak."

I planned this answer. "A free man must speak with many travelers. I've picked up a shape or two."

"How did you come to keep your tongue?"

Easy enough. Only Captains dock their boys, except for singers and some commanders. "The mothers of beast-borns leave their tongues."

"Ah." Cranox shifts his eyes to the coals in the brazier. "Did you know her? Your mother?"

"No. You?"

Cranox doesn't seem to mind the question. "Like you, I was beast-born. I lived for a time in the west. We travelled, my mother and I. She sold pots and pans. Ladles and locks. Anything, really, from the Weave to The Deep and beyond."

"You know The Deep?" I'm genuinely surprised. No man I've ever spoken to can say they've travelled to The Deep.

Cranox nods. "A strange place. Once you pass The Watcher, it's a steep path down into the jungle. When I walked it, Puerta was only a village."

"Puerta."

Cranox is amused. "Horse, you're not as well-traveled as you say.

Puerta. The last settlement before The Deep. Surely, you've seen The Watcher."

Ash pointed to The Watcher when we ice-climbed in the Splinters. I pull a meat shred from between my teeth. "What did you see there?"

Cranox shrugs. "One sees what one sees. The unnatural concoctions that escape the Weave. They and their spawn. Creatures you have to see to believe. Did you know, Horse, that there's a city there entirely ruled by apes? Yes. Some are intelligent, mark me. And another of conloors, but crossed with humans. Unforgiving, those creatures. We sometimes see them flying over Seven Lake. Spying for the Queen, no doubt."

Cranox settles his gaze on me. "Your mother did well by you, Horse. She gave you freedom, no small gift. She had no talent for naming, though. Decan, bring Horse some cranny to ease his bones. He must be weary after such a long journey."

Decan hands me a cup of carved horn. In it, he pours a red-tinted brew. The taste is more sour than sweet and has a spicy edge. Like the hilt the Queen gave me, the cranny burns its way down my throat.

"Drink up, my friend," Cranox says, "and I'll tell you of the Master you seek."

I intend to only sip. But every few minutes, Decan tops off the cranny. Cranox even makes the shape word for *drink up*. Once, I try to tip the horn over and spill the cranny, but Decan is quick to save it.

"A man who spills his horn must drink two to make up for it, Horse!" There's nothing merry about Cranox's expression. He means to make me drunk enough to spill secrets.

"You promised the Master's story." I pretend to be drunker than I am though not by much. "So far, I've heard only sprig tales about The Deep. Next, you'll be telling me apes talk!"

"Sprig tales!" Cranox laughs. There's no joy in the sound. "Very well. The Master was once like you, a boy beloved by his mother. Beast-born, pure. Tongued. She gave him to wildmen to save him from the Captains. Wildmen took him east. Perhaps you travelled the same paths."

Though he was still a boy, the Master rallied the older men. He founded the Hundred-Hundred, his army. They built Seven Lake stone by stone.

"Now, we rule." Cranox describes the city: dwellings and

workshops protected by a massive wall. Machines do most of the work. Every day, the Hundred-Hundred grows stronger as men fight the decima and win.

"The decima." I try to keep my voice even, to show that I'm not drunk. But I'm very drunk. The tent swims around me. Cranox's black eye goes in and out of focus. "What is the decima? Will those poison men in the cage fight this decima?"

"Those poor creatures?" Cranox waves away more cranny. Has he even been drinking from his horn? "They'll be fed to the speluks. We have many more to feed in the Master's city."

I should say something else, something drunk and silly and without a care for the poison men herded into the cage. But no words come. Cranox intended to daze me with cranny so that he could pluck the truth from me, a berry so ripe it practically falls into his hand. Not just my life is at stake. I risk the lives of my brothers.

"Decima," I mumble. "By the Master's breath, what is that?"

"A tradition of our kind, you might say. A battle in the arena. Every man here," he says, looking around the tent, "has fought and won or has had someone fight for him."

"Won what?" The Queen told me that any male who wishes to join the Hundred-Hundred had to fight for it.

"Why, the lives of his brothers and friends! For each victory the prize is ten lives." Cranox takes the empty horn of cranny from me. "Your name isn't Horse, is it?"

I ignore the question. "Shall I be made into entertainment for the Master?" Even soaked in cranny, I could reach over and snap Cranox's neck. With the strength the nektar gave me, it would be like snapping a meat skewer.

"If you wish to join us, yes, you'll fight a decima. You'd have your pick of those poison men in the cage. You can bring any nine with you."

"Nine?" I repeat.

"Nine." Cranox's smile is horrible. "Your life and nine more. Not one more, not one less. Whose lives would you choose, friend Horse?"

I try to stand. I search for my cranny horn, to drink to Cranox's health and get past this moment. But he's already taken the horn from me and is refilling it. I try to rise. I get halfway up before Decan's heavy hand pushes me back into the pillows.

"Have you doused me in cranny to loosen my tongue?" I say to Cranox. "My mother didn't birth an idiot."

Cranox lifts a single finger. "Men who have their fill of cranny say interesting things. What's your real name?"

I waggle my head. The tent swims in yellow and blue.

His eyes are greedy. "How did you come to be pure, Horse? Even wildmen have their markings. Did the Queen…did she give you nektar?"

Golden and sticky, sweet and sharp. "Sweet nektar!" I say. I play the fool, spewing words in a cranny haze as I try to stand again. "I wish nektar for us all, whatever it is. For you, for me, for them! Decan needs nektar, to sweeten him. You need nektar, old Cranox, to sprout a hair or two on that bald head. Bring the nektar," I shout, falling back into the pillows.

Decan's jaw works angrily. I want to laugh and there's no stopping it: a desperate laugh, a helpless, stupid, cranny-fueled laugh. It's weeping, too: for me, my brothers, Odide. And Dinitra, so far away in The Deep, threatened by vicious conloor-men and a city of terrible apes. I even lost that silly toy, the figure of 12, without even realizing. That's what brings tears to my eyes: 12 and Tanoak and Cedar and every way I've failed them.

"He'll sleep here," I hear Cranox tell Decan. "Put a guard on him. If he says anything in his sleep, anything at all, I want to hear it."

I wish for water, a barrel of water, to dilute the cranny and clear my head. I feel both exposed and pinned to the darkness. Maybe a moment passes or an hour. The tent is filled with snoring when someone shakes me awake.

A face swims before me. It's one of the horse boys or the cranny boys. Or the meat skewer boys. "No more," I say, trying to push him away.

But the boy won't let me rest. He kicks the toe of his boot right between my ribs. "You fooled Cranox, that murderer. You ain't fooled me, Fir."

I peer up. His hair is a dirty, snakey nest. Copper-colored freckles sprinkle his nose and cheeks.

Lark, the scuttle. Pretending to be one of Cranox's ragged horse boys. Spying for the Queen.

A boy who knows my real name for one, unforgiveable reason: I told him.

I sink back into a fiery sea of cranny.

17

The Mother Eyes

I n the morning, my head feels like Jarvon's battered me with all four fists. Cranny is everything nektar's not. Instead of healed, I feel weak. Instead of strong, I feel poked full of holes and limp as old rope.

I remember the beginning, but not the end of my conversation with Cranox. But I remember Lark. He was just like the other boys scurrying around the camp. He said my name out loud. He told me Cranox killed his mother and that I was just like him.

And that he meant to kill the general of the Hundred-Hundred.

Has he already told Cranox my true name, sealing my fate and the fate of my brothers? They'll bind me. Worse: they'll kill me and feed me to a speluk, like my poor brother Tanoak. But what will Lark get for me? Like he said when we caught him: he wants something to trade. Maybe he's biding his time, waiting for his moment to trade.

But he's no friend to Cranox. Lark wants to kill him.

That's my only hope.

Beside me sits a bowl of cold porridge. I push it aside. I've had enough food to last me a week. First things first. Piss, then see if I'm to be bound and killed and eaten. Or eaten and killed and bound. The cranny has fuzzed my brain.

The perfect remedy, if I can stand it, to nektar.

In the tent, men warm themselves at the braziers. When I stand, the tent whirls. I have to steady myself against a pole. Under my palm, I feel hair. The pole is hung with red, black, and blonde scalps. Human: braided with ribbon and beads. Warrior top knots, two dozen at least. The scalps are stiff as bark.

One scalp is still braided with red and black ribbon. *Tanoak.*

Cranox's men snicker as I stumble outside. The morning sun feels like thorns scraping my eye balls. I vomit up last night's stew, the soft bread, sour cranny, my own juices.

This is getting to be a habit.

I stumble toward my brothers' pen. The pen is empty. The speluks staked near the cage yesterday are gone, too.

Behind me comes Decan. A sneer curls his lips. He says, *Cranox wants to speak to you.*

I see no human remains in the cage. My eyes on Decan's, I unlace my breeches and drop them to my ankles. A cold breeze brushes my ass. I spread my legs and piss directly at his feet. He jumps backwards, grunting.

"A horse pisses where it stands," I say.

He opens his awful mouth and belly-laughs. *You're no better than a beast.*

"I said I was beast-born. A beast is free to go where it likes. Beast fits me just fine."

Follow me.

"Crook in or out?" My breeches are still at my ankles.

Decan spits. *Your crook's your own to handle. He's gets vengeful when he's kept waiting.*

He takes me to a little hut at the edge of the camp. The hut is made of derak hides stretched tight by a frame of bent branches. Steam seeps through the seams between the skins.

Crawl. Decan points to a skin flap, then guffaws. *Like a beast.*

Even strengthened by nektar, my eyes have to adjust to the dark. Steam packs my throat like thick cotton. Cranox lies beside a heap of black rocks baking in coals. Despite the terrific heat, he's buried in hyba skins.

Another man kneels beside him. Sweat pours from both of their faces.

"Bancat turd!" Cranox snaps at the man. "I'll feed your fingers to a speluk if you hurt me again. No more purgative. Ease my pain, damn your eyes!"

There's a soft pop as the man uncorks a bottle. Cranox slaps the bottle away and the glass shatters on the stones. There's a quick, stinging smell of hot peppers. "You know what I want," Cranox growls.

The man shakes his head. *Nektar doesn't work anymore.*

With surprising speed for someone in such pain, Cranox seizes the man by the hair and shoves his face close to the coals and shattered bottle glass. "I'm no sprig to be lectured." He releases him "Get out."

The man scurries through the hut's flap. Cranox falls back on some pillows. For a moment, I think Cranox has fainted.

When he speaks, it's more of a moan. "Hand me the bottle marked with a black X."

I have to curl his weakened fingers around it. Cranox uncorks the bottle with his teeth and drains it. The liquid has a sudden, foul smell, like rotted fish. "It doesn't touch the pain. Just makes me care less. That damned nektar! It's healed me just enough to hurt more."

If my eyes don't deceive me, the nektar's stopped working. Delphinia Arc told me the nektar can reach deep inside. It erased my virus. But whatever ails Cranox seems beyond its power.

His breath is shaky. "Put another dipperful of water on, whatever your name is."

From a wooden bucket, I ladle water on the stones. Steam billows up. Cranox's cracked egg of an eye flashes behind a half-closed lid "I was a Mother Eye," Cranox says.

I expected to be accused of being a liar and poison man. The steam hides my surprise. The Mother Eyes are warriors led by a Bounty Captain called Maraz. Cranox looks much older than Maraz.

"My mother was Oxeme," he says, noticing my hesitation. "A northerner like Rek."

By Cranox's age, Oxeme must be Maraz's mother or even grandmother. Steam draws gobbets of sweat down my face and chest. Cranox shivers. "She left me my tongue as your mother left you yours. I think we're not so different. Perhaps we could help each other."

Years before I was born, the Weave attacked the Mother Eyes at the Battle of the Bog. Oxeme died along with every one of her sons. It took her daughters years to recover and brew fresh warriors.

"Help me sit." Cranox's pale hand reaches for me. I pull him up and adjust some of the skins to support his back. I try to be gentle, but he moans with pain. His skin sags from his shoulders and arms like a too-big shirt. His chest is hairless, pure as mine. I'm no fysic, but I think he's dying.

"Among men, you find all sorts." The effort of staying upright leaves him breathless. "Just as you do among Captains. To know a man is to know nothing about men. I suppose you can say the same about females. There are bright ones, dull ones, tricky ones, nervous ones. There are the ones who would cut off their hands to save you— not many, to be sure—and those who would gut you and smile at their handiwork, just to pass the afternoon. Not even a drop of cranny would they spare to ease your passing."

He speaks as much to the steaming stones as to me. "Don't fear the stranger more than the friend. The friend is close enough to slit your throat."

Cranox's strange eyes seem to swim in his sweat-sheened face. I wonder if he knows that one of his horse boys is a spy for the Queen and means to kill him. "My decima was to find a lither bull and bring the skin tanned and trimmed to the Master. Have you seen one?"

I shake my head. "Only tales."

He nods. "A challenge, in other words, not a fight. To see if I was worthy. The Master wears the skin to this day."

His words betray no joy. "I hunted for weeks before I found a lither bull. How favored I would be, I thought. Perhaps I would be asked to sit at the Master's side. But I was a poor skinner. I had to kill three of them before I was able to cut a proper skin."

Cranox pants with the effort of speaking. "Lithers can spit venom, you know. If any touches your skin, you're finished. It burns through you and dissolves your skin and the organs too. It's because the lither has no teeth. It must drink its meals."

Cranox reaches for the bottle marked X but only manages to push it over. It doesn't matter. It's empty. "Every man who wins a decima wins ten lives. One decima for ten. Who will be so bold as to risk their life for others? Who will sacrifice for their brothers?"

I'm about to lie that I have no brothers when Cranox speaks again.

"Have you ever felt so much pain that you wished for death? That you dream of death like a blanket to warm you?"

I shake my head, but I don't know if he can see me.

"Some wildmen refused the decima." Cranox sways against the skins. "They vow to find another way. They don't see that hope is like lither venom. Once it hits you, you're finished. Hope is conjury, Horse. Hope is old, dry bones. Hope is nothing. The only thing that matters is strength. Power."

Decan enters through the skin flap. *Zong won't wait past two days,* he says. *We must make our way to the meeting place. Zong will want to talk to the poison men.*

My heart quickens. I wonder if Zong will be able to smell the Queen's nektar on me.

"I like you," Cranox says to me. "You're crafty. An excellent liar, I think. Fight the decima for your place in the Hundred-Hundred, Horse. Choose men to fight for and they will fight for you. The nine you save will forever be in your debt. Maybe one day, you'll take my place."

Right now, his place is the last thing I want. Surprisingly gentle, Decan takes him by the shoulders. I help with Cranox's hips. I glimpse an odd leather contraption around his crook. As careful as we are, Cranox whimpers with every touch. He's pitiful, like a wounded animal.

If he dies, would Decan still honor this offer of a decima? What about Lark? So far, he hasn't revealed my secret, but I know it's like coin to him, something he can trade for his life or Cranox's. I can save nine of my brothers. What about the remaining eight?

Decan carries Cranox to a wagon, well-padded with blankets and pillows. The wagon has a thick cloth canopy to keep away the sun and wind. There are several more wagons lined up, carrying the cooks, supplies, and tents.

"Bring him my horse," Cranox tells Decan. He grimaces. "Horse shall ride my horse."

Decan brings forward Cranox's horse, saddled and with fresh paint on its chest and flanks, the grinning white face with red horns. As I mount, the others laugh, too. Horse on a horse!

The road is deeply rutted and crusted with ice. When we cross a dry river bed, the mood of the Hundred-Hundred darkens. I recognize this. Warriors grow somber when they return to a battlefield where they've lost brothers. Soon, we're threading our way between boulders. We pass another wagon, smashed and burnt. Nearby, the carcass of a horse lies on its side, legs extended as if it's taking a great sideways leap. Like the horse I ride, it still bears a heavy saddle and streaks of red and white paint.

We catch up to my brothers. The speluk handlers has been whipping them to move faster.

Decan calls a halt so the men may rest and eat. From the wagon, I catch the stench of shit. When I peer inside, I see that Cranox is splayed on top of his blanket, sweat pouring from him.

A wild idea comes to me. In the hut, Cranox said the nektar had stopped working. Something beyond its power is killing him. I know of no more talented fysic than my brother, Thorn. Can a fysic help where nektar cannot? I don't know why nektar heals or how it works. But I do know my brother. If Thorn saves Cranox's life, we'll be able to strike a bargain for our lives. I have to move fast, before Cranox slips beyond even Thorn's talents.

Decan sees what I see in the wagon. Cranox is dying.

"I can cure him," I blurt to Decan.

Liar.

"I can. My name isn't Horse. My name is Fir. I command the Living Wood. I command those Trees. Ask them. Among those poison men is Thorn, the most talented fysic ever to fight for a Captain. He can save Cranox's life, I swear it."

Decan grabs me by the throat. *Why should I believe you, Horse or Fir or whatever your name is? You just admitted you're a filthy liar.*

"You have no choice. Without Thorn, Cranox will surely die. You see it as well as I do."

I see the struggle on Decan's face. He's afraid but he also loves Cranox. *Then heal him. Now.*

"You must promise first. No harm will come to my brothers. I want all of their lives and mine. On that you must swear."

I see the struggle on Decan's face. He's doesn't believe me but he loves Cranox. If nothing happens, Cranox will die.

Over my shoulder, I hear a croak. Cranox has pulled himself to the end of the wagon. His face looks pale as one of my plucked birds.

"You'll be spared for your lies if you cure me," Cranox vows. "If you take away the pain. I swear it. If you…"

He collapses against the wagon's wooden gate.

Decan shoves his face as me. His sharpened black teeth gleam. *Which brother, poison man? Which brother is the healer? Or I swear I'll give the speluks a feast they'll never forget.*

There's no time to dicker over the price. "The one with white hair."

18

Babe

Decan brings Thorn to the wagon. My brother's white hair hangs in rolls thick as fingers to the small of his back. His hands are tightly bound.

"Free my brother," I tell Decan. I recognize this type of male: he needs to be commanded.

But Thorn isn't so easily led. Once his hands are free, he turns his back on me to return to our brothers. I see where the speluk handler's whip sliced his tunic and the skin beneath with his whip.

I don't have time to explain. I run in front of him and force him to stop. "If we cure their leader, we can save our brothers, all of them. I need your help, dear brother. Listen to me." *Listen to me.*

I'd rather listen to one of those speluk creatures. You left us. You left us for...

He's too furious to speak. He hasn't learned the shape I made for Odide's name, so he makes a horizontal V over his eyes. *Creature.* The word Odide hated. *That creature,* he repeats.

I fell under her power, yes. She conjured me. I admit it. I failed my brothers. *But I escaped, I tracked you.* I shape my hands into the word *trust,* palms crossed at the base of the neck. *Now, I will save your lives. You must trust me.*

My brother claps his hands sharply: *Stop.* He won't meet my eyes. *Beside that man, you rode a fine horse, the man who killed Tanoak and with his own hands carved off his hair. Then he fed him to... those creatures.*

To him, Odide and the speluks are the same: creatures. When we fought the Legion, we saw warriors die, some because of battle dogs. But the dogs never conjured us. They didn't eat the dead.

I had to. There was no other way.

Better that murderer die in pain and fear, Thorn says viciously. *Like my brother.* He snaps his fingers before and after the shape word, putting the emphasis on *my,* as if Tanoak were his alone.

If Cranox dies, so will you. And so will Willow and Fig and all of the rest of our brothers, I say, echoing his snaps with my own. *You'll never betray them, as I did. I know this. You are a better brother. I am the betrayer. But have the sense to help me save them now.*

From Cranox's wagon wafts a putrid smell. Thorn knows the smell better than me: the smell of dying. Thorn's eyes find mine as he matches the sound to what I've been telling him. *They'll let us go if I save him?*

"They'll spare us. But if he dies..." The Hundred-Hundred will demand someone, anyone, to punish. *We will be first to make a meal for the speluks.*

Thorn's lips press together. *I need my kit.*

Miraculously, Decan stored Thorn's kit in the cook wagon. Decan brings it, then tries to climb into the wagon behind Thorn.

I bar the way. "My brother needs space. Quiet. Bring us clean water and rags. Make sure no one disturbs us."

When I climb in, Cranox is flapping his hands as if to swat away the pain.

Thorn pulls Cranox's tunic up, revealing his badly swollen belly. Even the brush of Thorn's fingers on his skin makes Cranox whimper. Gently, my brother presses at the point of his jutting hips, then just above the hair fringe of the leather cup covering his crook.

Something grows in his belly. My brother lays the back of a hand against Cranox's forehead. *He's burning. It's a mass. It needs to come out.*

I've seen Thorn split bellies and repair and reinsert the grayish-pink coils of intestine that spill out. Sometimes, he pries out stave points or bits of metal released by pulsar blasts and buried in flesh. He's cut into a warrior's head to remove hard skull and let the gray tissue within swell out. The brain itself, he's said, though it looks like a coiled mushroom. The armorer knows how to make a metal plate edged in tiny holes for Thorn to fix to the bone.

As Cranox moans, Thorn uncorks forgetting and pours half a vial down old man's throat.

The shape of the thing is strange. Thorn presses Cranox's belly again. *The mass sits on his lower bowels.* My brother's palms press together and twist. *The two are fused.*

Thorn opens my palm to mark words in my hand, an extra precaution in case anyone is peeking through the wagon's cloth covering. *If I open him, he'll likely die from blood loss. He's very weak, brother. This won't work.*

Even though his words are terrifying, I relish Thorn's touch against my hand. He's still angry with me and mistrustful. But we're working together. *If only I had something more powerful than forgetting,* my brother says.

The only thing more powerful is nektar. It's stopped working as a salve on Cranox's skin. I saw that in the sweat bath. But will it work on his insides? Will it work as it worked on me, curing me deep inside?

It has to. Odide told me she gives Lark nektar. He has to have some.

Decan paces outside the wagon. I beckon him, surprised to see tears glittering in his eyes. *Is he…?*

"He lives." I list what we need. Fresh bitter comfort, spikeweed, a pail of leeches. I ask for cranny, too, and a small brazier already lit.

To all of this, Decan nods eagerly. Then I grip his shoulder. "There's a horse boy. The one called Lark. He trades in nektar. Bring him to me now."

Decan is suspicious. *What use do you have for a horse boy?*

"This is no trick." I tell him we need the nektar for Cranox.

Decan hesitates, but I can see that he knows the boy. Better still, he doesn't seem surprised to hear me say that Lark has nektar.

Then Cranox groans again. "We call that the death rattle," I tell him. "You've heard it. Every fighter has."

I raise my fist, then the thumb, which makes a slow circle: *death rattle.* "He dies while you delay. Hurry."

It only takes Decan a couple of minutes to locate Lark. Decan carries the boy to me like a sack of wet laundry. Lark sputters and spits, held high enough so his toes only skim the ground.

Only then do I realize the terrible flaw in my plan. When we caught him, Lark claimed he wanted to slit Cranox's throat. Now Lark doesn't have to lift a finger to kill the rider on the painted horse. Whatever twists in Cranox's gut is doing that for him.

I have to use everything in my power to get what nektar he has.

Lark's tongue is sharp as when we pulled him from the rocks near Leech Lake. "There was a time when Cranox put the heads of liars on a pole," he spits at Decan. "This is no beast-born wanderer. This is Fir of the Living Wood. He's been with the Queen. Look at him! Smell the nektar on him!"

Decan drops him. Lark brushes off his shoulders, beaming victoriously at me. "The Master will make quick work of you, poison man. Decan, put them in the cage with the others."

Give Horse—Fir—whatever he wants, Decan says to the boy.

Lark is incredulous. "Have you lost your hearing?" Furiously, he makes shape words. *He lied to you. He is a poison man. He reeks of the Queen!*

I take a step toward him. The boy shrinks back. "You have nektar."

He doesn't deny it. "What do you have to trade?"

Bring him what he wants, Decan says.

Lark folds his skinny arms defiantly. "The nektar's lost its power on him."

I measure my words carefully. "Do you mean to kill the general of the Hundred-Hundred by keeping nektar from him?"

Real fear sparkles in Lark's eyes. Decan doesn't know Lark wants Cranox dead, but I do.

Bring the nektar, Decan says ominously, *or I'll cut a pole for your head.*

Within minutes, Lark delivers two wax globes of nektar. They're the size of fists, the nektar amber colored and gently swirling inside.

When I take the globes, I feel the nektar calling to me. I'm not prepared. It's as if the Queen approaches, still out of sight but with her lilyfire perfume already making me giddy. I have to take a breath, harden myself. This is for our lives, for my brothers, not for me.

I set the globes on a blanket in the wagon, then climb in beside Thorn. Quickly, I explain what I know of nektar. There's no shape word for nektar, so I use *potion*: fingers joined and pointed upwards, swirling.

This potion heals any wound. It makes people stronger. That's what took away my scars, my tattoos. The potion healed the wounds Jarvon gave me and even grew back my teeth and fingers. Once you fix what's wrong inside him, we can lay the potion there.

You'd better be right, or we're all dead.

Thorn lays out his instruments. Decan placed the small brazier on the lowered gate of the wagon. I place a blade over the hottest coals. The cranny Thorn wipes on Cranox's belly stains the skin dark red. We both rinse our hands in cranny, too. Thorn takes a deep breath, then presses a heated blade to Cranox's skin.

Cranox has so much forgetting in him that he hardly flinches.

Swipe, Thorn says to me, *to soak up blood. You must dose him with more forgetting on my command. A drop at a time—no more, no less. Too much and he'll sleep forever. Too little and he'll feel the knife and jerk.*

Thorn makes the second cut vertical to the first, then, peels back the skin in quarters. I apply clamps to hold the flaps in place and give Thorn a space to work in.

More forgetting, Thorn says. He cuts through the fat and muscle to the cavity beneath.

Thorn's hand slips into Cranox's gut and searches like someone who's lost a button in a basket. The old man's vitals glisten red, but also yellow, dark brown, and purple.

Thorn lifts a coil of intestine, then closes his eyes, trusting the wisdom of his fingers. There's a squelch as he pushes something aside. Briefly, he opens his eyes and nods for more forgetting. The hot blade makes a smell like cooking meat. With a smaller knife, Thorn makes several interior cuts.

A look of confusion clouds his eyes. He lifts out a bloody mass and places it on a cloth, quickly flipping a corner over it. Thorn makes several quick stitches. *It's time for the potion.*

My craving for nektar has been steadily growing. *You take it,* I tell my brother. I know I shouldn't have more.

I will not. I see what it does to you, brother.

I have no choice. I pick up a globe and already feel the nektar inside. The hole I carve in the wax with a knife releases the heady scent of lilyfire. A little drips out. I can't help touching it: liquid sunshine, and the tension I'm holding inside releases. Even though it's just a droplet, the nektar works on me like the most powerful elixir.

Fir! Thorn says sharply. *Pay attention!*

I upend the first globe over Cranox's gaping belly. Nektar moves out, slow and golden. I make sure the nektar reaches every part of Cranox's exposed gut.

After Thorn sews up his belly, I drop nektar from the second globe over the carefully stitched seam. I'm almost woozy with it, like I've emerged a second time from the chamber in the Arc. I feel like I've just eaten the most delicious meal, had the most restful sleep, drunk the most refreshing hilt.

I force myself back. I force myself to pay attention. With the knife point, my brother probes the mass he removed from Cranox's gut. *Now we wait.*

What did you take out? Some growth, some infection?

Thorn pulls away the cloth. At first, the thing looks like a lump of fresh derak meat. Then I see what appears to be tiny hand curled on itself, tender as a new fern. A tuft of black, curly hair. Two arms the length of my littlest finger. At the tips sprout five nubs that look like fingers.

It can't be human. I take Thorn's knife and lift what looks like a five-fingered hand. "It can't be," I whisper. The mass looks a babe, but no bigger than the palm of my hand. Every feature is miniature: a wrinkled plum head, two pinprick nipples, a belly the size and texture of a walnut shell. The babe's single eye takes up most of its face. The eye is butter-yellow.

It could have grown there for years, Thorn says.

How? Only females carry babes.

Cranox already looks less pale. Thorn's cut on his belly is fading under the power of the amber nektar.

Thorn smashed the two empty wax globes flat, then puts them with the bloodied cloths and ties everything together in a tight bundle. He hands the bundle to me. *Tell Decan this is the thing we removed. Tell him the mere sight of such a thing will infect them all. Say the sickness enters through the eyes and goes straight to the gut. Burn it to cinders. Bury the cinders. Say this must all happen quickly or they'll catch the sickness and die. I won't be able to save them.*

I stare at the babe. *Why?*

You were right, brother. This may save our lives, as you said. But only if we keep the babe a secret.

The babe? I still don't understand.

Thorn unbuckles the brown leather cup that shields Cranox's crook. Underneath is a thatch of gray hair. Where these should be a crook there is a cleft.

My brother takes my hand in his to shape words. *Cranox is female.*

19

Sower House

There's no telling how long the babe grew inside Cranox, Thorn says. *Years.*

The babe's eye blinks. With the knife tip, Thorn points to how the babe grew and developed and layered upon itself, through infancy and childhood and into a crumpled version of a fully-grown human, all while growing inside Cranox's gut.

Inside *her* gut. Without examining the babe more closely, I can't tell if it's male or female, if that even matters. The babe squirms and makes a gasping sound.

Will it live? I ask my brother.

He shrugs. *It should never have lived at all.*

The process of how warriors come to be born—of how I came to be born—never interested me. Being born was the way of things, what Vessels did and how we came to be and the fact that I arrived here, a brother among brothers, sworn to my mother's service. There was nothing and then, in the laboratory, I was brewed, then placed in a Vessel's body. She birthed me and a Keeper raised me and I came to be a warrior and now a free man.

I'd hear things from my mother—a laugh or comment, anticipation of what her new crop of sons would do and be—and the only thing I'd feel was happy, that all was well and things were as they should be. With every crop of new sons for the Living Wood, I looked forward to meeting brothers. I looked forward to teasing them, training them, and when the time came fighting by their sides in our mother's service.

Cranox's breath is no longer labored. But the babe shudders. It struggles with each breath outside Cranox's body.

This I'm sure of: Cranox's secret means life for me and my brothers. The Hundred-Hundred thinks he's a male. If his true identity is revealed, Decan would be the first to pick up a knife to slit his throat.

What Sower made this? I say to Thorn. *Why? How?*

Thorn looks as confused as I feel. The warrior we knew as Wonder, one of the Dreams, trained Thorn to be a fysic. But male fysics don't attend females unless there's an emergency. That's what happened at Quillka, when Rek's Vessel, Susalee, collapsed. On the ground she birthed Rek's twins. I remember how Susalee screamed. Her belly heaved before the babes emerged: first Ruin, then Rage.

I'd stake my life that Wonder would be just as shocked as the two of us at what Thorn pulled out of Cranox. The babe slowly blinks its one great eye. Its mouth, perfectly formed, opens and closes.

Crazily, I think it will be years before the babe is ready for docking. Or to be a Captain? I don't know where or how this poor creature fits into anything.

Is it even human? The tongue presses out: fleshy and glistening pink.

Timbe, my mother, carried not a single one of us in her body though she had dozens of sons. Here's something I'm sure of. Whatever methods that led to me are not what created this babe. The single time I entered the Sower House, I was a sprig. Ash sent me with a message for Timbe, making her monthly visit there. My brothers were eager to learn from me how many new brothers they'd have by year's end.

Fast runners, Ash said as we drank pogee around the fire, *and warriors able to throw a stave across the Rift into the heart of the Head Sower herself.*

Excited and proud to have been chosen, I ran all the way to the Sower House in the high summer heat. At the door, a Sower took note of my badge, my mother's maple leaf. I was to follow the red line painted on the floor until I reached Recovery, she said.

My eyes adjusted to the darkened laboratory. I made out dozens of lights along the walls. Beneath each one was a Sower, goggled and in a shoulder-to-toe white gown. They had no reason to speak to me or look up from their tables, and they didn't. To them, I was neither egg nor extract, but a born warrior and therefore no longer of any interest.

I recognized some of the objects they used to create new warriors. With my brothers, I'd been sent into the Weave to steal them: levers, metal fittings and, once, a sackful of dials. In the middle of the room stood a high table piled with dozens of thin, round containers. An orange jelly filled them. I remember thinking the jelly looked delicious, like candy. There was a sharp scent, not of people but of tinctures and potions and the other things necessary to brew a human being.

I sneezed. Still, the Sowers paid me no mind.

Through a heavy curtain was a nursery. Here, Keepers bustled around freshly-born babes. One cradle bore the starfish badge of Quor's Sea Hunt. Quor needed boys agile as seals to navigate the seas and dive beneath the waves. I checked to see if the babe's fingers were fused, like my friend Coral, and they were, a beautiful black web connecting each one. I was happy that all was as it should be, a new brother made, and I looked forward to telling Coral so.

Next to that babe was a boy with bright orange curls: a Harvest, the cradle marked with the wheat sheaf badge. Then a pink-eyed Dream and two Kettles, twins, placed in the same crib and plump as just-baked rolls.

When I found my mother Timbe in Recovery, she opened her arms to embrace me. I didn't ask what the Sowers did to her or how she felt. I was just excited to see her. I didn't want to fill the time with chatter. I so rarely saw my mother alone. I relished her attention, her cool palm on my cheek, the smell of her: leather and lavender.

That day, I noticed new lines at the corners of my mother's eyes and around her mouth. I remember the couch was worn, a little wobbly. She was paler than when I'd last seen her.

I delivered the message Ash had given me, something I no longer remember about our latest mission into the Weave. We'd brought back spare parts needed for the laboratory as well as two daughters belonging to Lam, a fellow Sower who'd recently fled the Weave to join the rebels in Bounty.

"Are they well?" she asked.

I helped carry one of the daughters up and over the Black Stairs. I did my best not to hurt her though she struggled.

"And you not much more than a sprig." My mother squeezed my shoulder. I felt so happy. "You make me proud, Fir."

"They cried, mother." This popped out of my mouth. When we camped, the daughter refused to look at me. She shrank back every time I tried to pass her food or water.

"Daughters are always sad at first," my mother said kindly, "until they know the truth. They're in their mother's embrace now, are they not? They'll learn to be happy. All children should serve their mothers. You've done a fine thing."

My mother lay back against her pillows. One hand lay flat on her belly, as if something inside pained her. With the other, she grasped my hand.

"These are my last sons." She seemed sad and also content. "Don't tell your brothers. You must care for these fresh boys especially. You'll be their wise, elder brother. I plan to make you Ash's second one day. He'll teach you to be leader, should he die. You'll help train your brothers, show them the ways of the Living Wood, may your deeds never be forgotten. You'll care for them as I've cared for you. They'll come to love you as much as I do."

I understood that those clear containers, half-filled with orange jelly, would be used to brew new brothers. At the time, I wanted only to dance with joy and bask in my mother's love for us all. Would new brothers look like me, with pecan skin and green eyes? Would they be broad as Willow, tall as Tanoak? Would there be fysics as skilled as Thorn?

As I kneel beside Thorn, I want only to scream at my younger self. New brothers meant new slaves, mixed and cooked according to my mother's wishes. She never saw me as someone who could be free. I was just a thing to her, something that had a single purpose: to fight for her and die for her. She mixed me like a soup.

It shouldn't be a punishment to be male or female. To choose how to live a life.

But what of this poor babe? If Cranox saw the babe, would he be as tender as my mother was to me? Would he have us wash it, swaddle it? Would he carve a sturdy cradle, like Odide did for our daughter? Would he feel a Bond?

Then I feel shame again for allowing the Queen to conjure me. I don't understand how her children are made or how many she must bear at a time. But they would have been born conjured, without any hope of ever being free. Since the nektar ran in their blood and was part of their tissues, perhaps no conjury would even be necessary. They—and by extension, me—would always be hers, in thrall to her every desire, their lives pledged to her and never their own.

Cranox kept his secret for years. I'd bet my life that he'd take one look at the babe and kill it. More: he'd make us burn it, just like Decan will do with the cloths and wax globes. He'd make us swear the creature never existed, that Thorn carved some common growth from him, a bit of putrid flesh and hair.

No: he'd kill it and kill us, to keep his secret. We're more in danger now than were before we climbed into the wagon.

Decan pounds on the wagon to demand news.

"Your general lives," I shout to him, "but we need quiet! My brother is still finishing his work."

Thorn leans toward me, pressing shape words into my hands. *Perhaps they have their own Sowers, but I don't think so. We haven't seen small children among them. Infants. Or females.*

Thorn brushes his fingers along the seam he sewed into Cranox's belly. The nektar is absorbed. The skin is pure and replenished, like the skin of a much younger man. One by one, Thorn picks off the sections of derak gut he used to stitch the seam, popped off like spent hairs.

Here's what I know. His grey eyes are bright with fear. *Only females can carry a babe. Only males have the extract to make a babe, at least until the Weave concocted its own. Only females have the eggs that make a babe.*

Eggs? I think back to those containers in the Sower House. As far as I could tell, all they had in them was jelly.

Too bad nektar didn't make you smarter. Listen to me, Fir! Thorn's jaws clench. *Human eggs. Did you never pay attention when our mother spoke of this?*

She never spoke of it to me.

Thorn stares at the babe as he speaks. *Eggs are too small to see with the eye alone. And they must be harvested with care. That's why our mother went to the Sower House. There, she delivered the eggs that made you and me, brother. But that's not my point. Any Sower would know to choose the egg wisely and join it to the right extract, to ensure that the proper qualities will result. They are careful to place the egg in the Vessel, in the nest, where a human grows. That's the whole of the Sower's art, after all.*

I know about extract. Warriors call it *the swirl*, since we produce it through pleasuring our crooks. The feeling before the extract emerges is like being swept up in the most wonderful wind, full of colors and scents. When we land, the extract delivered, the colors and scents fade.

But eggs and nests? *I'm lost.* We are talking about humans, not beasts. *Cranox is no chicken. What nest?*

My brother grimaces in frustration. *The egg isn't the point. This babe wasn't in the nest. But there is one. Cranox has one in his body. The nest was shrunk like a dried apple. Maybe the babe never got there at all. This creature fed on Cranox's gut. As it grew, it squeezed him until it began to kill him. That potion stopped working on the outside because this creature, this babe, was growing stronger on the inside. It was killing him.*

Shape speech doesn't make this conversation easier. I can say *Captain* with my forearm outstretched, but Cranox is no Captain. Neither is he *warrior*: my fists at my hips. Nor is he a *Vessel* who bears sons or a *Keeper* who raises them: my two longest fingers entwined. He is not even *wildman*: a flick of the hand with the fingers separated. I thought Cranox was a man who knew how to command men. Lark, the spy, thinks he is the warrior who killed his mother.

What is he—she—now?

What are you getting at? I want Thorn to tell me what to do.

There was no Sower. No Sower, he repeats. *A Sower would never have been so careless as to place an egg outside the nest. Yet there is was. You saw it. Outside the nest.*

Through some other means, this babe got inside the general of the Hundred-Hundred. The answer comes to us both at once.

Beast-born, we say together. So not a Mother Eye at all. No, I tell Thorn. *Perhaps a daughter of Oxeme.*

For a moment, we're silent. This is something we'd never even imagined. *The only way. He—she—lay with someone. Maybe not by his will, since Cranox says he is male. I don't know,* he finishes, cupping his hands. *There seems to be no end to strange things in the east.*

It doesn't matter how the babe got there, I tell Thorn, *we have to keep this secret. When he wakes, he'll know we know he is...*I struggle for the words. *That he has no crook. He'll know we opened him.*

Secret: a thumb to the lips.

Perhaps Decan knows, Thorn says.

I shake my head. *Cranox went to great lengths to hide this.*

What do we do now?

Like that, the tension between us is gone. Thorn looks at me like he did before the Queen's conjury: like a brother and the commander of the Living Wood. I look again at the babe. The one great eye has gone filmy and dark. It's dead.

Put that thing in your satchel, I say to my brother. Now that it's dead, I don't care how it got into Cranox. What matters is that we took it out and know his secret. *We might have to use this, to show him that we can destroy him with this secret.*

Thorn shakes his head. But his objection has nothing to do with my plan. Thorn is afraid the babe will haunt us if its body isn't handled properly, burned within the day with the feet, what there is of them, pointing east.

I promise you, I say, *this babe will be properly burned once we're free. He —she—will do us this service first. The Far Lands will always be there, once we are safe.*

Then we need more cranny, Thorn says, *a jug of it. Cranny slows the rot. It'll stain the flesh red, but this will still be a babe for anyone to see.*

Cranox lets out a sigh, just beginning to emerge from the haze of forgetting. *We'll tell Decan we want the cranny to celebrate our success,* I tell Thorn hurriedly.

Two jugs at least, Thorn says. *One we'll use for the babe. The other I intend to drink to wipe the memory from my mind.*

I leave Thorn with Cranox. Outside the wagon, I tell Decan the news. His general lives and will recover. Abruptly, Decan embraces me, then joyfully lifts me and thoroughly shakes me in celebration.

Two jugs of cranny are needed, I tell him, to complete the healing.

My brother and I drain a half jug of cranny through the wagon's floor slats, as if we've bathed the general in it. The jug's mouth is just wide enough to slip in the dead babe. From the second jug, Thorn pours in enough cranny to top off the first, then seals the mouth with the cork. He props the jug with the babe in a corner of the wagon, then buries it in blankets.

We each take a healthy swig of what's left. To Decan, I give the bloody rags we're pretending hold Cranox's disease. I tell him to burn everything, then bury the ash in a deep hole to kill the disease and shield everyone from infection.

The deepest, Decan nods eagerly. He lets out a howl that sets the other men to howling, too, a fearsome roar that could just as well mean murder as joy.

Joy it is. Decan lopes away, bloody bundle in his arms.

20

Brothers

On Decan's orders, the speluk handler, Cuarto, marches my roped brothers to me at Cranox's wagon. It's the first payment on the deal I struck with Cranox.

My brothers' clothing is shredded by Cuarto's lither-hide whip, the skin beneath striped in angry, red welts. They move like old men.

Cuarto looks nothing like his speluk drafts. Where they are spindly, like man-sized spiders, he is a lump. His nose was broken long ago, so his nostrils look like a fungus sprouting between his eyes and mouth. In one important way, he's like his speluks: he stinks of putrid flesh.

He frowns, unhappy. Perhaps he was planning to feed one of my brothers to the speluks today. I feel a twinge of regret for the wildman who'll be chosen instead for a meal.

I can't save everyone.

Thorn may have forgiven me, but the rest of my brothers haven't. In the ruins of that village, they expected me to claim them. More: they expected me to free them, however impossible that would be. Even pure, I was Fir, their commander. Even suddenly appearing after the Queen's conjury, I was their dear brother.

They never imagined I'd claim I didn't know them. Worse: I called them speluk food. I walked away from them roped like beasts. I promised them freedom then let myself be conjured by a draft Queen. I see on their faces not only fear of Cuarto and his speluks and the Hundred-Hundred. They fear me. Fear what they think I've become. For what I might still do to them. To them, I'm a stranger—*no, enemy*—with pure skin and a heart remade by a draft's conjury.

I see this in their faces: What fresh betrayal have I prepared for them?

I long for the simplicity of the tracker map. The blinking symbols showed me how to find my brothers. My mother's maple leaf symbol was a sign of home. In a way, the map tracked what I loved.

How do I track loathing? Like freedom, loathing has no shape or substance. No water or sweat bath will wash it away.

No nektar either. This is one affliction the Queen's nektar can't reach.

I search for words: *peace, sorry, forgive.* Each one dies before it reaches my hands or my lips. No: the words die pecking against my nektar-strengthened ribs. Strangled in my nektar-healed throat. Drowned in the secret about Cranox neither I nor Thorn can reveal.

Suddenly, Thorn steps forward. *My brother planned it all in our service. Out of love. Love:* hands clasped with fingers entwined.

Whatever he intended, he's just blown sparks into dry tinder.

A pox on love! Willow shoves forward: earnest, loyal, stubborn Willow. He usually wears his top knot bound, to keep it away from the grub fire. But after so many days of marching under the lash of Cuarto's whip, it's a rat's nest of leaves and twigs.

I know how I look to him: well-fed, with fresh clothes and Burn's stolen boots, my tattoos and scars erased, backed by the Master's Hundred-Hundred, having just saved from the dead their cruel general, Cranox.

Cranox, who ordered Tanoak killed and scalped. What would they think if they knew Cranox was female?

Twice I've betrayed them for a female. I'd hate me, too.

Thorn blocks our brother. *He never betrayed us to the draft Queen. He never left us to these murderers. He was her captive, then he made a daring escape. He came for us and now he's saved us. He had to do what he did. They would have roped him, too, if he'd called himself our brother. He's saved us, I tell you.*

Willow snorts. *Tell that to Tanoak.*

Thorn doesn't give up. *Saved us* now, snapping his fingers. *Our brother died in battle, with honor. You saw it as did I. His death wasn't Fir's fault. Would you rob that honor from Tanoak?*

Willow jabs his finger at Decan. *That one standing beside you shot Tanoak in the back with his arrow. He shot him even after our brother fell. He did it for sport.*

It's one thing to know a brother died. It's another to have the enemy who shot and skinned him standing within arm's reach. But I can do nothing. I *must* do nothing.

We should have killed her. Willow's arms hammer each word. *That concoction in the Hive and that concoction she keeps at her side. We should have set the whole Hive alight and watched them burn.*

Thorn struggles not to interrupt. With the dead babe we sank in a cranny jug or Cranox's hidden cleft, we could silence Willow. We'd prove that we've managed to gain a little power back. Cranox lives because of us. Freedom seemed to simple to me back at Dolor. Once Dinitra gave me the Remedy. I thought all we had to do was escape. Get beyond the edge of our mother's tracker map and we would find this Master.

Now freedom is as tangled and messy as Willow's hair.

If I said aloud any of what we've just learned about Cranox, Decan would shove his way into the wagon and drag Cranox out. They'd tear off the leather cup to reveal the cleft. They'd kill him, a female pretending to be male.

Then where would we be? Facing an enraged Decan with Cuarto flicking his lither-hide whip. It shouldn't be a crime to be male or female. Anywhere. Yet we warriors were to be exterminated by the Weave. Females are not allowed in the Master's city. How did being born one way or the other become a crime?

If my brothers had done what Willow says, destroy the Hive to save me, they would be dead. Before a single one of my brothers could creep close enough to put flame to the comb, Odide would have known their intentions, called the Swarm, and finished them.

A bubble of bile roots where my throat joins my gut. I have to lie to them. Again. "Let me explain."

Willow's hands twist as if he's snapping the neck of every word he shapes. *No. The great Fir, the one our mother chose to follow Ash. Look at him now! Scrubbed clean. Maybe the Queen scrubbed off your crook and kept it for a plaything. Hoo! Maybe she fed your crook piece by piece to her damned creatures. You're not one of us anymore. Horse. You belong to the Queen.* Willow clenches his fists. *You have no brothers. You left us, remember? For a* creature, he snaps. *You're no longer our commander.*

Then the brother who fed me practically every meal since I became a warrior folds his arms over his chest and turns his back on me. From his thick neck to the muscles on either side of his spine, the flesh is red and swollen with Cuarto's whip strokes.

For a long moment, I hear only the soft nicker of Cranox's painted horse. Not only my brothers wait for me to answer Willow. The men of the Hundred-Hundred who are listening would also know: what will the Queen's conjured warrior say in his defense?

Thorn lays a hand on Willow's arm. *Everyone must calm down.*

Willow shakes his head. *I left calm behind on Cedar's pyre.*

Explain, brother, Thorn says, turning to me. *Explain what happened.*

I'd have to go all the way back to Quillka to truly explain, before we even faced the Weave's fleet. Here's the truth: a part of me left my brothers the day I decided I wanted to be free. When I understood that girls my age were free and I was not. When the wildmen, with their rags and desperate eyes, were free and I was not. When Dinitra captured my longing for freedom and pressed it into paper with her charcoal nub. At the swimming hole, Dinitra and I watched young warriors swim, a Bond silently growing between us. 12, a brindled mountain range of stripes and fangs and tufted tail, dozed at her feet, devoted to her. I asked her to help free me and my brothers, to help me find the source of the Remedy we needed to cure the virus our mothers brewed into our bodies.

Months later, she said yes.

Long after I realized I loved her.

There was no change in my body, no ropes that fell. I had the same eyes, the same skin. Freedom, like love, was an idea. A way of thinking. When I imagined what I would do with this freedom, she was always a part of it. I built a place for myself on that peninsula I spied in the sunrise sky, before the Swarm approached. There was a fiery sea and blue cloud mountains. And there was Dinitra, with 12 at her side.

In her eyes, I became something other than a warrior. I was Fir. I was myself. She saw me as no one else ever has then put what she saw on paper.

Dinitra never ordered me to escape. She never conjured me. She saw me as Fir and I saw her as Dinitra. That's what I wanted from freedom. To be seen. To be myself. No: to become myself and not what anyone one else wanted me to be. Not warrior or Queen's partner.

Fir.

I'll do what I must to save my brothers. But I know I'm no longer just the creature my mother made. The concoction. I was born to be a warrior, but I've become Fir.

Cranox's horse stamps, then muzzles the brown grass. I do what Ash could never do. I drop to my knees, then press my face to the earth, eyes closed, mouth closed. I extend my arms with palms flat on the ground at Willow's filthy boots.

I plead. *Trust me. Trust me.*

Long seconds pass. Then minutes. My brothers shuffle, unsure of what to do. I hear the brush of skin on skin: shape language. They're furiously talking. I feel a kind of peace, like the peace I felt as I lay in the grassy pool as the Swarm searched for me. As that strange draft, knowingly or not, helped save me. The only way out is through. The Swarm would see me or it wouldn't. I have to accept my brothers' anger without trying to argue it away. I have to humble myself as no other commander of the Living Wood ever has because we're in a place no brother of the Living Wood has ever been. We're under the power of a man who is no man, in a place with no name I know, with brothers who fear I'm still conjured by a draft Queen and facing a future I can't even imagine. I am free and my freedom terrifies me.

I lose track of time. I could be back in the Arc for all I know, in my seven sun-days of nektar sleep. Then a hand grips my shoulder. Then another. My brothers pull me up. Tamarack brushes the dirt from my knees and draws me to him, clasping me to his hard chest so tightly I can't breathe. Also, he stinks. He passes me to Thorn, who then passes me to Fig and then to my other brothers, one by one, until Willow alone is left, his back still turned on me.

I'll never be the brother I was before we left Dolor. I'll never be the brother he knew. I'm the brother I am, free.

"Brother," I say aloud. "You're right. I betrayed you. I betrayed all of you. I'm weak. I let myself be conjured."

A voice from the wagon interrupts. "You escaped the Queen, the only man alive I know who's done it."

It's Cranox. He's pulled himself to the wagon gate. His face is still drawn, but already gaining color. "Fir, you are as like to your brothers as a leaf is to its neighbor on the stem."

"You are a murderer." Anger flushes my cheeks. "You ordered my brother killed and took his top knot."

"Your brother died in battle. With honor. And the top knot, well. It's our way."

"Release us. We healed you as promised."

"Ah." Decan steadies him as Cranox climbs out of the wagon. Although I know he's female, I see nothing of a Captain in him.

He stares at his hands, flexing the fingers, though Thorn found no sickness there.

"I told you my brother Thorn has great skill," I say. "There was a sickness in you, deep inside you. Thorn took it out."

Decan looks at me with moony eyes. If I asked Decan in this moment to gift me a finger or a foot for saving Cranox's life, he'd saw one off and ask if I wanted more. His black-toothed grin is terrifying and completely sincere. *It is as Horse says. As Fir says. It is as he says.*

Cranox's voice is deceptively mild. "Where did your brother cut?"

Before Thorn can speak, I step towards Cranox. "Where it hurt, of course. My brother has no small skill."

I flatten my palm over my ribs. Slowly, I move my hand down, then stop just above my crook. Between Cranox and me, a second, silent conversation vibrates. This is nothing like the communication Odide and I shared. Cranox can't enter my mind just as I can't enter his. But I know he understands me. Thorn saw his secret. I saw his secret. And now he knows.

"You burned it." Cranox desperately wants this to be true. "The sickness. It's gone."

Decan nods eagerly. *I burned it myself just as he asked.*

But Thorn and I stay silent. If we had burned the babe, Cranox's next order would be to kill us. *Bless Fire Brother for Thorn's idea to hide the babe in the cranny jug.*

"Thorn stitched you inside and out," I tell him. "Everything is as it should be, like it was the day you first took breath. Is this not so, brother Thorn? Your natural insides. As your mother made them."

I'm getting dangerously close to revealing Cranox's secret.

Thorn saves me. *You must take bone broth for strength. A tea of starry white for swelling. Brother,* Thorn says to Willow, *will you kindle a fire? Decan, bring fresh cow bone still with marrow. That's best for healing.*

Before Decan can leave, Cranox speaks. "There will be no fires. We must march to our meeting with Zong. We can still arrive in time."

Cranox points at me. "You'll ride with me in the wagon, Horse."

"Fir," I tell him. "My name is Fir."

21

Rule of Ten

The wagon rumbles on the rutted road. Cranox wraps himself in his blankets. "Show me what you found."

It's hard to keep my eyes from drifting to the cranny jug hidden just behind him in the wagon. As the wagon rolls and jerks, the cranny jug shifts.

I describe for him what we found: a babe outside the nest. Still alive.

Use your hands, Cranox says sharply.

We couldn't tell how old. It was gripping your insides, Thorn said. That's why the potion stopped working.

Potion?

"Nektar."

Cranox looks stricken.

It was killing you, I say. *We saved you. You owe us.*

Cranox closes his eyes. *Tell me more.*

With a single eye and curled in on itself. But it was—it is—a babe. Hands, feet. A head and a body a little longer than my hand.

His face twists with curiosity and disgust.

The babe lived, I say, *for a little while.*

Cranox sits before me, but if I had to say, his thoughts are in place where he's all alone. Where he relives however that babe came to be inside him. By the clenching of his fists, the memory is painful. Thorn saved his life and took away his physical pain, but something in Cranox's past strangles him still. *I must see it,* he says.

You'll destroy it and with it any chance I have of freeing my brothers. Let us speak honestly. We want our freedom. Let us go.

Violence leaps in his eyes. *You know I could beat it out of you. Or worse.*

You could. But what we took out of you would be revealed.

I could have you killed.

Yes. And you would be next. What will Master do to you when he learns the truth? I move my hands slowly. *You say you were a Mother Eye? Their Vessel, then? You left for a world of men. Why?*

I was no Vessel.

Even reclined before me, even knowing that Cranox has no crook, I see nothing in him that says female. But there's no mistaking what Thorn removed from his gut. Once, he was a female desperate enough to abandon her village, her mother. She also abandoned her place above men. I left my mother, too. But I could never leave behind my maleness.

If I'd known that bancat turd of a fysic would open me, I'd never have allowed it, Cranox says.

Then you'd be dead.

Cranox swipes his hand over his skull, fuzzed with new hair. *It seems we have something to trade.*

Your secret is safe once we're away. We'll…we'll take it with us.

Cranox snorts. *That's the one thing I can't do.* He gazes at me steadily. I can't imagine what would make him abandon his maleness, But I can guess how he survived: determination and a limitless capacity for violence. *I still don't know the shape name of the warrior who helped save my life. And who now bargains for his own. Show me.*

I make my name, *Fir*: the pointing and middle fingers angled across one another with the right hand on top and the thumbs overlapped, forming an inner fir cone. With Odide, my name was play, the delicious give and take of her conjury. In this wagon, Cranox displays no gentleness. He shapes my name crudely, quickly, as if it's just one more piece in a larger game I still don't completely understand.

We have laws I must obey, Cranox says. *Not even the Master himself may violate them. The law of the Hundred-Hundred is this. Any man we find may ask for a decima. A decima wins ten lives, you and nine brothers. That's what we call the Rule of Ten.*

I have seventeen to save and he knows it. If decimas were coin, I could only buy a portion of the lives I need. My heart thumps against my ribs. *I have no wish to join you. I want all seventeen lives.*

You must fight or be speluk food. If you win, you choose your own fate. Even I can't free you or bring in a man who has not won a decima before us all. Call this...equality. All of my men have won decimas or had someone win for them, ten lives each time. Just as I fought and won a decima. Your choice is the decima or death. If you refuse the decima, it's not me who'll kill you. It's the rest of them, he says, meaning the men of the Hundred-Hundred who surround us.

Cranox slaps the back of his hand: an offer. *I can make sure the decima is easier for your brother.*

I'm startled. "My brother?"

Surely, the leader of the Living Wood will not risk his own life? You'll send that great large brother. What's his name? He'll make a good show.

He means Tamarack. It makes sense. Like his brother, Tamarack is huge, with hands like hams and a fierceness in his eye that even caused Tanoak pause when they fought.

But I can't ask a brother I betrayed to fight a decima for me—for us. Whatever battle is to be fought, I tell Cranox, I'll fight it. I'll fight as many times as I must to win the lives of all of my brothers. *And you'll make sure I win.*

I sound more boy than man. But this is the right thing to do. The only thing. Thorn knows what's in the cranny jug. If I die in the decima, my brother will make sure the Hundred-Hundred knows Cranox is a liar. Worse: female.

I can make sure you win, Cranox offers. *Once. That's a worthy promise, warrior Fir.*

I have seventeen brothers, I say. *I would fight for them all.*

Cranox waves his hand, irritated. *It's the Rule of Ten, not seventeen.*

For a long moment, we stare at each other. How my mother would ridicule me if she knew I'd brought my brothers to this, placed their freedom in the power of a male with no crook. A secret female. Whatever Cranox is. I'm not afraid of the decima. I'm afraid of what comes after I win: eight brothers still at Cranox's mercy.

I'll fight two decimas. My hands move awkwardly. *I'll fight a dozen, for my brothers.*

Cranox flicks his hand as if brushing away a fly. *You'll survive one. More I can't promise. They are to the death, always. For you or your opponent.*

You'll do it or we'll bring the Master an interesting gift.

For a long moment, Cranox gazes at me—not angry or even upset, but with an unsettling calm. *The minute you show him what you took from me, you and I both die. He'll kill you and your brothers to save himself from shame. That you can be sure of. Have a care, Fir. You have less power than you think.*

The wagon lurches to a stop. Decan pushes his head through the canopy. *Come,* he says, and another shape word I haven't seen, all five fingers curling downwards.

"Bring me my robe," Cranox shouts to Decan. He grips the wagon side to pull himself up. "You're coming, too. Zong will want words with the poison man who escaped his sister. My belly was killing me, not my eyes," Cranox says dismissively. "I saw what you told your brothers. Zong will want to know everything."

The vision I saw of Zong from Odide's memories was of a huge bee draft armored in black, faceted yellow eyes delighting in his mother's murder. He was bigger than Jarvon, but with a human mouth like Odide.

Decan tosses a heavy red robe and a black leather belt into the wagon.

"Few men live to speak of the Hive." Cranox pulls the robe over his emaciated chest. Already, nektar has given him fresh energy.

And me. Even the few drops I touched make me pulse with fresh power. Does Lark have more? I should find him and demand more. How many globes do I need?

I stop myself. I need whole chambers of nektar to cure seventeen brothers. There's no way Lark has that much nektar hidden away.

But the Master might.

"Zong will ask about her workers. Her defenses," Cranox is saying. His hand, palm up, lightly bounces. "Her *weakness.* He'll know if you lie. Trust me. Tell him everything."

"I thought you despised drafts." That's what Odide told me, that the Master and his Hundred-Hundred hate and kill drafts. At least the ones they can't use to terrorize, like the speluks. They only tolerate Odide and her Hive because the Master wants her nektar.

"Zong serves his purpose," Cranox says curtly. "As do you. If you anger Zong, even I can't protect you. He is easily angered."

Cranox struggles to stand. When he throws off the blankets, the cranny jug wobbles and tips to one side.

He doesn't notice. "You are right about one thing. Drafts are unnatural. Sower cast-offs, as you know. Failed experiments and the like. You should be grateful you're not one of them. Drafts are owed no decima. But…" Cranox tries to cinch the belt around his waist, but there's no hole to accommodate his belly. "Drafts can be useful."

"Useful," I repeat. Is Zong useful because he'll kill his sister and do to her Hive what he did to their mother's? Then where would the Master get nektar? Why destroy the source of something so powerful? I feel a panic. If Odide's Hive is destroyed, I will never taste her lilyfire nektar gain.

Cranox notices. "Like all poison men, you know so little of the world you're so desperate to be free in," he says cruelly. "Did you think your freedom from your Bond to your mother would solve every problem? Cure every wound, satisfy every hunger? Bah," he says, tossing the belt at Decan. "Bring me the pergama links!" he bellows.

Decan delivers a silvery chain that Cranox is able to latch around his waist. He steadies himself on my arm as he climbs down from the wagon. It's as if he hears my questions and senses my fear. "Once we've destroyed the Queen, we'll get our nektar directly from Zong. Simple as that. Not the miserable droplets the Queen so reluctantly sends, but buckets of it, barrels, to make the Hundred-Hundred invincible. Can you not see it, Fir? An army of soldiers who never age. Who can be revived from almost every injury and made stronger with every battle?"

Cranox sits on the stool Decan offers and pulls on an elaborately stitched pair of boots. "Now that the Captains—your mother, I should say, and all of her kind—have crushed the Weave, why, all the easier for us to crush them in turn, with an army they can't defeat. You can help us. Once we have Zong's nektar, we'll live forever."

The prospect of living forever with Cranox makes me sick. But I try to compose myself. "Why not have two Hives and live in peace? Why destroy the Queen?"

"Ah," Cranox says, "an excellent question. Because like you, Zong has his price. We want nektar. He wants his sister dead. A fair trade, I think."

Cranox gazes at me, perplexed. "I thought you'd be pleased."

"Pleased?"

"The Captains bound you to them. They used you. Then the Queen tried to rob you of your freedom. You should want her dead."

I never once felt the need for revenge, on Odide or my mother. All I wanted was to get away, to be free.

Cranox shrugs. "I never hesitate to kill those who wronged me."

Cranox and Decan move away from the wagon. I quickly retrieve the cranny jug. Luckily, my brothers are nearby. *Carry this*, I tell Tamarack. His huge hands make the cranny jug looks like a child's toy. *If anyone asks, say you're fond of this new brew. Never let it out of your sight.*

I am fond of it. Tamarack balances the jug on his bicep, mimicking how he'll pop the cork with his teeth and take a mighty swallow.

Don't touch the cork! Just keep it safe. And for the love of Fire Brother, don't drop it.

Near a lone tree, Cranox and Decan beckon for me to join them. As I approach, I hear a rising sound, like knives sharpening on a whet stone. Zong and his Furies appear from behind a low hill. There are twelve Furies, identical to Zong but for the red striping on his chest.

I recognize him from Odide's memories. He's twice Tanoak's height and heavier than Jarvon. He walks on two legs with the other four tucked at his waist. His wings fold onto his back, scraping the ground behind him like a stiff cape.

His eyes are like his sister's, enormous, except that they're a deep greenish-yellow. I see myself in them as I saw myself in his sister's eyes, two dozen Firs staring at once. His lips are red strips over sharply pointed fangs.

His soldiers carry weapons I recognize: curved blades with wicked tips. These are from the Blazes. I wonder if my mother even knows about Rek's betrayal.

"You're late," Zong says to Cranox. His voice is harsh, but surprisingly high, almost like a mosquito whine.

I worry that Odide's conjury and her connection to her brother means that Zong will be able to walk my thoughts. Just as I think this, Zong turns on me. "This is the one who was with my sister."

"My gift to you," Cranox says.

I feel Zong's eagerness. Am I his enemy because Odide wanted me or his spy and tool because I fled her? He leans in to sniff, then softly growls. "You stink of my sister."

His hands are like his sister's, with four fingers apiece, though his are tipped in red claws.

"We can offer you food and cranny," Cranox says. "You must be parched, friend Zong."

Zong ignores him. "I would know everything of my sister's Hive."

He hurls questions. How many workers did I see. How many larvae? How many soldiers? Did I see winter supplies? Did I see weapons?

I answer: the Hive has supplies, I saw larvae in the comb. The Queen's soldiers are loyal. I've felt myself the bite of their weapons. After nektar healed me, I felt every part of Hive Home.

I don't tell him Odide tired easily. Thinking back, I realize how desperate she was for a daughter. She said I would be her partner and help strengthen the Hive. Without a such a partner, the Hive is vulnerable. Without a new Queen, Hive Home is doomed.

Zong's lips pull back. I can't tell if he's pleased or about to attack me. "You escaped her. Not many can say the same."

I drop my eyes to the ground. Until this moment, I hadn't realized how vulnerable the Queen is. I wouldn't change what I did. But I don't want to help Zong.

"Come, come!" Cranox interrupts. "We shall drink to this, the end of the Hive. Odide's Hive, I mean," he corrects himself. "Long live Zong and the hive of his Furies!"

Zong doesn't even glance at the horn of cranny Cranox offers. "Bring the gift," he orders one of the Furies.

"A gift for the Master," Zong says, nodding for the Fury to hand over a wooden box. "To remind him of his promise to me."

Cranox slides off the lid. He lifts out a necklace: a white stone set in a five-sided frame of pergama. I recognize the same design as the pendant Odide wears. Except Odide's stone is purple. She promised a match for me in green to celebrate our Jule, on a hyba-tooth chain.

Cranox lifts the pendant to the light. The white stone glows. "Where did you find it?"

"I've had it since I killed my mother. Your Master and his old scribe know it. Take it as a sign of how I honor my promises. Your Master should do the same."

Cranox smiles, but there's only coldness in his eyes. "His old scribe. Is that what you are calling him now?"

Zong jabs a red claw at me. "The Blazes want this one. Trade him and the rest. He's no further use to you."

Cranox places the pendant back into the box and hands the box to Decan. "They must come to Seven Lake to fight the decima. That's our way."

"My sister's Swarm searches for him. Kill him before she takes him back."

I don't need to be reminded of the Swarm. Zong's words are chilling. I may be more use to this Master dead.

"The Rule of Ten is required," Cranox replies, his voice deceptively mild. "If they lose the decima, well. Cuarto may need them to feed his speluks. Be assured they won't go to waste."

"Their purpose? Their purpose," Zong hisses. "Another decima means another delay. Another delay means we do not destroy Hive Home. Another delay means you break your promise."

"Patience, Zong. The Hundred-Hundred will take Hive Home for you. Then you can do with it what you will. And we'll bathe in your lovely nektar for eternity."

Zong steps toward Cranox. I see a flash of how Odide remembers him as he killed their mother. But for Jarvon, he would have torn off Odide's head. "Here's what the Master doesn't see. Here's what I know, because I fly with my Furies and see with my own eyes. We don't just face the filthy Captains. We don't just face my sister and that vagabond she calls a protector. While the Master delays and delays and delays, a new power emerges. Yes, a new power."

Decan's hand grips his knife, but it stays in the sheath.

The next words explode from Zong. "An army of drafts, you *idiot*. Seven-legged, three-mouthed. Some fly and some crawl, some ride others like parasites. Some cannot live without water and some cannot even bear the idea of water. One dies if his skin meets the sun. One never sleeps."

"A draft army," Cranox scoffs. "Friend Zong, you mock me. We have nothing to fear from these concoctions. They're nothing but chaff and cow spit, malformed, ridiculous, a soup of frogs and snakes and whatnot."

"I am one of them." Zong's eyes fix on Cranox. "I am no *soup*. I know what drafts are capable of."

"Zong." Cranox raises his hands to calm him. "You know the Master and I don't think of you as draft. You are a new and welcome creature!"

Creature. Zong stiffens. He hates the word as much as his sister does. "Don't mock me, *human*."

Next to Zong—enormous, armored—Cranox looks like a plucked chicken.

"Tell me this." Zong extends his four hands, each finger with a red-tipped claw. "How do you combat such a force? Tell me! Since you know *so much*." The last word ends in a hiss. "They may seem weak. But I well know they have powers we can't even imagine. They are not like me. For generations, these drafts have mixed in The Deep. They mean to destroy us." Zong jabs a claw at Cranox. "In The Deep, a new leader emerges. They prepare to make this world their own."

Cranox tries reason. "We have ten thousand men. Machines, horses, weapons. By spring..."

"Curse spring," Zong's pus-yellow eyes glitter. "The time to attack is *now*! I've seen the drafts send messengers to my sister. She plots with them to save herself. She sends them nektar. Don't look so shocked. That old scribe the Master protects lies to you. He has always been her spy. Look how he left my mother to die!"

Like Jarvon, Zong's body is encased in hard plates that shift as he moves. "I'm no friend of yours, Cranox. I'm no friend to the Master. I'm your ally. As your ally, I say we must attack my sister now."

Cranox's voice is even, but his fists clench. "I'll deliver your gift. I'll counsel with the Master. I'll tell him you wish to move soon."

"So long as that old scribe sits at his side, your advice is nothing. He listens to the scribe, not you. He only wants to dabble in books."

"Be assured the Master will do as you wish. Do not fear, friend Zong."

"I've just said I'm not your friend. And you call me afraid?" Zong steps toward Cranox. For a moment, I think his grasping claws will rip Cranox limb from limb.

The buzzing of Zong's soldiers stops him. One whispers: "Wait. Wait. Wait."

Another adds his voice. "The time will come."

"The old scribe's time will come."

"Wait."

Zong's great eyes glitter with hatred. His wings unfurl and lift him. For a moment, he hovers as his Furies lift with him. "They may be weak now, but their strength grows. Every miserable draft who joins them makes them stronger. My sister heals them, plots with them. She woos them, just as she wooed this pathetic human." He looks at me as if I'm some disease. "If your Master delays much longer, our alliance be damned. I'll exterminate the drafts myself."

With a throb of wings, Zong and his Furies are gone.

22

Seven Lake

ll night we travel. I'm grateful. The steady pace of Cranox's painted horse and the cool night air clear my head.

My brothers walk around me. Too much has happened for there to be ease between us. But their silence is no longer so angry. Several times, Fig touches my knee, as if to prove to himself that I'm still there, still Fir.

After the Furies departed, Cranox made a grim joke. Surely, he says, there's some poison that kills pesky insects and then something else about severing their wings and using the wings to pave a beautiful new road to Seven Lake.

There's no love in this alliance between the Master's Hundred-Hundred and Zong's Furies.

Before climbing back into the wagon, Cranox ordered more guards posted in the rear and more scouts at the sides and front. I remember the image of Zong's knife through Odide's eyes, the gift her mother gave to him in place of rule. This alliance sits on the edge of its blade.

If Zong is capable of killing his mother, he's capable of killing anyone.

Would I have yearned for freedom if I'd known of the dangers awaited in the east? I think I would have. But as Cranox's horse clops toward the Master's city, I curse the dangers one by one: hybas,

Blazes, that spy and scuttle Lark. Cranox and his vicious speluks with
their taste for human flesh.

Only Odide do I spare. Perhaps it's the lingering effects of the
nektar. Or what I now understand was her desperation. She is older
than she first appeared. I thought of her as a girl, but no girl builds
such an enormous Hive. The empty cradle for our daughter haunts
me. She cured me and, yes, she conjured me. But it was Jarvon's
decision to attack me. He did it for her and she was grateful. But she
never broke her promise to me.

After seeing Zong, I understand Odide a little better. She needs a
mate or Hive Home is lost. Her brother won't give up until she's dead
and he has Hive Home.

Cranox's horse has either taken a liking to me or wants to eat me,
frequently throwing its head back to nibble at Burn's boot. When I ask
Decan its name, he says *horse*, then laughs: *Horse on a horse.*

To him, the joke never gets old. Decan is as loyal as a dog to me
now that I've saved Cranox's life. From the wagon, I hear Cranox
complaining at every creak and groan. He's healed, but since his
encounter with Zong he's been irritable and quick to lash out.

Tamarack has proven an excellent bearer of the cranny jug. My
thoughts circle back to what he carries in the jug. How will we use the
babe?

However we can. We're on a knife's edge, too.

After two days of steady walking, we arrive at a large lake. In the
distance lie low, stony hills. Decan splays his hands and counts off
seven fingers: *Seven Lake.*

In shape language, the gesture is close to the word *death*: one hand
flat with the fingers splayed, with the two fingers of the other hand
on the palm. The lake's surface is lead-gray and still. A storm brews
to the north, over The Deep.

Cranox's wagon bumps past a narrow strip of white sand. His
men, normally boisterous, go silent. On a log half sunk in the water, a
large raptor perches. Its large wings seem frozen just as the bird is
about to take flight. By its large, hooked beak, it's a juvenile grabeen
gone grey with dust.

Odd, Fig says against my thigh.

As we come closer, I see that the raptor's spindly feet are fused to
the log. Did it land there then die? Further on is a furry woolott

crouched as if to drink, the long whiskers gray as the water. Still
further on, I see five warriors caught hip-deep. I can't make out any
colors in their hair since it's gone a powdery gray.

Seven Lake is poison.

Fruit of the Dark, we call these waters. The lake lies like a dead thing
on the plain, but Decan seems proud. *Seven caverns lie below the surface.
The seventh is so deep no diver has ever reached the bottom.* He points to
great pipes that travel from the lake to the hill beyond, like exposed
veins. *See how we take the Dark from the depths, for our fine city! Light,
fuel, what feeds the forges and the ovens, the loom, our fine machines. The
Dark, wondrous Dark, our light!*

Decan guffaws at the play on words. Now that we're close to
home, he's jolly, smiling often to reveal his hideous black teeth. No
trees stand on the hill we're approaching, no bushes, not even hardy
Remedy. Beneath my feet, I feel the steady tremor of the pumps.

The Dark. Decan's four fingers grip his thumb, like an awkward
fist. *Without the Dark, none of our machines would be worth the metal
they're built with. Or the sweat.*

A path cuts north and up the hill's flank, cresting at a low saddle.
There, a blue light sweeps by at intervals. The light reminds me of a
speluk's spidery finger.

Decan says, *The Dark will win us back what should be ours. All of
what's ours.*

Though final climb isn't steep, Cranox orders a rest to water the
horses and allow the men to strap on their armor. They use water
from the grub wagon, not Seven Lake. Cranox pulls on a robe even
finer than the one he wore to greet Zong. The red weave is shot with
blue thread. When he moves, the fabric seems to flicker like a blue
flame. Carefully, Decan smooths the blue cuffs and the blue lining
along the lower hem. On the back is stitched a jeweled mask with
curled horns of beaten plate. It's the same image I saw painted on the
base of the bell tower in the burned village and on this horse: the
Horned Mask.

Then Cranox slips the robe off to try on another one. These colors
are the reverse: a blue weave shot with red. Cranox catches me
staring. "The colors of the Horned Mask. The most feared of all of the
Master's men. We must make a fine entrance. Are these weaves not
beautiful? Which robe would you choose?"

It's threat and boast combined. The babe in the cranny jug proves him a liar: Cranox is no man. Yet his achievements are real. Weighed against everything he's done for the Master, why should the Master even care if Cranox had a crook or a cleft? What difference should a robe make?

"It makes no difference what a man wears," I tell him pointedly, "as long as he's a man."

"Watch your mouth, Horse," Cranox snaps.

"My mouth is my own."

"It was never your own. It was your mother's and now it's mine until you win a decima. You and every one of your brothers is more valuable to me as speluk food than anything else. I could kill you where you stand."

"You can't. You told me yourself that you must follow the Rule of Ten."

"Ten," he says, "not seventeen."

"I think there is another rule that may apply to you," I snap.

Cranox abruptly turns his back on me.

I have to be more careful.

The last thing Decan brings him is Zong's gift, the white, five-sided pendant. Decan clasps it around Cranox's neck.

Lark has been watching us from behind the grub wagon. Our eyes meet. Lark masks his spying with a smirk. I suspect he still means to kill Cranox. But how can he kill the commander of the Hundred-Hundred in his own city, surrounded by thousands of his loyal men? Lark is no idiot.

Lark is another danger I couldn't have imagined before fleeing Dolor. He could have told us about Hive Home and Odide's history of conjuring wildmen. If he had, we could have avoided the Hive. I wouldn't have betrayed my brothers.

At the same time, Lark saved us by leading us to the Remedy plant. Odide conjured me but she also cured me, as the ghost of my brother Ash foretold. "You'll find the cure," he said. "It won't save everyone."

What secrets save us or kill us? How can I possibly tell the difference? Freedom is like a marsh with no path, a dangerous place where any wrong step might send me and my brothers to our deaths. I never imagined being free could be so hard. Or so deadly.

Cranox examines the hats Decan has pulled out for his victorious return to the Master's city. In one hand, Decan holds aloft a cap adorned in blue stones. In the other is an elaborate headdress fit with carved wooden wings and a thick tail of yellow and red grabeen feathers. It's a bit ridiculous, but Decan turns the headdress admiringly. The stones and feathers catch the afternoon light.

But in the end, Cranox chooses the cap with blue stones. For the robe, he chooses the one that flickers like blue flame. On foot, he begins to climb the hill, preceded by a man with an enormous drum. My brothers and I along with Decan follow. The man strikes the drum with each step. Behind, us men fall into columns. The wagons follow. Cuarto, his speluks, and the remaining wildmen bring up the rear, the whip cracking on the wildmen's backs.

Though it's so soon after his operation, Cranox appears completely recovered. I have to admit he's magnificent. Around his shoulders he's draped a hairy shawl: the topknots of the wildmen and warriors he's killed, Tanoak's among them.

At the pass, we finally see the Master's city. The city itself is protected by a high stone wall topped in parapets and guard towers. Inside, I count more than a thousand roofs clustered around a great white dome. The blue light I saw from the lake is set into the peak of the dome and flashes over the roofs in relentless rhythm. I hear the clang of pots, a dog's anxious bark. Daily life I'd see in any human place, Quillka, Dolor, or here.

The massive gates are closed. As we approach, the air goes from fresh to oddly warm and greasy. The war drum echoes against the walls and hills that cup the city. In front of the gate is a plaza paved with flat stones. To either side, like hands reaching out from the gate, are seats banked from low to high.

I'm searching for the word to describe this arrangement when Decan supplies it. *This is the arena where you'll fight your decima.*

Arena: two hands vertical with palms together and the pointer and middle finger raised. As if to confirm Decan's words, I spot a single bloody tooth, unmistakably human, stuck to a paving stone.

The drum goes silent. Two enormous pipes blare a welcome. Alone, Cranox strides forward. Lark leaves the grub wagon to sidle up to Tamarack. I hear him ask, "Are you so fond of cranny you need your own jug?"

I have a powerful thirst, my brother answers.

"Yet I haven't seen you take a single sip."

I'm about to tell Lark to back off when a deep rumble shakes the dust from the stones under our feet. The great gate opens. Before the gates travel far, though, they screech to a halt. A single figure emerges.

A boy.

He's slender and long-faced. His hair is a black bristle over a pale forehead. He wears no armor, only a dark brown tunic cinched at the waist with rope. He's barefoot. He sings just loud enough for us to hear: *dum ta dum ta dum dum dum.*

Then commander and boy, one splendidly attired and the other barely clothed, stroll side by side. Cranox's hands clasp at his back.

Willow moves to my side. *What in the Mother's name is that?* He means the boy.

To my eye, Cranox looks like a warrior gently schooling a sprig. Cranox and the boy turn toward the gate, then Cranox pauses to reach behind his neck and unclasp the pendant Zong gave him. He presents the gift to the boy. The boy examines the pendant briefly, then flings it against the stone wall with a crack.

They continue walking as if nothing had happened.

The rumble begins again. This time, the gate swings wide enough for the men of the Horned Mask to follow Cranox and the boy into the city.

Broad tables laden with food fill a plaza. Cranny barrels fitted with brass spigots are tipped on their sides. Everywhere, I see metal machines. Men use machines use to walk, lift guards up and down the walls, deliver fresh trays of food and then open their serrated jaws to swallow the bones and peels of what the men discard. There's a machine that carries fresh barrels of cranny and drives in the spigots and a machine that loads the barrels once they've run dry.

Every machine spits out a trail of blue smoke.

Cranox and the boy climb a platform where there's more food and cranny. Cranny is everywhere, in barrels and cups and spilling down men's chests as they drink in celebration.

Tamarack notices and glances at me with concern. Lark would trade that babe for Cranox's life in a heartbeat. And we'd die, too.

There's no reason for my brother to have his own cranny jug when cranny is practically flowing in the streets.

As discretely as I can, I say to my brother: *We will deal with the jug. Keep it safe for now.*

Decan turns to me, his black-toothed smile terrifying and elated. *Is this not the most wondrous city you've ever seen? You and your brothers must follow me. You haven't yet won a place at the tables.*

He leads us up a gentle rise to the city's center, where the Dome stands. The lower levels have rooms behind cage doors. Ours has a sleeping area with bunks five high, an eating area with a long wooden table, and what looks like a training room ankle-deep in sawdust. Four little machines, two-wheeled and puffing smoke, lay out towels, bars of soap, fruit, and fresh clothes.

In the training area, weapons hang on a wall: axes and swords, spears, and throwing stars. None has a metal blade. They're for practice and already well-battered. There are huaracas, too, with colors corresponding to every Captain I know: Birds of Prey, Kettles, the Harvest, Cranox's own Mother Eyes, the Sea Hunt, even the Blazes and the Living Wood.

More warriors than I could have imagined fled east. My brothers are staring. Did these warriors win their decimas or die in the arena? Did any of our elder brothers flee east?

Does anyone even keep track?

Your decima is at dawn, Decan tells me. *Man to draft is most common.*

It's as if he's describing nothing more than plans for an evening meal. *The last decima was a pack of hybas. Quick to the kill. A little messy but the man felt little pain. There was no feast there!*

"Was he a warrior? From Bounty?" The question is out of my mouth before I think through why I even need to know. What difference does this make?

Decan shrugs. *Doesn't matter, does it? Once you're in the arena, it's just you against whatever the Master chooses. Worst is lither. Because of the scales, its only weak spot is under the chin.*

Decan demonstrates by prodding his own chin with a filthy finger. *Pain from beginning to end when it bites. The venom is the thing to watch out for. Burns through everything: leather, metal, skin. If a drop lands on your foot, it will burn through to the ground and make your foot mushy as porridge. If you're lucky, it'll be hybas.*

I've never heard of a hyba pack being lucky.

Decan grins. *A quicker death. If I were you, I'd tell your brother to ride in on a horse. Dignified,* Decan nods. *More applause. We like that.* He punches my arm. *We'll feast well if it's a horse.*

"You want a horse so that you can eat the horse after?"

If it doesn't get bitten by a lither, Decan points out. *Sweeter than tough old goat. Not too often do we get to taste it. You lot get the last decima of the season: ten for ten. Everyone will be there. There's always a surprise with the tenth decima. The Master, he loves his surprises!*

"We need two decimas. I have seventeen brothers." I told Cranox the same. Cranox also promised a decima we could win, in return for keeping his secret.

What kind of creature will he send into the arena?

Decan shrugs. *There are only ten a year. Yours is the tenth. Won't be another decima until next summer.* He leans closer. *By then some of these boys will be speluk leavings. Might as well get used to the idea.* Decan grins broadly, wiggling his eyebrows. *Already the wagering started.*

I have to keep myself from throttling Decan then and there. Doesn't he realize how much I love my brothers? I know he loves Cranox. I saw the relief on his face when he learned we'd saved Cranox's life. How can he rejoice at that, saving one life, then so cruelly calling my brothers speluk food?

Decan presses his signing hand into my chest. *Which of you will it be? I've yet to make my wager. If I have some warning, I'm sure to make a bundle no matter what happens.* Decan points to Tamarack. *I say that great one. Or that fat one?* Decan means Willow. *I'd bet on the draft if it was him. Who'll it be?*

"Wager everything you have," I tell him. "I'm fighting the decima. This and one more. I will win every one of my brothers. Tell that to Cranox. Tell that to the Master. Let that be his surprise."

23

Decima

Before dawn, a guard appears to escort me to the thermal baths. There, an attendant scrubs every one of my crevices, even wedging a sponge between my toes and under my crook. The end of his small finger delves into my ears and belly button, scraping out dirt that's been there, I'm certain, since my Vessel birthed me. The man finishes with a sound slap on my ass.

I'm passed to another man. He kneads my muscles until I either cry out in pain or delight. Afterwards, my body feels pummeled and weak and completely relaxed, as if I've been dunked into another, crueler vat of nektar.

I return to our quarters. There, Willow braids his own red and black ribbon into my hair. Perhaps my mother would be appalled that I'm fighting this decima as a free man wearing her colors. But these are my brothers' colors, too. They bind us to out past and give me a bit of hope.

As do Burn's battered boots.

Then I set to sharpening my stave, making sure the metal tip can split a hair down the middle. To test it, I use one of Tamarack's hairs: coarse and curly. A stave has saved me a hundred times, most recently on the banks of the Cursed River, when I killed the hyba cub.

As we wait for the decima, I practice hurling the stave against one of the training room walls.

You'll certainly kill any walls that attack you, Willow says dryly.

Willow, Thorn, and Hawthorn try to argue me out of fighting. Every brother volunteers to take my place.

I say no seventeen times. This is my duty, I tell them. I left them once. I won't leave them a second time.

I'm bathed and scrubbed, my hair newly plaited and with a hair-splitting stave point, when Lark appears at the cage door. He shoves something through the bars: a new pair of boots.

"A gift from the Master," he says. "Cranox told him how you came to him first as Horse. The Master laughed, then took these from his very own room."

The boots are white leather and lace to the knees. The shaft is stitched with the outline of a horse with red eyes and a flaring tail.

How my life has turned and twisted on a pair of boots! The leather is thick, yet still supple.

Lark's voice lowers so that only I hear. "Hyba skin. Very rare. Listen. I can tell you something that might help. A gift of information."

"Why?" Lark does nothing that doesn't serve him.

"It would be a waste to see a warrior die in such fine boots."

The boy has pluck, I'll give him that. "Why should I believe you?"

"I showed you Remedy."

"Then you led us to the Queen."

Lark shrugs. "I told you the Master wouldn't spare you."

"What do you want?"

"Cranox. Like always."

"Your man on the painted horse." I shake my head. "You could have killed him before we got here. You could have killed him in his camp. Why should I help you now, when we're surrounded by his Hundred-Hundred?"

"I would have killed him if you hadn't forced me to bring you nektar. He was practically dead. Maybe you're the one who owes me." He starts to whisper. "How did you save him, anyway?"

"If you want something, ask."

Lark looks over his shoulder. Decan will arrive at any moment. "There's a way you can pay me back."

"Pay you," I snort. "For what?"

"For this. Information. They're readying The Beast for the arena.

The Beast has won three decimas so far. No man has found a way to even land a blow. No man but—"

I cut him off. "Beast? What beast? Lither? Hyba? Out with it!"

"I don't know what it is! Hyba, for sure. I've never seen such a creature. It's fast and strong. It climbs. The Beast knows every move a man can make. You have to think of another way to beat it. Something no one has tried yet. Something unexpected."

Lark is speaking in riddles. "You expect me to reward you for that?"

Lark is serious. "You have to think like not a man. That's what I can tell you. That is the only way you'll survive."

I come within a breath of seizing him by the neck to strangle him against the bars. In return for keeping his secret, Cranox has already promised me an opponent I can beat. Now I'm supposed to not think like a man? Is Lark taunting me by saying I should think like Odide?

Decan arrives and immediately grins when he sees the boots. I'm guessing he's laid a wager on my win. He thinks these hyba-skin boots will help me.

I shove the boots back at Lark. "I'll stick with the boots you stole. They've given me luck so far."

In the arena, the spectates of the Hundred-Hundred are already in place. Every seat is filled. Each spectate has a distinctive flag. There's Cranox's Horned Mask. Beside it a spectate with a blue flag spread with a lither's bat wings. Another has the head of a grinning hyba and another a red field bordered by twinned speluks. Set over the gate itself is a silver flag marked with a speluk-blue flame.

The Master's own, I suspect.

I try to carry my stave lightly, but find myself clutching the shaft. Fight not like a man. What easy victory has Cranox arranged? I can only fight as myself: Fir, Horse, a poison man who was cured by a Queen's nektar. Of all of the things I've been, this is dearest to me: the boy who wanted to be free. The boy who kissed Dinitra and found himself in her eyes. Will this be my last hour, hearing the crowd roar, knowing that freedom cost me everything?

Dozens of machines climb up and down the arena steps delivering food and sweeping up the leavings. Several machines lift the great nets that will keep me and whatever creature I'm set to fight separated from the spectators. My brothers have their own section, but are surrounded by the Master's men. The sight pulls my heart into my throat. I can only help them by winning.

I push away the other cruel reality. Even if I win, I can only save nine brothers. Nine. Who will I have to leave behind?

I hide my despair with bravado. "What news of my opponent?" I ask Decan. "I hope you've told your friends not to lay their wagers against me."

His grin is joyful. *None but the Master knows. That's the beauty of it. None but the Master ever knows!*

If only the Master knows, how can Cranox promise an opponent I can defeat? It's far too late for questions. Over the closed gates, Cranox appears on the balcony, along with the strange boy. A third person walks with them, the old man with a long, scraggly beard.

A hush falls over the crowd. Even the machines pause their rumbling. The grey clouds are low and unbroken, promising snow.

Which of the two is Master, old man or boy? The great horns on either side of the balcony blare and belch thick dust. A new machine wobbles through the gate: the height of a man but squared and gray, with a dark mesh mouth. "Behold, the tenth and final decima of the season!"

The machine clangs and squeaks as it faces first north, then south, east, and west. "Called by our Master, the decima is a fight to the death," the machine squeals. "On the victor, we lay wreaths of victory and fond appreciation. Fond appreciation! Nine lives and himself he shall take with him into the Master's loving arms. Loving arms! To the beast and the draft go the work of serving him. The beast and draft serve! The beast and draft serve!"

The crowd roars. "The beast serves! The draft serves!"

The machine trundles away in a fresh haze. The great gates creak closed.

My breath scrapes my throat. There's nothing to be done, I tell myself, nothing to care about, nothing to prepare. This fight will be a fight, that is all. I've fought before. All I have at this instant is myself and the air and my stave and the stones beneath my feet.

Muscles fortified with nektar. Cranox's promise that he will select a creature I can kill. Fighting not like a man.

And Burn's stolen boots.

Beneath my feet, the stones shake. A crack in the stones widens into a mouth of perfect darkness. It's a hatch leading into an underground enclosure. Time seems to stop. Even the men stop screaming to see what will kill me.

Then there's a rush of brilliant green. A full-grown lither slithers swiftly into the sunlight, crossing to the far side of the arena. It's big as a horse, with a horse-shaped head on a snakey neck. Its chest, fully armored in dull, green scales, lifts as it moves. Black bat wings furl on its back. Behind them, the lither's body narrows into a long tail with a scorpion's barb at the tip.

Decan told me a lither's scales are hard as metal armor. The lither coils its tail around its body, then thrusts its nose high, nostrils flaring to catch my scent. Decan also told me the under-jaw is the lither's only weakness, a palm-sized patch of leaf-green skin.

How is fighting a lither easy? Cranox lied to me. Is this The Beast Lark told me to fight not like a man? I see nothing of hyba in this creature. How would *not a man* fight this thing?

I wish I could be there when my brothers reveal Cranox's secret as payback for this betrayal. Too bad I'll be dead.

I keep a good distance between us. My stave is angled up in case the lither strikes and exposes its underjaw. I race through what I know from sprig tales, from what Decan told me. Lithers were brewed with horse and constrictor and scorpion and scaly pangolin. They're night hunters, silent, and only fly when they must. This one is patient, its red tongue flicking the air for my scent.

What I would give for the mud I smeared myself with to escape Odide.

The men of the Hundred-Hundred scream and hoot in delight. Then they grow impatient and start to hiss. They want combat, not creeping. Some stand on the wooden slats of their seats and stamp with their boots. If I had to guess, the lither hears better than it sees. It smells best of all.

Fight not like a man. Am I supposed to think like a bee, a conloor, a grabeen? With the sun climbing through the blue murk of the Master's city, I notice the lither's eyes are chalk white. Unblinking. I wonder: is it blind? Was Cranox true to his word, sending a blind lither to kill me? The lither flaps its wings once and I see that they're tattered with age or past battles.

The lither's nostrils flare. Suddenly, the wings extend, slam down, and the lither strikes: right at my boots. I leap to the side and roll, kicking up dust. Where my feet were, metal-blue venom splatters.

Some made it to my boots and they start to smoke. As fast as I can, I yank them off.

So much for my good luck.

The lither seems oblivious to the crowd's howls. The creature strikes again, this time just missing my shoulder. Again, venom splatters. I tear off my tunic. The lither strikes at the ball of filthy cloth, and the tunic smokes and dissolves in a spray of venom.

Behind me, I hear a creak. The same hatch is opening again. The sun is in my eyes, so all I see is a mouth of darkness. The lither must be deaf since it doesn't seem to notice, still trying to find me in the puddle of cloth.

I feel the crowd's savage glee. "Beast," they scream, "beast, beast, BEAST!"

No one told me a decima could include two creatures. But Decan warned me: the tenth decima always has a surprise. The shape that emerges has a hyba's heavy snout. A broad, brindled chest. A long, powerful monkey tail.

The Beast. Except I know her. The lither strikes the stones where I rolled and smeared sweat, not even close to where I'm standing.

Paws big as frying pans, flanks that flash brown and black tiger stripes. Golden eyes. Snout held high, she smells me immediately and whines in delight. 12, Dinitra's hyba cross. 12, who killed my brother Ash. The draft I trained with a hundred times in Quillka. 12, who would never leave Dinitra's side. I smell her: burnt butter.

Before we parted, I gave Dinitra a piece of my tunic so that 12 could find me. Her tufted tail lashes. She's found me.

They're not in The Deep.

I search the balcony where Cranox, the boy, and the old man are watching. If 12 is here, Dinitra must be here. Or dead. Here, she must be here.

Trapped, like us.

I have to win the decima to save nine brothers and find a way to save eight more. But to win now means I must kill 12.

I won't.

The lither smells her and rattles the scorpion barb on her tail. I feel the lither's fear as it hisses and coils in on itself.

12 ignores both of us. Now that she knows I'm here, she gives herself a good shake, then heavily lies down and begins to clean her paws.

Slowly, the men watching start to laugh. Some throw bread heels, then rocks. A few make their way through the netting and roll close to 12.

She doesn't flinch. 12 lays her head on the stones with a groan and closes her eyes.

The lither is larger than 12, but slighter. It's blind and probably deaf. The lither insistently flicks its tongue. I look to the balcony again. The boy seems to be screaming at Cranox. The old man stares at the arena, his expression unreadable.

Where is Dinitra? Cautiously, I aim my stave. Lark didn't lie. He told us the Master would use The Beast. I'm supposed to fight her by not thinking like a man. He didn't mean think like a draft. He meant think like a female, like Dinitra.

Lark has seen her. I'm sure: Dinitra has to be in the Master's city somewhere.

Cautiously, the lither starts to slither toward 12, thinking she's asleep. I know 12 is very much awake. I've seen her play this trick dozens of times. She's waiting for the lither to make a mistake.

And it does. The lither begins to lift and unfurl its wings. The green skin of its underjaw pulses as the creature rises just slightly as it prepares to strike.

Just as the lither's jaws slam forward, 12 leaps up. When we trained with her, she'd wait until we committed to a movement, until we couldn't do anything but complete it. She'd shift faster than we could blink. Using her tail like a fifth limb, she'd be on us before we even realized she wasn't in place any more.

12 twists as the lither slams its open jaws on the stones. The creature struck too hard and is stunned. As the lither lifts its head to sniff, the leaf-green patch winks into view.

12 strikes. The lither whips back and forth, blue venom spraying. 12 hangs like a boulder from its thin neck, pulling the lither down. Venom droplets splatter onto 12's fur.

This is how she killed my brother, Ash. She won't release until the lither is dead.

The lither flips onto its back, trying to knock 12 off. Yellow lither blood from where 12 has ripped apart its neck pools on the stones. It's far too late. The lither's wings are pinned beneath it, useless. The scorpion barb strikes 12 again and again, but it's pointless. Already, the lither's green scales are fading into a greenish grey.

The men of the Hundred-Hundred scream. "Kill the Beast! Kill the Beast!" On the balcony, Cranox shapes words: *Finish it.* The decima will only be won when I sink my stave through 12's two hyba hearts.

Which I will never do. Only when the lither is dead does 12 come to me. Her tongue lolls. I remember it well: a slab, blue-black and warm. I whisper her name and 12's golden eyes fix to mine.

The fur on her back haunch smokes where the lither venom landed.

"Hold," I tell her. Dinitra's command. I rip my breeches off and try to wipe the lither venom from her fur. Quickly, I have to toss the smoking cloth away.

Now what? *Think not like a man.* I shape a command Dinitra spent so long teaching her, my fingers extended and tapping my thumb: *jaws closed.*

She obeys. I remember how Dinitra would sing to her: *No killing the nice warriors. Not even a little bit. No bites, no licks, my terrible, sweet creature.*

Think like not a man. I'm not going to kill her. I'm going to show everyone and especially the Master that I understand her. We understand each other. I will show him something he's never seen.

I'm going to show him a surprise.

I give 12 a command: *go!* Instantly, she obeys, circling the arena almost faster than my eyes can follow. Her tail is a snakey blur. Then I call her to me. With my hands, I open her jaws. I never did this with her in Bounty, but I'm hoping she understands. Our lives depend on it. She's confused at first, thinking I want her to lick me. Again, I open her jaws. "Open," I tell her.

My fingers extend like opening jaws, my thumb stiff. *Open your jaws.*

She seems to understand. She opens her jaws and I lay my arm on her soft tongue. The sharp tips of her fangs rest lightly on my skin as her tail lashes with pleasure. She bears down just slightly: play. The tips of her teeth don't break the skin, but I feel them like Thorn's needle poised to stitch a gash.

12's eyes are bright with happiness. She always loved learning something new.

My last command is something I watched Dinitra do with her at Quillka. I slap my shoulders. 12 plants her front paws there. We dance. Then I hold my fingers up—three, seven, nine—and she yips the numbers. To finish, I have her balance on her hind legs and tail and hop forward as I do the same, my hands flopping.

A naked, bootless warrior, a pure, dancing with The Beast. The arena explodes in laughter.

When I call her to me, I see that she's exhausted. Heavily, she lies down. There's still enough lither venom to burn through her skin and dissolve her back haunches and legs. Under her ribs, her belly looks swollen and bumpy. Something is eating her from the inside.

I lift her great head into my lap. Her golden eyes flicker with pain.

12 is dying.

24

The Master

A shadow falls on me: Tamarack. Thorn is beside him, his fysic kit already open. Behind them, my other brothers are still fighting the guards who tried to keep them from leaving their seats and entering the arena.

Thorn uncorks a vial of forgetting and dribbles it on 12's blue-black tongue. Willow pulls off his tunic and wipes 12 again. But the venom's already burned through the fur and has worked its way into the skin. 12's skin is surprisingly pale, now pocked with angry, black holes.

Before I can say anything, the stones rumble again. I'm thinking that now, the Master means to finish us with a third creature. We'll all die. But it's no creature. It's Decan trotting beside a large machine chuffing smoke.

Master's orders, he says. *The Master said that was the best decima he'd ever seen. The best decima ever. One for Melán's Illuminated Book. You won, Horse. You've won your eight brothers. Get her on the platform.*

Not eight. Nine! "I was promised nine!"

Eight brothers and The Beast. Usually, we eat the beasts who die. But hyba is much too sour.

Decan gazes at 12 with open admiration. *He orders you to save The Beast. She is dear to him. He would see her healed. The machine will take her to the baths.*

Thorn nods. *It will wash away the venom that's left. But what's inside her ...*

Maybe it's like... I stop myself, but Thorn understands. Could nektar heal the lither burns inside her?

The machine maneuvers to grab 12 with claw arms and lift her to the platform. My brothers steady her. She groans but doesn't wake, awash in forgetting.

As we trot beside the machine, Decan bounces between dismay and delight. First, he lists everything he's won in his wager. *Peach preserves! Sugar cake! Laced boots! Juicy blood pudding, by the Master's breath!*

He can't stop describing what he saw, his delight so intense he can hardly shape the words. *When the lither pounced, oh! I thought you were a goner. Then when the hatch opened! Hoo! I knew a surprise was in store, but The Beast!*

He adds to his list of winnings. *Eleven ounces of pickled bancat liver! A block of black salt from Far Eek!* He might as well have won the city and every morsel in it with my decima. Like a child, he skips with delight. *What a decima!*

But if 12 dies, he says, the Master will be inconsolable.

As the machine trundles into the baths, the men there quickly leave. The machine halts at the largest pool. It reeks of rotten eggs. Willow and I jump into the pool first. As the machine's platform slowly tilts, we guide 12 into the water. My brothers join us to keep her from drowning since 12 has not a speck of fat on her and would otherwise sink.

I stand at her massive head, careful to keep her snout above water. If 12's here, Dinitra's here, I keep telling myself.

12 can't die. If she dies, I couldn't bear Dinitra knowing and knowing I was there and didn't stop it.

Thorn examines 12, but can't find any injuries save for the venom burns. He presses on her swollen belly. *It looks as if she's been sick for some time. From before the decima,* he says. *Malnourished, too. Whoever heard of a hyba that doesn't eat?*

I whisper, "Can you cure her of the venom? Can you cut it out?"

I know something of humans, but nothing of drafts or lither venom. I'm afraid if I cut her, I'd do more harm than good. We've washed away most of the venom. I can ease her pain with forgetting. Remember hybas have two hearts. *She's strong, brother. With laurel, I can ease the pain. But brother...*

On my skin, Thorn forms words. *You've saved eight lives. We must find a way to win the rest. Why waste what power we have on this beast?*

My gaze is fierce. "She's here. She has to be. I will have the lives of all of my brothers and 12's. And her as well."

Thorn doesn't understand. Of course, he doesn't. He doesn't know that Dinitra and I have a Bond. I could say it's because we owe her or it's the right thing to do. The words crumble in my mouth. A half-truth is a half-lie, always. It's because I want to see her. It's because I long for her. It's because she saw me and saw my longing for freedom. It's because I still dream of a life where she's there. Where we can both take our freedom and make something of it, something that wasn't there before. Something we share. Together.

In my twisted logic, if 12 survives, then Dinitra is alive and I'll find her and maybe they'll be some chance for us to find a new land and live in peace.

Then I check myself. 12 looks diminished in the water of the baths: eyes glazed, tongue floating, her tail bobbing and even the white tuft limp. *Yes: we'll sleep on raindrops and eat raw flowers and never feel pain or hunger or fear. What an idiot I am.*

It's a dream, a boy's dream, a dream of clouds and light and fiery sky. It's a dream with brothers who speak in riddles on a river bank then vanish after they promise a cure. It shouldn't be the dream of the commander of the Living Wood.

Yet I'm sure: I'm Bonded to my brothers and I am Bonded to Dinitra and Bonded to 12. They all belong to me and I to them.

Willow says what Thorn won't. *You should have killed the beast when you had the chance. One more brother you would have saved!*

And lost 12. My anger is quick. "You choose."

Willow is as angry as I've ever seen him. *What do you mean, brother?*

"Shall it be Tamarack? Fig?" Over 12's head, I point at my brothers one by one. "Shall we go youngest to oldest, shortest to tallest, skinniest to fattest? Shall it be the most useful brothers? The best fighters? How about the ones with hair most like our mother? Or hair most unlike hers. Tell me, Willow. Which of them do you think should die?"

That's not what I'm saying.

"That's exactly what you're saying." I'm trembling though the water steams. "She gave us Remedy. 12 just saved my life. We fight for them all. That's my order. Male and female and draft. *All.*"

I've put 12's life equal to the lives of my brothers. Dinitra's too. *Equal.* In the past, we saved the Weave's drafts because we pitied them, not because we thought they were equal to us. But at this moment, I can't choose. I won't choose. I love my brothers. I love 12. And I love Dinitra, even though she is a Captain. Even though she's female. Even though her kind made us to serve them.

Equal.

Willow isn't convinced. But he is practical. If we're to save 12, then we must think of something to stop the venom that's killing her. Stop it inside. *The only thing I can think of that might cure her is what we used on Cranox.*

He doesn't have to add that it worked on me after Jarvon almost killed me. *I've watched you.* Thorn says. *The nektar cured you deep inside. You haven't eaten a bite of paddle loaf since you escaped the Queen. You should be dead.*

"Yes."

Perhaps it will do the same for 12. Heal her inside.

Will Lark still have nektar? How can I force him to give up more?

It's Decan who speaks next. *The Master has nektar. You must get it from him.*

"Then take us to him."

Decan grimaces. *No one goes to the Master without a summons.*

"No one has fought a decima like I did. Take us."

My understanding of men like Decan runs true. He follows my command. Spitting into the water, he says, *Follow me.*

Again, the metal arms of the machine reach for 12 and haul her out of the water. I feel like sobbing. Once so powerful, she looks weak and vulnerable. As we walk, I can't help but count. I don't have nine more lives to save. Now I have ten: my nine brothers and Dinitra. Fine, I think. A second decima will save them all.

At the Dome where the Master lives, the machine carrying 12 has to navigate a series of stairs leading to the top floor. It extends its jointed arms, then scurries like a beetle. All the way, 12's tongue hangs limp and pale. We pass a great room of cages holding creatures that fight in the decimas. I spot a lone hyba pacing. A young lither hisses at us, trying to spread its dark black wings. One cage hangs from the ceiling, with four grabeens inside. When the grabeens glimpse us, their hideous howls are deafening.

Even when the flock ate Burn, I was never this close to a grabeen.

Each time we pass a guard, they go gob-eyed. "The Beast," they whisper. Her mighty tail curls limp as old rope around her still-dripping body.

Decan's chest puffs with importance. *Move your carcasses!* he yells at the gapers.

The machine carrying 12 chuffs black smoke. I have no weapon, no grand plan. No boots, no clothes. Only my wits.

At the top is a large room. The first thing I see is the old bearded man seated on a plain wooden chair beside a table. Before him is an open book. The old man has flung his beard over his shoulder like a scarf. His gnarled fingers grasp a stick of charcoal. He's drawing.

I feel a stab of recognition. Dinitra draws in books. But this book is much larger, with thick, cream-colored pages.

Beside him stands the same boy who greeted Cranox outside the city gate, the same boy who watched the decima. In his hand, he holds a small cup.

Which is Master, boy or old man? The old man's beard is braided with black beads and black ribbon. That single color belongs to no Captain I know. His back is humped, pushing his face almost parallel to the table. His robe is rough spun and patched with squares of fabric that long ago lost any hint of color. I've never seen anyone, male or female, so old.

Cranox stands beside a window, his expression unreadable. I've won this decima. But he knows we still have his secret. Now that I'm a man of the Hundred-Hundred, what can he do about it?

The machine reaches the far wall. With a squeal, it sinks to the floor. 12's eyes are dull coins behind her eyelids. There's a fireplace I could use to warm her, but it's filmy with cobwebs. An odd little machine puffs out heat and trails blue smoke as it rumbles around the room. The heat dissipates immediately as the smoke coagulates into a greasy blue carpet.

The boy beckons, "Come closer, warrior Fir."

The boy isn't as young as I first thought. Maybe fourteen? About the age when warriors are docked. Even when I look at him directly, his face seemed blurred, as if I'm looking through cloudy glass. His prominent brow casts a shadow over his eyes. No tattoos or scars mark his skin, not even a freckle. He wears the same brown tunic I saw when we waited outside the city as he and Cranox strolled like a warrior with a new, young brother to train. He's still shoeless, his feet and legs speckled with dirt. The skin of his arms, face, and neck are so fair it looks like he's spent most of his time indoors. Even from several steps away, I can see a tracery of blue veins in his hands. Under the right light, I think I might be able to see right through him.

"I couldn't have planned a better decima." The boy takes a sip from the cup. The hairs on my neck rise. He's drinking nektar. Suddenly, I crave it. I have to kill the urge to swipe the cup from his hand and drain it.

The boy's hands tremble. He nods at the old man. "Mélan is sketching it. Come look."

On the page, the old man—Mélan—has laid out the arena. To either side are the spectators and machines. A single, sinuous line marks the lither. He's just begun on me: a head and arms, like a stick figure with no face. Like Fire Brother. Dinitra always writes stories in her drawings and so does Mélan, using black ink to make careful loops: *Fir of the Living Wood faces the old lither.*

Zong spoke of an old scribe. A coward, he called him. This must be him: Mélan. So the boy is the Master. How can the Master be so young?

"He bends the creature to his will," the boy says. The words sound too big for his mouth. "A surprise!" Abruptly, the boy turns to me and asks, "Why have you come to my city?"

I bow my head. "The Beast needs nektar or she'll die. She was hit with lither venom. It burns through her. Once she has nektar, I will tell you my story."

The boy steps closer, sniffing. His skin has a sheen. He smells strongly of lilyfire nektar. "You've tasted her nektar, warrior Fir."

I can't walk his thoughts, but I feel his emotions like a vibration through the air. He's curious and a little jealous. He's always thought of himself as a great warrior who could win a decima. He sees himself in me: a fighter strengthened by nektar. He's sad I didn't die but sadder still that he could lose The Beast.

I wish I could taste a bit of nektar. A cupful. I feel Cranox's strange eyes on me, alert to any weakness.

I force myself to look at 12. "I know nektar will heal her as it healed me."

The Master is suspicious. "Once you know where I keep it, you'll take it from me. She never sends enough."

I fight the compulsion to seize his cup, drain it, and lick it clean. She: the Queen. The Master is small and fragile-looking. I could overpower him, seize all of his hidden nektar globes for myself. For 12 and my brothers.

"Show Fir the first decima she fought, dear Mélan." The Master places his cup by Mélan's book. His dark eyes seem to dare me to shove aside the old man and seize the cup. "The one with the hybas."

Obediently, the old man shows me the page where he sketched 12: her powerful tail and tiger stripes. On a giant wooden structure, six hybas perch.

"We built that in the arena. Fighting on the stones and in the air, we thought. What a delight! She took them one by one. Thrilling! No force of numbers can defeat her. My heart was in my throat. She obeyed you. Remarkable. Just as she obeyed the female."

Female. My heart catches as the Master taps the page. Dinitra's crouching, her arm signaling, *Go.*

The Master's no fool. "You know her. You knew The Beast."

His eyes look too big for his face. The irises are pale and ringed in black. "My men ask: will The Beast succeed again? Battered by the previous decima? But I thought, 'Combine the familiar with the new.' The Beast: *familiar.* She's fought three times in my arena. Now, Cranox says, let's start with a *lither.* Were you not surprised?"

I hold my tongue. So this was Cranox's way of helping me win. I look quickly at him and see a flash of cunning in his expression.

The Master flicks his hand impatiently. "Surprised, warrior Fir! Were you not *surprised?*"

"Yes. I was surprised."

He looks pleased, then snaps his fingers. "The name of your mother! Show me."

I lock the five fingers on both hands. "Timbe. Captain of the Living Wood."

The Master's eyes narrow. "The Captains are terrible, are they not? Cruel and terrible."

I keep my eyes steady. Sweat beads on the Master's forehead. It's as if he's talking to himself alone. "Look at what a Captain did to me."

Abruptly, the Master thrusts out his tongue. A leather flap is fused to the charred stump. "If only I had the potion that would grow a new tongue. I could sing as I once did for my mother."

The Master lifts his chin as if he means to sing. Instead, he reaches for the nektar cup. He paces. "That's why the Captain took it. I sang. I sang beautifully. It was the Captain with the hunting bird, you know the one. The hunting bird!" he demands. "Was that Timbe? Was that the Living Wood?"

By his description, the Master is talking about the Birds of Prey. A raptor is their symbol.

"My mother's badge was—is—the maple leaf," I tell him.

But he doesn't seem to hear me. The Master's mouth gapes. Sweat courses from his temples. His skin has gone even more pale, a thin membrane over the flesh beneath. Before he collapses, a guard rushes to catch him. Swiftly, the guard takes a well-chewed stick from his pocket and wedges it between the Master's teeth.

The guard holds the Master's left arm. Thorn kneels to hold down the right. The Master's legs wriggle like a just-caught fish.

Mélan watches from his chair. There's no surprise in his voice, only sadness. "My dear. He will sleep the rest of the day."

I can't help myself. "Is it the nektar?" Odide wanted to keep me so submerged in nektar that I couldn't escape. If I keep sipping the amber liquid, will I end up like the Master: growing younger and more addled every day? Shaking uncontrollably? Will my craving for nektar wipe away every other thought? Who will bring me a stick to bite?

I can't touch nektar again no matter how much I crave it.

When the fit passes, the Master goes limp. Cranox and the guards carry the Master into the next room.

When Cranox returns, he's holding two fist-sized globes of nektar. I'm struck by how he doesn't seem to crave it. I wonder if it works differently on females. Does that mean it won't cure 12?

Without hesitation, he hands the globes to me. My resolve vanishes. I want the nektar, all of it, for myself.

Cranox sees nektar-frenzy in my face. This is deliberate. He could have handed the globes to Thorn, but he chose me, to remind me of my weakness. It takes everything I have not to kill him on the spot, seize the globes, crack them open, then drain them like the sweetest hilt.

25

Brood

Thorn kneels beside 12 and yanks open his fysic kit. With a knife, he drills a hole in a globe, then hands the globe to me. *Spread that potion well along her flank,* he tells me, *where there are burns.*

His eyes linger on me a second too long. He knows I want it all. Even touching the waxy globe sends a shudder of longing through me.

But there's no point in drawing Thorn into the same craving. I carve open the globe and upend it over 12's burned flank. The nektar soaks into the pocked skin. I layer on more until the first globe is empty.

I could run to Dolor and back on the surge of power through my hands. I wouldn't have to eat or drink a thing. My sense of smell is sharp: Thorn's sweat, even a hint of Dinitra's smell on 12's head, right between the ears, where I've seen Dinitra kiss her.

Then I smell something else: cranny. A red corner of a cloth hangs from Thorn's fysic kit. That's where Thorn decided to hide the babe.

Thorn lifts 12's snout to pry open her jaws. I can drip in nektar from the second globe. I have to fight with myself to keep from licking my fingers. How long until my skin is pale as the Master's? How long until I collapse in fits?

I tell myself I'll be different. I'll control myself. I'm strong, stronger than anyone could imagine. I'm no addled boy pretending to be

Master. I'm the commander of the Living Wood. My brothers depend on me.

12 and Dinitra depend on me.

The nektar has already smoothed away 12's burns. But it's not working on her insides. Again, her belly clenches. She bares her fangs, moaning in pain. She pants, her golden eyes squeezing shut in agony.

I don't know what is happening, Thorn says. *It's what I felt inside her. Like the babe...I think it's eating her.*

He catches himself. Cranox watches every move. Thorn pulls his kit closer to his thigh. This secret is our greatest weapon.

I stroke 12's soft muzzle. "She needs more," I tell Cranox. "Two more globes."

He shakes his head. "If two globes don't heal her, nothing will. What you've already given her would raise the dead."

"The Master has his supply as do you. Bring it!" Nektar fuels my strength and my rage. Again, I see myself seizing the nektar the Master has for myself. Myself and my brothers. I'm wiser and kinder. I'm smarter. I'd use the nektar to cure 12. I'd give each of my brothers their share, to cure them of virus. I'd make the Master's quarters into an Arc, with as many chambers as I could fit. I'd cure every wildman who comes to the Master looking for freedom. I'd build an army, a better army, an army of brothers bound by nektar.

Why should the Master and Cranox have all the nektar and not my brothers? Not me? My brothers watch from across the room. I'd make a better commander of the Hundred-Hundred. By the Mother's breath, I would make a better Master!

The old man, Mélan, rests his hand on my shoulder. I can tell from the smell of him that he, too, tasted nektar, but long ago. The lilyfire is weak, like the peal of a distant bell. "Whatever ails poor 12," he says kindly, "it's beyond the power of nektar to heal. Comfort her."

This time, 12 groans deep and long. She snaps at the air, as if the pain is a swarm of pesky flies. Can the nektar itself be killing her? Thorn said he didn't know what nektar could do to a draft. But drafts are brewed in nektar. That's how 12 was born, from a sac of nektar. Nektar can't be what's killing her.

I know so little about drafts, so little about her. What parts are battle dog, what parts are howler monkey, hyena, tiger? Perhaps what's poison to the tiger is life to the hyena?

Her tail lifts and like a club slams down. Cranox and Decan shrink back, still terrified of The Beast. Cloudy liquid gushes over the stone floor. At first, I think it's nektar coming through the holes made by the lither venom. I dip my finger in and taste it, expecting sweetness. But the liquid is salty, like sea water. 12 groans again, then expels a glistening mass from under the root of her tail.

For a moment, I think she's expelled her vitals. The mass looks like what I saw of Cranox's insides, red, yellow, and a faint purple. The lither's venom must have loosened whatever holds her together. Dinitra isn't even here to say goodbye.

Desperate, I grasp Mélan's soft hand, speckled brown as a hen's egg. "The Captain. The female who brought her. Where is she?"

"In my dwelling," Mélan says.

I'm grateful he's confirmed what I already suspected, that she's here. But I need more. "She should see 12 before she dies," I tell him.

Dinitra will never forgive me for losing 12. I've failed her. I've failed us. I've failed at everything I've done since leaving Dolor. I wanted to bring nineteen brothers to freedom. Two are dead and I've saved only eight from the speluks.

And I'm losing 12.

Thorn punches my shoulder. *Bring it to her, you dolt!*

12's head raises. Her fleshy tongue licks at the mass.

Don't you see what's happening? It's like that Vessel in Quillka. The one with the red hair.

The Vessel? Just before the Weave attacked Quillka, one of Captain Rek's Vessels birthed twins.

Birth. I pick up the glistening mass and feel it squirm. 12 is birthing, not dying.

I glimpse a black nose and tiny paw. Tightly curled around its body is a tail. The tail even has a tiny curl of hair at the end. A tuft, just like 12's.

12 chatters with anticipation as I bring the pup to her. With her blue-black tongue, she pulls apart the sac. A pup wriggles out and squeals.

"Bring towels!" I cry to Decan. The pup is white but for a brown on black stripe at the shoulders. The Master's quarters seem to shrink around us. Thorn and I bend over 12 as she heaves, pup after pup slithering out. I laugh out loud, then stroke her belly. I feel more lumps: more pups. I lose track of time, who's in the room. When she is finally finished, 12 rests her head on my lap with an exhausted groan.

The final count makes Thorn laugh out loud. Twelve pups. Twelve for 12. We set each one at a teat already leaking milk. They eagerly suckle.

I've helped birth Rek's twins and now a brood of hyba crosses, Thorn says. *Wonder taught me everything he knew about being a fysic. But he never helped birth twins or hyba cross pups!*

I want to embrace my brother, kiss him, raise him like a battle flag. He's taken every challenge and kept his good humor. After I betrayed my brothers for Odide, he was the first to trust me again. "What will you name them?" I ask him.

Name? He grins. *What kind of name do you give a beast like this?*

"We could name them for trees."

He shakes his head. His answer surprises me. *They're born free, not like us. Let's wait to name them. Maybe, they'll pick their own names.*

He points to the largest pup. Like the others, it's white with a brown and black stripe over the shoulders. Somehow, the long tail came out kinked. The kink looks like our shape word *to beckon.*

Kinktail is too obvious. Beckon, well. Maybe something like... He lays his hand on 12's flank. *We should call him Brother.*

Brother. I laugh. *Is it even male?*

Thorn's face collapses in laughter. He lifts the pup. *Brother it is.*

Did my Keeper treat me as gently as 12 treats her pups? Keeper, Mother, Vessel. 12 is all three to her pups. Does Dinitra even know that 12 was carrying pups?

I look at Mélan. "You said she is with you. The female, the Captain."

He nods.

"Take us to her. She must see the pups. She must see 12."

But Cranox bars the door. He won't let all of my brothers leave. "You may take with you only the ones you won in the decima."

Nektar heat surges in me. Can he really stop me from leaving? Even weakened, 12 could rip his head off. I could reveal his secret and end him here and now.

But the Hundred-Hundred would cut us down before we even left the Master's quarters. Cranox folds his arms across his chest. "Choose."

I've feared this moment. Cranox wants me to select which of my brothers will live and which may still die.

Then Willow steps forward. *I'll stay.* Tamarack joins him. Quickly, my brothers decide they'll all stay except Thorn, who will tend to 12.

I have to clench my fists to keep from weeping. They trust me to win them. They trust me to find a way. Even Thorn, who knows I'm craving nektar, still has faith in me. Our Bond is stronger than ever.

"You will not harm them," I say to Cranox. I still have his secret: the babe. "You will let my brothers return to our quarters. I will make sure the Master hears of any harm that comes to them. That he hears *everything.*"

How effective a threat this is I can't tell. Since collapsing, the Master hasn't reappeared. Will he even remember how much he enjoyed the decima? That he spared my life and 12's? Then I remember what the Master said about who docked his tongue. The Master may be addled by nektar, but his memory is intact.

The guards bring baskets for the pups. We load them three to a basket on the machine platform. I'm so eager to reach Dinitra that I'm about to run down the stairs of the Dome naked.

Quickly, my brothers share the clothing they have: Fig's too-small breeches and a too-large tunic of Tamarack's still cut with Cuarto's whip.

I refuse boots. If I can't have Burn's, I prefer to go barefoot.

Thorn and I leave the way we came, following Mélan as he hums, *dum ta dum ta dum dum dum,* the same song I heard from the Master the day we arrived.

Mélan uses a cane to steady himself. I come next, with 12 behind me, her pups mewling on the machine as it scrabbles down the stairs.

Has Mélan been kind to Dinitra? Is she his prisoner? I feel like racing past the old man to wherever she's waiting. I couldn't allow myself to believe it before. But now each step brings me closer. I'll see her soon. I'll smell her. I'll wipe away every memory of the Queen once I'm in Dinitra's arms.

26

Pentaklon

Mélan's dwelling is high on a slope at the city's northern wall. He guides us through a warren of dwellings, small markets, and workshops.

My thoughts whirl. Thorn doesn't know how I feel about Dinitra. I have to control myself, control how I act in front of him. What can I even say to her? *I've thought about you every day, every hour, every minute.* But that's not true. I almost forgot her when I was conjured by the Queen. My chest squeezes with shame. Surely, Dinitra will notice I'm pure: no more tattoos.

My brothers know she gave me the secret to Remedy. She's why we were able to escape. But they don't know how I feel about her. They don't know I have a Bond to her. That I crave her.

More than nektar? I'd gladly replace nektar with Dinitra. I could scrub the nektar away as I scrubbed away Odide's scent in the lake at Hive Home. Once I'm with Dinitra, I'll have the strength to fight the nektar. To forget what happened with Odide. To start something new.

To finally make a choice as a free man.

Frequently, 12 pauses to check on the pups. In their baskets, the pups curl around and over each other and gnaw on each other's still hairless tails. Already, their eyes are starting to open: golden, like their mother's.

I don't know if the Master's city has ever seen such a procession. An old man, a hyba cross, a pure, barefoot warrior in ill-fitting clothes, his fysic brother, and twelve pups that squeak like rusty door hinges. A blacksmith bent over his anvil stops his arm in mid-swing. Only the little machines trundling up and down the street and spouting blue smoke seem oblivious.

As he walks, Mélan stoops like a question mark over his cane. One man, caught eating soup, drops his spoon and clatters backwards and over in his chair. Thorn leans over to pick up the spoon and hands it back with a grin.

12 pays the man no more attention than she would a flea. Her great tongue hangs from her jaws as she walks, her tail sweeping back and forth.

Mélan pauses at what looks like a bakery. "They have my bread," Mélan says. "Fetch it for me, Fir? I know I should probably move lower down, but the light is much better in the heights. For my drawing."

I push open the door. 12 enters behind me, a sudden thunderstorm. The baker cowers behind a counter piled with round loaves. "Mélan's bread," I tell him.

"Pink or white?" he asks, trembling. The pink bread is for the men who need Remedy, the white for beast-borns. For every white loaf, there are a dozen pinks.

"Half and half," I say. I don't know what Mélan eats.

The sack the baker gives me has enough for a week's worth of both colors.

Mélan talks as we continue to climb. He moves slowly. I wonder if he's in pain. "When I first came here, there was no city."

I offer to carry him, to get to Dinitra faster. He waves me off. "This is good for the heart. When I first came here, there were no houses, no walls. Just rock and hills."

I don't really want to hear about any of that. I want Dinitra. But I feel like I have to pretend. "Were you a warrior?"

Mélan pauses to lift his hand from his cane. He flicks his hand with the fingers separated. *Wildman*. "Is the word still the same?"

I nod.

"Some days, I think I've forgotten most of what I ever knew. Other days, I remember too much. Look, here's the egg man." Again, I retrieve his food: a basket heaped with speckled hen eggs.

"In those days, free men lived scattered, no more than ten or twelve to a group. Prey to the creatures that grew more numerous every passing year."

Creatures. "Not like this one," he says, meaning 12. "Whoever brewed her had a mind for how she'd be used. I see how devoted she is to the girl."

The girl. Dinitra. My heart leaps even though this is just a reference to her. She could be around the next corner or down the next street. I feel waves of anticipation, then fear. Does she even think of me?

"Those of us who made it to each spring counted ourselves lucky," Mélan says. "One winter, I broke my leg. I was dying. Tyr found me, saved me."

"Who?" I say, distracted.

"Tyr. Queen before Odide."

That gets my attention. "You knew Odide's mother? And you survived?"

"I'm perhaps the only man alive who knows what you felt, friend Fir."

"But...she let you go."

"Not exactly." Mélan stops for a moment to catch his breath. "I didn't know what she was at first. I couldn't speak for lack of food and water. The cold. Couldn't see, either. Her people took me in, bathed me, fed me, clothed me. Healed me."

"Tyr saved you," I say, "with lilyfire nektar."

"A very long time ago. Come, we're almost there."

Mélan turns to the right and leads me up a curving street that ends at a rock face. A few wooden dwellings seem to hang like bird nests from the rock. The dwellings are interspersed with gray plants rooted in the cracks.

Most of the dwellings appear empty, cobwebs streaming in the windows. As Mélan said, the air is clearer here. We've climbed high enough to be able to look down on the city's blue haze. The haze obscures everything but the top of the Master's dome and its rotating, speluk finger of light.

At a battered plank door, Mélan pauses. "My rooms hardly fit 12 and the girl. And now these pups! Perhaps your brother could return to the Dome? He's safe in the city now that you've won his life."

Thorn's reluctant to leave me unguarded. "It's alright," I tell him. "Look, I have 12. She's worth an army of brothers. Just don't let that kit," I say, pointing to the bag strapped to his chest that contains Cranox's babe, "out of your sight."

As I watch him go back down the steep hill, I feel relief. My brothers still don't know my feelings for Dinitra. I'd rather see her first then figure out how to explain.

12 whines with anticipation as we reach the last dwelling. To me, every second's delay feels like an hour. After weeks of travel, after the hyba pack and the Blazes and the Queen, after falling into the hands of the Hundred-Hundred and fighting for my life, I'm about to see her again. Not in The Deep. Not in Dolor. Does she even know I'm here? Did she watch the decima? Will she recognize me: my hair a tangle, my skin pure, bootless? Suddenly I'm ashamed. What can I cover myself with?

I wish I at least had Burn's lucky boots.

Better she sees me as I am, a conjured warrior who lived and just fought a decima. And danced with 12 to the laughter of the Hundred-Hundred.

Once Mélan opens the door, 12 shoves past me. There's a clatter as something shatters, swept away by her tail or shoulder.

But there's no Dinitra inside. 12 sniffs at a chair next to a table crowded with pots of paint. In one cup, brushes stick out like thistles. A pot of blue has fallen to the floor and shattered.

A book—Dinitra's book—lies open.

"Where is she?" My voice is harsher than I mean it to be.

Mélan isn't offended. "She's always out collecting things. Herbs and flowers, leaves and shells. For her paints. It helps her pass the time when 12 is fighting a decima. She makes paints for me now. We might as well be from the same mother, she and I. Brewed in the same Vessel though years apart. We're both painters, sketchers. Come, warrior Fir. I'll make tea. She's never away for long."

My disappointment is intense, but there's nothing to be done but wait. I busy myself unloading pups from the machine and setting them against a wall. 12 inspects them, then starts cleaning them one by one.

"So…Dinitra is free to go about the city?" I ask.

Mélan nods. "A bargain I struck for her life. 12 fights the decimas and she isn't killed. Harsh, I know. Bex grown less patient with time. But now that you've won 12…"

Mélan sees my confusion. "Bex," he says, "is the Master. Bex is his given name."

As if he can hear my thoughts, he adds, "Nektar only makes it worse. His moods."

Mélan places a kettle on a metal grate. The flame lights with the flick of a switch: blue and oily-smelling. He pulls a tea pot from a shelf and dumps in a handful of laurel and winterwort. "Calming," he says kindly, "while we wait."

12 flops down heavily so her pups can suckle.

"Come, sit," Mélan says. In a side room is window with a large table, angled so that Mélan can stand as he paints. The light illuminates the book he's been working on. Unlike what he was drawing in the Dome, these pages are vibrant with color. I remember Zong spoke of an old scribe who busied himself with books.

"Still much work to be done, but you see more or less," Mélan says about the book. "Here is 12. The first decima she fought. There, the poor wildman. Dinitra wept all night. Someone who hadn't done them any harm, she said. She thought she'd never see 12 again. But Bex returned 12 without a scratch."

Mélan has captured 12 exactly: her golden eyes tracking her prey, her powerful haunches gathering. I can almost feel the hard muscle explode as she leaps. "That first time, no one but Dinitra knew her power. She warned Bex it was no contest at all. Not really even a decima. They're meant to be entertainments, not slaughters. But he insisted."

The tea kettle whistles. He has me place cups on a small table as he slices bread. From a cabinet, he takes a small wheel of cheese and cuts two generous slices.

Mélan motions me to a lumpy chair. On my plate, he's added a spoonful of apple jam. "The jam isn't as good as Tyr's, but it's passable."

I don't admit that the jam might as well be sawdust compared to what I tasted in Hive Home. Since I left Odide, no food has appealed to me. I just want to see Dinitra.

Mélan shuffles to his books. The wooden shelves are packed so heavily that they bend downwards in the middle, like sly smiles. "Book twenty-three, I think. That's when I saw Tyr for the first time." Starting at the lowest shelf nearest the window, he counts to the end, then moves his finger to the shelf directly above. "Like weaving," he says, as if answering a question. "Left to right, right to left, and so on. More efficient, Dinitra agreed."

I never imagined that my life—Dinitra's life, the lives of my brothers, 12 and her pups—would end up in the pages of books. With a flourish, Mélan pulls out the book he wants: number twenty-three. "There are many answers here, most to questions no one has thought to ask. I live in the past mostly. It feels kinder."

I'm on edge, waiting for Dinitra's hand on the door. Unless Mélan can bring me Dinitra or tell me how to win nine more lives, I don't think a musty old book will help.

Then I stop myself. Not nine anymore. There's Dinitra and twelve pups. I need to save twenty-two lives. At least three more decimas. The prospect makes me even more impatient. I'd fight all three decimas today instead of wasting my time with paints and brushes.

Mélan is oblivious to my darkening mood. The leather cover of Book 23 is decorated in a pattern of vines and flowers. "My mother taught me to draw. A book of days, she called hers. My books are years. Lifetimes."

He sets the book on my lap, then turns to the page he wants me to see. I see a Queen like Odide but with mandibles instead of lips. Like Odide, her skin is a polished black. Her eyes are black, too, and segmented into dozens of hexagons.

The pendant around her neck is like Odide's, five-sided and set in silver pergama. But the stone at the center is white. Tyr's pendant looks like the gift Zong gave to be delivered to the Master, the one he smashed.

Mélan sees the recognition in my eyes. "I know Zong gave it to Bex. He smashed it. The pendant was a message. Zong grows impatient with us. He wants to kill his sister and march on The Deep. Zong knows I love her. That I tell Bex that Odide isn't our enemy. Why should we fight those who do us no harm? Zong killed his own mother. Why would he not kill me or even the Master if we get in his way?"

"Kill you?" Why would Zong kill the old scribe?

Mélan looks pained,

"Shall I send a brother for the pendant?" I ask. "It may be there still."

Mélan waves his speckled hand. "I care nothing for the pendant. It was a threat. I prefer my books. We can't go back to the past, friend Fir. But we can remember it and learn from it. That's why I paint. Your friend and I have talked long into the night about why we draw. She is quite talented, you know."

The room smells of burnt butter from 12 and the pups. "I know," I say. "She drew me."

Mélan's smile is mysterious. "An excellent likeness. I recognized you immediately from her book."

My cheeks flush. I'm not used to being looked at so closely.

"Dinitra told me all about you. About 12's name," Mélan says. "About her past. She first saw the beast in the twelfth cage. What a thing! To be named for where you're kept a prisoner. How she and 12 came to be traveling together. It's a good story. You were in it."

"She spoke of me?" This pleases me beyond what I can express. Dinitra has been thinking about me, too.

"What else is there to do on long winter's nights but talk?" Mélan strokes his long beard. "And tell stories of lost loves. Those are the best stories." A smile plays on his lips. "Somehow, every story she tells leads to you."

I look to my bare, filthy feet. I'm not prepared for other people to know how I feel about Dinitra. Or how she may feel about me.

I change the subject. "How many books do you have?"

"You see all of the Hive books there, on the middle shelf. Twenty-three through one-hundred-and-sixty-five. Many happy years. Then the years of this city. One-hundred-sixty-six through, let's see, three-hundred and twenty-two. Twenty-three if you count the book on my table. The one where I'm painting your decima."

I'm careful with my next words. "During your time in Tyr's Hive, did you see…other men?"

"Oh no." Mélan shakes his head. "Tyr and I were joined in Jule. Odide is my daughter."

My mouth drops open. "You…"

"Lovely years they were. Times of great plenty. I took special care of the orchards. And I painted, too."

Hesitantly, I ask, "So Zong?"

"My son," Mélan says.

Cranox taunted Zong when Zong called Mélan "the old scribe." *Is that what you're calling him now.*

I notice that Mélan look a slice of the white bread, the same loaf that he cut for me. He has no virus, either. Like me, he was cured by nektar.

He shuffles to the bookshelf to pull out one of the Hive books. He explains that the Hive pages are made of honeycomb shaved thin and left to dry in the sun. The comb is supple and drinks in paint. "Once it's dry, the two are fused, paint and comb," he says. "They'll survive anything but fire."

He invites me to feel the surface. "Close your eyes."

The page is pliant, almost soft. I feel the faintest thrum of the lilyfire nektar that the comb once held: winds and summers and lilyfire long before I was born. The painting is of their Jule. Mélan is a young man, his hair black as Tamarack's. He sits straight, his shoulders square and powerful. Beside him, Tyr wears her white pendant. Her gown is black and she looks like a night sky with a single, brilliant star. Her four-fingered hand rests on his.

Mélan gazes at the picture. His love for Tyr shines on his face.

But does he also love the Master, does he love Bex? Can those loves be the same? Who am I to say what kind of Bond anyone should have? Or if they can only Bond once or to one person?

I'm trying to phrase the question when Mélan taps the top of the page. There, he's written a single word: *Pentaklon.*

"Penta," Mélan says, "means five. Like the five fingers on a human hand. Tyr's pendant was shaped this way as a promise. It's the union that made the hive strong. You see it has five sides."

The truth is I hadn't noticed. When Cranox examined it, all I saw was that it was like Odide's except for the color of the stone.

"Female," Mélan says, lifting the smallest finger, "then male. Both human. After that comes plant, then animal. Of these, plant is most numerous and therefore the longest finger. The final finger, the thumb, is the draft: the mix of them and what brings them all together. Pentaklon is what pendants like these are called. The five points bind us to the palm—the earth—and the back of the hand, the sky. All of us."

My first reaction is to shake my head. This Pentaklon idea is better than Fire Brother. Fire Brother is just sticks and moss. At least, the Pentaklon is beautiful.

I speak carefully. "You lay with her. With Tyr." I refuse to say beast-like. Beast-like sounds like an insult.

Mélan chuckles. "Why, of course! How else are children made outside of those cursed laboratories, Fir!"

With a fingertip, Mélan gently touches the paint he used for Tyr's face. "For many years, we built a hive. Our children came in spring. Every harvest more bountiful. It was a time of great joy. Our valley was filled with animals, birds, grasses. Our streams and lakes with fish and frogs. But one day, I noticed my beloved was tired. That is the way of all living things, I know. Somehow, I thought our Jule would protect her even from death. It came time to birth a new Queen."

I think of how quickly Odide tired when I was with her, how desperately she wanted a daughter. In her chambers stood a lovely, empty cradle.

"My son killed Tyr. Zong," Mélan says. "And he tried to kill Odide. The new Queen. His...ambition. Perhaps it was too much of the human in him. Too much of me."

I search Mélan's face for any hint of Odide: her human lips, her delicate nose. Where she has black skin, he's pale as moonlight. Her eyes are glittering black and segmented and his are human and clouded with age. But there is something of her temperament in him. Her laugh. It's like looking through a cracked glass. I didn't realize how important it was to birth a new Queen. When I first saw her, I thought she was no more than a girl.

I'm trying to think of the word for Mélan and a daughter. It's an old word, rarely used. "You are her...are his..."

"Father." Mélan closes the book. "Father to Odide and Zong. Grandfather and great grandfather to thousands more. I haven't said that word aloud for many years. Yes. Father. Do you know the shape?"

Mélan shows me: the palm of the hand horizontal and facing the sky, making a circle. The opposite of mother, when the palm faces the Earth as it circles.

Father.

27

A Perfect Number

1 2 leaps up. A sweep of her tail upends the small table sending the teapot, cheese, and crusts of bread flying. Robbed of their warm mother, the pups squeal in protest.

Then Dinitra bursts through the door. 12 is on her, a tempest of love and devotion. Her tail winds around Dinitra like a vine. Abruptly, 12 stands on her back legs and plops her heavy forelegs on her shoulders.

Dinitra buries her face in 12's dense ruff. "My dearest, dearest. Oh, come to me, you terrible, sweet creature. Are you hurt at all?"

12 tries to shift her head under Dinitra's chin. It's as if she's trying to fit her enormous body into Dinitra's. 12 satisfies herself by roughly licking Dinitra's face with her blue-black tongue.

Dinitra hasn't seen me yet. This gives me a moment to look at her. She's thinner. Her hair—her beautiful brown hair, thick and springy— is shaved to the scalp. On her forearm, I see the scar where a feral battle dog once attacked her. She wears the loose tunic and baggy pants of the Hundred-Hundred.

12 goes to the floor with a thump. Only then does Dinitra see me.

Something in me collapses. It's the badness, the fear, the not-knowing. I'm empty and full, weightless and as heavy as I've ever been, the only thing keeping me in place.

I don't have to move. Dinitra hurls herself at me. She even smells of 12: burnt butter. I never want to move from this spot, where she's in my arms.

She's the first to pull away. This time, she examines me. Questions mount in her eyes. "How? When?"

"I thought you went to The Deep," I say. "I even saw you."

"You saw me?" I'm saved from having to explain that I saw her through the eyes of the Queen and her Swarm by a sharp bleat from one of the pups. Dinitra's eyes go to them. Then she's kneeling among them, picking up first one, then two, then as many pups as she can fit in her arms.

The pups wriggle happily. It's as if they've absorbed their mother's devotion to her, tasting her with their blue-black tongues. Dinitra embraces 12 at the shoulders. "This was what you were hiding in your belly, you sneak."

"Twelve," I tell her. "Twelve for 12. A perfect number."

Dinitra's face glows with happiness. I notice again how drawn her face looks, the softness whittled away. She's suffered and that stabs me. "How?"

I shake my head, laughing. "You tell me."

It's so absurd and so unexpected that we both bend over laughing. Then she's back in my arms. This time she kisses me: warm, quick, hard.

Her hands go to both of my cheeks. "I knew she was fighting another decima. Was that you?"

I tell her I fought an old lither. Then 12 appeared from the underground chamber. 12 killed the lither, then we danced before the entire Hundred-Hundred. "Like I saw you do with her. The dance saved my life. She saved my life. The Master liked it. He freed her," I tell Dinitra. "No more decimas for her. 12 was wounded, but we healed her. We thought she was dying, but she was having pups."

"Free?" Dinitra looks at me with wonder. "But…"

She looks at Mélan. "Is this true?"

"12 and eight of his brothers," he confirms. "I saw it with my own eyes. The Master called it the best decima he'd ever seen."

Dinitra turns to me. "Only eight brothers." She knows we were twenty-strong in Dolor.

I force my voice to be steady. "Eight won in the decima. Cedar I lost in the river. Tanoak…" I have to collect myself to say the words.

It's like a song I can't stop singing: *dum ta dum ta dum dum dum.* Because of my failure, Tanoak died. "Tanoak after."

"I'm so sorry. So sorry." For a long moment, we embrace. "So there are nine more to save," she says.

I have to use shape language or risk breaking down. I've just found her again. I don't want her to think I'm weak. I take her hand and expose her palm. There, I shape the words. *Twenty-two. 12 pups, nine brothers. And you.*

"Twenty-two." She steps away. "Three decimas. By the Mother's breath. There won't be any more decimas until next year. Isn't that the rule, Mélan? I saw it in your book."

All I want to do is hold her, taste her, smell her. Be with her. Never leave this strange little dwelling with its tea and paints and pups. Our roles have reversed. Once I was bound by my mother's service. Now, I'm a free man in a world of men. Dinitra is the prisoner.

"We have to find a way," I tell her.

Her smile lifts me in a way nothing else can. "I wished for this," she says "I dreamed of you. But you're different. Your tattoos." Her brown eyes lock to my green ones. With the Queen, I saw myself reflected dozens of time. With Dinitra, I'm one: Fir. "In my dreams, you had boots," she says.

On or off, stolen or burned. *Boots.* All of what's happened and all of the distance we've travelled bound up in this: she sees me. No boots. I've lost brothers, fallen into the conjury of a Queen and her nektar. My laugh is a bark. She laughs with me, a yip that sends the pups yipping with her.

"Dear me." Mélan hobbles to the stove. With a clang, he places the kettle back on the blue flame. "We need more tea."

I sit on the one lumpy chair. Dinitra curls next to the pups, plucking one of them, Brother, from the basket and plopping him in her lap. My story gushes out, mostly spoken but some in shape language. It feels a little like when I stepped into the lake at Hive Home, vomiting out nektar and food and bile. I tell Dinitra everything except what's in Thorn's pouch: the babe.

That even kind Mélan can't know.

"The Queen's nektar cured my virus," I tell her. "Erased the tattoos. I no longer need Remedy. I guess I'm a pure now."

I want to make sure Dinitra understands that I didn't ask for nektar. I didn't ask to be cured or to be with the Queen.

Mélan stops spooning tea leaves into the teapot to ask, "Would you rather she let you die?"

I have to admit: no. Especially now that I've found Dinitra again. If Odide had let me die, my brothers would be speluk food. She tried to conjure me, yes. But it was Jarvon, not Odide, who attacked me and beat me so badly I couldn't flee. He did that out of loyalty to her.

Perhaps I can forgive Odide just a little.

Then it's Dinitra's turn. After the Captains destroyed the Weave's fleet at Dolor, she, the Vessel Susalee, and 12 fled north. They planned to slip past The Watcher and descend into The Deep, just as she'd told me they would.

"If it weren't for 12, we'd have been killed a dozen times." Like the Hunger and Burn, they were attacked by a grabeen flock. Even though 12 had never seen a grabeen before, she knew exactly what to do. She leapt high enough to seize the grabeen leader by the throat. With a yank, she separated its head from its body.

"They never bothered us again," Dinitra says.

At The Watcher, Furies ambushed them. They were blocking any draft heading for The Deep. Zong questioned them for days. He was especially fascinated by 12. He wanted to keep the hyba cross and kill Dinitra, but 12 was impossible for him to control.

"She killed five of his Furies that first day," Dinitra says proudly. Although Mélan is his father, she has no love for Zong.

Zong traded the three of them to the Master for barrels of the Dark. "He means to use the Dark to burn his sister's Hive," Dinitra says.

Daughter, son, father. I never knew words could tangle so much and mean so many different things. In the Weave, there are no *sons*, only males contained and used for extract. In Bounty, males are warriors or wildmen and a few despised beast-borns. *Mothers* are Captains who command their sons. For Odide, a *daughter* is life itself. If I'd stayed in Hive Home, I would have been a *father* like Mélan.

"Zong asked so many questions about the Weave," Dinitra is saying. "About how they made drafts. Well, I was never a Sower," she laughs. "Did I ever tell you about my carnivorous potato?"

"A carnivorous potato." With all that's happening, all we face, she's talking about a carnivorous potato. "You never mentioned it."

"Susalee made a plant thing that dripped honey and attacked its predators. She got a *merit*."

"A merit!" I have no idea what a merit is or why it matters, but I pretend it's the best thing in the world, like being named commander of your Mother's warriors. Most of all, I love this feeling I have when Dinitra and I talk. It's as if we've always been together.

"You were jealous," I say.

"Terribly." Dinitra's laugh is a kind of balm. "I admit it. I was jealous. She was better at everything. Except..." Dinitra reaches down to kiss 12 between the ears. "She was never much good at hyba crosses."

"Where is she? The Vessel?"

"Not the Vessel." Dinitra turns serious. "Don't call her that. Her name is Susalee."

"Susalee then."

"The Master keeps her as a kind of pet. She's in the Dome."

"A pet?" How can a human be a pet?

"He's...not like anyone I've known before," Dinitra says, glancing at Mélan. He seems to be dozing in his chair. "She has everything she needs. I guess he's kind to her. To be honest, she refuses to be near me. All she wants is to go back to the Weave even though I've reminded her a dozen times that it's destroyed."

"Kind" isn't a word I'd choose to describe the Master. But I'm quiet as Dinitra stares at her hands.

Dinitra arranges Brother back among the pups. "I feel responsible for her. I knew her in the Weave. I guess we were friends."

Friends. That's another word I don't use much. I have *brothers*, a *mother*. Some of my brothers had *lovers* in Bounty.

Is Dinitra a friend? No: I want her to be a lover. The thought makes my heart race. I don't know anything about beasts or male and female. I don't even understand how I was created. But I know I want her.

"After the twins were born, Susalee wanted to die," Dinitra tells me. "Maybe the only reason she's alive is because I dragged her with me. Still, I feel like I failed her."

My heart fills. I feel like I failed my brothers. She feels like she failed Susalee. I don't need conjury to walk Dinitra's mind or she mine. We sit with our failures, silent companions.

"What if there was a place for us away from all this. All of it," I blurt. "Bounty, the Weave. Hive Home. This blasted city. What if there was a new place that we made ourselves? Anyone who wanted freedom and peace would be welcome."

There's no time for this. No place. I have to stand to work out my frustration, startling the pups who nervously thump their tails. It's all impossible. I can't see the path to leave all of this behind. Carrying 12 bleating pups? Where would we be safe from Zong? Where could we live unafraid? "If only that miserable Lark had told us to avoid the Scarlet Valley. If only we'd gone to the Deep!"

"Then you would not have ended up here," Dinitra says. "But what's happened isn't as important as what we'll do next. Now that we have twenty-two lives to save. How are we going to do it?"

I'm speechless. I watch her repeat the shape language. I've never seen anything that makes me happier.

We, Dinitra says. The pointer finger circling. Dinitra and Fir together.

28

Kind-in-Kind

Even if we manage to save everyone, what sort of life is there for us? Even Mélan with his stories of a Jule with a draft Queen ended with loss. Fire. Murder.

"We've told you our story, Mélan," I say, "but how did you come to this place from Tyr's Hive?"

"Another long story, but I am happy to tell it. Dear daughter," he says to Dinitra, "please bring me book one-hundred-and-sixty-five."

I'm surprised by the word *daughter*. But Dinitra doesn't hesitate to pull the book from the shelf and lay it on Mélan's lap. "It's the thickest," she says.

"This is a very long story," Mélan says.

Dinitra and I stand behind him as Mélan goes through the pages. "I depended on nektar then. I thought I needed it to live. I took just a taste every several days. Enough to last me several years, I thought."

He runs his crooked finger under a title on the first page: "The burning of Tyr's Hive." The page is full of smoke and fire. I see the comb of Tyr's hive melting. Their children—workers, drones, Arcs— twist in the flames. The next page shows Mélan alone in a dark forest, three globes of nektar roped to his back.

"Doesn't nektar make you young?" I ask. As the words leave my mouth, I'm ashamed. I'm telling him he looks very old.

Mélan chuckles. "I know what I look like to you young ones. I'm a painter. My gift is to see, sometimes too clearly. I'm not sad about my wrinkled skin, my old bones, though I'd like a little more sleep. This is what should happen to all creatures. We're young, we grow old. We die. I'm not afraid of it."

In his mouth, the word *creatures* isn't an insult. It's loving, a word that unites human, draft, plant, and beast. We're all *creatures*. We're all part of the Pentaklon.

When I saw Tyr's death through Odide's eyes, I didn't see Mélan. I wouldn't have known him, anyway, as a young man. If Zong hadn't killed Tyr, maybe Mélan would have stayed in her Hive.

I'm making myself crazy with could-have-beens, should-have-beens. Dinitra is next to me: warm, breathing. How can I give up now?

"In your world, boys don't grow very old, do they?" Mélan says to me. "Tell me, how old is your oldest brother?"

That's Thorn. I count back from our escape from Dolor. "Twenty-eight."

"And you?"

I feel like I've lived several lifetimes since the Weave's attack on Quillka. We become warriors when we're eleven or twelve. "Seventeen."

"That was how old I was when Tyr saved me."

"If I can ask, how old are you now? How old is the Master?"

Mélan thinks for a moment. "Let's see, I am 123 last spring. Bex is thirty years younger. Ninety by my count. Very old the two of us, by now. Twenty-six years I spent with Tyr. Almost your eldest brother's lifetime."

I can't comprehend what it would mean to be that old. How much they both have seen! Mélan's body shows every passing year. And the Master grows younger and more crazed with each passing day of nektar.

"How did you and Bex meet?" I ask.

"After Tyr's hive burned, I wandered a year or more. Hid. Zong was searching for me. It took me many months to feel again. It wasn't just her death. I lost hope. I had lost everything, you see. Everything I held dear. Except nektar."

The nektar gave him strength to travel. He could bear hunger and cold. I remember how I felt as I fled Odide: like I could run forever. I needed no blanket, no fire.

But the nektar also confused him, Mélan says. He'd circle back to Tyr's hive even though it was ashes. "I came upon my dear one just east of here, at Seven Lake."

Dinitra's hand is on his shoulder. He pats it. "Pour us a bit more tea, daughter."

Once she delivers the tea, Mélan starts again. "Just as Tyr found and rescued me, I found Bex."

I think from the way Dinitra nods that she's heard this story before. "You said there was no city then. No walls."

"You don't need a city to care for someone. I hunted, drew water. I made our shelter. It was hard, but I came to love him."

"Bex was alone?"

"Alone and dying." Mélan looks to the shelf of books as if to call out another number so that we can look at new pages. Then he gazes back at his tea.

"Would you like for me to fetch the book?" I ask.

He shakes his head slowly. "Some years, I prefer not to remember."

For a long moment, we go page by page, the only sound the snoring of 12 and her sleeping pups. They're in a heap, Brother buried beneath the others. The sun is sinking and a gentle yellow light fills the room.

"Tyr's nektar saved him," Mélan tells us. "I thought only of getting more, so that my love would recover, be strong again. It's all my fault." Tears slide down his wrinkled cheeks. "My curse that I brought him nektar. I tied him to nektar. I loved him and I still love him. The nektar will never let him go."

I can't help glancing at my own arms, torn to pieces by Jarvon, then put together again by nektar. Every time I hear the word, I remember that I want it. Dinitra seems to sense my agitation and moves her hand to mine.

"How did you stop?" I ask Mélan.

"It wasn't easy. It isn't easy. The craving never goes completely away. Bex didn't always take this much nektar. A sip here and there, to ease his aches. He would share it with men who needed it, to heal them. To cure them of virus."

"I wish this for my brothers," I blurt. "Just once would do no harm, would it?"

Mélan suddenly looks very tired. "They will live happy lives eating their pink Remedy. Lives free of the craving. Nektar never lets go."

There's a long pause. I think he must be finished with his story. But in a whisper, he asks for another book. "One-hundred-and-seventy."

This time, I go to the shelf, counting left to right, then up and to the end, then right to left. The page he turns to is almost completely red: a battle with a touch of gray ash. Mélan has captured the colors of battle. I know that color like I know my own hands. It's a terrible, fine power to be able to capture war on a page.

"That was a time of war," he says. Instead of feeling love and gratitude to Tyr and then Odide for their nektar, Bex grew to hate them. "He especially hated my daughter, Odide. Jealousy, perhaps. Need. He wanted nothing to do with my past. That's why he threw the pendant."

"What pendant?" Dinitra asks.

"My dear daughter, Zong send Bex a terrible gift. Tyr's Pentaklon. It wasn't sent in friendship. Zong was telling him that time grows short. He promised to help burn Hive Home. Kill Odide. Then march on The Deep and exterminate the drafts."

"Why does Zong hate them so?" I ask. "They're drafts like him."

"It's precisely because they're like him, I think. He's spent too many years hating his sister to love any draft."

The last thing I want is to lead my brothers into another war. If Bex marches on Hive Home, will Thorn and I be forced to fight with him? As much as Odide conjured me, I have no desire for revenge. I wish no harm to Hive Home.

Dinitra leaves to go to a back room, then reappears with a full bowl of mash for 12. In the street, she scoops up a handful of pebbles to mix with the meat.

12 eats the mash in three bites. Then she drains a bucket of water, licks each pup, and lies down again to sleep.

Mélan sips the last of his tea. "If Bex could erase my time with Tyr from my mind, he would. He wanted me and he wanted her nektar. And me to have Bonded only to him. He thought he was better than other men, that he would use nektar wisely. With the power of nektar, he thought he could right the wrongs of the world: humble the

Captains, stop the Weave from eliminating men. End the Weave's power to make drafts. Use nektar only to heal."

I hear the echo of my own vow to use nektar for good. I could heal my brothers. Heal every man in the Master's city who still carries the virus. I could return to Bounty and heal every warrior, giving them the chance I had, to be free.

Bex thought the same thing and ended up a prisoner of nektar.

I shift to face him, then kneel at his feet. I take his hands in mine. "I need to save twenty-two lives. Dinitra, my brothers. These pups. We need to go someplace where we can be free. A new place, maybe where the Pentaklon isn't a pendant or an idea, but something real. If we stay, some of us will die. I'll pay any price."

I stop myself, my cheeks burning. I sound crazed. "I mean, how can *we* do that? How can we find a way. And finally be free."

"My son." Mélan stares at his tea cup. Only my mother has ever called me *son*. "Never have I painted a single perfect page. There's no such thing as perfection. That's one reason nektar is so dangerous. It gives humans the illusion of perfection. To this day, Bex believes himself as he was when we first built this city. Young and strong. Capable. Brilliant. You may think you'll find perfect freedom somewhere. Everything as you dream. But unless you carry freedom here, in your heart, there's no place that will truly satisfy you."

"What choice do we have?" I say. "If we stay here, we'll be forced to fight Zong's war against your own daughter. That freedom's worthless. Less than worthless. It's what we're all running from. I'd rather have some freedom than none at all."

Mélan's face looks like an old rag hung on a hook. "You must understand that what you'll be asked to pay will be more than you bargain for. A Kind-in-Kind is the only way to win that many lives."

"Then tell me what a Kind-in-Kind is."

"Very well." Mélan asks for book one-hundred-sixty-eight. "That has the first decima."

"But..."

Dinitra places her hand on mine. She shapes the word *patience*. Mélan must tell this story in his own way.

"Here it is," he says, opening the book I bring him. "The first decima. There I am, as I was, a young man."

In the drawing, Mélan is a little older than he was in his Jule with

Tyr, but still powerful, with muscular arms and a chest that bristles with hair. His hair is black and streaked with gray down to his elbows.

At the top of the page, Mélan has written the story.

The first and most glorious of the decimas. Men come to us as slaves and win their place in the Hundred-Hundred. Only the strongest. Only the smartest. Nine they may choose as their companions. Men alone.

"Forgive the words. It was a different time. I was a different man."

To show everyone that he meant what he said, Mélan volunteered to go first. He fought a speluk. On the page, the speluk tears viciously at his leg. On the next page, I see how Mélan managed to get behind it and crush its windpipe. It's a common move I've practiced with my brothers hundreds of times.

"I asked only for my love in return. For Bex. One life. I wanted to make it clear that Bex would lead us all. I saw that in him, this talent for leading men. He was the one who designed this city. He understood the Dark. He built the first machines and fueled them with the Dark. We would be a place of freedom for men. A place of strength even as the Weave grew and planned for men's destruction. That light at the top of his Dome. It was not always blue. We first put it there to be like a star, showing men that they had reached safety. The color was white."

"Why not take all the men who come?" I ask.

"We wanted to!" he cries. "But there were too many. We didn't have enough food or clothing, shelter. I said we could take only the strongest, the ones who could help. They'd have to fight to stay in the city. The decima was the best way, the fairest way."

Mélan's fingers tremble. These aren't fond memories. Something in him compels him to draw just as Dinitra is compelled to have her paper and charcoals always at hand. I used to think that drawing something would remove terrible memories like a piece of shrapnel. But for Mélan, the hurt is still deep inside, deep as a virus but impervious to nektar.

"Tyr had her defenses, too! An army more magnificent than even Odide's. Yet she gave her army to Zong as commander. She believed he would be loyal to his sister. She thought his love for her would bind that loyalty."

For a long moment, Mélan strokes the page with his knobby fingers. "It only led to her murder. It was my fault, my fault."

I'm beginning to worry about my brothers. Nine of them are still vulnerable. If I spend too long here, they'll wonder if I've been taken again.

Mélan is still talking. I can't leave before I know how to win twenty-two lives.

"All things truly wicked start from innocence," Mélan says. "Even Zong's heart was not always this way. My son. When I took the nektar from Tyr, I thought its only power was healing, strength. I soon found that nektar also gives youth. I didn't age. In fact, I grew younger. For a price. Over time, nektar creates a Bond even love can't break."

Mélan turns to me. "You've tasted nektar how many times, Fir? Some would cut off a limb to have nektar just once more."

To myself, I count. The first time was in the Arc. The second time was when Thorn and I healed Cranox, my hands smearing nektar along Thorn's careful seam. The last time was with 12. Three times.

"If you take no more, the desire will fade over time," Mélan says. "But it will never go completely away."

"You spoke of a Kind-in-Kind, Mélan," I remind him, growing impatient with these old stories, these old books. We're talking about the future, not the past. "And that I wouldn't like it. But I need to know. How do I get it?"

"It means more killing."

"Show me." I correct myself again. "Show us."

Mélan turns the page. "The regular decima is based on the Pentaklon, on the five groups. Remember, I told you, Fir: male and female human, animal, plant, and draft. I said there must always be a balance. Human must fight draft or draft must fight animal. There must always be a balance, you see? Never can a human fight a human. And no draft can fight a draft. No Kind-in-Kind."

But this makes no sense. In my decima, there were two drafts.

Mélan nods. "Normally, Cranox suggests what beast or draft will fight. But Bex heard you had been with the Queen, that you'd tasted nektar. Bex thought it would be entertaining to pit you against a draft that owes its life to nektar. That was how 12 was brewed, after all. Less and less does he follow any rules. And the lither, well. She was very old."

"So a Kind-in-Kind is not a regular decima." This is starting to sound like a riddle. I hate riddles.

The old man asks me to place book one-hundred-sixty-eight on his drawing table, where the light is better. "A human may request a Kind-in-Kind at any time. That is the key. Humans can always demand to fight other humans."

Mélan warned me I wouldn't like the choice. "I won't fight a brother. Or Dinitra," I say hotly.

"You don't have to. You ask for your opponent by name. You can't be denied. If you win, you get all you ask for. There's no limit to the lives you can gain. Or riches."

Mélan needs my help to stand. He leans on my arm to go to Book One-Hundred-Sixty-Eight on his table. The light is strong enough to make him blink rapidly. On the page he selects, two warriors face off with only their huaracas. Around them, the arena is packed with men. By the landscape Mélan has painted, I see that it's early spring.

One of the figures is bald, reminding me of a young Cranox. The other fighter is painted over with a black rectangle.

"You know him," Mélan says. "Cranox himself. He asked for a Kind-in-Kind. He wanted to kill the commander of the Hundred-Hundred. He asked for three things in return: to be named commander and to have that man's name and face be erased from all memory."

Dinitra touches the black rectangle. "You must remember the man's name, Mélan."

"I believed this was a fair trade. After I finished the page, I painted over the man's figure. See what I wrote?"

The man called Cranox won his decima. He asked that his name alone be recorded. So it was done.

"You see, I didn't even record the other man as a fighter. Cranox won. He got what he asked for. I went back through all of the books and painted out his name and likeness wherever it appeared. At the time, I thought this was just. I have no memory of the man's name, daughter."

How Cranox must have hated this man. Then I wonder. Could this man have been the one who put the babe in Cranox's gut when he was female? That's the kind of memory Cranox might do anything to erase.

But the truth is I don't care about this nameless fighter. What I hear is this: in a single fight, I can win twenty-two lives: my brothers, Dinitra, the pups. To please Dinitra, I could even ask for the Master's pet, the Vessel. *Susalee.*

"Tell me what I have to do," I say to Mélan.

The old man doesn't seem pleased. "You must be clear about what you want as your reward. Anything you want that you don't ask for will be denied to you. Even your own safety."

It feels strange to be bargaining for lives this way, like I'm trying to get a better price for tomatoes or fresh rolls. "My own life, then. My brothers, all nine. I want Dinitra. Susalee. And the twelve pups."

Mélan asks, "What about nektar?"

I think of what Mélan told me. My brothers can eat Remedy for the rest of their lives to tame the virus. They don't need to be cured by nektar and risk craving it, like I do. But what would it hurt to ask for a couple of globes?

The room is deep in shadow. Dinitra lights the lamps. Even their warm light doesn't reach the chill I feel. I have to leave her again. Only if I win the Kind-in-Kind will I save her, save 12 and the pups. And my brothers.

We'll have to figure out how to carry the pups, at least until they're big enough to walk on their own. We'll need food and clothing. Weapons. Maybe a wagon and horses.

The list of things grows longer. Charcoal and paper for Dinitra. Thorn probably needs new vials.

And I need boots.

Then I realize Mélan didn't finish his story about Cranox and his Kind-in-Kind. Cranox asked to be commander and have the man he replaced be erased.

"What was the third thing Cranox asked for?"

Mélan tries to wave the question away, but I insist. This might be useful to me. It might be something I wouldn't think of asking for but need.

"Very well." Exhaustion softens Mélan's voice. "Cranox asked that the man be skinned and tanned so that he could make his war drum. You marched behind it when you entered the city. The Great War drum of the Horned Mask, Cranox's Spectate. It's made from the skin of the commander he ended up killing with his bare hands."

29

Bonds

I don't want Dinitra or 12 with me. Or Mélan. Too much can go wrong. Better that they stay with the pups, with tea, in the warm light of the lamps.

And I don't want Dinitra to see me with the Master. He's sure to be sipping nektar. She'll see that I still thirst for it.

I don't want her to see me weak.

I leave quickly, with barely a goodbye. I can't wait another second. If I could fight the Kind-in-Kind tonight, this very hour, I would. When I walked up the street earlier in the day, all I could think about was seeing Dinitra. Now I run with her still in my thoughts. I feel the moment when I descend back through the blue haze into the lower part of the city. The haze congeals into a fog that sticks to me like spider web.

I find my brothers playing Snaps. They've just eaten, their plates and cups scattered everywhere. Willow's made a stack of paddle loaf. They're still chewing when I burst in.

Fig hoots, having just won a pair of bootlaces from Tamarack. When they see me, my brothers clap me on the back and kiss my cheeks.

They're in a fine mood. The Master himself sent a barrel of cranny in honor of my decima. My brothers have been filling and refilling their cups all afternoon.

Quickly, I tell them about the Kind-in-Kind. I tell them I'm going to the Master immediately to demand it. Now that I know there's a way out, each minute in this city is like nettles in my boots.

If only I had boots. I add that to the list of things I want from the Master.

A Kind-in-Kind is the only way to save all of us, I tell them. *We,* I say, circling my finger, *will all be together. Finally free.*

I tell them I'm also asking for Dinitra and 12's pups. Dinitra came with the Vessel who birthed Rek's twins in Quillka. Susalee will come with us, too. We'll have all the supplies we need.

Cranox fought the first Kind-in-Kind, I tell them. *He killed the man who was commander before him. His prize was to replace him and command the Hundred-Hundred.*

I don't add that Cranox asked for the man be erased, skinned, and made into the war drum the Hundred-Hundred played as we approached the Master's city. My other suspicion about their connection I keep to myself.

Thorn is the only one who hasn't been drinking cranny. I wonder if he lost his thirst for it after he removed the babe from Cranox's belly and slipped the babe into the cranny jug. *This sounds risky. Which human will you fight?*

Tamarack interrupts. *One of us will fight in your place. I will fight.*

I lead the Living Wood. I told them we'd be free. I'm the one who has to fight. *I'll ask for Cranox in the arena. Avenge our brother.*

Tamarack grabs me around the chest and lifts, squeezing me with such savage joy that my head whirls. *Surely, our brother brings you strength from the Far Lands.*

Willow isn't convinced. *If you kill Cranox, that puts you in place to be commander of the Hundred-Hundred. Is that not what happened with Cranox? What's to stop that from happening to you? We'll be just as trapped.*

That's not the rule, I say. *I won't ask for that.*

Even as say this, I curse myself for not asking Mélan that question. Mélan himself said Bex doesn't always play by the rules. If the Master is so crazed by nektar, could he break the promise of a Kind-in-Kind? Could the Master force me to stay?

Force us all to stay?

Thorn's gray eyes are wide with concern. He echoes my fears. *That addled boy will cheat. He'll lie. He'll find a way to trick you. What's to stop him? We should just escape like we did with that Queen.*

"With 12 pups? We wouldn't get past the gates."

The past is our best weapon. Paint and leather and hardened comb. "They have their rules," I say, "and this is one of them. Once I kill him, I get what I ask for: your lives. We'll be free to go."

There's a long silence before Willow speaks again. *What if we don't want to leave?*

"Say again?"

Some of us want to stay.

The room is weirdly quiet for seventeen cranny-soaked warriors. Have they been celebrating their decision to stay? With the men who slaughtered our brother Tanoak? After we crossed the Cursed River, I wondered which of my brothers would be the first to say aloud that he wouldn't follow me.

It's no surprise: Willow.

I try to argue him out of it. I go down the list of dangers. Zong and his Furies want the Hundred-Hundred to go to war with Odide and her Hive. Zong allies with Rek, who hates us. Somewhere in The Deep, an army of drafts gathers.

An army of drafts? Tamarack opens his hands in a question.

If you stay, you'll have to fight the wars the Master chooses. Is that what you want?

But I've misunderstood the question. It's not just Willow who's thinking of staying.

Tamarack's meaty fist turns at his cheek. *Why not fight the drafts? We should join the Hundred-Hundred. Kill the Queen who tried to take you from us and the Captains who enslaved us. What are drafts to us? They're not our kind.*

Dear brother. My breath catches and I have to start over. *We fled our mother with no thought to kill her. We simply wanted to be free.*

I understand his anger at Odide, but why kill the drafts we've never met? Drafts we once saved? *Brother, I'd never raise a weapon against our mother. Or an innocent draft.*

Tamarack cuts me off. *I would.* He turns to our brothers. *We've already wasted so much time protecting drafts. They're unnatural. They don't love us. We get nothing from them. We're men and belong with men. That's what I think.*

"Where did you get these ideas?" I ask.

The Master's men talk. I like what they say.

Listen. I can't lose my brothers at the moment I need them most. *I know it may not have seemed that way, but the Queen didn't mean to harm us. Whatever she did, she did for her Hive. That doesn't deserve death.*

Tamarack responds hotly. *She took you. She conjured you. You wouldn't have been free. You would have been bound to her more surely than you were bound to our mother. After all that running! She would have used you to make more of those* creatures. He snaps his fingers angrily.

The very word Odide hates: *creatures.* "She made a mistake, that's true. But I escaped. All of that's behind me. Behind us."

We haven't had our revenge, Tamarack says. *Revenge* is one of our most violent gestures. The hands touch between the thumb and pointer fingers, then twist, as if throttling a small animal.

"Then why would you stay with the men who killed our brother?"

But you already said you'd kill Cranox in this Kind thing. That's revenge enough. It's the Queen I'd like to finish off.

I counter, "She doesn't feed wildmen to speluks. She never whipped or shackled you. She never forced you into an arena to fight and die. She fed you."

You owe her nothing, brother, Tamarack insists. *We owe her nothing. Drafts should serve us because we are men. We're the most powerful.*

Is that what the men of the Hundred-Hundred say?

It's what I say.

"Brothers." Mélan told me that I'd have to pay more than I bargained for and that I wouldn't like it. "I owe her my life. Without nektar, I would have died. The things I learned from her." I point to Thorn. "Those things helped saved us."

More I can't tell them without revealing what Thorn and I know about Cranox. I choose my next words carefully. "The Queen conjured me, yes. But she also helped me. Helped us. Did she stop my brothers when they chose to go?"

A few brothers shake their heads: *No.*

"We didn't escape our mother to fight at someone else's order, male or female," I say. "We're not just warriors, we're not just males. We are ourselves: Tamarack, Willow, Thorn. Brothers, if the Hundred-Hundred kill a draft because it's not pure human, how long will it take for the Hundred-Hundred to say only men with brown eyes are pure? Or men who are tall or men who still have their tongues? Anything can divide us. But what unites us doesn't change until we walk to the Far Lands: we live. That should be our most cherished Bond."

My brothers talk among themselves. *I carried a draft over the Black Stairs.* Then, *There was the one who died before we reached Quillka. I never could understand what that draft was trying to say.*

I liked that frog draft, Sil. He brought me fish, says Fig.

Willow stares at me for a long moment. I struggle to keep my expression calm, but all I can think about is when we crossed that the Cursed River months ago and Willow joked with me as we faced the hyba pack. What saved us was not my skill or our speed or even our weapons. I killed the hyba cub daring enough to attack despite its fear of water. I killed the cub that left the pack.

Then the pack devoured its own. If we split up, we'll die.

"I'll go to the Master and demand the Kind-in-Kind. I'll ask for your lives in return. If I survive, then you can decide," I tell them. "Come with me or stay. You're all free men."

I can't hide the hurt in my voice but that's the only way to say something like that: with the hurt.

Wait. Willow goes to a corner. Since the lither burned Burn's boots, I've been barefoot.

We did our best. See? The boots are old with a shaft that's slouched. But Whitebark managed to burn our symbol, the tree, on the side. On the sole he carved lightning bolts.

The boots are Blazes and Living Wood both. My good luck. *Every time you take a step you're still a filthy Blaze,* Willow says. *They're ugly as you, but maybe they'll help keep you alive in the arena. Be careful, brother.*

Alone, I climb the stairs to the Master's dwelling in the Dome. Now that night has fallen, the blue speluk finger of light looks like solid flesh. I don't allow myself to think too much. Get the Kind-in-Kind, I think. Kill Cranox. Then free. The rest will have to sort itself out.

The guards at the Master's door let me pass. By now, the warrior who danced with The Beast is famous.

The Master stands alone at a window, humming his little song to himself. "I didn't expect a visitor. What brings you, warrior Fir?"

Without Mélan there, I'm not sure how best to demand the Kind-in-Kind. On the small table is the delicate cup he uses to sip nektar. The cup is empty. Yet my thirst for it leaps up just as strong as before.

The Master is irritated by my silence. "Don't stand there, warrior Fir. Speak."

Why not kill him here and now? Why even ask for a Kind-in-Kind? If I'm Master, I'll rule. All the nektar will be mine. Dinitra will be mine. Everyone and everything I love will be mine. My brothers and I won't be parted. They'll come to me and I'll protect them and they'll always be with me.

Again, the Master insists, "You came for something. What is it?"

I tear my eyes away from the nektar cup. I blurt, "I demand a Kind-in-Kind."

The Master doesn't seem surprised. He waves his hand, small and smooth as a boy's, as he turns away. "That Mélan and his books. They are precious to him. Just because it's written, warrior Fir, doesn't make it true. What he drew is what happened. Not what can or should be. Every book can be burned. Think no more about such nonsense."

The Master—Bex, I remind myself—turns his back to me. "I know you spoke to the girl," he says. "I have her book."

I was so focused on the Master's nektar that I didn't notice Dinitra's book sitting on a table with its dark leather casing. Her mother gave it to her in Quillka. The Master goes to the table and sets the nektar cup down. Then he lifts the book so that I can see the page with her drawing.

The drawing is of me.

"So informative! The weapons the Captains have, their leaders. Why, I even know what they are called. Susalee told me. Your mother, Timbe. Lam of the Birds of Prey. Poor Ular killed by Captain Rek, painfully drawn and written. The one who took my tongue is long dead. But they're all the same."

If I kill him, all the nektar in the city will be mine. Surely, Odide would send more. We'd deal with Zong together. We'd deal with the Captains, too. This time, the alliance between men and Odide would be real. There would be no need to attack The Deep. No need for more war.

No more decimas. My brothers would be cured. Dinitra would never leave my side.

The Master flips to another page. "Captain Rek! Here she stands with her metal arm."

The Master's fingers are long, with milky-white nails. I have to remind myself that I'm talking to a very old man. "She's impressive. Captain Rek and I have been communicating for some time. Planning."

The Master sees that my eyes are drawn to the nektar cup. "You knew The Beast. I didn't know that when I awarded you those nine lives. Your dancing was pretty. Perhaps I should take those lives back."

"I thought you enjoyed the pleasure of a surprise."

He barks a laugh. "Cranox isn't so fond of you."

This isn't going as I planned. Maybe my brothers were right. There are no rules. The nektar clouds my thoughts but seems to sharpen Bex's.

"Let us call this conversation an exploration. It helps me see who you really are." Bex moves his hands as if he's weighing stones. "Weigh your strength."

My life, I think, against the lives of my brothers, or Dinitra, or 12. Cranox.

"We can't hurt you," I tell him. "We'll leave. You'll never hear from us again."

There's a flicker in his eyes. His eyes are the only part of him that hint at his great age. "But that can't be. If you go to The Deep, well, Zong would be furious. You can't go back where you came from, Rek will make sure of it. There is really no place for you, is there?"

I have a hard time imagining Bex and Mélan together. Mélan is gentle and kind. Bex is cruel.

The Master's eyes slide off me to the empty nektar cup. "Wouldn't you like a taste?"

"No," I lie.

"We know the power—we know the wonder—of nektar, do we not, us two? You have drunk deep of it, I can tell. I can smell the lilyfire on you."

I can't deny it. Even now, watching him touch the cup, I crave it.

"We have a Bond, warrior Fir. You and I. This Bond between us could be *useful*. Other Bonds, well. They don't last."

I'm starting to wonder if I'll ever leave this city. He's refused the Kind-in-Kind. What else can I do?

I can offer Cranox's babe. But Cranox said I would die too, since the Master would be humiliated that he gave command to a female.

"You'll have every comfort in my army," the Master is saying. "You can even have her for your own. That female. Not the one with red hair. She's precious to me. Did you know she sings?"

I step back. "I'm no slaver."

The Master blinks. "A pet, not a slave. You shock me, warrior Fir. We enjoy each other's stories, she and I. Zong brought her to me as a gift," he says. "Now The Beast, as you know, is a marvel. But that female she came with? She doesn't sing. I don't like books."

The Master cocks his head. "What a pair we two would be, warrior Fir. Cranox grows old. Tired. Perhaps you could be my new general. Would you like that?"

This is exactly the danger my brothers warned me about. As I watched him choose a robe and a headdress to enter the city in triumph, I sensed this fear in Cranox: that he could be replaced, then exposed. He has to be the commander of the Hundred-Hundred to hide his secret and stay alive.

I don't feel sorry for him. He killed and scalped my brother, Tanoak. But it helps me put aside any lingering doubts. If someone doesn't kill him, he'll kill me and every one of my brothers to keep his secret hidden.

"I demand the Kind-in-Kind," I repeat.

The Master shakes his head petulantly. "I already said no. I'd rather have you at my side."

I push down my desperation. "Mélan showed me Book One-Hundred-Sixty-Eight. He said you must grant the Kind-in-Kind. It's the rule."

"Mélan." The Master turns his back on me. "We made that up so long ago. It's just another story, warrior Fir. We were children."

"You weren't children. You were grown men. You are grown men."

Bex scrapes the nektar cup with his finger, then pops the finger in his mouth. "Those books. I shall have them burned. But very well. I was pleased by your decima. Perhaps I'll be pleased again. Go now. Prepare. The Kind-in-Kind will be at dawn."

I feel dizzy and not only because of how desperately I want that nektar cup. I have to tell him exactly what I want if I win. "In exchange, I want…"

The Master waves his hand, irritated. "Tomorrow. Tomorrow you'll make your little request for all that will hear." This time, his grin is sinister. "As you know, I love *surprises*."

30

Book One-Hundred-and-Sixty-Eight

All night, I prepare for the Kind-in-Kind. I sharpen the metal tip on my stave. I hurl the stave again and again at the training room wall to make sure I have the weight balanced properly. The stave is light enough to travel further than Cranox will suspect. I must drive the point straight through his heart.

Willow makes no snide remarks. My brothers watch me silently, then stay together after I go to sleep in one of the bunks.

I imagine the sound of the stave hitting Cranox. I don't want to kill anyone, but I see no other way. When we left Dolor, I thought I wouldn't have to fight other people's battles ever again.

But this is my first battle as a free man.

I wonder if Dinitra will watch. I don't know what's worse: that she sees me kill or be killed. What will become of her if I don't survive? Mélan protects her, but he won't live forever. The Master keeps Susalee, the Vessel, as a pet. Dinitra and 12 may have to fight the Master's wars, too. Each of those pups is worth ten men on the battlefield.

You terrible, sweet creature, she called 12. As long as the hyba cross stays close to Dinitra, she'll live. But how many of the pups will die before Dinitra's heart breaks for good?

At dawn, I don't eat a bite even though Willow made my favorites: derak stew with onions and tiny purple potatoes, paddle loaf, little honey cakes drizzled with burnt sugar. It would all taste like dust, anyway. It's been a day since I last took nektar. The craving is intense. At the table, I sweat even though I'm sitting perfectly still. My hands are steady, but I feel weak.

Wouldn't that be rich! The nektar that gave me such power enfeebles me just when I need it most. In my mother's service, I've killed battle dogs and their legionaries. My first victim was a legionary who'd stopped to examine her tracker map. She thought she was hidden in a thicket. I heard her breathing. As I crept closer, I saw the map's light on her face. She was crouched, her face shining with sweat. She was afraid.

I thought all of that was my good fortune. She had no idea her death crept close.

My cross bow was loaded with fine, new bolts a brother had just made. I'd polished the stock that morning with some of Willow's fresh derak fat. Before I even touched the trigger, I imagined returning to Ash to report the kill. I craved his approval. The look he would give me, that I had been a fine choice of our mother's to second him.

The killing was almost an afterthought. What I looked forward to most was the praise. My status in my brothers' eyes.

The bolt was so well-placed the legionary didn't even cry out.

Now, the thought of killing Cranox fills me with revulsion. He deserves it a thousand times more than the legionary. Still, I wish there was another way. Why can't the Master just let us go? I don't care if Cranox has a crook or a cleft. He could have both or none for all I care. I just want to find that place where my brothers will be safe. Where I can be with Dinitra. I want to lie with her, yes. I also just want to be with her: to talk to her, to laugh with her. To have her see me as I truly am, sick of killing. Sick of running. Sick of war.

I crave nektar and I crave Dinitra. I crave the solid thunk of my stave hitting Cranox, so that this is all over. I crave the sweet give of the waxy globe as my knife tunnels through it, to the nektar inside.

This time, 12 can't kill for me. Kind-in-Kind: humans alone.

At dawn, every seat in the arena is filled. More than filled: men sit two to a seat and crowd the narrow aisles. Machines steam up and down whatever gaps appear in the human blanket. I smell everything. There are sausages and hot rolls and cups of cranny and sugar spun in elaborate shapes and stuck on sticks: lithers, bancats, bright blue speluks. Among them, I spot figures shaped like 12, with tiger stripes and a long tail with a white tuft of sugar.

All tasteless to me. All dust on my tongue.

On the balcony stands the Master with Mélan at his side. The Master sips from his nektar cup. The old man is bent over so far I only see the top of his gray head. Will this Kind-in-Kind make it to his illuminated books? Soon, I may only be a swipe of color on a stiff page. Fir, who once fought and died, captured in red and blue ink.

Or maybe the Master will order me erased, as he erased the man Cranox killed. Will my pure skin be made into a new drum that announces the Horned Mask's return to the Master's city?

I hope Mélan writes down my name even if he has to black it out. It will be there, underneath the paint. Someone might find it again long after I'm dead.

With them on the balcony is Cranox. The Master wanted to wait for the morning of the Kind-in-Kind to know my choice. He wanted it to be a *surprise*.

Cranox may die of the shock alone. He is wearing one of his fancy robes, the one that flickers blue flame, to celebrate.

But the real surprise comes as a shape darkens the doorway. Zong has arrived with two of his Furies. Zong and his father together on the balcony. Mélan stands to the far right. Zong stalks to the far left, then turns his insect eyes to me.

I spot my brothers in their seats. Somehow, they've managed to find cloth, paint, and several long sticks. They've made their own banner for the Living Wood: a black tree spread on a white field. I realize: that's why they stayed up after I went to sleep. They were making a banner for us made of sheets.

Despite everything, they follow me.

The Master beckons me to approach the balcony. "I grant the Kind-In-Kind. What would you have in return for victory?"

"My brothers. All of them."

The Master nods. "You shall have all of them. Five, is it?" he says slyly.

"All seventeen." I remember Mélan's words of caution. Make sure to ask for everything you want. Once you've finished, there's no going back. "The eight I won in the decima and the nine who remain. All seventeen."

"Mélan will record this."

"I want more."

The men of the Hundred-Hundred strain to hear my voice. I already won 12 in the decima. "I would take all of The Beast's pups. Twelve."

The Master sounds almost hurt. "But they're mine! They birthed here, in my city."

"They're mine if ask for them and I win."

"Oh, very well," the Master says, irritated. Over his shoulder, Zong watches, his yellow eyes unblinking.

"I'm not finished."

This time, Cranox steps forward. "You overstep, warrior Fir. The Master has been generous."

"This is my right. So says Mélan. Ask him yourself. Book One-Hundred-Sixty-Eight."

Cranox tries to whisper in his ear, but the Master waves him away. "Speak, warrior Fir, and be quick about it."

"I ask for the life of the two females. Dinitra and Susalee. The one you keep as a pet."

"You presume!" Cranox has to restrain Bex from pelting me with the nektar cup. "No Kind-in-Kind has ever included a female! Mélan has no such page. That's not our way. No, that is not part of the Kind-in-Kind."

"Before all of the Hundred-Hundred, I claim it!" I bellow. I know I'm pushing what Mélan told me, but it's worth the risk. "Book One-Hundred-Sixty-Eight! Nowhere does it say that this is only the male. Human, it says. Human against human. I can take any human as my prize!"

"Let him ask for the moon and stars," Zong hisses. "He won't survive the day."

"Do I have your word?" I shout again. "This is written in Mélan's own hand. I've seen this with my own eyes. It is written! It is recorded! I may ask for whatever I want if I fight and kill another human. Male or female. It makes no difference in Mélan's book."

"But she sings to me!" The Master means Susalee, his pet.

The roaring from the stands drowns out my reply. Finally, the Master lifts his arms. The Hundred-Hundred goes silent. "Someone must die, warrior Fir. Two may not leave the arena alive. If all is fulfilled? I'm willing to give you what you want. The female, Susalee, will be yours."

"And Dinitra. With The Beast and her pups. I must have your word."

The Master flicks his hands "Mélan, write it down. You have my word."

A machine trundles toward me from the gate. "The humans fight! The Kind-in-Kind shall be fought to the death! The Master is generous, he is kind! He follows what is written in the illuminated book!"

Then I think: I forgot to ask for supplies, wagons. Charcoal and paper for Dinitra, new vials for Thorn.

At least I already have my boots.

This time, Cranox speaks to me from the balcony. "Who will you fight, warrior Fir? Who will have the pleasure of killing you? And with what weapon?" His grin is malicious. "The Beast cannot fight for you in a Kind-in-Kind. I wonder if you would have even survived that lither, old as she was. You're truly on your own."

I don't know if Lark is with my brothers or somewhere else. I wish I could see his face as I speak. The thing he asked for is here. I point to the commander of the Hundred-Hundred, to Cranox. "I choose him. For my Kind-in-Kind, I will kill Cranox with a stave."

I see everything as if in slow motion. Cranox realizes he's trapped. The Master himself shapes his mouth into an O of surprise. My words hang over the arena like the blue haze.

Cranox argues with Zong and then with the Master. But the Master abruptly turns his back on him.

Zong must be pleased. He thinks Cranox and the old scribe both tell the Master not to kill his sister or march on The Deep.

Cranox has to fight me. At the entrance to the arena, he drops his beautiful robe. Underneath, he wears a simple tunic and breeches. His boots are dyed the blood red of the Horned Mask.

A brisk wind kicks up the new fallen snow. Two men run out with staves, one to each of us. Cranox looks at me as he weighs the stave in his hand.

He comes within range, then stops. Only I can hear him. "You saved my life only to ask for my death. Why is that, warrior Fir?"

"Necessity. You mean to kill me."

He doesn't dispute it. "Why not ask for Decan? Or Cuarto? I'm an unworthy prize."

"You're commander. You killed the commander before you. That's not unworthy."

Cranox shakes his head. "You didn't know him."

"What was his name?"

Cranox narrows his eyes. "What does it matter?"

"Was he the one who put the babe in you?" The stave is sweaty in my hand. It feels nothing like the practice stave I threw all night at the wall. I'm surprised Cranox remains so calm. He lifts and balances his stave. He cocks his arm, preparing to throw. The crowd roars, expectant. Behind him, I see the Great Gate, the Master's eyes fixed on us, Zong by his side like a menacing shadow.

"What does it matter to you, Horse?" Cranox sneers. "You and your brothers are already dead."

Cranox hurls the stave with a quickness that surprises me. With the nektar still coursing in my blood, my eyes see the stave coming. Every detail is revealed: the damp spot where Cranox's hand gripped the shaft, the nick in the sharpened tip, a practiced spin. A slight wobble means the stave should hit right at my heart.

If I'd been standing still. I twist. The stave brushes my tunic and lands skittering on the stones.

Cranox's face pales. "You cheat. This should be humans alone. Not spoiled with nektar. You are the Queen's *creature*."

"Nektar saved you, daughter of Oxeme." Mention of his mother, his cleft, are the best weapons I have. I balance my stave and lift. This is too easy, like killing a creature in a pen. Like how Cuarto feeds his speluks with helpless wildmen. But I must do it: for my brothers, for Dinitra, for 12 and the pups.

Suddenly, Cranox sinks to his knees. He begs. "Spare me. I will send your brothers on their way, I swear it. Take the girl. Take 12 and the pups. I'll help you. Let me live."

"Spare you? After what you did to Tanoak?"

"I didn't know he was your brother. If I had known, I wouldn't have killed him, I swear it. Did I kill any other brothers? No, I allowed you to win their lives in the decima."

"Eight lives." Behind him, I hear the creak of the hatch. Bex can't help himself. Something else is coming. The gusting snow makes it impossible to tell if the black spot is the hatch or the thing that's coming for us. The balcony comes in and out of view between gusts of snow. "How many brothers have you killed, brave Cranox? How many sons? How many daughters?"

"I'll go away," he pleads. "I'll leave today for Far Eek. You are commander now." He's weeping. "I'm old. I only wish to rest."

"Liar."

"I arranged the decima for you! The old lither..."

"Why was 12 there?" I lift the stave, ready to aim at whatever's coming.

"It's the Master! He does what he wants. I didn't know, I swear it. We can get rid of him together. He's too..."

I'm waiting for the next word, but nothing comes. Cranox's chest shoves out. I think he's having a fit like the Master, some nektar madness. Then colors bloom in his chest: bright silver and red. The tip of a crossbow bolt coated in blood.

Blood gushes from his mouth. Cranox falls face forward to the stones. Dead.

Behind him is a shape: human. Through the snow, I see a smear of red-gold. Footsteps, a chime of armor, and she's before me, crossbow aimed at my chest.

Susalee. The Vessel. The last time I saw her with my own eyes, she was birthing Rek's twins at Quillka. Through Jarvon's eyes, I saw her as she trekked with Dinitra and 12 toward The Deep.

She loads a fresh bolt, fletched with the bright red and green of grabeen feathers. She aims, this time at my chest.

Her armor is Zong's black plate. Her boots are fine, black leather stitched with golden flowers. Dinitra told me that when they were still in the Weave, Susalee brewed a new flower that dripped honey and ate its predators.

She's a predator, not a pet. "Fir," she says calmly. "Lark told me about you."

"He asked you to kill Cranox, too."

She nods. "Move to your right."

Her crossbow follows me as I circle to the right. Without taking her eyes from me, she cocks her weapon. I can't tell if the spectators are outraged that a female just killed their general or eager for her to kill me.

I'm half-crouched, my back to the Great Gate. "I won't help you kill me."

"I have no intention of killing you." Apple and pear cores thud around us. Then chicken bones, shoes, eggs. If she waits any longer, the Hundred-Hundred will batter us with breakfast, too, and tomorrow's dinner.

"I asked for your life in the Kind-in-Kind. Dinitra wanted me to," I say.

Her mouth twists. "She got me into this mess."

"She wouldn't leave Dolor without you."

"She should have. I saved myself. I just won the Kind-in-Kind, not you."

I hear the pounding of feet. The Hundred-Hundred will kill us both. The men came for blood and death, not to see their leader shot in the back by a female.

Susalee angles the crossbow up, as if she's aiming at the sun rising just over the Great Gate. She catches my eye. "I never miss."

I whirl just in time to see Mélan peering at us through the swirling snow, as if memorizing every bit of what's happening for another page in one of his illuminated books. The blue speluk light sweeps over him, then moves back towards his dwelling above the city's murk. In front of the Hundred-Hundred, in front of Zong and the Master, in front of my own brothers, I fall to my knees. I've lost the Kind-in-Kind. I've failed them all.

Susalee's bolt buries in Mélan's chest.

And then she laughs.

31

Furies

A ngry men lift me, then smash me to the stones. I lose track of where Susalee was standing. I try to defend myself, but it's pointless. The men are enraged. A female has killed two of their own. I did nothing to stop her.

Then there's a sudden stillness. I lift my swollen face. The Furies have formed a ring around us, forcing the men of the Hundred Hundred back. Zong himself lands next to Susalee. He takes her by the arm and helps her stand. He's almost tender as he loops her arm around his shoulders and lifts her into the air.

Two Furies take me, but they're not gentle. I'm like a dirty scrap no one wants to touch.

My left cheek is taut and hot to the touch, so swollen I can barely see out of my left eye. Not that my right eye sees much. Beneath me, the Great Gate passes. We're going to the Dome.

By my count, I have broken ribs and a cut gushing blood over my eye. Thorn would call me lucky, for just being alive. Soft clots of blood hang from my nose.

In the Master's quarters, the Furies set me next to Susalee.

With a single shot of her crossbow, she killed Cranox. Then she killed Mélan. One easy shot, one impossible one. Why? Why didn't she just kill me? I can't help the tears that squeeze through the swelling around my eyes. The salt stings. I'm weeping for myself and my brothers. For 12 and her pups. For Dinitra. The Kind-in-Kind, wasted.

Mélan is dead. He called me *son*. What will happen to Dinitra, 12, and the pups now? To my brothers?

Just as easily, Susalee could have shot Zong or the Master himself. But she picked Cranox and Mélan.

Why?

Zong knelt at her side. She wore his black armor. Furies brought us here.

This is Zong's doing. He's finally rid himself of that old scribe. His *father*. And the general who stood in his way.

Just then, I hear a scrape. An intake of breath. At the door is Lark. The Furies let him pass.

"He's dead," I manage through my swollen jaw. I mean Cranox. "Are you happy now?"

"She did what you couldn't."

"Now that he's dead, why are you still here?"

Lark's voice sounds different, happier. "I still have things to trade."

"Why Mélan? Why kill the old man?" Mélan harmed no one. He painted books. He sheltered Dinitra, 12, and the pups.

"You heard Zong," Lark says. "Mélan kept the Master from attacking Hive Home. Killing Odide. Zong wanted him dead on the day he killed Tyr."

"The Kind-in-Kind was my only chance. I've lost them."

Lark shakes his head. "Not at all. You're more powerful than ever. Zong has won a great victory. Finally, he has control of the Hundred Hundred. And he has a new commander."

"A new commander?" My gut roils. Then I realize what he's about to say: exactly what my brothers warned me about.

Lark walks me through what will happen next. Zong made a deal with the female: be the Master's pet and gain his confidence. When the time was right, she would move quickly to kill Cranox and Mélan. "She has a pretty low opinion of men. It wasn't hard to convince her. The right word in the right ear is a powerful thing. We all got something."

"What does Susalee want? What would make her kill two people like that?"

"Her freedom, of course. Just like you. Zong promised. You of all people should understand that."

I wait several seconds before speaking. "Why not kill the Master? If Zong wants his army, he could take it by getting rid of him."

This time, it's Susalee who speaks. She wasn't beaten as badly as me, but her voice is thick with blood. I'm startled to see that her eyes are the same color as mine. "The men of the Hundred-Hundred won't follow Zong. They won't follow a draft. They certainly won't follow a female."

Lark nods as if this is the most obvious thing in the world. "The Master is too scrambled by nektar to lead. He cares nothing for where or how he gets it. He'll remain in the Dome. They'll bring him out for this and that. He'll barely notice. Neither will his men."

Susalee tries to laugh but gasps with pain. "They'll follow you, Fir. You danced with the Beast. They love you. And Zong will force you to do as you're told."

"I refuse."

"You can't. Dinitra. 12. The pups. Your brothers. Their lives depend on you."

"Some of your brothers want to stay, you know," Lark adds. "Wise, if you ask me."

"You're the one who's been poisoning them," I growl.

Lark shrugs. "If you mean by poisoning that I've been talking to them like free men, then yes. Poison it is. You told them yourself they get to choose."

"Don't you care about your kind?" I challenge Lark. I mean males.

His voice turns ugly. "What have males ever done for me? Men killed my mother, remember?"

Just in the weeks I've known him, he's grown taller, ganglier. His mop of hair is just as unruly. But I see the man he's becoming. "The Blazes almost killed me. When you and your brothers caught me, I saw the disgust on your faces. To you, I was a *scuttle*. A beast-born."

I had no idea the word was so hurtful. "But we saved you."

"To use me. I know you lied to me, Fir. You had no intention of letting me go."

"What about the Queen?" I push myself to standing. The room whirls. "What will the Queen say once she hears that Zong killed

Mélan? Her *father*. And you helped him. She said she was like a mother to you."

"Like I said, warrior Fir. My mother's dead. If you ask me, there's no more Queen or Captain or Sower. No more wildmen. No more Cranox, the murderer. Zong is in charge now."

"You betray your kind." But why wouldn't he? What love did the Captains ever show him? The Blazes? He saw Cranox kill his mother. I meant to use him and so did Odide.

"My kind is me, Lark. I will always choose myself." He smiles cruelly. "I told you he'd never spare you."

He meant Zong.

32

Lilyfire

I hear a humming: *dum ta dum ta dum dum dum*.

The Master wanders into the room carrying a full cup of nektar. He's been drinking deeply and has the rosy skin and satisfied look of a babe who's just feasted on his Keeper's rich milk.

The Master barely notices the three of us. There's a small balcony and he steps toward it, but stops before going outside. As before, a little heating machine trundles haphazardly, pumping out little gasps and a heavy trail of blue smoke.

As the Master hums, I hear the clomp of boots on the stairs. I groan as I lean against one of the walls.

One by one, soldiers of the Hundred-Hundred enter the room. The first two men carry a heavy iron brazier. They set the brazier at the fireplace, just as covered with cobwebs as the day I first met the Master. The rest bear heavy sacks on their backs.

One man sets a sack down. Through my swollen eyes, I see the flash of leather binding, the flutter of painted pages as the contents are removed.

Mélan's books.

When Decan arrives, he lights the brazier and starts feeding Mélan's books into the flames. *Welcoming you, warrior Fir,* Decan grins. *Or should I say commander. A fresh, warm start.*

Decan announces that he's my second. The motto Cranox and the Master devised—"The beast serves, the draft serves"—is no more.

Zong devised a simpler one. "Death to the Captains and the unnatural drafts. Death to all who do not praise the Master."

Zong and his Furies are no longer unnatural because they're in command.

Death to my mother, death to Bounty. Death to all warriors who refuse to pledge loyalty to the nektar-addled Master and his ruler, the murderous Zong.

The flames consuming Mélan's books turn from orange to bright blue and green.

The fireplace sucks up most of the smoke. The exhaust from the heater is heavier and swirls over the floor. "I need air," I tell Decan.

He's nothing if not quick to serve. He helps me to the balcony. We pass the Master, who comments: "What use is the past to those who make the future? We are better rid of it."

There's no sadness in him, no grief for the dead lover who saved his life. "*Dum ta dum ta dum dum dum*," the Master hums.

A curl of paper ash wafts past and is lifted outside on an air current. It's only mid-morning, but already bitter cold.

When Zong arrives, he stays on the balcony with us, like his sister afraid of fire. He tells me what I already know from Susalee and Lark. I'll lead the Hundred-Hundred. Although the Master will remain in the Dome, Zong will be the true commander.

My first task will be to take Hive Home. I must choose one of my brothers to join with Odide in Jule. It doesn't matter which one. Just not me, since I will have to return to the Master's city to prepare for an assault on The Deep.

I must let Odide live long enough for a new Queen to be born. Then I will rid him of his sister. The new Queen's nektar will flow to his allies.

"I expect no less from a creature that killed his mother and father," I say.

Zong's mouth opens and closes over his sharp fangs. "You seek to provoke me. I cannot be provoked. I won't hesitate to kill those you love. Do not doubt me."

I don't. But I won't bend to him, either. "I'm a free man."

Again, his mouth opens and closes. "You're free to leave. Alone."

I feel like he's been following my thoughts, but that's impossible.

If he could follow mine, he'd know I have no intention of obeying him.

"If you leave, you cannot take anything with you," Zong says. "Your clothes, of course, your boots. But no food, no weapons. No brothers. How much, warrior Fir, do you value this freedom? Is it worth abandoning your brothers? That female and her draft, her draft's spawn?"

The cruel fingers of his four hands clench and extend. "I'm not bargaining. You have no power, Fir, except what I give you. Do as I say or leave. You're no slave. This is your choice."

I see myself reflected in Zong's terrible yellow eyes. He's neither glad nor angry; triumphant nor concerned. He will get what he wants no matter what I do.

"You'd be a fool to refuse me," he says. "Go and speak with your brothers. Converse with those shapes you make. I would have your answer by nightfall."

In their quarters, all is quiet. The merriment I saw yesterday, as my brothers drank and played Snaps, is gone.

I order Decan to wait outside.

Thorn breaks out his fysic kit. Over a bowl of Willow's healing tea, I make my apologies. They warned me the rules would change--or there would be no rules at all.

I tell them everything. Zong offers to release us in exchange for taking Hive Home. More: I command the Hundred-Hundred, with Zong the hidden power. One of us must join Odide in Jule and birth a new Queen. Then we march on The Deep.

Just as my brothers warned.

Tamarack is first to speak. *We must do this.*

I refuse, I say. *Odide is not our enemy.*

Willow agrees with Tamarack. *I volunteer to join with the Queen. What of it? It seems a small price to pay.*

Tears of frustration build behind my eyes. I thought I would win our freedom. One Kind-in-Kind and I would save every one of their lives. I would free Dinitra and 12 and all of the pups. We would leave the Master's city with all that we needed.

And paper and charcoals for Dinitra.

I wonder if we'll ever be free of Zong.

Odide will see us coming, I tell them. I'm still connected to her through lilyfire nektar. Likely, I always will be. I correct myself. *She'll see me coming. It's impossible for me to get close to Hive Home without her knowing. Once she knows our intentions, she'll send out the Swarm.*

Or she'll just grab me and conjure me and get her daughter. I'll be one of those husks for the lake fish. The closer I get to Hive Home, the more powerful she'll be. I'm ashamed to admit that Odide will always have this power.

Then you will stay here, Tamarack says. *We'll go. We'll take the Hive, complete the Jule.* Then he pauses, perplexed. *How long does it take to make a new Queen? And...how?*

I have to laugh. *I have no idea. But none of that will happen. I'm not letting my brothers risk everything without me. We have to find another way.*

Thorn says there's a cut over my left eye that needs stitching. I take a quick gulp of cranny, then close my eyes as he sews.

You're pure no longer, he says when he finishes.

I've never been more grateful for a scar.

Thorn rocks back on his haunches. *I have a proposal.*

How to kill the Queen? I ask. *I won't allow it.*

He presses his hands in mine to speak. *I don't propose to kill her. I propose to join her.*

What do you mean?

The potion. His fingers join and point upwards, rubbing against each other. *We can make a deal with her. Isn't that what this is all about, that potion? Once we have it, we'll offer it to the men of the Hundred-Hundred who still have virus. We can heal them. We can heal ourselves.*

We need a shape word for nektar, something that can be *healing* and *making oneself young again* and *conjury* combined. It comes to me: pointer fingers sliding up my cheekbones and ending in a twist at the temples: *nektar.* Newly sewn, my skin is sore, but I make the gesture anyway: *nektar.*

Nektar, Thorn repeats. *The men of the Hundred-Hundred tell us that the Master keeps the nektar from them. Even when they're injured or dying. None but the Master may have it.*

Thorn knows I crave nektar. "Go on," I say.

What if we were to give nektar to them? What if we offered all men nektar? All creatures? We could heal ourselves, too. We wouldn't need Remedy any more. The Hundred-Hundred would follow us, not the Master.

Nektar is no solution. It conjures, I say. Conjures: my palm circles my ear. *Men can't stop craving it.*

For the first time, I confess to them that I'm conjured by nektar. *I have no desire to be another Master and grow so addled by nektar that I kill other men. Force the decima on them. We have to find another way.*

We could distribute nektar carefully, Thorn says. What if a sick man had only a drop or two? What if he brewed one of his tinctures, reducing the craving, but keeping the nektar's healing power? *Only enough to heal. Only to those who want it.*

"Once it's in your system, you want it always," I tell them. "Mélan told me. It's dangerous."

Thorn shakes his head. *You've gone without nektar. Since we used it on 12, at least. It can be tamed, brother, can't it?*

Maybe he's right. But there's still the problem of getting close to Hive Home. I don't trust myself, I tell them.

Willow raises his hands in a question. *Perhaps another could go in your place?*

A smile plays on Thorn's lips. *The Captain.*

He means Dinitra. Perhaps. But I already felt Odide's anger toward her, her jealousy. Might Odide harm her to get to me? How could I protect her if she walked alone into the Hive?

Sometimes, Thorn says, shaking his head, *you aren't the smartest brother. The answer is obvious. 12. She enters Hive Home with 12.*

So 12 comes with us to Hive Home. And the pups. The pups have as much to gain as any of us. If Zong had his way, they'd be weapons as soon as they're capable of walking. Not just against his sister. He'd use them against the draft army in The Deep.

I have a hard time shaping words. My emotions ball up inside me: love for Thorn, love for my brothers, even sour Willow. Fear for 12 and her pups. Dismay at how we got here. Regret. Two brothers I've lost. I grieve for Mélan. All of his beautiful books burned. Sadness and fear of what's to come: more war.

And Dinitra, always Dinitra. From the day I first saw her in the training pen at Quillka until today, clasped to her in Mélan's tiny dwelling. Of course, she found the one person who understood her, who saw the world through paint and brush. Mélan: *father*. Dinitra: *daughter, lover*. And Fir: *free*.

I don't have words for what I feel. Maybe, it's a glimmer of hope.

Crazy hope. Addled hope, groundless hope. We're planning together: male, female, and draft. We mean to save Odide, Odide and her lilyfire. It's the Pentaklon, the union. Tender still, no more than soft roots and a stem. But it's something.

I think back to what Dinitra told me about her failed experiment. A carnivorous potato, she called it.

Well, I have a carnivorous potato of hope.

Of all the places we've been, this is the worst: trapped in a city of blue, greasy smoke, occupied by murderous drafts who care nothing about us, about the ones we love. The awful decimas Mélan devised and then regretted until Susalee killed him.

I love my brothers. They love me. I love 12 and every one of those pups. Though Odide tried to conjure me and led me to abandon my brothers, I know there's good in her. She conjured me so that she would have a daughter. She was desperate and now I understand a little better, because I'm desperate, too.

Sometimes, being free means making hard choices to protect the ones you love.

I don't know what kind of shape my love will take or what it will do to me. I don't know if Dinitra feels the same way. To me, love feels like nektar, like conjury, but not against my will.

This is my will. I choose it. As a free man, I choose to be conjured by love.

I tell my brothers to prepare to leave in the morning. We'll need horses, wagons, food. And a gift for the Queen. I know exactly what the gift should be: Tyr's pendant, still abandoned where the Master threw it. Smashed or whole, it will say something words cannot.

We're returning to her a memory of someone who loved her. And someone she loved.

It's for her daughter, we'll say. For the future. For love.

33

Parade

I tell Zong I accept his terms. We'll march on Hive Home in the morning.

Zong says, "We?"

"My brothers and I. Dinitra, 12, and the pups. We." I make the shape word for *we*, the pointer finger circling.

He shakes his head. "That sounds like a parade, not an attack. You'll go with Decan and Cranox's Specate. Your Specate," he says, correcting himself. "The female goes with you."

Female: Susalee. That's a complication I didn't anticipate. "I have another condition," I tell him.

His lips curl. "You're in no position to impose conditions. I could kill you where you stand."

"You could, but you'd have a problem. What male would you put in my place as commander? Decan? He's a man born to be led. Vile Cuarto? His own men loathe him. You'd have a mutiny on your hands if you put one of your drafts at the head of the Hundred-Hundred."

Zong's yellow eyes darken with anger.

I bury my fear. "You need me."

In the background, I hear the Master humming: *dum ta dum ta dum dum dum.*

For a long moment, Zong considers me. "What's your condition?"

"I attack my way. You must not interfere."

I know he'll follow me. He and the Furies will watch every move. So will Susalee, sent to spy. Probably, Lark, too. But I think we can do what we need to do even if there's an army spying on us.

Zong isn't able to walk my thoughts. But he's a careful observer. I feel him picking apart my every movement with his faceted eyes. I keep myself absolutely still. As a free man, I get to make my own choices. And I choose to find a way for us—me, my brothers, Dinitra, 12, and her pups—to survive.

No, better than that. To live. To grow the hope I feel rooting inside me. Like Mélan said, we may not find a perfect place. But maybe we can make a place that's ours.

"If you betray me," Zong says, "I'll make sure that every human and draft you love suffers for it. You'll watch as they suffer, warrior Fir. I won't let you die. You'll watch and then every day of your life you'll live and regret what you've done to the very last of your days."

I nod. "We are agreed."

From the Dome, I climb back to Mélan's little home. I find Dinitra weeping in the lumpy chair. The book shelves are a splintered chaos. Paint is splashed everywhere. They even took a mallet to the stove and Mélan's teapot.

In the wreckage, 12 nurses her pups.

"We'll leave in the morning," I tell Dinitra. "You and 12, with my brothers. We must bring the pups in the baskets."

"What are you saying?" Dinitra is shaking her head. "Leave? How? Where?"

"We have a plan."

"What plan?"

I start to laugh. "A crazy one. Pretty impossible. One we'll have to pursue even though Zong would kill us if he found out what we're really doing. Or the Queen will kill us. Not sure yet."

I sink to my knees. I wish my tears were nektar, so I could shed every drop of nektar from my body and refill myself with my love for her. But nektar is a part of me. Odide is a part of me. Cedar and his death are a part of me, Tanoak's, too. My mother, my brothers. And Dinitra. As I take her hands in mine, I feel like I'm holding everything: my faults and failures, my doubts, my past and my future. My love for her. I carry all of it. Like my single scar, these burdens mark who I am.

Who will I be for her? For myself? A free man.

I'm conjured by love.

Either I'll die on his journey or I'll die on another, after all of this is over. There's no magical place. There's no perfect safety: no perfect at all. There's only what we do when things are hard. The choices we make. What we go through.

I choose Dinitra. I choose my brothers. I choose 12 and her pups. I choose the Pentaklon: all of us.

"We're going to Hive Home. Zong wants us to kill his sister, but we won't. We'll ask for her help. You'll ask for her help."

Dinitra stares. "That does sound like a crazy plan."

I tell Dinitra the truth: I don't know if this will work. If there's a more likely path, I don't see it. I need her. I have no tracker map. Who could even make one? Our map is the path we make, our vow to be together, not to be divided—draft or human, animal or plant—ever again.

"The only way out is through," I tell her. The last time I thought this, I was hiding from Odide's Swarm. The words served me well enough then.

Her hand presses over my heart. "I'm sorry it's come to this. I'm sorry for Susalee. I never imagined she'd hate me for bringing her with me from Dolor. I thought I was doing the right thing."

"You were doing the right thing. Rek would have forced her to be a Vessel."

"She doesn't think so."

"Zong is sending her with us to Hive Home. She's to be his spy."

Her laugh is bitter. "So we change places again. In the Weave, she was the best of the best. So many merits. For every one of her merits, I had an infraction. Then my mother brought me to Bounty and Rek took Susalee and made her into a Vessel. Now she'll spy on me?"

"On us," I smile.

"I wish I could draw this, but it would be a scribble. No one would understand."

"Then scribble," I tell her. "The only thing I care about is that you choose to come with us. I won't force you. No more orders, no more demands. Choose us. Choose me."

"You mean choose the warrior who danced with 12 in front of all the Master's men? Choose the warrior who helped birth twelve hyba-

cross pups? Hyba-cross crossed with who knows what 12 found as
we walked? Choose the warrior who tried to win my life and the lives
of his brothers and the pups in a stupid fight, a fight he should never
have fought in the first place? A fight he lost? That warrior?"

"That warrior," I say.

"I can't."

Dinitra smiles at my stricken expression. "I've already made my
choice. I chose you the moment we sat together in Quillka. When you
told me you would be a free man."

That night, hidden away above the murk of the Master's city, we
lie together. If this is beast-like, then it's also kind. It's urgent, but also
soft and slow and sleek. As the night chill creeps under the door, we
warm ourselves in each other. What we do seems effortless, as if it
was always deep in our bodies, waiting. I feel her hips, her breasts.
She breathes against me and I breathe with her, our breaths twinning,
as if we share the same lungs, the same skin. As if we are the same.

We compare our hands--mine perfect, hers perfect, even with their
scars.

12 snores in the other room. The pups sometimes squabble and
squeal in their sleep. I've never felt more at peace. Maybe, this is our
land: this room. There are no fiery lakes, no blue cloud islands. A
table, a chair, the little heater as it chuffs. Splatters of paint and the
smell of burnt butter.

Perfect.

In the morning, I hear the great war drum of the Horned Mask
calling me to march on Hive Home. I run down to the Great Gate to
join my seventeen brothers. Eight of them climb back to Mélan's
home to collect Dinitra, 12, and the three baskets of pups.

I mount Cranox's painted horse. My brothers were never riders, so
they perch uncertainly on their beasts, jangling the reins and speaking
to them in shape language.

Dinitra prefers to walk, 12 pacing at her side. I don't see Lark, but
I know he's following behind and watching.

Susalee has her own painted horse. Did she get what she wanted?
No one but she knows for sure.

As we climb the low hills between the city and Seven Lake, Thorn
calls a halt. He's brought some sticks and tinder for a quick fire. From
his fysic pouch, he draws a cranny-red bundle: the babe.

Now that Cranox is dead, we don't need the babe anymore. It's time for us to let it continue its journey. Thorn carefully feeds the flame. When the tiny pyre is ready, he lays the babe on the coals and points the feet east.

Once we reach the crest, I see Seven Lake before us: a dull, gray disk of death. The blue speluk finger of light is dimmer here, barely a flash. To the west is our destination: Hive Home.

Walking beside me, Dinitra takes my hand to shape words against my palm. *Zong will realize something's wrong. He'll try to stop us. He'll send the Furies. What will we do then?*

What do you think we should do?

She thinks for a long moment. *Someone very wise once said to me that the only way out is through.*

Then we go through, I agree.

END

Acknowledgments

The same people who helped bring *The Bond* to print also helped shepherd *The Hive Queen*.

As always, I owe a special thanks to the Magic Ifs, who I met through the Vermont College of Fine Arts program in Literature for Children and Young Adults, a magical experience. YAM. Residencies with Artcroft in the Kentucky Knobs, Wildacres in North Carolina, and the Yeonhui program in Seoul, South Korea gifted me a precious resource: time.

Blue Crow's Katie Rose Guest Pryal and Lauren Faulkenberry's careful eye helped shape and sharpen this story in ways I am still discovering. Additional thanks to Tamiya Anderson at Blue Crow for her editorial help. Adam Versényi's love of story inspired me to write a book he would finish and thump down with a satisfied nod.

My daughter, Frances, continues to inspire me as she begins her service as a teacher to the kids I hope will now love Fir, his brothers, and Odide as much as I do. To my son, Ray: this story exists because you thought it should. Thank you.